Jim,

With a sister like [illegible] you will certainly understand the presence of Bon Cat. Enjoy The Parade.

John B. [illegible]

The Last Parade

The Last Parade

by

Hiland B. Doolittle

Rome Publishing, Inc.

Albany, New York

All characters in this novel are fictitious.

Published by Rome Publishing, Inc.
Albany, New York
Manufactured in the United States of America
First Printing
Designed by Beryl Frank/Lisa Hanifan

Library of Congress Cataloging in Publication Data

Doolittle, Hiland B.

Title

LCC - 98-091277

ISBN - 0-9662742-0-2

For Suzanne

who ended the nightmare and began the dream

The author wishes to thank the following persons who assisted in the creative process

Margaret Mirabelli
Spring Harbor, Ltd.
Delmar, New York

Mary-Arthur Doolittle
Slingerlands, New York

Lorraine Tallcott
Loudonville, New York

Bernard F. Connors
Loudonville, New York

John Q. A. Doolittle, Jr.
Newport, Rhode Island

Andrew Casano, M.D.
Loudonville, New York

Larrie Calvert
Morristown, New Jersey

Beryl Frank
Albany, New York

The Gin-Group - Dave, Herb, Joe
Menands, New York

The Last Parade

September 19, 1968

Into the night... into the night... I go.

Hodges reached for the receiver. It chilled his ear. He let it ring until finally she answered.

"Hello?"

"Hello, ma'am. It's me, again," said Hodges.

"I see. How are you tonight?"

"Well enough, thanks. I'm hoping he's home."

"No, he's... he's still not home," she sighed. "I'm sorry. He's not here."

"You know who it is?"

"Yes, this is the fourth time."

"Right, the fourth time I've called."

She hesitated. "Hold on... please." Her hand covered the receiver. She was collecting herself. Hodges felt it.

Talk to me!

She removed her hand, but lowered her voice. "You're not making this any easier. We're all anxious."

"I don't mean to make it harder. I just..."

"We all want the same thing," she interrupted. "Like I told you before, he said he'd call. When he gets home, he'll call," she sighed. "We're still hoping."

"Yuh, we're hoping. I guess you're right, we all want the same thing. It's just that," Hodges paused. "I... I miss him. There are things I need to know."

"We all miss him," her voice cracked. "It's hard. Look, I told you about the letter. Told you what he said... It's over. I don't know if that means over for me, for him, or for all of us. Not a day goes by, not one day, I don't think about it. I just know he said it's over."

"Not for me."

"But that's what the letter said. And that when he got back, he'd call. I have your message. I have the numbers," she began to sob. "These calls, I... they just got to stop."

"I'm sorry. I just need..."

"Please, no more. No more calls," she cried. "Life goes on."

Hodges flinched. "He would never... say that."

The phone clicked dead. His chin fell to the cups of his hands.

What might have been was lost, lost forever.

"Into the night... into the night... I go... the way," his eyes filled. "The way? The way... I no longer know."

January 24, 1967

Ton Son Nhut Air Force Base, Vietnam

The plane idled on the runway. The cabin door opened. All eyes turned front. The flight attendant appeared before them. In time they would remember her even more vividly blonde. The navy blue uniform subtly accented her full figure. She was crisp, impressively crisp. Their anxiety peaked.

"On behalf of the captain and crew of Pan Am flight 357, we wish you the best of luck. The prayers of your nation go with you. Remember, one year from today, we'll be back to take you home! Be there!"

A pause. A practiced smile.

"Please check for all carry-ons. When de-planeing, exit in single file. Thank you!"

Nobody moved. The impatient mental preparations begun at 30,000 feet stalled completely. To a man, the 341 fresh recruits suffered a sudden uncontrollable reservation. Twenty-four hours earlier they had departed Maguire Air Force Base in New Jersey. In Anchorage they had changed from their military transport to this luxurious Pan Am liner. After a brief refueling in Tokyo they had arrived at their final stop, Ton Son Nhut Air Force Base, Vietnam.

A gruff first sergeant took charge. "Gentlemen! Fall-in! You heard the little woman. Single file! At the bottom of the ramp, follow the white line. Now! Move out!"

There was no escape. The thing! The thing was happening.

The GIs slowly rose and cautiously approached the door. The sun's brilliance startled them. They clung to the comfort of the air-conditioning. The flow pushed them ahead.

The first sense. Choking heat.

The first vision. Blinding sun.

The first smell. Engine fumes.

The first sound. Choppers.

The first taste. Fear!

The first thought. Unprepared.

They fumbled for bearings.

The parade began. Hodges followed Mac down the ramp. Part of him lagged behind.

A white line was painted on the ground. The line led to a walkway along a chain link fence. Behind the fence, disheveled Americans watched their arrival.

Each replacement wanted assurances. No way! Not today.

The veterans pointed. They laughed. They were done. The ritual began.

"Yo GI! Welcome to the Nam! It's Number Ten. It's all yours! We're going home. We made it!"

"Hey you! Yeah you. You! Boy! You are a long GI. Look Mammasan! There goes a hopelessly long GI. He's so long, he ain't here yet!"

"Hey GI! Hey GI! I am sooo short! I am sooo short I may not be here now! Good God Charley! I'm gone. You missed me Charley! I am his-story! What's that make you GI?"

Laughter from the left. Stunned silence, grave doubt to the right.

A hairy-chested American with a yellow bandanna over his head held his right hand high. "Ears! Ears here! I got ears! Gook ears. They make you feared. Wear em round your neck! Scares the shit out of em." He looped the string around his neck.

"Yo! Man! PFC! You hot? Get used to it! This is a cool one! An a dry one! Wait'll it rains. It don't stop. I mean it rains foreva and then some! Welcome to the land where wet dreams are your worst nightmares! Least ya got a dry one to start."

"Hey man! We're goin home. Got any messages for the women of the world? We'll be seein em real soon. Sweet Jesus! We made it! Praise the Lord!"

Applause from the left. Thirst to the right.

"Hey GI! We're gettin on that plane. Yeah, that plane, right behind you! Goin home and just in time. It's gettin too hot. Too hot to handle and I ain't talkin weather. And I ain't talkin those VC fuckers! The big guys from the North are here. They're on the prowl. Time to go! Whew!"

"Yup! Those regular army gooks are bad asses! And more comin every day! Courtesy Ho Chi Minh. Like weasels round a chicken, just lookin for a few fresh recruits. Fresh blood for the weasels!"

"Hey baldy! Yeah you! Baldy! Over here! Welcome to the Nam. They're here. Yeah, they're here, even right here on this base. Oops there's one! Yeah that little dishwasher over there. She's one. See her, lookie there! She's lookin at your name tag. Damn, she's got your name. She'll be checkin it twice. Tonight, tonight she's gonna tell her pappysan. He'll be lookin for ya. Tomorrow, he'll be tellin his friends to be lookin for ya. See! That's how it works."

"Hey GI! Nice threads. Joe, ya see that? Brass buttons! Ain't seen them in a while. A long while. Cool too! Anybody hot in those threads? An lookie there! Now how bout that! Shined shoes! We don't see much a that round here... do we Joey baby? Hey GI! You, you keep that shine. That's the Nam for ya. Dressed for the body bag! Lookin good GI!"

Uneasiness to the right. The pace quickens.

"Don't listen GI! Don't listen. It's Number One here. Ya know that dump ya took on the plane? Yeah, that dump up there. The one you took. Well, that'll be your last flush for one hell of a long time. Think about it! Soon, we be flushin all the way home!"

"Hey GI! You're gonna love these slant eyes! They're really somethin. Had one last night. No shit! Deodorant for hairspray. Right Guard! Had Old Spice last week! That's a gook for ya!"

And then, there, left of the walkway, was Dudley. At parade rest, Staff Sergeant Alonzo Dudley, two-time survivor, stood motionless. With his hands clasped behind his back and his broad chest thrust forward, he raised his granite chin defiantly. The sergeant prevailed without expression. He wore meticulously pressed jungle fatigues. The beret shielded his eyes. His holstered pistol empowered him. The sergeant needed no designation of rank to convey his authority. He stood in the sun. He did not perspire. The sergeant was a serious man. He was there for his squad, the twelve of them.

Dudley stared ahead. "MacKerry! Hodges! Fall out!" he called. The other GIs followed the line.

"Balman! Parker! Fall out! Behind me. No talking."

The line continued. Lost.

"Ringhyter! Hosmach! Lavelle! Velasquez! Fall out!"

Only a few were left. The heat, the heat!

"Weaver! Jones! Cortes! Fall out! Behind me. No talking!"

"Hodges!"

"Yes, Sergeant."

"PFC Scott was on the plane?"

"Yes, Sergeant."

The Ghost materialized behind them. "Sorry Sarge, I'm not one for parades."

"PFC Scott! Glad you could join us."

"Yes! Sergeant!"

"Good Scott. Good. Squad, follow me. That includes you, Scott."

An unfamiliar sense of gratitude overcame them. For their six months of training, Dudley's presence had meant exhaustive activity. Now he was order, order amidst chaos. The transformation was dramatic.

The whip became the man.

Day One.

364 to go!

Laureen

The journey from the village of Ben Cat to Saigon necessitated painstaking disguise. Earlier this day Laureen had muddied her face and worn a wide-brimmed straw hat along with Grandmother's oversized clothing, complete with residue from the oxen. Now, submerged in the luxury of a hot, soapy bath, she closed her eyes. With the cleansing of each pore, the village retreated. "There were still bubbles!" she mused.

Hearing movement downstairs, Laureen arose, wrapped herself in the softness of the towel, and proceeded to her dressing area. After fastening the turquoise *oa yai* she lifted the silver brush from the mahogany bureau. Standing before the full-length mirror, Laureen arranged her long, black hair. Satisfied, she clasped a gold brooch to the dress, then went down the stairs, through the screened door, and onto the patio.

Monsieur Chocart sat under an umbrella at a round table overlooking the spacious lawn and gardens. Relaxed in white flannels and a loose-fitting silk shirt, Chocart was especially dapper this afternoon. His greying hair neatly combed to the right revealed an aristocratic profile. A silver ice bucket rested in the middle of the table near an arrangement of flowers. He finished a sip of Chivas Regal, set his glass on the table, and rose to hold Laureen's chair. A paper-thin glass of iced tea marked her spot.

"Laureen, child, fresh as a daisy," he motioned to the tea. "This will complete your transition from country to city."

"Thank you, Godfather. You and Madame always make the trip worthwhile." She seated herself. Chocart settled her chair before reclaiming his own.

He raised his glass to her. "I think to Paris! Paris would be nice, *non*?" He winked.

"Paris!" Laureen blushed. "Could life take such a twist?"

"La Sorbonne, le Louvre," he teased. "Your father would be proud. So many of your countrymen have made the journey that, for you, it would be a homecoming of sorts," he smiled. "And certainly safer than your present surroundings. Think, child, no more checkpoints," Chocart chuckled. "You make such a wonderful impression and with the success of your work here at the National Library, perhaps a job in the embassy? I have confidence we could create a good situation."

"From Ben Cat to politics in France, *mon dieu*! Another transformation." Laureen stared into the elaborate sprinkler system watering the lawn.

"No more radical than your present venture," Chocart said emphatically. "What has it been, eighteen months?"

"Seventeen. Seventeen months since leaving your home, leaving my job. The experiences are missed, but the village is home. It feels right, although we do have our disagreements."

"That surprises you?" Chocart laughed. "How? For three years you were here at the school, then eighteen months at the library. You visited Ben Cat, what, once a month?"

"As with Saigon now," she answered.

"Laureen, you came a child. You left a lady."

"Unqualified for Ben Cat..."

"Overqualified, I imagine," he chuckled. "And now we see you but once a month. You are missed. Madame and Alicia, they do not bridge the grandmother, granddaughter gap so easily."

"Godfather, you tease me! Between Madame and Alicia there are no gaps."

Monsieur laughed. "That is true. They are inseparable. Sometimes I wonder if the little one will be permitted her schooling." He sipped his drink. "How fare Mai Nin and Tranh?"

"Well, thank you, they are well. Filled with resistance to the idea of leaving, untroubled by my fears, but well," she looked to him.

Chocart deliberately crossed his legs. "Yes, I see. You realize Mai Nin has outlasted many, shall we say, severities?"

"Yes, Godfather, and with each severity Grandmother's resolve solidifies. Mai Nin's vision is narrow, but, oh, that constitution. It is iron."

"So it has had to be," he assured her. "Saigon could use her constitution. And what of Tranh?"

"Ah, Tranh Nhu Lam, my alert brother. The narrowness of village life reduces his aspirations. Ben Cat influences him beyond his advantage." She sipped. "Do you suppose they could endure a trip to Paris?"

"Goddaughter, with proper planning the most difficult part would be from Ben Cat to Saigon. It would be my pleasure to handle the Paris arrangements for you. You overestimate the difficulty. After all, these old bones are not without influence," chuckled Chocart. "Perhaps you should go ahead of them, make living arrangements, then return for your family. By eliminating the unknowns, the opportunity for success increases."

Laureen reached for her tea. The reality of her family was incomprehensible to Monsieur, yet his solutions soothed her. Placing her foremost in his equation, he unemotionally put complications aside. Laureen realized her best interests were his sole consideration.

"Godfather, they feel unthreatened. They have so little communication beyond the village they are unaware of the danger surrounding us."

"Take them a newspaper! Take them photographs. You must explain. Even we, residents of Saigon, feel threatened."

"Ah, but Saigon is not Ben Cat," she paused. "Besides, the photographs would be seized at a checkpoint. Suspicion would surround me. Even now, disguise is mandatory."

"You do arrive... rather ignominiously," he laughed. "The sentries don't know what a pearl passes them by."

"Ignominiously, but safely," she smiled.

Chocart shook his head. "Yes, I see. Here," his hand circled the lawn, "we forget the complexities around us, around you. Of course, you realize, those complexities necessitate your departure."

"Yes, Godfather," she sighed. "How wonderful Paris would be! The possibilities are most... invigorating. Is that the word?"

Chocart laughed. "As usual, your command of French is impressive. Do you still study?"

"At home. Reading, studying never tire me. The lighting is difficult," she shrugged, "and it seems something always deters me," she laughed. "Do you think we could afford such a trip, and then to live, live in France?"

"Ah, you consider this! This is good. Finally, a question I can answer with some authority." He reached across the table to take her hands. "I am pleased. This is what your father would have wanted." Relinquishing her hands, he noticed two new arrivals on the sprawling lawn. "Ah, Grandchild! Grandmama! Come, see who visits," he called.

He rose and offered Laureen his left arm. She stood, delicately sliding her right hand inside his elbow. "Laureen," he said as they approached the newcomers, "your trust would release the funds for such a move. As you know, the investments grow steadily. You use but a meager portion. Your father wanted you to benefit from this money. I know he would be pleased should it transport you to safety. What better use? Money should not concern you."

She squeezed his arm. "You are so good to me. My father was wise to have such a friend."

"Laureen, I am only as good to you as your father allowed. He loved you very much," he patted her hand.

"La! Oh La, La, La! Come! Play with me," called Alicia.

Laureen laughed as the nine-year-old wrapped herself around her legs. Looking over the child's head, Laureen addressed Madame, her only true female confidante. "Madame, today, as usual, you are lovely. Beautiful Alicia resembles you more with each visit." She patted Alicia on the head. "Do you enjoy the garden together?"

Madame Chocart extended her hand to Laureen. "La, my dear, how wonderful to see you. You are stunning, as always. I love that color," Madame nodded at Laureen's *oa yai*. "Your Ben Cat air perfects your complexion." Madame perceived Laureen's radiant beauty already surpassed her mother's. The strength of the French, the delicacy of the Vietnamese splendidly showcased themselves in Laureen. The *oa yai* accentuated her petite waist, complimented her bust and hips while extending her legs. Unlike the raw beauty of her mother, Laureen imparted latent sensuality encased in resolute innocence. "You honor your mother. Now, child, tell us of the Highlands. Are you safe? Is Mai Nin well? And what of Tranh? Has he slain his first tiger?"

"Grandmother says we are safe. Ben Cat has a good harvest, so the village is busy. Tranh, let me see where to begin? He grows tall and each day more handsome. Recently we discussed Alicia," she teased. "But even with such an enticement, he will not come to Saigon. He is blessed with Mai Nin's resolve. Was my mother so stubborn?"

Madame Chocart clasped her hands together. "She would certainly have preferred determined. What do you think, Papa?"

"Yes, determined is good. Ah, the memories! And now," he said sadly, "now they are both gone." He shook his head. "So many changes in one lifetime. Change and transition. Here, life is transition."

"Are there new blossoms since my last visit?" asked Laureen looking at Alicia.

"Please, Grandmama! Oh, please may I show La the gardens. There is so much to see."

Alicia loved Laureen's visits. At the child's insistence, Laureen was always given the room adjoining her own. The closet remained filled with Laureen's brightly colored *oa yais*, which Alicia loved. But most of all she liked Laureen's treasured plaster-of-paris model of the rubber plantation at Lai Khe where her father had been the chief engineer. Every element–the laboratories, the residences, the water lines and reservoirs, the power plants, the roadways, the pools, and even the peasant village, where one thousand Vietnamese laborers had once been housed–had been meticulously duplicated to scale.

Porcelain figurines, representing ladies, gentlemen, soldiers, Vietnamese laborers, and children of both nationalities, were busy in the scene. Trucks dotted the roadways. Cattle grazed in the fields as chemists stood outside their impressive laboratories. One of the grand homes had a large pool. A fancy automobile was parked on the circular driveway. Soldiers directed labor efforts. Dogs prowled the village.

Each trip to Saigon Laureen would visit her favorite store to purchase another figurine. Each new arrival further enhanced the spectacle.

On the last night of each visit Laureen would rearrange the scene. She knew that Alicia spent hours noting every alteration. When La returned, Alicia would ask, "Why did you move the car? Where do the trucks go now? Did the workers change shifts? What did the chemists discover? Are the ladies having tea by the pool? What do they discuss? Why does the soldier point? Shouldn't the children play together?"

That night Alicia would snuggle into Laureen's bed. Holding up a figurine, always a Vietnamese character, Alicia would plead, "La, tell me about this one?"

Laureen would close her eyes, reflect back to her other world, then commence a story more enthralling than any book. Alicia was spellbound.

They loved the characters.

Saigon

The waitress shifted her thigh against Sergeant Alonzo Dudley's massive bicep. She blushed but held her ground.

"What you want, boss man?"

"Sir?" Dudley looked across the table to Major Timothy White.

"Bloody Mary, light on the Tabasco, please," White smiled up.

"Right, light on the Tabasco..."

"And nothing fancy, no celery, thanks."

She leaned into the bicep. "And one *bas-mui-bas*, right?"

"Right," Dudley looked up. "The sooner the better."

"Okay, boss man. The sooner the better." She pivoted toward the bar.

"Well, Sergeant, you satisfied with the training?"

"With the paces? Yes sir. They've done the paces. As ready as I could get em in six months."

"That's all we can ask. If you're satisfied, I'm satisfied. How was your leave?"

"Leave? Didn't take much leave, sir. Stayed at Fort Campbell. Worked out, read, worked out. How about you, sir?"

White folded his hands on the table. "They never really understand, do they Sergeant? It's a lonely career. Lonely for us, lonely for our close ones. Tough. A lot to ask of wives, children, lady friends."

"I guess," Dudley shrugged. "You spoil em a little?"

White smiled. "We spoiled each other. It's a little unreal, but it works. For now, it's all we can do for each other."

"Yes sir." Dudley leaned back. "Twelve months from now, you can spoil em some more, probably with a higher rank."

"One Bloody, light Tabasco, one *bas-mui-ba*s, ugh!" The waitress set the drinks on the table. "So, boss man, you come back again?"

"For a while."

"You bet, for a while. You good at that. When you settle down with number one girl?"

Dudley looked up. "When the time is right, Kim. When the time is right. Right now I do... goodbyes."

She smiled. "You do first-class goodbye. Too much, but very good."

Dudley shrugged, "Those goodbyes, they make for powerful hellos."

"You very good at that." She turned back to the bar.

White smiled. Dudley raised his glass. "Major, to the thing?"

"The thing, Sergeant!" The bottle and glass clicked.

White lowered his drink. "They go home for their leaves?"

"All except Scott."

"The Ghost, that what they call him?"

"Yes, sir."

"He's the, uh, convict?"

"Yes, sir. It was jail or us," Dudley shrugged. "Sentenced to the thing."

"How's he coping?"

"A good soldier. He'll be out front. He understands."

"I see. The game's the same. The stakes have changed."

"A little." Dudley drew from the bottle. "He's good."

"That'll help. The others?"

The corners of Dudley's lips turned up. "Ten flat bellies... and Balman."

"Balman? New Joisey, right?"

"Fifty pounds lighter, but still no flat belly. He'll have one of the M-60s."

"Okay, Balman's got a rock. Who's on the other?"

"Ringhyter."

"Ohio?"

"Yes, sir. As big as the state."

"That going to work in the bush?"

"They can handle the rocks, sir. They're ready."

"Under your tutelage, Sergeant, we have come to expect nothing less."

"Thank you, sir."

"The rest marching to the same drum?"

"The usual. The preparation was demanding. They clustered."

"Oh?"

Dudley placed an ashtray on the left edge of the table. "Over there, that's Balman, Cortes, Parker..."

"The radio?"

"Yes sir, Parker," Dudley moved another ashtray left of the table's center. "There, there I got Velasquez, LaVelle, Weaver..."

"Grenades?"

"Weaver has the cannon, yes sir, the M-79." He placed his bottle to the right. "There, there we have... Jones, Ringhyter, Hosmach..."

"Explosives."

"And way the hell... over here," Dudley tapped the right edge of the table, "are MacKerry, Hodges, Scott. Scott, he may be even further away. Sometimes even he's not sure where the hell he's at."

"That's why the Ghost?"

"Yes, sir, he gets around."

White stared into the corner. "So they're clustered."

"Always happens. They are as ready as..."

"Your last time?" White raised his eyebrows.

"Better... than my last time."

"Right. So, Sergeant, how do you read them?"

"They know. The temperature is rising. They know."

"They should know," White shrugged. "They should. Hodges, he's the squad leader, right?"

"College boy, yes, sir. Still thinking he's going to brush every day. Yes sir."

"Do the others respond to him?"

"Now, no problem, sir. At first, they didn't respond to much of anything."

"Except you, right Sergeant?"

"That's correct, sir. They don't like it, but they do."

"You are ready, aren't you Sergeant?"

"This time," Dudley looked up, "yes sir. This time, I had em the whole six months. That works better."

"Six months training, then their leave. They going to remember your tutelage?"

"Sir," Dudley smiled," "I do bring em back, real quick, real hard."

"I'm sure you do, Sergeant. Sure you will." White sipped his Bloody Mary. "Our initial orders are confirmed."

"Sir?"

"We're attached to the First Infantry."

Dudley leaned back. "The Big Red One. Could be worse. The Highlands, the Central Highlands."

"You been there?"

"North... and South, not the Highlands."

"Let our men rest two days, then you bring them to Long Binh for final Ready Vietnam Training."

"Ready Vietnam, in the Nam," Dudley tapped the table.

"Ironic, isn't it?" White grinned. "I'll be there getting final orders, polishing the details. This liaison stuff can be tricky."

"Caressing the brass, sir?"

"You could call it that," White shrugged. "Third Vietnamese Army Corps, they're in the Highlands."

"Yes, sir. They're all the same to me," Dudley hesitated. "Watch yourself."

"Uh huh, Sergeant. I've been thinking about this. How about we call our operation Matchmaker? During our leave my wife and I saw *Fiddler on the Roof.* This liaison thing, it just clicked. Matchmaker."

"Matchmaka? Sounds good. 'Matchmaka, Matchmaka, make me a match,' that the one?"

"You have it, Sergeant." White raised his glass. Dudley tapped his *bas-mui-bas* against it.

Kim slid a tray of refills onto the table, then settled herself into the chair alongside Dudley. "You soldiers, you solve the trouble of the world?"

"Not yet, Ma'am," White answered. "Not yet."

"Well, you off to good start. This round is on that very handsome PFC over there," Kim nodded toward the bar.

Dudley and White turned to acknowledge their benefactor.

The Ghost raised his bottle.

White

Major Timothy White was the Citadel. There was more. The tightly clipped hair was regulation. His blue eyes and clean-shaven face were calm, but the jaw, the jaw set discipline. His shoulders pressed back, his chest elevated, the major regarded the sluggish squad seated before him with an easy confidence.

"Gentlemen, welcome to the Nam. Long Binh is Headquarters for the First Infantry Division. The Big Red One. This is the major fortification in the Big Red One Theater of Operations. Make no mistake, in this theater, like everywhere in the Nam, there are no secure areas. There are unfriendlies, Victor Charleys, in the zone. In this neck of the woods, Long Binh is as good as it gets. Now don't get your hopes up. Long Binh will not be home for long. Here you receive supplies and orientation." White nodded toward the door where Dudley loomed. "And here the good sergeant," the corners of his mouth edged upwards, "gives you your final Ready Vietnam Training."

The squad tensed.

The major moved to the center of the room. "Ready Vietnam Training is time well spent. After six months you probably feel you have trained enough." He hesitated. "I doubt it." He turned away walking behind the metal desk. "In the Nam we learn something every day. Don't forget that! Every day is a learning experience all its own. Now it's a popular practice to count... count each day down to the end... the end of your tour of duty. Sergeant Dudley and I, we don't recommend it. If you want to count, I suggest you count the lessons... and remember them. One thing you can count on... what you learn in the Nam will last you a very long time. That is for sure. The other certainty is that no matter what you learn, there's more... more to learn."

The squad groaned.

The major scanned his clipboard. "Sergeant Dudley will inform you as to base procedures and acceptable conduct." White squared his shoulders. "This is no time to forget the valuable lessons you have learned. Not one soldier in this squad, not one soldier on this base, or in this country can afford the luxury of a breakdown in discipline. In the Nam you cannot have a bad day. Those are reserved for your friends back home. Here, every day... is a bad day. Don't make it worse."

"Your final destination will be up north, still in the Big Red One Theater. You will receive further orders on a need-to-know basis. In the meantime, write those letters. The good people back home are worried about you. Any questions?" White connected with each of the expressionless faces resisting him.

"Sir! Thank you sir! Ten hut!" Dudley snapped the squad to attention. The sergeant saluted the major, who returned the gesture before briskly departing.

The door swung closed behind White. The squad remained at attention. "Gentlemen, the Man, the Man was talking to you. Get your shit togetha. When the major talks, I talk. You got it? No questions? Good! You got it all figured, right? We'll see! Reconvene at 0600. Full gear! We got work to do. The vacation is... ova. Dismissed!"

Dudley spun through the door.

"We learn somethin' every day," Balman mimicked. "Count the lessons. What the fuck! I lost forty-five pounds, I learned enough. No one trained me for the frigging heat, the shitty food, or trying to sleep through artillery. Now, goddamit, Dudley's gonna run our asses in the bush. Christ, we might as well be back in basic. Who needs it?"

"The major's right," said MacKerry. "We got lots to learn. Me? I'm just glad we're stayin together."

Ringhyter moved toward the door. "One thing's for sure. Dudley didn't train us for six months to split us up. We're here to help the gooks learn to fight. That's our ticket."

"Another day, another scratch," Hodges began. "If it stays like this, I'll take it."

362 days

Mai Nin

Centuries of greenery surrounded her. Succumbing to the rich fragrances, Laureen placed her books in her yellow backpack and leaned back, enjoying the scene.

Below, the village of Ben Cat proceeded soundlessly with its timeless existence. The golden steeple of the abandoned church reflected the sun's bright rays back to her.

Her grandmother led a stray calf, her prize, back to the herd. The eight oxen preoccupied her.

"Mai Nin, will you sit beside me?" Laureen called.

"Have we lost your brother? Like the yearling, Tranh wanders in search of himself?"

"He looks for wood," Laureen laughed, "or more probably signs of a tiger."

Mai Nin seated herself. "He chases his tail hunting a tiger in these woods," she laughed. "His thrill is the suspense of a possibility which far outweighs our meager reality." Mai Nin tucked a patch of betelnut into her mouth. "So, child, what news from the city?"

"From Saigon? Migrations from the provinces overwhelm her. And more Americans arrive each day. The city yields to the swelling."

"Saigon," Mai Nin released a stream of betelnut, "she admits no limits. It seems her way."

"Yet all around her bear her burden. To the north, terrorists purge Ben Suc. To the south, the plantation changes hands again. Now the Americans fortify Lai Khe. Our little Ben Cat seems a pawn awaiting the sacrifice." Laureen shook her head. "We have discussed leaving before. Perhaps, Grandmother, perhaps this is the time, while we are still removed."

"Before we are removed, you mean!" Mai Nin placed a blade of grass between her teeth. "Ben Cat is our home. Danger is a familiar companion. The Chinese, the Japanese, the French, they have all visited Ben Cat. Fortunately we remain unworthy of their sustained attention."

"Yes, Grandmother, but in those times was the village ever so unsettled? Our young men leave. Villagers bicker. Lifelong friends oppose each other. How will the crops be harvested? How will Ben Cat survive?"

"Laureen, Ben Cat bends forever in the winds from beyond the paddies. One day all return. Like your friend Guyan." Mai Nin turned to Laureen. "What has he learned from the world beyond?"

"Guyan is steadfast in his commitment to the National Liberation Front. He resents the Americans and resists Saigon." Laureen stared across the pasture. "He seems well. Hungry, but well. His friends, they seem less distinguished, do they not?"

"Indeed! Our rice is depleted! You are honored by friends with convictions as deep as their stomachs," Mai Nin chuckled. "Their conversation leaves little time to savor the taste. When do you suppose we should brace ourselves for their return?"

"They never say," said Laureen. "They are secretive, always secretive."

"Aye, his friends from Ben Suc are from a serious mold. Guyan is the same cut, just less experienced."

"He ignores his family. It puzzles me. So many of his friends ally with Saigon. Chiang Xi, our playmate, greeted me last week. He is impressed with his uniform and shiny boots."

"Child, each soul determines its path. While youth arranges the details, Ben Cat perseveres. They will come home, as did you." Mai Nin lifted her walking stick. "Ah, that foolish calf! He knows no boundaries.

We must fetch him before your brother mistakes him for a hungry tiger!"

"Let me." Laureen rose, heading across the pasture.

Mai Nin admired her youthful grace. As Laureen rescued the calf, her half brother emerged from the woods. He carried a bamboo pole. "Undoubtedly his gun," chuckled Mai Nin as her grandchildren greeted each other.

At age thirteen, Tranh already stood taller than Laureen. His round face was dark, like his father's, while Laureen's thin, fair face exemplified the finest features of their mother and her first husband, the Frenchman. Basking in their beauty, Mai Nin enjoyed their obvious affection.

"Ah, Tranh Nhu Lam, were the woods filled with tigers?"

"Not today, Mai Nin," he laughed. "but, Grandmother, your yearling's manners show no improvement. Does he not know your age?" Tranh stretched his full length on the ground next to his grandmother. "And when will my sister wed Guyan, the tiger of Ben Cat? Has this been the subject of the afternoon discussion? After all, such a celebration might soothe the village."

"Tranh Nhu Lam!" Laureen exclaimed. "Your talk resembles the squirrels. You spend too much time in the woods. Foolish words are more hurtful than foolish thoughts. This you know. Guyan is my friend since childhood, nothing more. Certainly our friendship does not merit the attention of the village."

"Ah, children, no more of this!" Mai Nin pointed to the herd. "Shall we take them in?"

Tranh stood. "Ben Cat needs me. My friends work the paddies. La, perhaps you and Mai Nin can manage the herd?"

"What do you think, Grandmother? Are we capable?"

"The oxen heed my instruction better than either of you. Even the calf pays me more mind than my grandchildren." Mai Nin looked to Laureen. "La, let the boy go. We need not worry about Tranh. His stomach never forgets the whereabouts of the evening meal."

Tranh chuckled and Laureen laughed as they parted company.

Long Binh

It was not panic. The granite chin never faltered. There was urgency, not panic. The thing, the thing was happening.

"Gentlemen, yesterday's attack concluded your training. Consider those mortars your last lesson in Long Binh."

Weaver stood. "Sergeant Dudley, I learned incoming from outgoing. It sounds different. I got it figured now."

"Weava, the important lesson is that you, Weava, very definitely, you, Weava, can die anywhere in the Nam. There are no safety zones. None. In the middle of Long Binh, you can take a hit."

Weaver sat. Dudley looked at his squad. "Think about yesterday. Charley is out there. He wants you to know he's out there. He's advertising. Why else throw eight mortars into Long Binh? What the fuck can eight mortars accomplish? The little bastard just wants us to know, know he's there, watching. That is Charley." Dudley looked at the ceiling, then paced to the middle of the sleeping area.

"Look how he fired. Look at the time of day. What do we have? We got one slippery weasel. He knows when we eat. Boom!" His hand traced the trajectory. "Incoming! Eight rounds. Think about it. We still got light at 1800 hours. Mortars mean Charley was close. Close to our perimeter, too fucking close. Why didn't the towers see the fucker?"

Scott, the Ghost, stood. "Sergeant, they were already there. Probably from the night before. He spits the mortars, creates confusion. In the confusion he slips away."

"You got it, Scott. Just like home, right?" Dudley almost smiled. "They were there. Our towers missed them the night before. They lay eighteen fucking hours in the dirt, the heat. Could you do that?" He hesitated. "Boom! Eight mortars. Boom! Then they disappear. Standard Operating Procedure for Charley. His modus operandi. You don't pay attention, Charley takes advantage. You get it, Ringhyter?"

Ringhyter shifted uneasily. "Sergeant, he did good. He got what he wanted. If he hits the mess hall, minimum thirty officers go down. He scares the shit outta the base. What's the risk? Eight to ten guys. What could they gain? Beaucoup casualties. Like you said, pretty smooth."

"One squad," Dudley's eyes pierced them. "One squad!"

"Sergeant Dudley," Lavelle stood next to Ringhyter.

"Lavelle?"

Wrestling with his shyness, Lavelle tilted his head, but kept his eyes steadfastly ahead. "Sergeant, aren't they probably still there? Probably going to do it again. I mean why not?"

"Because, Lavelle, it is not necessary. Charley knows we're looking for him. If he comes, he won't come from the East. Charley neva, eva takes the same trail twice. Neva, eva." Dudley strode to the center of the hooch. "But, LaVelle, you and G-6 are thinking alike. Intelligence says they're still out there, somewhere."

"The base is on Red Alert. Major White has volunteered your services for night patrol outside the north perimeter. If they're there, you find them. You do what you been trained to do. Assemble on the chopper pad at 1500 hours. Full gear. You receive drop and lift coordinates at that time. Corporal Hodges is in charge."

He looked at Ghost, his pointman. "This ain't no drill. This is for real. You," he pointed at Ghost, "get em there. You," he pointed at Hodges, "get `em back. No fuckin' around. This is... Mission Number One. Dismissed."

Always first to prepare, Ghost imagined himself the Doctor of Camouflage. On point he would be alone. He travelled light, carrying only his weapon, his ammunition, a machete, and five grenades. Invisible! He must be invisible. Ceremoniously applying the varying shades of camouflage, Ghost quietly chanted their prelude to courage.

"Into the night... I go.
The way... I must show
Into the night... I go
Hunting... friend or foe
Into the night... I go
The signs... I know
Into the night... I see
It's either... you or me!"

Ghost understood his role. His mission remained unchanged. He was to search, to uncover, to find. In the past three years he had made only one error. The judge had given him two options: the military or incarceration. Ghost reluctantly opted for a 24-month stint with Uncle Sam. The locale was problematic, but the role was familiar.

At 1545 hours the choppers hovered over the landing zone. The doorgunners aligned their sights. The co-pilot waved them out. Ghost hit the ground in full stride. Lavelle followed him to the treeline. The rest of the squad lay in the tall grass. The choppers spun upwards, away, gone.

They were alone.

Lavelle turned, waving them to the trees. They sprinted to him.

Somewhere ahead Ghost lowered himself into a thicket. His hand cupped his senses. He inhaled, pulling them in, holding them. It began. He exhaled the chant.

"Into the night... I go.
The way... I must show.
Into the night... I go
Hunting... friend or foe."

This was it. Mission Number One. It was his, his and Hodges'.

Four pulls. Perfect! The confident awareness arrived. It was not his vision. It was not his hearing. Ghost knew. It was his senses. He had them. They were not Dudley's. They were his, the Ghost's. Dudley knew that. Ah, the Ghost was ready... ready to disappear... into the night... into the night... where it's either you or me!

Lavelle was sixty meters behind searching for their invisible point. They were waiting, waiting for him. Ghost rose. Lavelle nodded. The squad edged ahead. It was understood.

Two hours later their ambush was in place. Hosmach laid trip wires to their rear. Ghost roamed the flank. In a rotating sequence Hodges motioned each man ahead to set his claymore mines.

MacKerry's adrenaline surged with the coming of darkness. His panic would not subside. Fearful that any move could betray him, he struggled to occupy his mind. He lifted his M-16 and peered through the starlight scope. Closing his left eye and opening his right, Mac tunnelled into the scope.

Magic! He could see everything. The scope detailed the jungle surrounding them. Slowly he focused on his far right quadrant. He strained for a motion, a sighting, a signal.

The denseness stared back. Taut with tension, the questions arose. Would a body erupt from the blackness? Would a shrub lunge at him? Would there be a warning? Would there be time, time to react? Could he stay alert? Was someone scoping for him?

"Memorize the background!" the trainers had said. He tried.

What was that? Had the branch quivered? His eyesight deceived him. He strained to hear. Nothing. He focused on the tree. Nothing. Again he strained to hear. It was nothing. A cloud crossed the moon. The background changed.

Shit! Would the cloud diminish the effectiveness of his scope? Shit! He felt it. They were close. They were out there. They were coming!

Mac yearned to speak. Was Hodges feeling it? The scope blurred to his left quadrant. With imperceptible moves, he began the reverse scan. He was the most patient, the most careful. If they crossed his path, he'd see them first. He saw nothing.

Mac set his weapon down. Even in the heat, his sweat chilled him. In the stillness his skin crawled. The ground twisted around him. Shit! This was insane. What were they doing out here? Back home nobody would believe this insanity.

To his right, six feet away, barely visible, he studied Hodges' motionless form. Shit! He's looking back at me. Wonder what he's thinking?

Mac raised his weapon for another scan. Everything had already changed. Whoa! A familiar tree. Couldn't miss that sucker. Must be a thousand years old. Look at the vines! Man! Oh man! A sniper could hide forever, foreva, in Mister Big Tree. The moon flickered to Mister Big Tree's left.

Or was it a reflection?

Shit! He focused the scope. It was near his left claymore! He felt for the triggering mechanism. Yeah! Got it! Safety's off. Good. Nothing. Disappeared. He wanted to blow the mine. Sweat dripped onto his lips. He lowered his rifle, brushing his mouth with the back of his sleeve.

Dear Mom, Boy, do I miss you and the girls. Please give everybody my love. Tell them I'm fine. Well, Mom, every day's an adventure.

Tonight I'm layin in the jungle just waiting to get myself shot or to shoot some poor VC who walks into me. Fun, huh! Twelve hours from now, it'll be over. Glad you're not here.

Up scope. Gonna start left this time. Still, very still. Too still. Crawling. Things are crawling. I hate that.

Mac saw Hodges scratch his neck. He shouldn't be doing that. Damn! He's relaxing.

Well, Mom, there's nothing out there. That's the good news. The bad news is I am scared shitless, sorry, to death.

Up scope. Slowly now. Yeah, Yeah, Yeah. Nothing, Mom. There's nothing out there.

Getting thirsty. In a minute. Uh, huh. Let's see now. This scope is really something. Wonder if Charley has em. Probably a Russian thing. Whoa! Something moved. What? Stay on it. Hold it. There! There it is. C'mon. Move! You mother! He fingered the claymore trigger. Shit! The cloud inched past the moon shifting the shadows. Damn! Gotta relax.

Down scope. Mac felt for his canteen. He rested his weapon on the ground. After loosening the container top he held the water below his head and dropped his mouth around the opening. By tilting the canteen, he was able to sip. As instructed, he held a swig in his mouth swishing it from side to side. Okay. Back to the scope.

So, Mom, how'd you like the automatic deposit. Pretty good, huh? Two hundred bucks a month. That should help. Save it, if you can. I sure don't need any here, laying in the jungle.

Another double scan. Down scope. Another drink. Gotta talk.

Mac looked over at Hodges, who was scoping the stillness. Maybe intelligence was wrong. Maybe they weren't coming. Mac listened. Would he hear them before he saw them? That would be bad. He wanted to see them first.

The insects were noisy. Maybe it was like the movies. If the crickets stopped, the bad guys were coming. Go, crickets, go. An electric caterpillar wormed up his arm. Resting his weapon, he raised his shirt sleeve and flicked the caterpillar toward Hodges. Heh, heh.

Yeah, Mom. Here I am. Laying in the jungle, flicking stinging caterpillars at my best friend. What a place! Wonder if those critters bother Charley. He probably eats em. That's what Dudley keeps saying, "All the elements are on their side."

Mac curled and uncurled his toes, clenched and unclenched his fingers. He hunched his shoulders forward, then back. He rotated his head from left to right, back again, then up and down. It was good. He was tired, but alive.

Up scope. First to the familiar stump in the right quadrant. More slowly than before, he started left. Now he scanned higher. He went twenty feet above the ground.

Up. Down.

The same cloud lingered motionless. Many stars. Unbelievable stars. Bright up there. Dark down here. This sucks. Shit, what am I thinking? This is good, right?

Up scope. Start with Mister Big Tree. Nothing. A little right. Hold it! Hold it! What's going on! Freeze! Right there. No! His pulse jumped. He fought to stay still.

The crickets screamed!

Leaves were moving. Something was crawling through a shrub to the right of Mister Big Tree! Did Hodges see it? Hodges, are you on it? What the hell! Charley! He's moving right. Shit! He's near the mine. His fingers gripped the trigger. His hands shook.

The movement stopped!

Mac positioned his M-16 on the log, shrinking further behind it. He set the claymore trigger near his right hand.

The shrub quivered.

There! There it is!

He locked on the movement. Still going right! Hodges! Shit! He's gonna clear the shrub. He's gonna be in the open. Shit! Mac's forefinger caressed the trigger.

He took a breath. Another breath.

No movement. Charley was in the bush. He wouldn't leave cover. Were there more? Where?

Move, you sucker!

He wanted to fire. Move! One more foot! Nothing. How long you gonna stay? Is he underground? Oh shit! He might be underground.

Two deep breaths.

Every part of him shrieked with frustration, screamed with that thing. Fear!

He was afraid. Could he pull the trigger? In his mind it was always Balman. Never Mac. Balman could do it. Mac filled with self doubt.

Can I pull the fucking trigger?

The shrub moved! Into the clearing! Shit! Charley!

What the fuck! He's... he's two feet tall. He's... he's got a tail, like a rat.

Shit!

A fucking anteater! An anteater!

Almost blew away an anteater! Jesus Christ! I almost killed a fucking anteater.

He wanted to cry. To apologize. To go home.

His being collapsed.

Dear Mom, can I come home?

348 days.

Tranh Nhu Lam

The blindfold was off! His first meeting. Dizzy with excitement, Tranh grasped each detail around him. Thirty sentries armed the perimeter. Their uniforms shown with buttons, brass buttons, and colorful patches. These victors from the north were significant men.

The Viet Cong were everywhere. Dressed in the more familiar black garb of the National Liberation Front, fifteen other men and women were interspersed among the audience.

Heavy tree limbs hung over the clearing, where the audience sat facing an empty chair and table. Lanterns illuminated the setting.

Tranh squatted down absorbing the scene. Two hours earlier the thirty villagers had set out from behind the temple in Ben Cat. Blindfolded, clasping the hand of the person in front, they had been guided by Guyan, Phong, and two men from Ben Suc to this spot, deep in the jungle.

Mai Nin, Laureen, and Ben Cat were far away.

From all directions groups of believers continued to arrive. Tranh lost count. He turned to his right, where he beheld his grandmother's oldest friend. Embarrassed, he lowered his eyes. Bent from a lifetime of labor in the paddies, Ching Phor seemed an unlikely participant.

"Tranh Nhu Lam, does Laureen know you are here?" she asked.

"No, Ching Phor, Laureen again visits Saigon, but Phong assured me all were welcome."

"Ah, the ambitious Phong. He is correct. All, even my decrepit self, are welcome. And what of Mai Nin? Is she aware?"

"Very, Ching Phor. Nothing escapes Mai Nin," Tranh whispered. "It seems my experiences are hers."

"Then you are a most fortunate grandson. To accept such tutelage, either willingly or unwillingly, says much about you," she chuckled. "Does the grandson of Mai Nin know these meetings are secret?"

"Secret? How could such a gathering be secret?"

"Through our oath. This night will require your decision. Are you prepared for such an oath?"

"An oath? Phong did not explain this oath. Why? Why is this necessary?"

"For your protection. Your oath is a serious matter. It does not conclude this evening, nor next week, nor next year. Such an oath endures throughout one's lifetime. No matter the circumstance, you must honor the oath of your brothers and sisters. It transcends friendship and family. Neither Laureen nor your Ben Cat playmates will ever know of your participation. You see, the oath protects us all. It binds us to our beliefs." Ching Phor waited. "Many youths, indeed, many adults, cannot comprehend such an understanding. The decision is yours."

Her directness put him off. Keeping his participation secret would diminish his personal glory, but simultaneously it would shield him from Laureen's criticism. "Ching Phor, have you taken such an oath?"

"Aye," she laughed. "Too many years ago, long before you were born."

"Before my birth?"

"Aye."

"What will convince me?"

"Yourself. You will convince yourself, perhaps sooner than you expect. Tonight's meeting will be especially pleasing. We sing happy songs. Wise men make wonderful speeches. You will not easily forget this night."

"Will you need my assistance returning to the village?"

"Tranh, you are your grandmother's grandson. The journey home is not unfamiliar to me. For too long the land beyond the paddies has accepted me." She leaned toward him. "Out here, life is less complicated. Stay close by me. We will explore together."

Before them, a guitarist tested the chair. Unhappy with its placement, he moved it three feet further right of the table. Resuming his seat, he tuned the strings.

She arrived from nowhere. Watching the guitarist, Tranh had not seen the girl enter. Wearing a white silk *oa yai*, she stood before them. Her hair glistened. She glowed! Her eyes flashed in the darkness. Tranh sat breathless. Her delicate hands cupped at her waist. She opened her palms, spread her arms, then raised her hands to shoulder height. Her proud figure pressed the top of the *oa yai* until her palms came together beneath her chin. Lowering her eyes, she bowed, completing her greeting.

They were welcome.

The guitarist struck a chord. She smiled at them. And then, without warning, her song embraced them. Overwhelmed, Tranh lost the words. Where had the songbird come from? Was she real?

Ching Phor grasped Tranh's hand, but his eyes remained riveted on the girl.

She was the song swirling around him. Gradually she led him through Vietnam's history. When the guitarist stopped, Tranh felt miraculously alone with her. He jumped to his feet.

The gathering applauded.

"Tranh Nhu Lam!" Ching Phor rose to his side. Grudgingly, he turned to her. "Young man, you have found your place. This is clear. You have my support." Her eyes lowered.

Confused, speechless, Tranh nodded, then turned back to the girl. At that precise moment, her gaze fell on him. He was standing! She had noticed him. Heat rushed through his face. Pandemonium surged within.

Instinctively he lowered his eyes and bowed. Suspended in the pose, he calmed. When he straightened, the astonishing black eyes were still focussed on him. She smiled. The audience turned to observe the tall, handsome youth. She bowed in return and then, once again, their eyes locked. Totally enchanted, Tranh succumbed.

The girl raised her arms to the throng, smiled, and was gone.

Disappointment swept through him. Tranh slumped to his seat.

An impressive soldier moved center stage. His visored cap shadowed his face. The audience hushed. Certainly this was a leader of soldiers, a leader of men, victorious men.

"Welcome, brothers and sisters! I am Major Yuang Chi Xian. I bring greetings from your brother Ho Chi Minh. He wishes you well. He wants you to know he feels your suffering. He feels your deprivations. He shares your shackles. He understands your efforts. We are your brothers from the North. Like all brothers, we have much in common. We are farmers. We rise with the sun. We also work until nightfall. We grow your crops. You grow ours. Yours are ours. Ours are yours. We are men, we are women, we are children. We are Vietnam. This is why our leader, the great liberator of Vietnam, overwhelmed the Westerners before. He envisioned that we, the brothers of Vietnam, would take possession of our country. That we would have our crops, our land, our natural resources, just as the enemy from the West has theirs. Brother Ho loves Vietnam. He loves us all. Ho Chi Minh believes all Vietnamese are still his brothers. Still his sisters." The major moved two steps closer.

"When you have such a large family, you have much responsibility. Your liberator is a most responsible man. He is gifted with honor, endowed with courage. His vision is blessed with wisdom. Brother Ho does not understand the conduct of the leaders in the South. Ho is responsible. Saigon is not. They encourage the Westerners... again."

"Have they forgotten so soon?" His anger encompassed the audience.

"Have you forgotten so soon?" He moved left of the table.

"In our humble country we strive to preserve our birthright. The foreigners, the outsiders, do not understand our history. And some among us forget our traditions. They are blinded, blinded by greed, blinded by personal gain. They forsake their countrymen. They care not for our land. They want our resources. They want our servitude."

He shook his fist. "Ho Chi Minh refuses to grant them your lives, the lives of your children. Ho denies them your land, your resources."

The major walked to the edge of the clearing. The audience followed his movement. "Brother Ho does not understand these false Vietnamese who encourage the outsiders. Brother Ho wants you to know he will not disappoint your trust. He asks you not to forget our glorious victories. At Diem Bien Phu we taught the world a lesson, a meaningful lesson. It was not that long ago." He smiled. "Apparently the West learns slowly. Now a reminder is necessary. The lesson needs re-stating."

The major moved back to the table. "Why do your leaders forsake their past, forsake their people? You must ask these questions!" He slammed his fist on the table.

"We have friends! We have allies around the world! Ho Chi Minh has worked diligently to secure these honored friends. These allies know Vietnam must have independence. Our friends share their successes in order that we may build our own successful nation. This is why these friends already assist us! What does Saigon share?"

"Ho Chi Minh is a man, a man of action. Decisive action. His tolerance runs short. Soon he will effect your liberation. The enemies of Vietnam will tire of our persistence. Their families do not understand why their children die in our land!"

The major straightened. "In return for his support, Brother Ho asks for yours. He understands you have families to feed. He urges you to continue. He understands you must be cautious. He encourages prudence. But support has many forms. A bowl of rice, a safe haven, a place for storage, an errand, a song, an observant ear, silence. These are significant things. They will hasten your liberation. You must do what you feel you can, and then slightly more. On the path of your destiny Brother Ho asks that you consider your heritage. Consider the future of your offspring. We share the same path. We share the same destiny, the same future. We shall again be victorious!"

Tranh heard no more. His mind spun frantically. He turned into the waiting arms of Ching Phor.

Lai Khe

Tower Three rose high above the Lai Khe perimeter. While offering an unequalled view of the horizon, the elevation rendered the post an appetizing target for snipers. Tower duty was no bargain.

He toed the rubber. You want this don't you, big guy? Think you can handle it? Bullshit! His weight shifted back to his right foot. The left turned sliding into the pit beneath him. The right knee crossed over in front of the left. He pivoted. The right foot kicked high. Higher. His fingers gripped the seams. It would rise. The left hand took the ball from the glove below his waist. His left arm raised directly over his head. His cheeks inflated. The right leg reached ahead landing solidly. The left leg pushed forward. He exhaled. The ball flung to the target. Smoke! "The Mick" swung! Thud! "Strike Three! You're out!"

Hodges manned the watch.

A swivel-mounted starlight scope stood at the center of the platform. Four feet above the deck, binoculars rested on a shelf. A three-foot square map detailing coordinates and elevations beyond the perimeter was attached to a board to the right of the scope. A radio, linking Tower Three to an artillery coordinator and the numerous bunkers below, was mounted into a panel under the map. The ground troops relied heavily on the towers for surveillance.

A bench crossed the rear of the platform, where MacKerry, with arms folded over his chest, lay half-sleeping, the American way.

Hodges put his eye to the scope, beginning a scan from right to left.

Dying for a cigarette! Five more hours! A real pain in the ass. Like the bunkers better. Man, it's flat out there. Clear night. Not much goin down. The stars, they're like the lake. So many, so bright, peaceful. Who would ever guess? My favorite time of the day. Quiet out there. Could probably doze off. Dudley! Better not.

Well, big brother, you were right. I should have stayed in school. Here I am in scenic Lai Khe. Once upon a time you might have liked this place. Used to be a Michelin rubber plantation. Seems like the French knew how to live. Unbelievable buildings, unbelievable setting. Thousands of rubber trees. Now Headquarters Third Brigade, Big Red One. Beaucoup artillery, an airstrip. Seems pretty safe.

As usual the officers have it pretty good. The high rankers live in plantation homes. Big, beautiful homes. Some have pools, can you believe it? Not like our pool, but a pool here in Vietnam?

What's best about Lai Khe? The airstrip. Lots of commotion, lots of instant firepower. Supplies coming and going all the time. We got Air Cav, we got Tank Corps, we got us. The grunts. Lots of us.

We have a screened hooch. That's good. Our own hooch. Just the twelve of us. Still wish we were eleven. Figuring out how to trade Balman for a player to be named later. So far, no takers.

Dudley's around. Not seeing much of him. Every day he and Major White take a couple of Vietnamese policemen and zip off in a chopper. No clue where they're going. We'll find out soon enough.

We have a nightclub! Not the Copa, not even the Embers. Just a club. The Paddy Wagon. It's about 100 meters from our hooch. Twice this week that was too far for Balman and Parker. We found em in the morning about half way home.

It's clear out there. Must be two clicks from here to the treeline. Two rows of barbed wire in between. Mines and flares all over the place. It's not Long Binh, but there's plenty here. Charley likes to harass us. Advertising, Dudley calls it. Every now and then he'll throw in a few mortars just to let us know. For the eleven days we've been here, nada. Nobody's complaining, except Balman! What's new?

There's a village here. The only base with a village inside the perimeter. Used to be where the laborers lived. Laborers? More like slaves, I think. Anyway, where they lived. It's a secure area, surrounded by barbed wire. MPs patrol it. Not supposed to be in there, but the veterans say it's better than the shopping center. The shopping center! What a joke! There are a few shops, souvenirs, stuff like that. Then there are the bars. Two huge ones. Saigon tea, anyone? The bars feature Lai Khe's ladies of the evening. Guess what! They're government-inspected, prime cut. Each week, our medics give em the onceover. If they're clean, they keep their number. With a number, they're in business. No number, no business. The medics are like gods. From what Mac and I saw, there are no–zero–goddesses. For sure! Anyway, the shopping center is open til 1800. That's when we go to work. Night duty's a pain in the ass, but it could be worse, a lot worse.

There's nothing out there. No movement. My guys are probably sleeping on the job down there in the bunkers. Time for the wake-up call.

"Good Morning Vietnam! Bunker Three-Fiver, this is Tower Three. Anyone alive down there? Over!"

No response.

"Bunker Three-Fiver, this is Tower Three. Hello! Rise and shine! Bunker Three-Fiver, this is your Tower calling. Do you read me?"

"Uh, Tower Three, Three-Fiver, here. What's up?"

"It is now post time down there. Someone should be on their toes. Like, the thing is happening."

"Yeah? Where, brother? Don't seem like it," answered Cortes.

"Well, my man, if you don't stay awake, you may miss it. Then what'll you tell your grandchildren?"

"No sweat! I just want to live long enough to have grandchildren. You know where you can put your thing."

"Tower Three rogers that! Bunker Three-Four, this is the Tower. Do you read?"

Silence.

"Bunker Three-Four, have you been overrun?"

"Uh, Tower. This is Three-Four. We ain't been overrun. I say again, we ain't been overrun. Uh, wouldn't you know?" Parker asked.

"Not really. We've been grabbing some shut-eye ourselves up here. Can you bring me up to snuff on the activity level?"

"Yeah, well, let's see. Lavelle's asleep in the hole. He's got a death grip on his trigger. Think I should wake him?"

"Bunker Three-Four, this is your Tower. Proceed with caution. If he manages that thing like his sex life, it'll go off in his hand."

"Hey! Good one, Tower!" Bunker Three-Four was awake.

"Tower Three, this is Bunker Three-Three. Before you make any remarks about our sex lives, we're here, we're awake, we've been expecting your call. What's happening, amigo?"

"Three-Three, kemo sabe, this is your Tower. You win first prize! A visit to the freshly stocked, recently renovated House of The Rising Sun right here, in downtown Lai Khe! Way to go! Attire is optional, condoms are required. A local custom. Way to go guys! Dudley is proud of you. I am proud of you and I am sure in his infinite wisdom, LBJ himself is sleeping better knowing that you will not be part of tomorrow's body count. Keep up the good work."

"Bunker Three-Two, anybody home?"

Silence.

"Bunker Three-Two, come in."

Nothing.

"Bunker Three-Two, this is your Tower. Like to hear from you!"

Again, no response.

"Bunker Three-One, this is Tower Three. Do you read?"

"Loud and clear, Tower."

"My man Hoss, that you?" asked Hodges.

"Yes, indeedy, old buddy. The one and only. Weaver and I were just talking about your girlfriend. He's got her picture here. She's mighty fine. We miss her. Weaver's got a hard-on. Wants to know if you'd mind?"

"Bunker Three-One, that's my sister, you bozos! Keep the bullshit up, I'll introduce you. She'd straighten your ass right out. Bossiest woman alive, believe me!"

"Uh-huh, I see, Tower," replied Hoss. "Uh, Weaver says he's lost interest. His big guy just went off duty."

"Say, good buddy, how bout checkin out the stiffs in Bunker Three-Two? You wanna get back to me on that?"

"Will do, Tower."

Hodges set the microphone down and began to scan. He was hungry. A cigarette would be good. It would have to wait.

"Tower, this is Bunker Three-One."

"Tower Three, go!"

"Balman and Ghost are wide awake in Bunker Three-Two. Fact is, they're havin a little party. The Do Not Disturb Sign is out. They said to ring them up only in an emergency. They think you can handle the watch without their help. Their words, 'Don't be a pain in the ass and do not, under any circumstance, fall asleep!' That's a quote."

"Roger that, Bunker Three-One." Hodges hesitated. "Bunker Three-Two, wherever you are, party on! Glad to know all is well down there!"

"To all my Bunkers, this is your Tower, Tower Three, bringing you up to date. The front is quiet. Wire One is clear, Wire Two is clear. The bush is still. Despite your vigilance, there are no visible unfriendlies inside the wire. But the really big news, at this time, zero four three zero, is that The Rising Sun opens in just... one two zero minutes. Have a good day. Out."

334 days

Ben Cat

Her step seemed shorter than usual. Laureen slowed to remain by Mai Nin's side. The round brim of her grandmother's hat nearly covered her shoulders. Her tattered black shawl fell loosely across her breast.

"You are right. There was no sanctuary." The events of four years ago replayed tensely across Mai Nin's face.

"Were you frightened? Where did you hide?" asked Laureen.

"Horrible blasts struck the jungle." Mai Nin's face contorted. "Before we heard them, the airplanes were over the village. They disappeared in an instant. Before the village understood, before we could react, they returned. The second time they discharged their bombs. We had never seen anything like it," she shook her head. "Explosions beyond comprehension. The ground shook beneath us. The north fields were aflame. Our crops were devastated. We were helpless, helpless to save them. The village wept early that day." Mai Nin prodded the calf. "Then the helicopters, they landed amidst us. The noise was deafening. Soldiers were everywhere. We hid under the ground. It had been a long time." She paused. "The soldiers were frenzied. They were shouting and pointing their weapons. The village shook with fear. There was no protection, no escape. It was sudden, so unexpected. We were unprepared."

"Poor Tranh," said Laureen. "His world turned upside down."

"He stayed by my side. We comforted each other."

"What of the other villagers? What of the Elders? Was there resistance?"

"Who could resist such a force? The village was stunned. We accepted them. They stayed a week. They searched everywhere. They had many questions. Yuang Tien, his wife, and two brothers from Ben Suc were arrested."

"Yuang Tien? What had he done?"

"Child, you confuse me. Details escape me. Why must you know? It was four years ago. You were still studying in Saigon."

"Aye, but from history there are valuable lessons. We must rely on our history."

"But history from such a forgetful woman?" Mai Nin shrugged. "Yuang Tien was unwise, careless. The soldiers removed him, his wife, and his two brothers. They have never returned." Mai Nin stopped, turning to look at the village below. Her stick pointed to the southeast corner of the village. "He lived there, near the edge. When the soldiers searched his house, there were weapons under the flooring. He and the others were beaten. The house was set afire. When the flames reached the roof, there was ammunition woven into the thatch. The explosion injured two of the soldiers. Smoke and fear thickened the air." She shook her head. "We, we were frightened."

"What did the soldiers do?"

"At first they were shocked, but anger overcame them. Had the Americans in berets not been there, our own soldiers might have destroyed Ben Cat. The Saigon soldiers were inexperienced. Children, really."

"And what of the paddies? What could the Elders do with the paddies destroyed?"

"La, soldiers come, soldiers go. Why must you continue these questions? Saigon sent us food, insufficient food, but a beginning. Later, the National Liberators supplemented the repayment. The village returned to work. This year we shall have a full crop. We have come full circle. That is the way of Ben Cat. It was not the first such incident."

"Nor, Grandmother, will it be the last. Does this not demonstrate that we should leave? Beyond this place, there is life without jeopardy."

"And where would we go? Now that we have you back, why must we leave? Ben Cat is our home. Are you not content with your peace, with your books? With us? Certainly, we are more fortunate than most."

"Yes, Mai Nin. We enjoy good fortune. Ben Cat is my home, the home of my family. We can never be separated again. Mother would be pleased that we are together, would she not?"

Mai Nin smiled. "Most certainly. Your mother, my daughter, is fulfilled. You have studied well. Tranh benefits from your teaching. He reads wonderful stories."

"But he could do more, so much more. He needs challenge. He lacks inspiration. Away from Ben Cat, he would have real teachers, real challenge. Mother would want Tranh to be educated."

Mai Nin accepted Laureen's cleverness. "Aye, she would, but Tranh is not ready. His mind is elsewhere."

"He grows like a weed," observed Laureen. "He will stumble on the way to manhood."

Mai Nin halted. She turned to Laureen. "La Nhu Lam, Vietnam endures danger. You must see that Ben Cat is a haven. We remain unbothered. The intruders from the North and from the South may pass through, but they will pass us by. The Elders have control. They are experienced. Certainly more experienced than those soldiers we saw years ago."

"But, Grandmother, suppose they take our rice? They want our harvest. In Saigon there is never enough food. Never. The number of Liberators grows and they can no longer feed themselves. Our plentifulness may be our downfall."

"The Elders understand these things. This is not a matter of your arithmetic," chuckled Mai Nin. "This is a history lesson, or do you forget?"

Laureen laughed. "What of our oxen? Will the Elders protect them from the intruders?"

"La, as in the past, the Elders will represent us. They have earned our trust."

"Aye, Grandmother, they have earned our respect, but these enemies, both these enemies, are dangerous. Ben Cat is but one stop along the road to Saigon, another on the path to Hanoi."

"Laureen Nhu Lam, hear my riddle. If the intruder is not acknowledged by the homestead, has the homestead been intruded upon? If the homestead arises, prepares the meal, goes about its chores, then retires, who, then, notices the intruder?"

"Mai Nin, the riddle is unrealistic."

"That the intruder gains strength through recognition, that is the dilemma. We of Ben Cat must steel ourselves," Mai Nin tapped the ground twice, "steel ourselves to be disinterested in the presence of these intruders. For righteousness to triumph again, we must allow certain injustices to momentarily pass through our domain. In the span of our lifetime, they cause imperceptible disruption to our tranquility, to the tranquility of our village. These are the significant lessons of the past. The Elders know these things."

Laureen spoke carefully. "Your philosophy is clear, but it is merely philosophy. The intruders care not for philosophy. The American equipment in Saigon is terrifying. They have much power. And now they assemble in Lai Khe, merely fifteen kilometers away. Ho Chi Minh will resist to the end. The National Liberators have his support. The struggle seems endless."

"Ah, Lai Khe! We know Lai Khe well, do we not little one? Do you remember?"

"Not very well, Grandmother. Not well enough. Father's model reminds me."

"Aye, such bittersweet memories. You are certainly the most beautiful flower to grow in Lai Khe," beamed Mai Nin. "A magnificent bloom from the shade of the rubber trees. Very rare! Now, my flower, may we end this discussion for today? Our oxen are ready to fill their stomachs. As you know, it is still our work."

Lai Khe

Days became nights, nights became days. Boredom emerged as the enemy.

At 1500 hours, Thursday, March 2, the squad assembled inside the officers' mess. Twelve chairs faced a table. Left of the table was a blackboard and a map hanging from an easel.

"Yo, Mac," Hodges whispered, "show and tell."

"Uh huh."

"I never liked this stuff."

"Me neither," Mac smiled. "Think it's serious?"

Hodges laughed, "Is Dudley here? It's for real."

"Yeah. He's wearing his Sunday best." Mac nodded toward Dudley standing at the entry.

His fatigues were starched. His boots shone. His holster gleamed. Dudley was a thing of beauty, a large thing of beauty.

"Ten Hut!" Dudley barked.

The squad snapped to attention. Carrying a crooked cane with a brass duck head for a handle, Major White strode past Dudley to the table.

"As you were!" the major commanded.

The squad sat.

"Gentlemen, I trust you are acclimated to our environment. You have trained well." The major nodded at Dudley. "Now is the time to earn your pay. We need your assistance and your attention." The major crossed to the easel. With the tip of the cane he pointed at the map.

"This is an area we call the Iron Triangle. The southern tip of the Triangle is here, just east of Cu Chi. The northwest point is this town, Ben Suc. To the northeast is Ben Cat, here." The pointer marked a line from Ben Suc to Ben Cat.

"The Iron Triangle is designated a free-fire zone." The major moved to the blackboard. In big capitals he wrote:

IRON TRIANGLE – FREE FIRE

The squad stared at the board. White moved behind the table. He opened his file, nodded twice, then looked up.

"You will consider the Iron Triangle enemy territory. As you can see, the northernmost point is less than seventy kilometers from Saigon. This area is a threat to the security of our allies. Your mission is to assist in the elimination of this threat." He moved to the front of the table.

"We have designated two components to this process. The first commenced last month. Operation Cedar Falls. This operation is designed to make the presence of our airpower and superior firepower felt by the enemy. As part of this operation we have intensified our efforts to destroy enemy supply lines. The Ho Chi Minh Trail receives our daily attention. The second component is to destroy supply bases within the Triangle. These areas remain under heavy pressure. We find them, we hit them. We do not presume to know the whereabouts of all enemy strongholds in the Triangle. We do not presume to differentiate VC forces from civilians. We know their tendencies. We acknowledge their existence. They must be destroyed."

The major moved to the blackboard. He wrote:

CEDAR FALLS

Under that entry, he inscribed:

JUNCTION CITY

"Gentlemen, like the five squads you trained with, you belong to Operation Junction City. Each squad has been designated an area of responsibility. In your area you will assist in all operations identifying, destroying, and securing enemy supply bases."

"The secured areas will then be relinquished to the Army of the Republic of Vietnam, the ARVNs. You will assist the ARVNs in the creation of a military base and in whatever police actions are necessary to maintain that base. These, gentlemen, are your orders."

Again, the major moved to the blackboard.

ARVN–POLICE

"In your designated zone, the first such operation is Manhattan."

OPERATION MANHATTAN

"You will be attached to the 2nd - 28th Air Cavalry. The Black Horses."

2ND - 28TH – BLACK HORSES

"The Black Horses are a formidable, experienced, combat unit. They have the full support of the First Infantry Division and necessary elements of the Air Force." The major eyed the squad. Skepticism stared back. "Questions?"

Squad members shifted uncomfortably.

Hodges stood. "Sir, where, exactly, is our area?"

"Corporal, we are getting to that," answered the major. He returned to the blackboard.

BEN CAT

"Ben Cat is your area of responsibility. Sergeant Dudley and I have been spending some time around Ben Cat." White looked to Dudley. "We think you'll like it."

"Yes sir!" Dudley agreed.

"Intelligence indicates increased VC interest in this area. We do not believe it is active. The enemy does, shall we say, have influence in Ben Cat. We must discourage civilian interest. On the other hand," his cane touched the northernmost point of the Triangle, "Ben Suc is active, an enemy fortress. Ben Cat is not Ben Suc, yet." He shrugged. "VC fortresses lose." He scowled. "Ben Suc must go. It will, soon. That is when we expect the VC activity around Ben Cat to increase. We must be ready. We will hold Ben Cat."

Again, to the blackboard.

COSVN – PENTAGON

"The National Liberation Front, the VC, have used the Triangle as the base of their resistance for forty years. Our sources indicate their headquarters are underground, literally underground, somewhere in the Triangle. This headquarters they call the Central Office for South Vietnam, COSVN, the VC equivalent of the Pentagon. We want it. I say again, COSVN goes!"

"Now, wherever COSVN is, North Vietnamese Regulars, the NVR, are there, on the job. They assist in all COSVN operations. Make no mistake about it, they are trained, they are equipped, they are the real thing, the real thing."

"Junction City seals the Triangle," White's cane moved from Ben Suc to Ben Cat to Cu Chi then back to Ben Suc. "Next we shrink it." The cane moved inside the Triangle. "When we flush them out, we deal with the NVR, on our terms." He moved to the table, sitting on the edge.

"Sounds easy, right? Get this straight. Ben Cat is not Lai Khe. Our primary concern is VC. The VC have many faces. In a free-fire zone, suspicious activity is dealt with... aggressively. Farmers do not wear black pajamas! I say again. Suspicious activity gets immediate aggressive response."

"This is war! We are not in the hostage business. We do not want to waste one life, not one, taking a hostage. Understand that. If you don't, or if you have questions regarding this session, direct them to Sergeant Dudley, who, by the way, is one fine soldier." The major walked to the door. There, he turned. "Today's information is sensitive. Keep it to yourselves."

His jaw relaxed. "If you haven't been to downtown Lai Khe, I suggest you get to know the locals. Thank you!" He was gone.

"Ten Hut!" Dudley moved to the front of the desk. "Questions?"

"Sergeant, how many civilians in Ben Cat?" Ringhyter asked.

"Good, Ringhyter, you are thinking. Six hundred, give or take."

"Sergeant," Hodges began, "do they know we're coming?"

"Not from us, college boy. Not from us." Dudley paused. "Probably, you understand?"

"Got it Sergeant. Probably."

"Sergeant Dudley, when do we go?" asked Hosmach.

"When you are told, Hosmach. When you are told."

"Sergeant, what the hell? I mean, what's it all about?" Balman asked.

Dudley pointed to the board. "Balman, you see this? Read the board! That, Balman, is your tour of duty."

They read:

IRON TRIANGLE – FREE FIRE

CEDAR FALLS

JUNCTION CITY

ARVN – POLICE

OPERATION MANHATTAN

2ND - 28TH – BLACK HORSES

BEN CAT

COSVN – PENTAGON

320 days

Ben Cat

It was their special Wednesday. The Elders had determined that every fourth Wednesday was to be a day of rest for Ben Cat. For the children it was a day of recreation and enjoyment, of poetry interspersed with games.

Laureen sat on the steps of the neglected Catholic church, the children surrounding her. Beside her was her yellow backpack, their library. Each time she unzipped a compartment, their world expanded. Each time it closed, they were back in the village. They loved the zippers.

Today they had been especially rewarded. Before withdrawing her first book, Laureen had given each of the seven girls brightly colored ribbons. Each of the nine boys had received an elastic wrist band. The day had begun well.

As she completed the afternoon reading, Laureen acknowledged the children's restlessness. She closed the book and slid it into the sack. The children jumped up.

"Bite the Carp's Tail" invigorated them. Away from work in the paddies the children eagerly embraced childhood. Ticklish laughter, a rare sound in Ben Cat, filled the air.

Tranh stood apart, between childhood and manhood. "Bite the Tail" was beneath him.

"Tranh! Help Lin!" Laureen called.

Holding her scraped knee, Lin Qua Lac lay on the ground. Tranh smiled sympathetically. Lin, the cheerful, younger sister of Tranh's good friend Phong, basked in Tranh's gallantry.

The awkwardness of the game amused Laureen. With their hands placed on the hips of the person in front, the sixteen children formed a line. The first person was the head of the carp, the last the tail. The object of the game was for the head to "bite" or catch the tail without any participant breaking contact. This necessitated a coordinated effort by the entire body. The movements were resisted by the tail. When the head caught the tail, a great celebration ensued. The old head then became the new tail and the game would continue. The children tripped and fell until the inevitable arguments and tears.

Lin was always near the front. Never the head, never the tail, she somehow commanded center stage. Today was no exception. She glowed with boundless energy. Restored by Tranh, she resumed her position. Until she fell again, she would continue to radiate her contagious enthusiasm.

"So, brother," Laureen observed, "you have rescued her. You are her hero forever."

"La, hero or not, the game grows tiresome."

"Not for them," said Laureen. "The game is filled with irony, do you see?"

"Irony or awkwardness? Lin has already fallen three times."

"Does it remind you of anything?" Laureen asked.

"La, it is a game. A game for children. Why must it be more?"

"See how they struggle. The tail's slightest refusal creates enormous obstacles. And if the tail has a sympathizer, then all is lost. The obstructions are plentiful, the gains momentary."

"Who in line would side with the tail? They could never become the head," said Tranh.

"Aye, but who has more fun than Lin? She is never the head, never the tail, yet she enjoys herself more than the rest."

"Yes, sister, she has the most fun," he agreed, anxious to escape. "Are two caretakers really necessary?"

"Necessary? Well, handsome brother, if the game reflects Vietnam, think of yourself as a leader, a leader of our Saigon..."

"Your Saigon, Laureen. The city is unknown to me."

"Our Saigon, Tranh. You must oversee the game, organize our efforts. Where would Lin be without you?"

"If left alone, she would fall less. The children deserve happiness, but as a great leader from your Saigon," Tranh suggested slyly, "my responsibilities should change. My people need food. The crops, they need me." He pointed to the paddies. "Seriously La, though you and Grandmother need my help, my friends think me lazy and irresponsible. They lose respect for me."

"Tranh Nhu Lam, who treats you with disrespect? Why? You read, you write, you practice math. Someday you will help Ben Cat more than they realize."

"La, my friends see me just as you treat me, as a child. Do you see my height? Do you recognize my strength? Grandmother sees a grandchild, you see a younger brother, but, La, my childhood has ended."

"Is that so?" she smiled. "Yet one more reason to leave Ben Cat. You would benefit from real teachers, real schools. The world is larger than Ben Cat, larger than Saigon, larger than Vietnam. You could learn important things. With education, you could bring back knowledge to advance the village."

"The world beyond is not my concern. Must we always have this discussion? Like this day, it grows tiresome."

"Tranh, Grandmother ages. She would be safer in a larger city with proper medical care."

"Grandmother will never leave. If our mother could not move her, how shall you? She despises Saigon. There is no air. There are too many people, too much filth. How many times must she say Ben Cat is where she started, where she will end?"

"Grandmother is stubborn. You could help. She would never deter you. If she saw you wanted schooling, then she would relocate. We would be safe. My friends in Saigon would welcome us. Where they live is quite beautiful."

Tranh waved his hands across the surrounding hillside. "More beautiful than this?"

"The beauty is different. Accompany me to the city. See for yourself."

Tranh shifted. "Laureen, may we end this? Grandmother awaits you, the crops need me."

"Aye, aye. Children!" she called. "We must stop now! Your meals await. Your parents will grow angry, your meals will grow cold."

The children began to disperse.

"La, have you a boyfriend in Saigon?" Tranh asked.

"No, brother! No boyfriend. My heart is not in Saigon. It is with you, with you and Grandmother. In Saigon there are books and friends and much advice. Always, advice. We are both of us so very young, so inexperienced."

"No boyfriend? What about Guyan?"

"Guyan is a friend. My oldest friend, but certainly not a boyfriend."

"Is Guyan too daring for Saigon?" Trank asked archly.

"In Saigon we do not discuss Ben Cat. There is never mention of Guyan's daring. That is the business of Guyan." Laureen hesitated. "However, in Saigon arrangements are under way for *your* bride. Indeed, a rare plum has been located. She will bloom in about ten years. Does that suit you?"

"Ten years! How rare a plum that must be. Sister, will this plum bear fruit?" joked Tranh.

"Tranh Nhu Lam!" Laureen blushed. "You spend too much time with the likes of Guyan!"

"So, sister, there is the problem. Guyan proposes fruit?"

"Tranh! Stop this chatter. Someone will overhear." Laureen laughed, but her color heightened. "Besides, Guyan is devoted to his politics, which do not necessarily agree with mine!"

"Ha! You blush! What does this blush mean?" Tranh briefly enjoyed her annoyance before changing the subject. "So, when do you return to the city?"

"On Sunday. The trip is tiresome. There are so many checkpoints. The bus is overcrowded with many people from the northern provinces," she answered. "You will help Grandmother?"

"Aye. You and Grandmother can rely on me."

"Thank you, brother. You are a good brother, a better grandson." Laureen kissed his cheek and turned for home. Tranh watched her progress out of sight, then raced toward the temple.

They were further apart than when the day began.

****

"Ching Phor, there are so many," Tranh whispered.

"Tranh Nhu Lam, you join us? This pleases me. Yes, there are more tonight. There are others on other nights."

"Others? More than this? Where are they? Will they be on time for the meeting?"

"The meeting? This night there is no meeting. Tonight we work. This night is a test. If you succeed, your reward will be other nights. Remember, you must only help when asked. Guyan or Phong will come to you. Do not seek them out. Your enthusiasm must remain unnoticed." She paused. "The Americans will be coming."

Tranh recoiled. "The Americans? Coming to Ben Cat? How do you know?"

"Informed people, well-advised people, know these things. This is why so many work so hard. We prepare the village."

"How many Americans? How long will they stay?"

Ching Phor placed her hands on Tranh's cheeks. "It matters not. Preparation, that is our concern. Do not become excited or confused. If we succeed, Ben Cat will have no attraction for the Americans. How interested can soldiers be in a village of farmers whose rice they do not eat?"

"Yes, Ching Phor, but what of the songbird?"

"Ah, the songbird! The voice of an angel. She flies to many meetings. We will not see her this night."

"No songbird? No meeting?" Tranh's enthusiasm waned. "Perhaps Grandmother needs me."

"Tranh Nhu Lam, tonight we need your strength. We carry those baskets," she pointed to forty baskets neatly lined up behind the temple, "to the safety of the jungle."

"Those baskets?" Tranh balked. "They are huge!"

She smiled. "Aye, big for the shepherd, not for the oxen."

Two long poles resembling a yoke firmly attached to the middle of each basket. "This seems the work of oxen," Tranh muttered. "What is in the baskets?"

"True oxen never ask."

"But where do these goods come from?"

"From the neighbors of the oxen."

"From the village? We have so little."

"From the village and our neighbors beyond. It is a good harvest, is it not?" She put her hand on top of his head. "Be not concerned with these questions. Pick your course. The right one has the answers."

Tranh absorbed the reprimand. He must not appear too young for such responsibility. "Will we be late?"

"Ah, you worry that you will be missed. Does Laureen know your whereabouts?"

"No, Ching Phor. She cooks for Grandmother."

"Ah, tomorrow you must tell Mai Nin you spent the night with me. She will understand."

"Are you certain?"

"Mai Nin understands your eagerness. Tomorrow, tell her we were together. Now let us see if you can handle the basket as easily as you ask questions," Ching Phor said, bending to test the weight of one basket.

"Ching Phor, you carry an end!" Tranh was horrified.

"Aye, Tranh, this old farmer carries an end. And you, ha! As a grazer of cattle you will struggle to maintain the pace."

Guyan appeared from the side of the temple and methodically began checking each basket. He fastened the lids, tested the yokes. Occasionally he rearranged a pair of carriers. Then he summoned Ching Phor to a position near the rear of the column. As he instructed her, he studied

Tranh. Twice she nodded before returning to his side.

"Come Tranh, we shall hoist this one at the end." She moved to their basket. "Guyan says it is the lightest."

"Guyan noticed me. What did he say?"

"He asked about your sister. He is disappointed she does not know."

"Guyan will not tell her?"

"Tranh, Guyan has already forgotten that you are here. Tonight we are oxen. One old, one young. That is what Guyan sees. Like your oxen, we must now get in line with the others. They will lead us. Let them smooth our trail."

They took up their position. Tranh tested the worn handles. Then, as he looked around, he noticed Phong dressed in black. All nine Viet Cong escorts carried Russian-made AK-47 automatic rifles. No longer an ox, Phong was a soldier!

Guyan waved the column forward. The escorts spaced themselves along the sides of the column.

Before they lifted the baskets, Ching Phor handed two scarfs to Tranh. "Wear these over your shoulders, under the yoke," she instructed. "They will ease the journey. Tomorrow, you may not be so sore. Now, little ox, put your shoulder to the yoke. Tonight, you become a man. Wonder no longer about your songbird, this is why she sings to you."

Tranh crouched, then slowly rose lifting the heavy weight. They followed the carriers in front of them. Guyan stood where the line had begun, counting the baskets, prodding his oxen.

"Ah, my most determined carriers. Of this pair there is no doubt. Be strong and steady. Maintain your distance and all will go well," he instructed.

After struggling through the heavy jungle, the group turned south. The thickness became a defined trail. Tranh gratefully accepted the transformation. Under a roof of heavy limbs, they had entered a living tunnel.

The pace quickened.

Lai Khe

Thunder erupted ahead. The Air Force paved the way, doing their thing.

On the runway fifteen carrier gunships lined up behind their six pesky Bumble Bee escorts.

Two captains, two lieutenants, and four sergeants, all wearing the distinctive Black Horse Emblem of the 2nd-28th, listened as Major White gave final instructions. Two ARVN officers nodded occasionally. Dudley stood silently next to the major.

The Black Horses lounged under the trees near their choppers. Their gear lay around them in the lucky arrangement of the day.

MacKerry and Hodges shared a tree facing their chopper, Bulldog Eight.

"You feeling it?" Hodges asked.

"Uh huh."

"The gut?"

"Yuh. The gut."

"Me too." Hodges nodded toward White. "Maybe they'll call it off."

"Right, you bet. Then it'd be tomorrow. Might as well get it over with."

"Mac, you wanna be an airborne ranger? You wanna live through hell and danger?"

"Please Mr. Hodges, can I?"

"Wanna go to Vietnam? Wanna kill the Viet Cong?"

"Right."

The major turned to the choppers. Above his head he circled his right hand. The engines roared.

A Black Horse captain faced his troops. With hands at waist level, he motioned his palms down, alerting the ranks.

The other captain handed White a headset. Covering his left ear, the major placed the receiver to his right.

The Black Horses shuffled their gear.

Hodges surveyed Bulldog Eight. Its two doorgunners arranged their bandoleers and swivelled their M-60 machine guns, checking the sights.

Hodges lowered his head. Two deep breaths. Get it together! This is not an ambush. This is an invasion. They are out there. You are going to them. Casualties! Not me. Not me. Pick yourself up!

"Mac! This is it!" Hodges shouted over the roar of the engines. "Keep your ass down!"

"Yeah, will do! You too!"

With another circling motion White rounded up the troops. The Black Horses scrambled to their feet, grabbed their gear, and sprinted onto the choppers.

Go! Go! Go! Dudley's squad clambered into Bulldog Eight.

The pilot acknowledged Dudley, the last to arrive. Dudley raised his right thumb. The pilot nodded.

They lifted up into panic. Airborne! Shit!

One hundred thirty-six Americans and ten ARVNs headed to Ben Cat.

At full altitude, Ringhyter paled. He leaned left, quaked twice, then vomited. Parker heaved violently.

"Jesus, Ringhyter! Jesus, Parker! What the fuck!" screamed Balman. "What assholes! Don't anybody over here even think about it!"

"Hoss, don't look down!"

"That's got nuthin to do with it!" shouted Hosmach covering his mouth.

"Way to go Hosmach! Jesus! What's with you assholes?" yelled Balman.

"Shut up, Balman!" barked Hodges.

"As you were!" Dudley ordered. "Ringhyter, Parker, clean yourselves up. We are. Going in!"

Bulldog Eight swooped around a hillside and into the war.

Black smoke billowed up from the jungle.

The thunder!

Small fires raged around the fields.

Burn you fuckers!

The helicopter shifted south. The village! There it is!

A church?

Two Bumble Bees buzzed the perimeter. Their bullets poured into the fields. The Americans had arrived.

"On your toes! Count of three!" Dudley commanded.

This is it!

"One!" The squad rose to their feet.

Helmet on! Can do! Can do!

"Two!" The chopper hovered near the ground.

Land soft! Run! Run!

"Three!"

"Go! Go! Fuck em! Go!" Hodges hit the ground running. Struggling to maintain his balance, he locked and loaded.

Run fast! Run low!

Look! Look! Fence! Fence! Go! Go!

Hodges dove behind a sparsely wired fence where Bravo Company had already assembled. His helmet rolled forward. Shit!

Bravo Six, their captain, barked at the radio.

My helmet!

Bravo Six fisted his lieutenant.

Delta Six is in place! The north is covered. Here we go!

Bravo Six checked his watch. He tapped his lieutenant's shoulder, pointing to the wooden archway over Highway Thirteen, the entrance to Ben Cat.

The lieutenant jerked his thumb right, then left.

Two sergeants barked. Bravo Company ran to positions on either side of the archway.

Hodges crawled to his helmet. Goddamit!

Sporadic pings snapped at the invisible enemy.

Hodges dove into the tall grass left of the arch. He looked down. His arms were bleeding from scratches.

Can't breathe! No air! Hodges gasped. Yes!

He stared through the grass.

Nothing! Where are you?

His arms throbbed. Fuck this! Okay! Okay! Now what?

Hodges looked to Dudley lying to the right of the arch.

Dudley! You look ridiculous!

The lieutenant signalled one sergeant right, another left.

The sergeants stared back, waiting.

The lieutenant pushed his hand forward.

"Tiger! Move out!" barked the first sergeant.

"Snake! Go!" shouted the second.

Troops on both sides of the arch jumped up and sprinted down the sides of the road.

Hodges focussed on Snake. Get there!

Snake stopped behind a wooden cart filled with hay. He looked back at them, paused then swivelled to the rear of the cart, firing into the hay. He ducked back.

Nothing! Jesus!

Snake beckoned. Two Black Horses sprinted to the cart.

Snake darted ahead to the first hut.

The backups at the cart stabbed the hay. Two more men arrived. They lifted the side of the cart, tipping it over. Hay spilled over the ground.

"Yo! Mammasan! Anybody home?" Snake fired into the hut then spun back to the side of the entrance.

Nothing! Fuck this!

Snake ran ahead. The backups stormed the hut. One stood right of the door. One left. They nodded. The first dove left through the door. The other right.

MacKerry and Hodges raced to the cart.

Black Horses crashed into the huts of Ben Cat.

"Knock, knock, Pappysan. Come out, come out, wherever the hell you are!" Sporadic bursts. Nothing!

Somewhere down the line. "Hello! Lookie here! Yo! Lookie here!"

A discovery!

"Yo! Pappysan! C'mon out. C'mon now. Easy! Easy! Don't give me no reason to waste your ass! C'mon Mammasan! Bring those little ones up here. Easy now! I see! The neighbors! What! More neighbors! A friggin block party! Yo! Sarge! We got a block party here! Jesus! Ya gotta see this! Must be thirty of 'em. Right here in the pit."

Black Horses surrounded the hut.

Civilians straggled onto the dirt road.

Hodges looked at them. They're dazed, not surprised!

These were not the Vietnamese of Lai Khe, or Long Binh, or Ton Son Nhut. Sparse clothing. Worn footwear. Weathered skin. Stooped posture. These were peasants.

"Mac, they're dirty."

"Man, they been under ground."

"Yeah."

By 1330 hours Bravo and Delta Companies had completed the initial sweep of Ben Cat.

By 1945 hours the American and ARVN intelligence teams had completed their initial inspections.

At 2030 hours Bulldog Eight took the squad back to Lai Khe. They would return in the morning.

White and Dudley remained in Ben Cat with the Black Horses.

At 2100 hours the peasants of Ben Cat returned to their homes.

Thirty-two rockets had blistered the jungle.

Thousands of American rounds had been expended.

The paddies lay quiet.

Ben Cat

"Obese! They are obese." Tranh pushed his bowl forward.

"Ching Phor, honored guest, please forgive Tranh," Laureen began. "The Americans preoccupy him." She motioned to his bowl. "Tranh Nhu Lam, eat your rice."

"The excitement is understandable," Ching Phor nodded. "Grandmother, old friend, what do you think?"

"My oxen missed their work. Ben Cat lost a day."

"The paddies are damaged," said Tranh.

"But we are unharmed," Laureen reminded.

"You are fortunate. They entered my home," said Ching Phor.

Tranh set his chopsticks down. "Your home? Were you there?"

"Aye."

"What did they do? What did you say?"

"*Chao*!" Ching Phor laughed. "They seemed surprised."

"No wonder," said Laureen. "Were you frightened?"

"Perhaps, but my fear was less than their surprise." Ching Phor looked to Mai Nin. "Did they come here?"

"They did," answered Mai Nin.

"Grandmother kept them out," said Laureen. "She sat in the rocker on the porch. They pointed at her. She played dumb. One came halfway up the steps. She spit betelnut at his feet. He jumped back. They walked around the house, looked in the windows. They yelled at her, but they left," Laureen laughed. "What do you suppose they think?"

"That Grandmother has rocked too long," Ching Phor laughed. "Tell me, old friend, have you lost your mind?"

"Just my memory."

"They were angry," added Tranh. "Do they always yell?"

"They are afraid," Ching Phor shrugged. "Home is far away."

"Not far enough," said Tranh.

Mai Nin patted Tranh's forearm. "The visitors will see we are harmless. Harmless and poor. When they are convinced, they will leave. We will rebuild, as we always do."

"But the crops?"

"The heart of the paddies still beats," said Ching Phor. "The limbs, they are wounded, but the heart, the heart is strong. Soon the Americans will bring us food. And their doctors will mend things that we do not know make us unwell."

Laureen rose, taking Tranh's bowl for refilling. "Ching Phor, are you certain? How do you know these things?"

"Ah, Laureen," said Grandmother. "Ching Phor is wise in the ways of the world. Before you were born, she brought knowledge of the world beyond to Ben Cat. We have progressed since then." Mai Nin turned to Ching Phor. "You see, old friend, occasionally my memory still works."

"Ching Phor, you are not of Ben Cat? From where then?" asked Laureen.

"Grandmother, what meddlesome children you have! They are too long with the animals," Ching Phor laughed. "Do they think that Ben Cat has never changed, that new citizens never arrive?"

"Ching Phor! Please excuse me!" Laureen blushed.

"Laureen, do not be so serious. Your apology is unnecessary. My life is like one of your books. When you have more time, perhaps we shall turn the pages together," Ching Phor smiled. "It might be unwise to read just one chapter."

"That would be wonderful."

"How many Americans are still here?" interrupted Tranh.

"Who would count?" answered Ching Phor.

"They have many guns."

"Aye, fancy guns," Ching Phor shrugged. "But no targets."

"Are the black soldiers different?"

"Different but the same," said Ching Phor.

"They do not live equally," Laureen began. "According to my reading they often disagree."

"Like our disagreements, perhaps," reminded Mai Nin. "Sometimes we do not live together, but we are Vietnamese, are we not? Ching Phor is correct. They are different but the same."

Ching Phor reached into her straw bag. "Old friend, do you remember these?" She handed two scarves across the table to Mai Nin.

Mai Nin accepted the scarves, stretching them across her lap. "Green and black," she smiled. "My favorite colors. These scarves are old but not forgotten."

"While you do your work, they may shield you."

"Years ago they brought us good fortune, did they not?"

Ching Phor smiled. "Like the lucky scarves, we are tattered, but not without purpose."

"Aye, tattered, not purposeless."

Ching Phor rose. "My stay must end. We grow weary. After such a day, the young should let us sleep. Your generous table is appreciated. Thank you all."

Mai Nin stood across from her. "Ching Phor, you must come more often. My old bones need more attention than the children provide. And thank you for returning the scarves. To see them again is no surprise."

****

Budweiser was the order of the evening.

Stripped to their scivvies, MacKerry, Hosmach, and Hodges lay on their bunks, beers within reach.

"They're small. Wiry and small, like jockeys," MacKerry said.

"Nice teeth," laughed Hosmach. "They're either black or missing. Can't figure which is worse."

"You hear how they talk?" asked Hodges. "They speak so fast, sound so angry. Mean, you know?"

Hosmach laughed. "Looney Tunes at 78 speed."

"They were excited. They're scared," explained Mac.

"I don't think so," said Hodges. "I think fierce, yeah fierce."

"Bullshit! They're scared. Christ, who wouldn't be? What a day! They woke up hearing everything around them blowing up..." began Hosmach.

"If they were sleeping to begin with," interrupted Hodges.

"Yeah, well then, while the shit hits the fan, the Bumble Bees spray bullets all around the village. They couldn't get out..."

"Or back in," said Hodges.

"Yeah, or back home. Then a bunch of choppers drop sixty armed GIs to the north and sixty more to the south. They know we're locked and loaded and gonna shoot first, ask later," Hosmach shrugged. "They're scared."

Hodges lowered his beer. "Unless they expected it."

"Shit, Hodges! What d'ya mean expected it? How could they expect it?"

"I don't know. Somebody should have panicked. They were too calm, like they knew. That's all."

Mac put his empty can on the floor. "They don't look like trouble. If you ask me, they look like jockeys."

"Yeah, jockeys that never won a race," laughed Hosmach. "Maybe that's what this is, the place where losing jockeys live forever."

"Foreva!" said Hodges. "I'd like to talk with them. See what makes 'em tick."

"Good luck!" Hosmach chuckled. "Who says they tick to begin with?"

The east door of the hooch swung open. Ringhyter and Parker stumbled in. Behind them Weaver and Balman pretended to vomit.

"It ain't funny, Balman," defended Ringhyter. "Wait'll it happens to you."

"It ain't gonna happen to me, don't you worry."

Hodges closed his eyes. "Where's the Ghost?"

Ben Cat

Republican. Democrat. Democrat. Republican, Republican, Republican. Good, we're ahead!

The Elders had submitted.

The government of South Vietnam mandated that all residents register. Each household was compelled to identify their domicile and list the occupants and their ages. While ostensibly creating a list of eligible voters for the free election scheduled for the fall, the process further served to identify the permanent villagers.

Hodges could barely tolerate the last of his ten-hour shift. The day before he had been assigned to the same registration table. Aided by a non-English-speaking assistant, an ARVN translator conducted the tedious interviews. Twenty residents of Ben Cat still awaited processing.

Hodges' squad mates supervised more active work details which were staffed by villagers. They had established a defined, defensible perimeter and fortified the command bunker in the southeast corner of the village. Other projects were also underway. In exchange for work, the villagers received food and medical treatment.

Bravo and Delta Black Horse Companies still manned the defenses. Impatiently, they trained two ARVN companies to take over.

After clearing the checkpoints at the newly constructed south and north gates, selected men and women worked the paddies. The crops were not receiving their usual care, but Ben Cat was busy.

Hodges was not. The villagers ignored him. In their excited animated language they spoke only to the ARVNs.

To Hodges' right a bent, elderly woman vigorously chewed betelnut. Wearing a large straw hat, and brandishing a six-foot bamboo walking stick, the woman stepped forward confidently. Her deft signature caught his interest. Amused that she could write, Hodges studied her. He could see that she noticed his surveillance. Completing the form, she stepped to her right, half turning her back to the American. She addressed the boy with her.

"Tranh Nhu Lam, now you must sign. The loyal soldier will show you where," she nodded at the ARVN translator. "Do this quickly, for this speechless American shows surprise that we are able to write. Sign neatly so he will know that we are not completely unintelligent!" The boy glanced quizzically at Hodges, then leaned forward to sign.

The translator looked at the uncomprehending Hodges and laughed heartily.

"What did she say?" Hodges asked.

The translator hesitated. "That you have the look of a python snake. That her grandson should think of you as such."

"What?" Why would she say that?"

"Maybe she has lost her mind," chuckled the translator.

"Uh-huh, too bad," said Hodges, looking past the woman to the boy. "What is this boy's name?"

The translator checked the signature. "Tranh Nhu Lam," he responded, then in Vietnamese he said to his assistant, "this American asks the boy's name. Do you suppose he has a yearning for his behind? Ha! Ha!"

The assistant leaned across the table, cynically scrutinizing Hodges.

Mai Nin turned on Hodges. In Vietnamese she barked, "American, you behave like a goat. We are Vietnamese! You are a guest in our village. If you approach my grandson, you will feel the wrath of his grandmother. And of all Ben Cat! You, visitor, must show my grandson respect!" Emphatically, the old lady slammed the end of her walking stick on the table in front of Hodges.

Startled, Hodges jumped up, knocking over his chair. The villagers laughed uneasily.

"What the hell? What did she say now?" Hodges towered above her.

Confronted with the unexpected, the translator wavered.

Protectively, Tranh stepped in front of his grandmother. Villagers circled about them.

The translator sprang to his feet. "Apologize GI!"

"Apologize? For what?"

"Honored Grandmother, the American apologizes for the impropriety of his remark. He begs your forgiveness! He is unfamiliar with the ways of Ben Cat."

Tranh glared at Hodges. The old lady raised the walking stick. Again she slammed it down. Bristling, she spit betelnut at Hodges' feet. The villagers laughed.

"Tell the American that his manners must improve, or he will be an unwelcome guest in our village."

The translator turned to Hodges. "The woman is crazy. Bow to her so she will leave and we may return to our work." He shrugged. "We lose much time."

"What has happened here? Why should I bow to this crazy lady?"

"Because, GI, it is the only way she will leave."

Flushed with humiliation, Hodges deplored his inability to reverse the situation. He bowed, mumbling, "Go away, old lady, go away!"

"Mai Nin," the translator began, "the American apologizes. He will never approach your grandson. Perhaps it was a bad joke? May we return to the registration? It grows late. Your neighbors await."

"Aye!" she spat. But they did not leave. Placing her arm around the boy's waist, she turned her back to Hodges and faced the next registrant.

Unprepared, Hodges was captivated.

Dark, bright eyes blazed with intelligence. A stunning woman with long, glistening hair studied him.

Hodges stumbled back.

High cheekbones graced a delicate, serene face. Fresh and flawless, the skin was fair, soft.

Hodges faltered. She was with the old lady! A granddaughter! No!

The granddaughter lifted the pen and leaned over the table.

Breasts!

Finishing her signature, she set the pen down. She turned toward the American, smiling radiantly.

Remarkably, they connected. Incredibly, they realized it.

While waiting in line Laureen had observed the American. He did not appear discourteous. Understandably bored, he had been analyzing the villagers. He was uncomfortable, but not unfriendly. She had detected a spark of interest.

Softly, slowly, clearly, she spoke. "*S'il vous plaît, parlez-vous français?*"

"French!" Hodges started. He groped for the words. "*Oui, oui Mademoiselle. Un petit peu*. A little. *Merci*! Thank you. *Merci beaucoup*!" More words would not come.

It was a beginning.

"Mai Nin," Laureen said, "there is most certainly a misunderstanding. It seems that we have misjudged this guest. Should we not acknowledge the error?"

Tranh spoke first, "We should leave. The American is a fool."

Mai Nin turned to the American. He was tall and red from the sun. "Tell the American that we regret any misunderstanding. That is all."

"Monsieur, there seems a misunderstanding. You have been treated unfairly. We shall explain to the villagers. We regret this incident. Please accept our apology."

He knew it was French. She, she was apologizing for whatever had happened. Yes!

She looked up at him steadily and smiled brightly. "*Comprenez-vous?*"

"*Un peu. Merci.*"

The boy shrugged, the grandmother sighed.

The three turned to leave.

He must stop them. He fumbled for words.

"Mademoiselle, *s'il vous plaît. S'il vous plaît*! *Un moment. Quel est votre nom?*" Damn! The pronunciation! Please stop. "Mademoiselle, *s'il vous plaît?*"

She stopped!

"Monsieur, my grandmother is named Mai Nin. This is her grandson, my brother, Tranh Nhu Lam. My name is Laureen, Laureen Nhu Lam," she bowed.

Laureen Nhu Lam! Hodges could not afford an error.

"*Merci*!" Jesus! Merci! Is that the best you can do!

He faced the old lady. "Mai Nin." He bowed.

Then the boy. "Tranh." He bowed.

He smiled to her. "Laureen Nhu Lam." He bowed.

In his slowest, most gentle English, "My name is Hodges. Caster Thompson Hodges. Your kindness overwhelms me. Thank you."

Ben Cat

"A chance meeting?" quizzed Mai Nin.

"Grandmother, a chance meeting. Inconsequential, really,"

"Rarely do such things happen in Ben Cat."

"He wanted to thank me. That is all."

"Laureen Nhu Lam, you have encouraged the American. You have called attention to our household. This is serious, a serious breach."

"Grandmother, please! My intent was to be courteous."

"Courteous? How curious! Courteous to the people who burn our paddies! Courteous to the visitors who enclose us like dogs! Courteous to those who show us no respect!"

"Grandmother! No." Laureen softened her voice. "Courteous to a young man whose people give us food and medicine. Courteous to a man from afar who comes to protect us. Of respect for his parents, who send us their son, should we not at least make him welcome? He does us no harm."

"Laureen Nhu Lam, history is trustworthy. Do you remember?" Mai Nin squeezed her granddaughter's hand. "If the intruder is not acknowledged by the homestead, then has the homestead been intruded upon? Laureen, you have acknowledged the intruder. This is unwise."

Unsettled by the rare disagreement, Tranh drummed his fingers on the table.

Sensing his discomfort, Mai Nin turned to him. "Tranh, this

conversation is not for you. Leave us to resolve our differences. Today Ching Phor works at the new medical tent. Please walk her home." Mai Nin reached to the shelf behind her. "Give her this green scarf. It will give her pleasure."

"Yes, Grandmother." Tranh took the scarf and eagerly raced to the recently erected hospital tent. When he got there, he watched for a while before seeking out Ching Phor.

An American doctor brandished a needle. An anguished mother appeased her crying child. A man, dressed in village garb, but unfamiliar to Tranh, was being treated by a different doctor. The villager had a bewildered look as the doctor withdrew a syringe from his arm. Outside the tent twenty people waited in line.

Ching Phor was cleaning an empty examination stall. She wiped a metal tray near the table. Suddenly Tranh saw her drop several packets into her loose shirt. Tranh stifled a laugh.

"Tranh Nhu Lam!" Ching Phor exclaimed as he approached her. "What a surprise. Will you walk with me?"

"Aye," Tranh nodded, reaching into his pocket. "Mai Nin wanted you to wear this scarf."

"Ah, the green one. It is a favorite. However, tonight the scarf will not be necessary. You must return it to Mai Nin. It is a game we play. Remember to extend my appreciation to Mai Nin. Tell her our people grow healthy."

Tranh placed the scarf carefully back in his pocket. "Your message will be delivered along with the scarf."

"But first," said Ching Phor, "we visit Buddha."

"Buddha?"

"Aye, Buddha. Today we are more fortunate than usual. Many believers were treated," explained Ching Phor as they walked toward the temple.

"Are the Americans good healers?" Tranh asked.

"Aye! But when they understand our lifestyle, they will be better. Their training is evident. Far superior to our own countrymen, who are careless and disinterested."

"Disinterested? What does that mean?"

"The Saigon healers resent us. The country is not the assignment they choose. To the Americans, we are foolish, but they dislike suffering. To the Saigon healers we are beneath them, unworthy of their attention. To heal is their privilege, not their motivation."

At the temple Ching Phor gave him instructions. "Please Tranh, worship for me. We will enter together. You must remain until my return. Concentrate on Buddha. Do not allow my wanderings to detract from the sincerity of your gratitude."

"Worship? For you? How?"

"Imitate the others. Sometimes we must all be imitators."

Although unfamiliar with the temple, Tranh would not disappoint her. He sat passively on the floor. His thoughts returned to the American, to Laureen's baffling indiscipline. Somehow she seemed misplaced in Ben Cat.

Attempting to subdue his inner conflict, Tranh closed his eyes to meditate. Ching Phor moved to the front of the temple. Looking back to Tranh, she smiled, then disappeared behind the Buddha.

Ben Cat

Hodges squatted and waddled three feet forward. "Quack, quack, quack!"

"*Vai bo*!" shrieked the old woman.

MacKerry laughed. The elderly woman next to him roared hysterically.

"*Vai bo*?"

"Aye, *vai bo*!"

Hodges got on all fours. "Woof! Woof!"

"*Cho*!" shrieked the woman.

"*Cho*?"

"*Cho.*" Betelnut splattered on the ground.

"Ah, two more words. You see Mac, it isn't that hard."

"I see, man. I see. You're nuts."

The two old women, MacKerry, and Hodges were waiting to begin the weekly distribution of food to the village. Sixty meters away from their cargo truck, Ben Cat formed a line. Two ARVN policemen checked names against the registration list. At first the villagers had been hesitant to accept the food. Now the line formed early every Friday. The small people of Ben Cat seemed to have grown large appetites.

During their first detail Hodges had removed one of his contact lenses, completely astounding Xiam Thong. Believing that without the magical lens he could not see, she had promptly announced to each recipient of food that he was blind, "*Dui.*" The villagers were awed. Hodges had become a celebrity. Now even strangers greeted him, *"Chao Dui"* or "*Dui, eh dui!*" Hodges enjoyed the notoriety.

MacKerry had relayed the story to the squad, and the nickname stuck. To the Americans and Vietnamese alike, Hodges was Dui.

"C'mon, Dui, we got work to do. The natives are restless. Up or down?"

"Down," Hodges answered.

"Okay, Quam Thi, up you go," Mac offered a hand to help the old woman up onto the truck's platform.

Quam Thi grasped Mac's well-muscled arm instead. She feigned light-headedness. Hodges and Xiam Thong laughed. Mac was the strongest man the women had ever seen. He hoisted her onto the truck, then jumped up behind her. She moved forward to pass cartons to Mac, who then lowered them to Hodges. Xiam Thong completed the delivery. She relished the prestige.

"So they're gonna leave," Mac began.

"Next week," Hodges shrugged. "No more Black Horses." He handed a carton to Quam Thi. "This place is changing."

"Yeah, well that's one change I could do without. You think the ARVNs are ready to take over?"

"What we think doesn't matter, does it?"

"No, it doesn't." Mac lowered another carton. "I don't like it. We're gonna be alone."

"Not quite, Mac. Not quite."

The transformation of Ben Cat was nearly complete. Bunkers and barbed wire ringed the perimeter. Satisfied with their training of the ARVN guards, the Black Horses were ready to move on.

At the north end of Ben Cat the principal ARVN encampment was segregated from the village by barbed wire. To relieve their cramped living quarters, many soldiers sought informal living arrangements amongst the villagers. Some were welcome.

At the south end of the village two exclusive units of ARVN police resided next to the American quarters. Encased in sandbags, a mounted M-60 protected the roof of the American command bunker. Dudley's squad preferred to sleep near the bunker rather than in their tent, which served primarily as a storage and eating area. A gate, supervised by ARVN police, protected the compound entry.

Major White and Sergeant Dudley managed the bunker, aided by Major Yuang Keh Thiut and two ARVN MPs. The bunker maintained constant contact with artillery and air corps units stationed in Lai Khe. The area now received regular air reconnaissance.

Each end of the village featured newly constructed gates where ARVN police inspected all traffic. Generations of villagers who had never submitted to a checkpoint tried not to notice.

Mac checked his watch. "Six more hours. Six more hours and we're outta here. Back to Lai Khe."

"Yuh. Back to the ranch for three days of R & R."

"And downtown? What d'ya think? The guys are going," said Mac.

"Screw that. They're just whorehouses. Not me. Not interested," Hodges chuckled. "Now the other side, the Dark Side, that might be interesting."

"Why?"

"Because, my man, because it's real. We're here, we oughta do the real thing."

"Dui, in case you didn't notice, we're doing it." Mac turned to Quam Thi. "Mammasan, you bring the laundry?" He pulled at his shirt, stained with perspiration.

Quam Thi hesitated. "Aye! *Sac sir giat!*" She pointed to six straw bags resting near the ARVN policemen.

"Sac what?"

"Clean laundry," Hodges said.

"Oh, clean laundry. Yeah," Mac laughed. "Whatever."

Quam Thi extended her hand. "That I understand," Mac reached for his wallet. As he handed the money to Quam Thi, she pointed to a figure beyond the expanding line. Mac shaded his eyes, "Hey Dui!"

"What?"

"Lookie there. That must be her. The girl you been telling me about. Whoa! Must be! Wow, I see what ya mean, even from here!"

"Where?" Hodges looked up.

"Over there. With the white hat."

"Shit, that's her. Hey Mac, cover for me?"

"Yeah, we'll handle it. Mammasan, look!" Mac pointed at Hodges, then banged his chest just over the heart.

"Aye... *duc tinh*!" Quam Thi pounded her breast laughing heartily. "*Di, di mao*!" she waved Dui toward Laureen.

"I'll be back!" Hodges walked briskly away.

"Laureen Nhu Lam! *Chao annoi*!" he called.

Laureen burst out laughing.

Progress! This was progress.

"*Qu'est-ce que c'est?*" he asked, bracing for her French.

Laureen pointed at him. "Males are *anh* or *annoi*." Pointing to herself, "Females are *em* or *emmoi*. You are *annoi*, not *emmoi*. *Comprenez-vous*, Dui?"

She knew his nickname!

"*Emmoi*." The word had intimacy. "I am sorry," he stumbled in French, "I need lessons in Vietnamese."

"*Oui, annoi*." She lowered her eyes. "And English," she said, "interests me."

"Laureen, *emmoi*, will you teach me? And perhaps I can help you."

"We shall see. The situation is... difficult."

The village is watching! "Why?"

"*Annoi*, you are American."

"Yes, an American who cannot see. If you do not teach me, I will be both *dui* and stupid. You must help me." Hodges dropped onto his knee before her. "Please," he begged.

"Upon my return we shall see." She motioned to the bus beyond the checkpoint.

"*Emmoi*, where do you go?"

"To Saigon. On the autobus. Seven days."

"A week? What is in Saigon?"

"Friends, books, some business," she hesitated, "professors. Saigon has English teachers." She lingered. "Do you like your Vietnamese name, Dui?"

"My name is Caster Thompson Hodges," he enunciated carefully, "but Dui is fun, is it not?"

She turned toward the checkpoint. He walked beside her.

The policeman waved Laureen forward. Hodges followed.

"This name Thompson, what is its meaning?" She drew a strand of hair away from her eye.

"Thompson is from the family of my mother."

She beamed comprehension.

Please don't leave!

She stepped onto the bus. On the first step, she turned back to him. "Your mother. Ah! Then this name is good." She paused. "Thompson..." Their eyes met. "*au revoir... annoi.*"

"*Bon voyage*, Laureen... *emmoi.*"

Oh my God!

299 days

Lai Khe

The Ghost took them to the edge.

Mac lifted the wire. Hodges slid under. He raised to a crouch and gripped Mac's hand. Mac crawled to his side. They joined the others.

Lights!

They hit the ground. The MPs passed.

They were in.

Alcoholic courage and the mystery of the Dark Side had lured Balman, Hosmach, MacKerry, Ghost, Ringhyter, and Hodges off limits to the old village in Lai Khe. The rules were simple. Watch your wallet, avoid detection, survive.

The moon provided light.

After the MPs vanished, Ghost led them across the dirt road into an alley.

"Here we are, gentlemen, welcome to the Dark Side. This is where the action is. Keep it down. The deal is... anything goes. You want it, you can get it. Stick together."

The Ghost had made this trip before.

"Some of those Air Cav assholes are partyin here tonight. They're more trouble than the gooks. Watch your ass." Ghost winked at Hodges. "Into the night, my man. Into the night."

"Mac, look at this." Hodges pointed to a hut behind them.

"Jeez!"

"Now that, that is an aluminum siding job. This I gotta see." Hodges walked to the side of the hut. MacKerry and Hosmach followed. "Can you believe this? The whole side is Schlitz."

"Weird," said Hoss. "Let's see the other side."

They walked around the corner. "Jeez, Budweiser!"

"I'll bet the south side is Miller," offered Hodges.

They rounded the next corner. "I'll be damned," exclaimed Hoss. "Look at this street. They're all like this. Aluminum-sided huts with thatched roofs. Ha! You were wrong, this one's Piels. The first round's on you, Dui."

They looked down the street. Thirty similar huts dotted each side of the dirt path.

"Pretty ingenious," Hodges said. "Not coordinated, but ingenious."

"Yeah," said Mac, "and there's one hell of a lot of beer bein drunk on this base. The whole damn village is like this."

A boy approached them. "Hey, GI, you wanna fuckie my sista?"

"What?" asked Hosmach.

"I say, you wanna fuckie my sista. She number one fuckie, you know?"

"Man, this is too much," laughed Hosmach, "let's get back with the other guys."

"They're long gone," said Hodges.

"Great!"

"Hey, GI, you queer? I find you boyfriend, you suckie, fuckie, okay GI?"

"Hey kid! I'm gonna kick the shit outta you if you don't get lost."

"C'mon, Hoss," Mac started, "he's just kiddin. Hey boy..."

"I no boy!"

"Yeah, well, where's some beer?" asked Mac.

"Not here. You follow me. You want number one cigarette? I get for you. I take you round the village. I show you everything. You pay me five dollar. Five dollar, okay GI?"

"No way," said Hoss.

Hodges shook his head. "I don't know. We need someone to show us around. Christ, we don't even know our way to the wire. What do you think, Mac?"

"I'm not payin. We'll find our way."

"Yeah, that's right," agreed Hoss.

"Hey, I'll pay! Okay kid, you work for us. Two dollars now, three when you take us back to the wire. Okay?"

"Okay! Okay, GI. You number one!"

"This is Mac," Hodges said, pointing him out. "Mac the cheap! And this short one is Hoss, Hoss the queer..."

"That isn't funny, you asshole!"

"And me, I'm Dui."

"Dui! Dui eh, Dui? You no can see? Ha! Ha! How you get that name? I think you dinky dow, you know, like crazy GI."

"Yeah I'm crazy. And thirsty. What's your name?"

"My name Sam. Everybody know Sam. I take you round. Who call you Dui?"

"Friends. Friends from Ben Cat call me Dui. You know Ben Cat?"

"Yeah, I know Ben Cat." Sam made a circular motion around his head. "The people there, they crazy. For sure. Too many VC. You know VC?"

"Yeah, we know VC. We didn't see no VC in Ben Cat," said Hoss.

"No VC huh? You lucky. You be lucky tonight too. C'mon, we go. Get beer."

He led them between two huts. "You watch out for clothes line, okay GI? They hang you." He pointed to the neck-high lines behind the huts. The men crouched behind him.

The boy stopped in front of a hut. "You wait here. I come right back." He darted into the house. Sam's high-pitched voice was answered by a deep American voice.

"An adventure!" said Hodges.

Hoss shrugged. "Some adventure. They'd have a tough time explaining this to our families. Three GI's killed off limits in Lai Khe!"

Sam returned. The sweet smell followed him out the door. "This place no good. We go other place."

"Why? They sell beer here?" asked Hoss.

"They sell beer. This place no good tonight. Crazy GIs. Air Cav, you know? Bad for us. We go."

They arrived at another hut.

"I never been to Milwaukee," Mac pointed to the Old Milwaukee siding.

"Sam, Mac likes Milwaukee, let's do it," said Hodges.

"Dui, you wait." Sam peered inside, then said, "this good place. Your friends be back later."

"Our friends?" asked Hoss.

"They come back."

"How do you know our friends?" asked Hodges.

"Your friend Ghost, right? He send me to you. He say take care of you." He pointed to their Big Red One insignias. "Your friends same-same."

"Ghost!" The three men laughed. "Okay, let's see how the natives live," Hodges said.

They entered a dark room. A small table was in the center with benches along the sides. Two doors led to other rooms. Flaps hung over the entries. The room was lit with candles, but the hut was empty.

"Mammasan come soon. You sit down." The men sat around the table. The room was harmless. Sam tuned a portable radio. Stringed instruments whined in the background.

"*Chao* GIs." An elderly woman entered through the rear door. "I am Phan, mammasan this house. Who are you?"

"This Hoss," Sam pointed at Hosmach. "This black man, Mac. This GI, he Dui. Ha! Ha!"

"*Chao*, Mammasan," said Hodges. "Got any beer?"

"You like *bas-mui-bas?*"

"What's that?" asked Mac.

"It means thirty-three," said Hodges.

"Right, thoity-three. Beer. Vietnam beer," said Phan. "Not too cold."

"You got any American?" asked Hoss.

"No, GI, no American."

"Too flat, right Mammasan? *Bas-mui-bas* is fine," said Hodges.

"Yeah, let's try it," agreed Mac. "Three thirty-threes, Mammasan."

Phan opened three bottles, passing one to each of them.

"What about me?" asked Sam.

"What about you?" growled Hoss.

"I thirsty too."

The GIs laughed.

"I no kid. I drink beaucoup beer."

"Okay, okay."

"You want cigarette? Got number one cigarette. Mac, you like my cigarette, eh?" Phan pointed at MacKerry.

"What the heck? Why not? Let's light em up."

Phan handed them each a joint. "You like my music? Can get Armed Forces, too."

"No, that's fine, Mammasan," said Mac.

They inhaled. Hodges and Hoss coughed harshly. Sam laughed raucously. MacKerry chuckled.

"White GIs no can smoke! Ha! Ha!"

"Man, this shit's strong," coughed Hoss as Hodges wiped tears from his eyes. "Look at this. Look at the paper. Mine says Camel. Look at this!"

They read the print on the cigarette. "Sure enough, mine says Camel," said Mac. "This ain't no Camel. Where'd you get this Mammasan?"

"She got filters, too," explained Sam. "You want L & M or Salem?"

"Mentholated pot?" said Hodges. "I'll be damned."

"She sell you one pack. One dollar fifty cents. Right mammasan?"

Phan nodded.

"We'll think about it," said Hodges.

"Your friends be back soon. We have big party!" Sam waited. "You want girlfriend?"

"A girlfriend? I don't see any girls." Hoss chased a drag with a gulp of beer.

"Girls come, soon. You use rooms." Sam pointed to the closed doors.

Phan nodded.

"We'll see," said Hodges. "Mammasan, how long you live in Lai Khe?"

"Long time." Phan looked away.

Hodges studied her. She wore baggy black pants and a white shirt. Her hair was pulled back into a bun. Her weather-beaten skin was heavily lined, but she lacked the humble stance of a farmer.

"You have a husband?" Hoss asked.

"My husband a soldier. He away. Fight the VC."

Three women entered the room. "We got girls. We got party," Sam exclaimed. "Dui, I have another beer?"

"Sure, Sam, help yourself," agreed Hodges. "Hoss, yours has a big ass!"

"Mine has a big ass! What about yours? She's got no tits!"

"I got number one tits," said the woman, abruptly raising her red shirt. The Americans roared with laughter.

"That settles it. Mine's got tits," said Hodges. "Yours still has a big ass!"

"Sure enough," agreed Mac.

"Hey you! You black GI. You wanna dance?" asked a girl in a green blouse.

Mac regarded the girl. "Maybe. What's your name?"

"You call me Bong. This my friend Nam," she pointed to the girl in red, "and this my friend Sow." She pointed to Hoss's girl. "We like to dance. We smoke, okay?"

"Sure. Mammasan, give the girls the weed," said Hodges. "Let's see, you're Bong, Nam, and Sow. That means four, five, and six, right?"

"You smart, GI. What your name?"

"My name is Dui."

"Dui!" The girls squealed. "That funny name. We have good time tonight, eh Dui?"

"Sure, Nam, tonight we have a good time."

"You have girlfriend back home?" asked Nam.

"I do!" interrupted Hoss. "I get letters too. These guys get no letters. My girlfriend writes all the time. She's waiting for me."

"That good for you," said Sow caressing his cheek.

"Wonder what she'd think now?" laughed Mac.

"Hey, that's not funny. This is here, ya know. She'd understand."

"You bet," said Hodges.

Balman, Ringhyter, and Ghost burst through the door.

"Lookie, lookie, lookie," said the glassy-eyed Ghost.

"Hey GI, you beaucoup deb," Bong pointed to Ringhyter's blond hair.

"Deb?" asked Ringhyter.

"Pretty," said Hodges. "Like beautiful."

"Thanks," said Ringhyter, sitting beside Bong.

"Where you guys been?" asked Hoss.

"Around," answered Ghost. "Checkin it out, man, checkin it out. All's cool."

"Who's the little shit with my beer?" Balman pointed to Sam.

"My beer! You dinky dow, GI, beaucoup mop," said Sam.

"Mop, what's mop?" asked Balman.

"Mop," began Sow, "mop is fat. Your name Mop." The girls giggled.

"Mop? My name's Mop! Well, give me a beer and I'll show you mop." He sat near MacKerry. Ghost slumped to the floor near Phan, who rose and opened beers for everyone.

"Hey Dui, yours is sorta nice. You remember me?" Ghost asked Nam.

"I never see you."

"Oh, well, you all look the same to me," he laughed. "Yo Mammasan! You got a number one cigarette?"

Phan handed him a joint, then turned to Sam and spoke in Vietnamese. The room hushed.

"Is okay," said Sam, defusing the tenseness. "Phan say I get more beer. I be right back."

"Man, I am feelin no pain," said Mac.

"We go next room?" Bong pointed to one of the flaps. "I make you happy." She stroked his thigh. "You number one, Mac."

"Yeah Mac, you're number one... tonight. Take her in the next room," Balman yelled.

"Here? In the next room?" Mac asked.

"Sure, we won't pay no attention. Who gives a shit! Right, Ghost?"

Bong rose, took Mac's hand, and placed it under her shirt. "You like?"

Mac looked to Ghost, who shrugged. "Into the night, my man, into the night... We'll be here."

Mac and Bong ducked under the flap.

Sow slid next to Ringhyter. "What your name?"

"Ringhyter."

"Too long! I call you Ringhi, okay?"

"Sure. Ringhi, now I'm deb Ringhi." Everyone laughed.

"You're a new man, Ringhi," said Hodges. "I'm Dui, now we got Ringhi and Mop. What a group. Dudley won't recognize us!"

Sow took Ringhi's hand, pulling him toward the other empty room. "You come, Ringhi. I make you happy." Ringhi followed her.

"Easy come, easy go," shrugged Hoss. "No clap tonight! Turn up the music, mammasan."

Nam studied the GIs. "Where you men been?"

"Man, oh man. Where we been? We been a little north. Some of us even been in the bush," Ghost teased Dui.

Suddenly Phan jumped up extinguishing the candles. "Get down, GIs!"

"Incoming!" yelled Ghost.

They bellied to the floor.

"Mac! Ringhi! Incoming!" yelled Hodges.

Phan scurried into Ringhi's room.

"What the hell?" Ringhi scrambled to cover himself.

"You move, Ringhi!" Phan pushed the bed aside, exposing a bunker. She jumped in. Balman, Ghost, Nam, Sow, and Bong followed.

Mac rushed from his room, half tripping over his pants.

"Comin' in!" yelled Hoss.

Mac and Hodges remained on the floor. A siren blared from the base. Incoming rounds poured in. One struck close by, shaking the hut. Shrapnel ripped through the siding. A lantern crashed to the floor.

"Jesus Christ!" Balman yelled. "Keep down! Get in here, you assholes!" Mac and Hodges squeezed into the shelter.

Outgoing artillery blasted the night.

"Get the fuckers!" shouted Balman.

Two more rounds landed in the village. The outgoing rounds intensified. The marijuana magnified the noise.

"That's it!" announced Ghost.

"What d'ya mean?" asked Hoss.

"That's it. They're done." Ghost raised himself out of the hole. "Any more beer mammasan?"

Sam raced through the door. "Dui! Dui! Come quick! GI beaucoup hurt!"

"What? Where?"

"Outside! GI beaucoup hurt. You come now!"

"C'mon Ghost, let's go."

"We gotta get back," Balman yelled.

"GI! You give me money!" demanded Phan.

"Balman, pay her. You guys go back. Ghost, you and Mac come with me!" said Hodges.

Hodges, Mac, and Ghost followed Sam out the door. "Over here." Sam ran around the corner of a hut.

A GI lay in the dirt, his head twisted to the side. Smoke lifted from his pants. Blood oozed from his leg. He was still.

"Shrapnel!" Ghost said. "We gotta get him to the checkpoint."

"Mac, grab his shoulders," Hodges whispered. "I'll take the feet!"

"His neck don't look so good," said Mac.

"We gotta get him out. He's bleedin bad!" Hodges removed his belt. "Ghost, fasten this tight around his thigh."

"Shit!" Mac drew back. "His arm's bad, too!"

Ghost tightened the belt, then carefully placed the arm across his stomach. "Let's go, fast!"

Mac and Hodges lifted the GI. Ghost led them to the checkpoint.

Gaining consciousness, the GI groaned.

"You're okay, man. You're gonna be okay," Mac murmured.

"Halt! Who goes there?" from the checkpoint.

"We got a man down!" answered Ghost. "We need help!"

"Bring him on! You assholes ain't supposed to be in there!"

"Yeah, yeah! We shouldn't be anywhere near here."

"Shit! He's been hit. You guys take the jeep," said the MP pointing to a jeep behind the bunker. "You know where the hospital is?"

"Yeah," said Ghost.

They laid the GI across the back of the jeep.

"Drive slow, no lights. Move out!"

The thing was real.

297 days

Ben Cat

He would be there. There was no question. He would be there for them, the twelve of them. He always would be.

Bulldog Eight swung over the Ben Cat perimeter. Their eyes strained toward the landing zone.

"Shit! There he is!" said Hodges.

The squad jumped from the chopper, which spun away back to Lai Khe. Dust swirled around them.

Dudley stood at Parade Rest. "Fall in!"

They dropped their gear, forming up a proper column.

"Ten Hut!"

They stood for fifteen silent, motionless minutes. The sun bore down.

"Chin up! Eyes front!" The sun. The sun.

Suddenly Dudley snapped to attention. He executed a crisp right face and marched parallel to the column. Arriving at the north end, Dudley halted. He faced left, took four steps forward, halted. His beret brushed Ghost's forehead.

The sergeant stared. One, two, three minutes. The sun!

Dudley took one step back.

Left face. Two steps. Right face. One step forward.

Dudley's chest thrust against Parker.

Parker blinked. "Eyes front!" Dudley stared.

One step back. Left face. Two steps. Right face.

LaVelle flinched. "Chin up!"

The sergeant worked his way back down the line. The heat rose.

No one moved. No one spoke.

The sergeant faced right. Dudley's eyes blazed into Hodges.

Hodges swayed forward.

"Ten Hut!" Three more minutes of the sun, of Dudley.

The sergeant took one step back.

"Hodges! You are one dumb fucka!"

One minute.

"Hodges! You are... a college boy?"

"Yes, Sergeant, sort of."

"Sort of. Sergeant?"

"Yes, Sergeant! Sort of! Sergeant."

"That's right! Sort of Sergeant!"

One minute.

"Hodges! You want me to write your mother one of those lettas?"

One minute.

"One of those lettas saying that you, Hodges, her, sort of, college boy son just bit it in a Lai Khe whorehouse?"

One minute.

"I do not write. Those lettas!"

The sergeant faced right. Twelve paces. Halt. Face right. Six paces. Halt. About face.

The chin protruded.

"Now, 'Sort Of' tell me... How was it?"

One minute.

"Was it good enough to die for?"

Dudley waited.

"Hodges! I do not... hear you!"

"Sergeant, no, sergeant! Not good enough to die for, sergeant!"

"Thank you, Hodges."

The chin edged up. "This is the Republic of South Vietnam. This ain't no fucking picnic. This is a fucking war zone. I did not train you to die. In whorehouses."

Their shoulders sagged.

"Ten Hut!"

"Ova here, you do not forget. Ova here, we learn something every day. We do not... forget. What we learn." He paused. "We rememba! We rememba everything! Because when we forget, someone writes lettas!"

He glared at them.

"The vacation is ova! Now you, every one of you, will be doing night patrols. This is what you were trained to do. There is no room, no time, for people who forget!"

He pointed across the column. "There are no second chances. None."

Two steps forward. Halt. Chin up.

"Rememba. Your last parade!"

One minute.

"You got off the plane. You knew. You were not ready."

He waited.

"You betta be! Your Vietnam is coming. Right now!"

He straightened.

"Rememba motion! Motion kills! Motion takes away the night. Takes away the surprise. The only good motion comes from the other side. From the little people. In the bush. And you won't see much. They neva forget. They know. Motion kills. Rememba. No motion!"

One step closer.

"A bug bites, you freeze. No motion. You tired? You wanna stretch yourself. Forget it! You sweat, you drip. You do not wipe. That is motion. You wipe, you die."

"You blend... into the dark. Feel the dark. Treat the dark with respect. It is your friend. And out there you do not have many."

He faced right. Six paces. Faced left.

"Rememba smell! Smell kills! Charley smells you. You die! Think about it. Charley smells you, you die! You wear cologne. You smell. You die. No motion. No smell. Hide in the dark."

Left face. Two paces. Right face.

"Rememba cigarettes. They kill every... body! You smoke, you create motion. In the dark. You create light. In the dark. You create smell. In the dark. Charley neva smokes in the dark. He just puts out your butts. In the dark."

Left face. Two paces. Right face.

"Charley loves the dark. Charley owns. The dark. He moves battalions. In the dark. He launches invasions. In the dark. He walks under you, ova you, through you. In the dark. He takes your weapon, your best friend. In the dark."

Left face. Two paces. Right face. Chin up.

"He measuahs you by day. Fits you at night. And we, we just keep sending those lettas. Those fucking lettas."

Left face. Four steps. Right face.

"Think like Charley! You must listen for Charley. Look for Charley. Feel, taste, think. Charley."

Left face. Two paces. Right face.

"I hate Charley! He is. My enemy. I respect Charley. I know. What he can do. Charley wants your ass. In a sling. You keep dicking around, he's gonna get it! Wise up! This is. The real thing!"

Two crisp steps back. Halt.

"You are going out! Onto his turf. In the dark. You dumbasses. You take nuthin. Not one little thing. For granted. You see a can on the ground, you leave it! That fucker'll blow your foot off. You see a doll in a tree, on your bunk, in your hooch, forget it. Leave it. Call the bomb squad. Something ain't right."

Two steps back. Halt.

"And something ain't right! Right here. In Ben Cat. Something. Ain't right."

Right face. Two paces. Left face.

"We are feeding them. More than they ever ate. They're still hungry! Where is it going? The medics are busier than hell! The patients neva come back. You get my drift! Something ain't right."

Right face. Two paces. Left face.

"Every little thing you do can kill you. And your friends. Your very good friends. Now! Get this straight. Charley knows about you! More than you know. About him."

He waited.

"He's the little boy or girl gonna sell you his sista. Charley is the sista, who looks sixteen, but is twenty-nine with five mouths to feed. Sometimes Charley looks like a friend. He might even have a friendly uniform, but he hates your guts. You are. On his block! You are. At risk. You! Are at risk. At all times. Don't eva forget it. The one time you do, he'll know, and he'll be there."

Right face. Two paces. Left face.

"He's the old guy. Wants to know your name. The old lady. Wants to see pictures of your family. He's the dishwasher. The shitburner. The bicycler. The cute one. The deformed one. The light one. The dark one. He's the one. Gonna bag you. And send you home. Unless. Unless you are ready! Ready for Charley!"

Left face. Two paces. Right face.

"So you listen. You listen good. You shoot first, you ask later."

One minute.

"This. Is the real thing. No bullshit! You think you see him, you shoot. You blow the claymores. You call artillery. We ain't here... to fuck around! We are here. To win. It is that simple. You see him. You kill him. Or he kills you! Not sure? Bullshit! You pull the fucking trigger. You might be right. If you ain't. We deal with it!"

Left face. Two paces. Right face.

"One more thing, dumbassses! Don't you be talking to him. The one you tell. Tells someone else. Soon the whole fucking VC batallion knows where we are. And you neva, eva go anywhere alone. There is no privacy. Here! When you think you are alone in Nam, you are not alone. Charley is there!"

"Like he is now. Like he's always been. The Fuck!"

Left face. Two paces. Right face.

"Dis-mis-sed!"

296 days

Ben Cat

Singularly uncommon. Guyan stepped onto the porch of the stone house and knocked on the door. "Laureen, are you home?" Muffled voices came from within. He swung open the door and stepped inside. To his right were two spacious rooms. A large hearth, opening to a cooking area behind, centered the left wall. Across from the hearth, a plate glass window let light flood the room. Charcoal silhouettes of Vietnamese laborers adorned the walls. He peered through a curved archway into the library where bound volumes were shelved in bookcases. Colorful rugs partially covered the wood floors throughout both rooms, which were further enhanced by delicate chairs, polished tables, and fragile ornaments. Guyan thought the house belonged elsewhere.

Voices came from the library. An American man! "Laureen, are you home? Mai Nin, are you here?"

Guyan strode through the sitting room to the library. Completely engrossed, Laureen sat at a table before the window. Her yellow backpack rested next to the chair. The American voice came from a recorder on the table. Laureen repeated the words. She stopped. A Vietnamese woman's voice explained the meaning. Laureen wrote something in a notebook.

"Laureen, did you not hear me?"

Startled, she shut the recorder off and turned to face him. "Guyan, you surprise me." She laughed. "How nice to see you."

"What is this? What do you do?"

"This? This is an English lesson. The accent is puzzling." She picked up a book. "This is a Vietnamese-English dictionary. It clarifies the meaning of words."

"How can this language interest you? Why do you concern yourself with the intruders? This exercise demeans you."

He sat down across from her. "You realize our people suffer due to the American presence. Our actions should not dignify them."

"Guyan, is not their presence beyond the control of this household? If we understood the language, could we not better understand the people? Maybe then we could reduce the tension."

"Laureen, the struggle is beyond these purposeless victims. Their senselessness does not justify their thoughtlessness." Guyan's voice became stern. "In their own country there is dissension. They are not brothers. Left alone, they fight amongst themselves."

Laureen weighed his vexation. "Guyan, my reading suggests our countries have more in common than we may realize. Their country consists of many cultures. Those cultures do not agree on many issues. They struggle to resolve their disagreements. Are we really so different?"

"Laureen, do you not see? They lack integrity. They invade our homeland to divert attention from their differences! They accept the unacceptable, the unjust. They compromise our heritage. To them we are meaningless, without honor. For these mercenaries we are an inconvenience to be tolerated for a brief moment. The damage they do will last beyond our lifetime. And you! Will you who has such wisdom, encourage them?"

"Guyan, no! Perhaps, my friend, you are misinformed. From what experiences come these judgments? The Americans offer protection. They feed our village. They care for the sick. Yet to you they remain contemptible because their work opposes your political beliefs. You and your sympathizers contradict each constructive contribution they attempt. It is easy to critique, to find fault, but could Ben Cat not benefit more by cooperating?" She swept her hair from her face. "And what of our Vietnam? The country divides into factions more concerned with daily existence than progress. Not all citizens in the south agree with the efforts of their government. Not all brothers in the north agree with their leaders. It seems politics widens the gaps, reduces hope."

Guyan's eyes revealed his frustration with her, but he persisted. "The American's weak resolve makes them surmountable. They underestimate the determination of the National Liberation Front and Brother Ho Chi Minh. Our commitment will surpass their weaponry. We shall emerge the victors!"

"Victors!" Laureen gasped. "There will be no victors. Before and beyond our lifetime, suffering was foredoomed for Vietnam. Our children's children will still bear the suffering unless, unless there is change, positive change."

"The colonizer will bear the guilt," he interrupted. "So shall the Americans suffer! Does your reading not explain how they succeeded with their independence? Yet they arrogantly deny us ours!" Rising from the chair, he stood before her. "Our children suffer now. They lose their identity. They become less than Vietnamese. We must restore them, restore their definition so that future generations will honor our homeland."

"Guyan, your beliefs are strong. Mine are contrary." She stared beyond the window. "My family is my first concern. The future is beyond us. Perhaps we should depart Vietnam."

"What? Is this why you study? Where would you go? To America? You will be unwelcome." Guyan lifted the dictionary. Dropping it loudly to the floor, he kicked it across the room. "These people do not open their doors to you. They are not your heritage. You and your family would be outcast. If you do not believe me, ask them. Ask the black ones!"

"My friend, this is a bad conversation for us. My interests are languages and cultures, all cultures. You struggle to protect Vietnam. My purpose is simpler. To protect my family."

"And how will you do that? By surrounding them with this?" The sweep of his arms encompassed the room. "This household that once subjugated our village?" He faced her. "Surrounded by foreign objects, you have become confused, as was your mother. My concern is to protect all the families, all the families of Vietnam. We deserve an honorable future. We must build a self-sufficient Vietnam. This is the objective of our great liberator. How can you disagree?"

"Guyan, my mother has nothing to do with this. And it might surprise you that theoretically we agree. The objectives of the conflicting governments seem similar, do they not? As we do, they disagree over means, not the end."

"Only you see similarities, Laureen. Only you. Perhaps your mixed heritage dissolves your reason." He strode to the doorway.

Her face colored. Guyan hesitated. Both struggled to get beyond the disagreement.

"Guyan, how long will you stay?"

"Until tomorrow." His voice was empty.

"You move about so easily?"

"Yes, Laureen. Very easily." He looked to her. "Laureen, my intent is not to offend you. You are my friend. At one time we might have been more." Laureen lowered her eyes. He began again. "You follow your heart, but you must heed my advice. These feelings that you have expressed today are dangerous. Dangerous to you and your family.

You must be more discrete with your opinions. This is not the university. Here, life is reality, not theory. Do you understand?"

"Guyan, you are my friend, a friend of this family, so shall you always be. The welfare of my family is personal, not political, not national. Sometimes, the responsibilities of our beliefs are burdensome, more burdensome than we deserve."

Ben Cat Perimeter

The Ghost dropped his pants. Good shit tonight, baby! It's happenin'. Into the night, mother fucker, into the night. I'm comin, yeah I'm comin. You ain't ready Charley. I know you ain't ready! I see, I see.... It's either you or me. It ain't gonna be me, you fucker... One more hit. Yes!... All right... all right... gonna stand up here an show my man LaVelle the moon.

At 2100 hours Corporal Eugene LaVelle stood left of bunker fifteen on the Ben Cat perimeter. "Holy Shit!" LaVelle lowered his scope.

"What?" asked Hodges.

"He's moonin me!"

"His ass isn't that good," Hodges laughed. "Saddle up, we're movin out."

Two days before, a reconnaissance flight had discovered a wide ravine two miles beyond the east paddy. Closer air observation had recorded no activity, but Dudley was not satisfied. With Ghost pointing the way, LaVelle, Hodges, MacKerry, Ringhyter, Parker, and twelve ARVNs would circle around the east paddy, enter the jungle at the easternmost point, and proceed to an ambush site at the ravine. Their late departure was intended to keep their mission a secret.

Hodges turned to an ARVN MP. "*Mui tam*, eighteen in the bush."

Last week a patrol had returned with two more ARVNs than had departed. By the time the irregularity was discovered, the two extras had already disappeared into Ben Cat. Counting departures and returnees was now mandatory.

"Aye, *mui tam*," the MP nodded.

Hodges moved alongside Parker, who raised his thumb confirming the radio's operation. Effortlessly clearing the paddy, they infiltrated the jungle.

Parker handed Hodges the microphone. "Matchmaker, this is Long Ball. Over."

"Long Ball, Matchmaka reads you. Ova."

"Matchmaker, we are at Checkpoint One. Over."

"Long Ball, Roga that. Choppas are on the pad. Big sticks are zeroed. Ova and out."

Lai Khe gunships were ready to support. Estimated time of arrival fifteen minutes. Artillery had their coordinates. Estimated time of arrival four minutes.

Quietly piercing the darkness, the squad reached the ravine at 2300 hours.

From the crest of the west bank, Hodges checked the terrain. The ravine dropped seventy meters below them to the flat base twenty meters wide. Across the way the ground rose steeply up again. The span was wider than anticipated, but overall the site suited their purpose.

Hodges designated a tree just below the ridge as the southernmost point of the ambush. LaVelle would hold that location while the rest of the detail spaced themselves out along the ridge.

Ghost scouted and secured an exit lane to their rear.

Ringhi's M-60 loomed in the center of the column. Taking his bearings, Ringhyter sighted the weapon. An ARVN assistant aligned the bandoleers.

At the north end another ARVN burrowed behind a boulder.

LaVelle lowered himself down the bank, strategically set out his three claymore mines, and strung the wires back up the slope to his tree. Immediately, the ARVN to his left moved down the ravine. When the northernmost ARVN completed the cycle thirty claymores covered the trail.

Scopes mounted, weapons locked and loaded, the watch began.

Hodges and Parker hid behind two stumps to Ringhi's left. MacKerry was north.

Hodges took the microphone from Parker. "Matchmaker, this is Long Ball, over."

"Matchmaka here."

"Matchmaker, we are in position, over."

"Have a good night, Long Ball. Out."

Hodges returned the microphone to Parker. "I'm cold."

"Tell someone who cares."

Hodges contemplated scenarios.

Ideally Charley would enter the ravine from the north. Hodges scoped the imaginary trail. They would be moving fast. The squad would wait until they crossed Ringhi. Then, then the shit would happen.

Charley could come from the south. Hodges surveyed the route. LaVelle would be ready. Charley could not come from the west, behind them, or from the east, across the way. Charley's route would be parallel to the their ridge, across the claymores.

"Too simple," he mused.

"Dui, what's happening?" Ghost materialized.

"Ghost! Jesus! Don't do that. You gotta stop sneaking up on me!"

"Sorry, man," smiled Ghost. "We got a number one exit lane up there," he pointed, "behind that gook near LaVelle."

Hodges marked the spot. "Sounds good. Spread the word. What else?"

"Nada. There ain't shit. Nothing's been back there in a hundred years. Give me a gook to watch the exit, then I can keep an eye on things."

"Uh huh, take him," Hodges designated the ARVN to his left.

"Will do. First, I spread the word, then take the gook and I'm outta here," he patted Hodges on the shoulder. "Into the night..."

"Yeah, you too."

Ghost moved down the line.

Parker set the radio on the bank behind them. Hodges returned to his scope.

All clear at 0100 hours.

No activity through the night.

Another senseless exercise, another scratch on the calendar.

Sunlight edged over the east bank into the jungle mist. Nothing.

At 0700 hours, the mist evaporated. Hodges checked his column. Everyone was awake.

"Son of a bitch," he tapped Parker pointing north where an ARVN was smoking.

"Jesus Christ," said Parker.

Suddenly a black arm emerged from the underbrush grabbing the cigarette. The surprised ARVN gasped.

"Glad Ghost's on our side," whispered Parker.

"Glad we weren't smoking," chuckled Hodges.

The vigilance continued.

At 0900, Hodges looked to the south. LaVelle stared back. Hodges signalled him down to retrieve his claymores.

Nimbly, LaVelle lowered himself to the mines.

Carefully he disconnected the first, slung it over his shoulder and bent down to detach the second.

The ground exploded!

Debris spewed through the air.

Screaming!

LaVelle writhed in agony.

"Booby trap!" yelled Hodges. "The claymore's booby trapped!"

The ambush stared at LaVelle.

A shot rang out. The bullet thudded into the ground just behind Parker, near the radio.

"Mother Fucker!" Parker yelled.

"Sniper!" Hodges reacted. "The radio!"

Ringhi answered. His M-60 sprayed across the east bank.

Now the entire ambush opened fire. The reckless rounds betrayed their cover.

Sniper! Sniper! Where is he?

"Cease fire!" Hodges' voice cracked. He waved the ARVN nearest LaVelle down the ravine. The ARVN grimaced in protest before proceeding. All weapons trained on the east bank.

"Parker! The radio, give me the hook!"

Parker handed Hodges the microphone.

"Matchmaker, this is Long Ball! LaVelle is down. I say again! We have one man... down. Send E-VAC. A-S-A-P!"

"Long Ball, this is Matchmaka. Roga that." Calmly, much too routinely. "Your position? Ova."

"We're in the ditch, goddamit. Bringing him out due west."

The ARVN began dragging LaVelle's unconscious form up the bank.

Hodges balked at the bloody torso. "His hand! Jesus! They got his hand!"

"Long Ball, this is Matchmaka," the radio suddenly barked. "Two are in the air. I say again, two are airborne. Proceed to 16 Foxtrot - 32 Papa. Ova."

Hodges groped for the map. 16 Foxtrot - 32 Papa! That was close!

"Long Ball, do you copy? 16 Foxtrot - 32 Papa?"

"Copy, goddamit."

"Easy soldiah. Your ETA? Ova."

"This is Long Ball. Copy 16 Foxtrot - 32 Papa." Get it together. Get it together. "ETA is... is... 0-3-5. Out."

His temples throbbed. We gotta go!

Ghost rose from the debris and hoisted LaVelle over the ARVN's shoulder. They started up the bank.

The northernmost ARVN unexpectedly opened fire.

LaVelle's ARVN ducked, dropping the wounded man.

Suddenly, Ghost lifted LaVelle over his back and rushed up the bank.

Blood poured from the severed arm.

The column rose to retreat.

The claymores! Shit! The claymores! "Blow the mines!" Hodges squeezed his trigger. The base exploded. In an instant a series of detonations scorched the ravine.

"Move out!" Hodges barked, raising his hand and pointing to the exit lane.

Hodges ran to LaVelle. His lower wrist and hand were gone. Hodges knotted a tourniquet above the elbow. LaVelle opened his eyes. Hodges turned away from his silent plea.

"Where to?" Ghost asked.

"16 Foxtrot - 32 Papa."

"Uh huh. The clearing we circled?"

"That's the one." They exchanged a look. "Jesus Christ! How?"

"Yeah man. He's fucked." Ghost grabbed Hodges' arm. "Move out man!" Ghost surged forward.

"Hodges, ya look like shit! Here's the radio, here's the map. Get on the hook!" Parker directed.

"They got his hand!"

"Yeah. Get on the hook."

"Matchmaker, this is Long Ball. We're moving out." A branch whipped across his face. A welt swelled under his tearing eye. "Shit! ETA 0-2-5."

They hustled ahead to the clearing.

Ghost discharged a flare marking the LZ for the E-VAC.

Everything turned red. What a mess! What a fucking mess!

"Long Ball, this is Matchmaka. We got two on you."

Two hueys surged toward them.

Hodges scanned the LZ. They would have to run sixty meters into the clearing. Exposed! A sniper's dream! Jesus Christ! We're hanging out to dry.

The hueys hovered nervously. Doorgunners sprayed the jungle. Furiously, the co-pilot waved them on.

Shit! Not me, you fucker. Not me!

"Go! Go! Go!"

They sprinted from the trees.

The ARVNs hoisted LaVelle into the first chopper. Hodges sprawled into the second.

They lifted away.

286 fucking days

Ben Cat

Laureen had wrapped a copy of her dictionary in plain white paper. Addressing it simply "To Dui," she had handed the book to an MP at the command compound.

Two days later Hodges had arrived at Laureen's house with a soccer ball for Tranh and candies for Mai Nin. Their learning had begun.

Now, two weeks later, the sun's last rays spread across the sprawling valley. Mai Nin enjoyed the scene from her wicker rocker on the porch. Tranh bounced the ball in the path below her. If the surprising American were to visit, he would arrive within the half hour. His politeness had softened Mai Nin.

Laureen's linguistic progress was remarkable. English was now the language she shared with Hodges.

His visits attracted curious neighbors filled with questions. The household was lively.

Tying a blue ribbon in her hair, Laureen joined her grandmother on the porch.

"So, Laureen Nhu Lam, will Dui visit this evening? Certainly you dress the part," teased Mai Nin.

"Do you think so?" asked Laureen. "Who stands before you, the teacher or the student?"

"Aha! Turn about, let me see."

Laureen spread her arms and pirouetted twice. "Now, oh sage one, you must decide. Is this the student or the teacher?"

Mai Nin drew her hand across her face. "The attire is of a teacher. From a distance, most definitely the teacher, but, as close as we are, there is no mistaking the color of a student. Indeed, a student filled with eagerness," Mai Nin lowered her eyes. "As your mother was once."

Hodges strode past the last hut up the hillside toward them. Laureen smiled radiantly. Tranh continued to bounce the ball.

"*Chao*, Mai Nin," Dui bowed.

"Dui," Mai Nin nodded.

"*Chao*, Tranh." Hodges motioned with his foot. "Any goals today?"

"*Chao* Dui," Tranh moved near the porch steps.

"Laureen, *emmoi*, how was your day?"

"Thompson, *annoi*, today is now a... par-tic-u-lar-ly... good day for me? Thank you for coming," she blushed. "And for asking."

"Ah, par-tic-u-lar-ly, that is impressive. Your vocabulary expands. Your success makes me jealous."

"Jealous? What is jealous?"

Hodges shrugged. "Jealous is, let's see. Jealous... is envious. For example, if I had something you wanted, you might feel jealous or envious of me." He looked around. "Like Tranh's ball. If Tranh had a ball and I did not, and I wanted a ball, I might be jealous of Tranh. Do you see?"

"What does Dui say about the ball? Does he want the ball back?" Tranh asked Laureen.

"No, Tranh, no. Thompson does not want the ball. He uses it to explain the meaning of an unfamiliar word," she returned to Hodges. "Jealous is an emotion then. Emotions are important." Laureen addressed Mai Nin. "Grandmother, have you seen the dictionary?"

"In your study, La, on the table," Mai Nin chuckled. "For one so bright, your memory seems short."

"On the table? Aye, from before." She faced Hodges. "My dictionary is still needed."

"Not now, Laureen. We should not waste time with such a word."

"Thompson, emotions are significant, even the bad ones. We cannot choose emotions. We must understand them all." She noticed the magazines under his arm. "What do you bring tonight? Your gen-er-os-ity is more than we deserve."

"Ah, these are for Mai Nin and Tranh. The April and May issues of *Life* magazine. There are many pictures, pictures of America, pictures of the world. I thought they might like to see."

"These we shall enjoy! A wonderful gift. You realize that each picture will raise many questions," Laureen laughed.

"Your neighbors ask interesting questions. I hope I don't run out of answers."

"Thompson," she beamed, "you are blessed with answers. This you and Mai Nin have in common. Perhaps you are more alike than you think."

"Uh huh," he handed the magazines to Mai Nin. "I think Mai Nin would not take kindly to the comparison."

"You might be surprised," Laureen laughed. "She is very unpredictable."

"Grandmother, Thompson brings us pictures of the world. They will be interesting, will they not?"

Tranh came up onto the porch to inspect the magazines. "Are there pictures of Vietnam?"

"You must look," answered Laureen. "Now, the dictionary." She went into the home.

Mai Nin stared at the cover of the May issue. An unfamiliar aircraft was surrounded by flames. "Tranh Nhu Lam, gather our neighbors. They will like these pictures. And we must include Ching Phor!" She reached to the shelf behind her. "Perhaps the black scarf will encourage her."

"Aye, Grandmother!" Tranh took the scarf, jumped from the porch, and ran toward the huts of the village.

"Where is Tranh Nhu Lam?" Laureen asked returning with the book.

"Gathering our neighbors. They will like Dui's gift," Mai Nin answered.

"Well, *annoi*," Laureen thumbed the dictionary. "The village is in-tri-gu-ed by your customs. It seems you must learn about us through your teaching?"

"Tonight Laureen? To be honest, I was hoping the neighbors might study the magazines while we walked."

Two women and a man already approached the house. More would follow.

"That would be nice," Laureen smiled. "Perhaps some other time. In Ben Cat per-son-al plans must often be put aside."

"Some other time, some other place. The story of my life," Hodges responded.

"The story of your life?"

"Well, the way things seem to go for me."

"Ah, but now your life will be different," Laureen smiled. "As with all who come to Vietnam, your life begins anew. It is our... myst-ique. Yes, it is our mystique.

"*Emmoi*, the mystique... is you. You give me hope. Do you understand hope? You are the light."

"Yes Thompson, and for me, you are the same. Very much the same."

****

After directing six villagers to his home, Tranh found Ching Phor walking toward the temple.

"Ching Phor! Ching Phor! Mai Nin requests you."

"Ah, Tranh Nhu Lam, the eager one. Do you bear a greeting?"

"The black scarf again. Do you think she forgets?"

"Mai Nin's favorite scarf. All is well then. No, she does not forget. Her memory is longer than you realize." Ching Phor accepted the scarf. "So, Little Ox, now that your home has guests, what are your plans this evening?"

"Tonight? Tonight there are no plans. The American visits Laureen. They study language. It seems so foolish."

"Your sister is far from the fool. The Americans are modern. There are things to be learned from them. In her learning, Laureen expands."

"Do you think so? Do you not think she, she forsakes the village?"

"Laureen! Forsake Ben Cat! Do you not see she is dedicated to you? To you and Mai Nin. This you must never doubt. She is driven to learn, driven to betterment. We traditionalists are short-sighted. Thus your discomfort with the American." She began to walk. "Are you tired? There is work for the oxen."

"Tonight? What will Grandmother think? What of Laureen?"

"Tomorrow tell Grandmother that you stayed with me. She will understand. Laureen will not question you."

They entered the temple. Tranh followed Ching Phor to the wall behind the Buddha. She removed a panel, exposing a laddered shaft. Climbing down, she led Tranh through a passageway where she removed another wall panel. They crawled ahead until she pulled away a tree root which revealed yet another laddered shaft. They descended further. At the bottom Tranh stared down a long tunnel. A solitary lantern illuminated the silent forms seated along the walls.

****

The magazine was open to a photo of Westinghouse appliances in a sparkling kitchen. A cheerful brunette pointed at a refrigerator.

"She is very pretty," said Laureen, passing the picture to the woman next to her.

"Yes," Hodges smiled, "but not as pretty as you."

"She is tall."

"Yes, she is tall."

"Does she always wear shoes with heels to prepare the meal?"

"I doubt it. That is for effect."

"E-ffect? Spell that, please."

"E-f-f-e-c-t. Effect."

She thumbed the dictionary.

"Oh, yes. Effect. She wears heels for effect?"

"For the advertisement."

"Ad-ver?"

"Tisement. A-d-v-e-r-t-i-s-e-m-e-n-t."

"Ah!" She thumbed. "Advertisement."

The neighbors chattered about the picture. Finally, their spokesman asked Laureen a question.

"Thompson, you must explain the magical kitchen."

"Explain the kitchen?"

"Aye, do you mind?"

"How could I mind? Let's see, you will translate?"

"As much as possible," Laureen smiled.

"Uh huh... Okay. This," he pointed, "is a refrigerator."

"*May trop*, refrigerator," Laureen announced.

"*May trop*?" The neighbors stared at Hodges.

"Uh huh. I see. We're gonna move slowly here."

An older man with thinning white hair offered Dui a cigarette. He inhaled then coughed twice. The neighbors chuckled as Dui checked the cigarette. "Well, well. What we have here is not your everyday Marlboro." He winked at the man who smiled toothlessly.

"Okay. The refrigerator has two sections. One for regular refrigeration, one for freezing to, uh, save things for a longer time. This is not my favorite area of the house. It's a work zone," he laughed.

Laureen smiled and began the translation. The villagers listened intently until she stopped. Immediately a rapid discussion broke out which halted just as suddenly. Another question.

"For how long do things freeze?" Laureen relayed.

"As long as you want. They're frozen."

"Frozen?" She checked the dictionary.

"F-r-o-z-e-n, frozen."

"Ah! Past tense. For how long then?"

"Forever."

"Forever?"

"Forever."

She turned to explain. The neighbors stared at Hodges.

"What?" he asked.

"Are you certain... forever?"

"Definitely," he nodded.

The villagers quietly marvelled the refrigerator.

Hodges looked to Laureen. "I think we're going to have some real trouble with the dishwasher."

"Dishwasher?"

****

The figures rose to a crouch. Tranh's height forced him to bend forward. The line shuffled through the tunnel away from the temple. After 800 meters, moonlight framed an opening. As Tranh approached the portal, a small corridor appeared to his left. Glancing down the alley, he noted four figures. Faceless but distinctive, two wore ARVN uniforms. Tranh exited the tunnel into the jungle. He focused on Ching Phor's step. Naturally bent, barely raising her sandals, she moved across the ground at a startling pace.

After thirty minutes they stopped. Ben Cat had disappeared behind them. Tranh whispered to Ching Phor. "Where do we go?"

"Where we are told," she said knotting the black scarf over his face. "Wear this to protect you from the branches. You must not return with scratches."

When the column resumed their march, they climbed two large hillsides. Three hours later they squatted at the edge of a clearing.

"Ah! Our most reliable team." Guyan arrived, accompanied by Phong. "You have done well to hold the pace. We are half way. The return will be slower. You must restore your strength."

Phong patted Tranh on the shoulder. "This bearer, my friend, is strong and fast. He earns respect for his family, eh Guyan?"

"His family need not prove themselves," said Ching Phor. "His has always been an honorable family. The Little Ox has his grandmother's soul. Save your counsel for your less hardy oxen."

Guyan patted her shoulder. "Aye! Wise One, Phong means no harm, only encouragement. The journey tires us all. Our effort requires harmony."

"Aye, Guyan. Tranh and Phong will learn we must depend on each other. Perhaps my short temper and my age betray me."

"As my youth betrays me," Phong apologized. "Your efforts surpass all expectations."

Across the clearing the treeline shimmered. Tranh started. "Ching Phor?"

"Do our friends surprise you? They have been there since we arrived."

"Are you certain? There are many."

"Aye, and look to the west," she pointed to a column of basket toters filing into the clearing.

"What is happening?"

"Little Ox, we take their baskets. Ben Suc no longer needs the goods."

"But?"

"Yes, the journey will be difficult. These baskets, you see, are heavier than rice."

"Heavier than rice?"

"Aye, much."

June 1, 1967

Ben Cat, South Checkpoint

"Old friend, how many times have we walked this path?"

"More than can be counted."

"Would you not think the oxen would know the way? Perhaps they lead us?"

"They are like my grandchildren," smiled Mai Nin.

"Ah, then they do know the way," Ching Phor laughed. "They just need our guidance."

"At least."

"But our gait has slowed. It is good they are mindful."

"The children or the oxen?"

"You are worried?"

"One is north, one is south. Tranh Nhu Lam embraces tradition, but my little flower, Laureen, encourages the American. As with her mother, she will follow her heart." Mai Nin shook her head. "To forbid? To encourage? My heart agonizes for them, for Ben Cat, for myself."

"This time an American. Laureen's world is a dream, her mother's dream. And Tranh, he has the heart of a lion, but the experiences of an ox. He is of the village. Do they ask advice?"

"Advice! Who seeks advice from such a decrepit old woman? Did their mother listen? Their paths are as different as their two fathers', but they share a determination as great as my daughter's. The only certainty is that my life will end here, where it began."

Ching Phor laughed. "Then we must stay the course together so that we may enjoy the results." She hesitated. "This time the danger is greater. Not because the commitment is less, nor because the intruder is unfamiliar, but because their instruments are so unforgiving."

"But Ching Phor, the crops, they come back well, do they not?"

"Aye, they receive experienced care," Ching Phor began. "Soon we begin the harvest. Our young men will be missed. Your oxen will be tested."

"Ben Cat will not be disappointed by my oxen. Is it not typical that when the men are needed most they disappear?"

"Only men are surprised by men," Ching Phor chuckled.

"Aye, they are predictably unpredictable." Mai Nin turned to her friend. "Do you miss your husband or do you bide your time?"

Ching Phor hesitated. "Life is the same. My husband gave me happiness not fulfillment. Without children, my path has been less complicated than yours, but who will carry on? Ben Cat is my reward. Her children are my children, her elders my parents, her adults my friends. The village has given more than can be returned." Ching Phor put her arm around Mai Nin. "What about you, are you lonely?"

"Lonely! Ha! With eight stubborn oxen and two ambitious grandchildren, who could be lonely? Their future, their dreams, those are my worries."

"Then, old friend, you must guide with a steady hand for their future and their dreams are at the crossroad."

****

In the Marketplace

"We're both left-handed." Mac sipped his beer.

"You know what I mean. His right hand, Jesus. He can't write, eat, throw... things we just take for granted."

"Yeah," Mac lowered his bottle. "I don't know what I'd do. At least he's alive."

"Mac, if it was me, what would you have done?"

"I don't know. I almost threw up when I saw LaVelle go down. It'd be worse with you. That what you wanna hear?"

"Mammasan! *Hai, bas-mui-bas?*" Dui called for another round. "You know it could've been one of us. Think about no arm, no leg, blind. Shit, so many things. Mac, I couldn't live without my arms or legs. I just couldn't."

"We'd have to. We'd just have to."

"Mac, we're young, real young. We get out of here, we're gonna live a long time. Like what? Like a vegetable? Bullshit!"

"Dui, you got to relax. We're here. We do the job, we go home. You watch my backside, I watch yours. We finish watchin each other's backsides, we go home. You get all worked up, we might have ourselves a problem, ya know?"

"LaVelle was good. But, as good as he was, there was a better one across the ditch." Hodges slammed a fist onto the table. "Jesus, how could someone slip into that ravine, booby trap the mine, get his ass out of there, and when all hell breaks loose have the balls to take a shot at the radio. Think what might of happened if we'd lost the wire. Christ, the way we were firing away, he probably had us in his sights."

"I didn't fire a shot."

"What? What d'ya mean?"

"I didn't fire. I didn't see nothing to shoot at. Since we've been here, I have not fired my weapon. Have you?"

"Well, no, no I haven't."

"Weird, huh? Why we feelin it so much? I mean, I feel tense, but I don't see anything goin on."

"Well, we've seen two guys take hits. That guy in Lai Khe and now LaVelle. There's a war out there," Hodges stopped. "Mac, what if one of us takes a hit? If you knew it was bad, if you knew you were lookin at a vegetable, if I could never walk, or throw, or, you know, screw, could you... do me?"

Mac pushed his bush hat back on his head. He stared past Hodges into the marketplace. "I don't know, and I don't know's I'd want your answer either."

The two sat in silence for a moment until Mac changed the subject. "You know you been seein an awful lot of that girl, Laureen. What's the deal?"

"The deal? It's out of control. A situation I shouldn't be in, but there's nothing I can do. Truth is, I've never felt like this." Hodges shook his head. "Laureen is different. When I'm with her, it's, it's not the Nam. The minute I leave her, I gotta get back."

"Dui, this is the Nam, no matter what."

"Yeah, I know. It's hard to figure. The minute I saw her, it happened. Maybe before she smiled, before I saw her, it had already happened. The way she moved, her eyes, I don't know."

"The way she moved? You said she was standing still."

"She was. She was standing still. Maybe everything around her was moving, I don't know. I just know it was... instantaneous and powerful, real powerful," Hodges shrugged. "You believe in destiny?"

"Destiny? Who knows? I do recognize a man with a case. And you got one. What about her?"

"Man, that's a tough one. She's smart, smarter than me. Her grandmother busts my chops. Always arranging these neighborhood seminars, ya know? Christ, there's always a crowd. We're never alone. But Laureen likes me. A lot. I felt it at first. It's stronger now."

"You're doing heavy-duty time there. She must like you or she'd throw you out," Mac teased. "You're learnin the language. Mr. Congeniality in Ben Cat, that's you." Mac leaned forward. "Maybe I should meet her and granny, ya know. And the kid, what's the kid's name?"

"Tranh, Tranh Nhu Lam."

"Yeah, Tranh. I should meet em. Maybe I could cover for you two love birds."

"Hey! That," Hodges smiled, "is one good idea."

****

Saigon

"And now English! What next, my child?" asked Madame Chocart.

"He speaks French. Very little," answered Laureen.

"French? Then he is not without merit," laughed Madame.

"Oh, but the pronunciation is hopeless. Fortunately his reading and writing surpass his diction."

"So he has schooling? But never to *La Belle France?*"

"Not to France, but good schooling, a private school. He relives the experience."

"Don't we all, *cherie*? Don't we all? For some of us, those memories are harder to recall," laughed Madame. "More tea?"

"*Merci*. And you, Madame?" Laureen rose to pour.

"Thank you, my dear. And how does Ben Cat receive the Americans and the ARVNs?"

"Miraculously. The village fills with barbed wire, soldiers, policemen, trucks, jeeps, helicopters. Ben Cat absorbs them all."

"Absorbs them? With such turmoil, how is this possible?"

"We have a hospital. Trucks leave cases of foodstuffs." Laureen shook her head. "The ARVNs sell everything. The black market flourishes."

"The black market? Who in Ben Cat offers currency?"

"Most probably the Viet Cong. The ARVNs even sell their own weapons. It goes beyond insanity."

"Oh! This sounds precarious. Are the Americans aware of this?"

"No, Madame. There are but a handful of Americans. The rest are gone. Now policemen oversee the ARVNs and the village. To miss the bartering one must be confounded or blind."

"Confounded or blind? This sounds like Saigon, or Paris, for that matter. Possibly these are universal qualifications for policemen?" Madame laughed. "So, tell me more of the American? Is he confounded and blind?"

"Thompson?" Laureen blushed. "Thompson is as naive as myself. He tries to understand the villagers. He struggles to converse. It is quite humorous, but he sees the fun. He is very popular."

"I see. But how popular with you?"

Laureen evaded Madame's gaze. "He makes me laugh. His presence fulfills me, his absence leaves me empty. It is new, new and unsettling."

Madame smiled. "Laureen? So it has happened? You are overcome. These feelings should not embarrass you."

Laureen turned from the table to view the garden. "Madame, how did mother know she loved my father? They were an unlikely couple, were they not? How did she entertain such an idea?"

"Entertain such an idea? Dear child, we do not plan to fall in love. Love happens. Even we French, who profess to know everything of love, know it is inexplicable. Your mother knew she was in love the same way all women know. From within, it comes from within, and certainly we do not control it. Love is the tidal wave within us all. Sometimes we survive, sometimes we succumb, and, worst of all, sometimes we allow it to pass us by. Occasionally, as with your mother, the greatest love comes from adversity, when we least need or expect it. Your mother loved your father without reservation. It was quite touching."

Laureen hesitated. "Then, how did she take another."

"I am not privy to that," Madame began. "Love changes. Our expectations change as do our circumstances. Love at twenty-two is different than love at thirty, or forty," she laughed, "or more. Love confronts loneliness, despair. When Michelin lost the plantation, your father was fortunate to escape. Your mother was devastated."

"She was lonely, desperate?"

"Laureen, your mother was filled with life, yet practical. I can only guess that she yearned for companionship. Later, love takes on a practical side. But make no mistake, once tasted, love leaves us insatiably unsettled until the next bite."

"The next bite?"

"Tranh's father."

"It confuses me so," Laureen looked back to her.

"Well, child, you are not alone. Not alone at all."

****

The Buddhist Temple at Ben Cat

"Brothers," the stern Viet Cong officer pointed to the map of Ben Cat. Guyan, Phong, and Tranh strained to see the details in the dim light. "Without Ben Suc, your village must serve as a sanctuary and supply depot. We need information concerning the fortifications. On this map we have detailed the northern sectors. Unfortunately our knowledge of the south is less specific."

The three studied the map. The checkpoints, the temple, the abandoned church, the marketplace, the medical compound, and all the streets were accurate.

The major pointed to some figures. "Here we have coordinates for the village landmarks, but more important is what we do not have."

"How may we contribute?" Guyan asked eagerly.

"Brother Guyan, there is a plan." The major looked at Tranh. "Your name is Tranh Nhu Lam, is that correct?"

"Aye, Major. Tranh."

"Tranh, you have a basic understanding of mathematics?"

"Aye. My sister has taught reading and mathematics, but she says my skills are limited."

"No matter! We will provide instructions." The major looked at the map. "Do you understand three-sided figures?"

"Aye. Triangles, squares, rectangles, these are familiar to me. My sister understands more of these things. She can teach me more."

"That may not be necessary." The major lightly circled the map with his pen. "Here is the perimeter of Ben Cat. You see the bunkers, the wire, the checkpoints. We have accurately documented the coordinates of these sites, but several items are missing."

"Major," Guyan began, "these are two eager workers, but they lack experience. This may be beyond them."

"Hmm, lack of experience?" The major turned to Phong. "Do you observe the Americans?"

Phong shrugged. "Not seriously."

"And you, Tranh, do you observe the Americans?"

"Somewhat." Tranh colored. "One American tries to learn our language from my sister."

"Aye, so we have heard."

Tranh looked up.

"Do not be alarmed. In turn, we must study our enemy. To be more effective, we should know his habits. How often does the American visit?"

"Too often," Phong interrupted. "He jeopardizes Tranh's movements."

"What do you say, Tranh? How do you feel about the American? Does he suspect your allegiance?"

"Tranh Nhu Lam has been very loyal, a hard worker," Guyan said. "He tutors under a veteran loyalist. His sister is a scholar who avoids the conflict, but her loyalty to her family is unquestioned."

"But what say you, Tranh?" The major pressed.

"The American does not seem a soldier. We call him Dui. He," Tranh looked to Guyan. "He pursues my sister. He is never the soldier with her."

"Ah, yes. And are you? Are you the soldier with her?"

"She is my sister, my sister the scholar, the teacher. To her there are no soldiers. We are all her students."

"So, the American courts your sister, and around her there are no soldiers. He learns our language..."

"Not very well."

"Not very well? But he may overhear something recognizable. You must be careful." The major thought. "And the American, Dui, you say, he has brought you gifts?"

"Aye, he brings gifts. Mostly for Grandmother and Laureen."

"Tell me, what gifts does he bring?"

"He brings candy, senseless things."

"But what does he give to you?"

"A ball. For kicking. A game ball."

"Ah, a kicking ball. For soccer, is it not?"

"Aye."

The major nodded. "The Americans love games. They play with great enthusiasm. And are you proficient with the ball? Do you play with friends?"

"No," interjected Phong. "We have no time for games!"

"Understandable, Phong, understandable. However, we would like you to play. In fact, we would like you to play with the Americans, near their compound. They are unable to resist a game."

"Play a game with the Americans?" Guyan repeated.

"Aye! We should encourage the game near their compound." With his pen the major designated the compound's location on the map. "Do you see this fence post? This is the tenth post from the checkpoint. We should like to know the distance from that post, the tenth post on the perimeter, to this post," he pointed to a dot on the wire encircling the compound, "the third post of their compound. We should also like to know the number of paces from this post," he pointed, "the easternmost post of the perimeter to the third post of the compound fence. You see, Tranh, we build a triangle." He connected the points.

Guyan repeated. "Phong and Tranh are to encourage a game near the compound. They are to pace off these distances yet remain unnoticed? That seems difficult."

"Aye, difficult. But Phong is a good soldier. Are you proficient at counting?" the Major asked.

"No, sir. Not proficient."

"Aye, then your role is to recruit other players and distract the Americans. Tranh will do the counting." The major rose and lifting a bundle of sticks from under his chair, he spread them out on the floor. "Each of these sticks is one-meter long. You, Tranh, must learn to walk with a one-meter stride. Brother Guyan," the major nodded to Guyan, "will practice with you, here, in the tunnel. He will place these throughout the tunnel, and then, Tranh, then, you will practice until your stride is consistent." He turned to Phong. "You are to practice kicking. You are to study the Americans. Learn about them. Do not rush this project. We have time. Accuracy, not expediency, that is our objective."

"But what of the bearings inside the compound? Are they not significant? Should we not work on those?" Guyan asked.

"A reasonable question, but not your concern. Even more than their games, the Americans admire cleanliness." He smiled. "Our laundresses are very proficient."

****

Command Compound

Dudley and Major White sat at a table sipping sodas.

"What are we overlooking, Sergeant?"

"Sir, nothing has changed. The ARVNs are the key players. We are as invulnerable as they are loyal. I'm not real comfortable with that, but that's the way it is."

"You still don't trust them?"

"Neva have, neva will."

"Some residual bitterness there, Sergeant?"

"Probably," Dudley shrugged. "They're unprofessional, unmotivated. Part-time clowns, like our National Guard. If the shit hits the fan, ya neva know what you'll get."

"Are they manning their posts?"

"Yes, sir. They show up. Around this village they're big news. Spending money, giving food away, trying to get laid, who knows what else?"

"I see. What about the MPs?"

"Sir, they got a buddy system going here. You don't piss them off, they don't piss you off. They're tough on certain civilians, piss poor on their ARVN pals." Dudley shrugged. "Can they be bought? Probably. Do they find stuff? Definitely. Yesterday they found a mammasan with two grenades stuffed down her shirt. My guess is she pissed somebody off."

"Christ! What did they do?"

"Took the grenades, beat the shit out of her in front of forty civilians, then called a chopper and sent her packing. She won't be back."

"I didn't know about this."

"Out of our jurisdiction, sir, you know? Our gook major, Major Thiut, he knew."

"He never said anything."

"That figures," Dudley said. "He only tells us what he wants us to know."

White poured more soda onto his precious ice. "This will not do! The ARVNs and the MPs must shape up. Any ideas?"

"A change of command would be good," Dudley grinned.

"Right!"

"Sir, Thiut, he's a soldier, but his cadre, that's another story. Real amateurs. We get to crunch time, they'll let us down. These ARVNs need discipline. Thiut cannot do it by himself, and he cannot do it while he's helping us in the bunker. He may have one or two good officers, but my gut tells me we got more trouble than we know."

"A change of command?"

"Well, either that or we trade the team. That won't happen. We need an asskicker."

"Like you, Sergeant."

"Like us, Major."

"Interesting," reflected the major. "Very interesting. I'll mention something in Lai Khe."

"Very well, sir. Probably won't go anywhere, but you could mention it."

"Now, Sergeant, what about our guys? How they doing?"

"Some good, some bad. The new guy's a lifer. Greenfeld. Wally Greenfeld, Cleveland. Five years in. Just came from Korea. Experienced RECON. Too early to tell."

"I see. He getting along?"

"They're feeling their way. LaVelle was popular. They took it hard. They been together a year now."

"LaVelle," The major shook his head. "Shit's happening."

"Yes, sir!" Dudley agreed. "Sir, there is one situation."

"Oh? What's that?"

"Sir, we got one man, Hodges..."

"Yes, Hodges."

"Seems he's taken a fancy to one of the locals. Christ, the whole village knows him. They got a name for him, Dui."

"Dui?"

"Means blind."

"A blind man fraternizing with the locals?"

"Yes, sir," Dudley waited. "You can bet it's noticed."

"By the other men? They're always lookin to get laid. What's the difference?"

"This guy, he's giving us good PR, but he is establishing a pattern."

"A pattern?"

"Yes, sir. When he's not in the field, he visits. When we're in the field, he doesn't, it's that simple."

"I see," White deliberated. "I see. And you think this is, uh, observed?"

"Everything is observed, yes sir."

"I see. What do you suggest? Restrictions? Do we talk to him? He seems smart enough?"

"Sir, I've been thinking. We could use this, not discourage this. He is excellent PR. We can use some."

"True. That we can use around here," White smiled. "You have a plan, right Sergeant?"

"Like to test my theory, sir. Keep MacKerry and Hodges on the day shift, working the perimeter. Keep sending out the patrols without Hodges. See what happens."

"More guerrilla stuff, eh, Sergeant? Can't hurt, can it?"

"No, sir!"

"If Hodges is in, who leads the squad?"

"Glad you asked, Sir!" Dudley grimaced. "Don't want to get too rusty. With your permission, the men need to see me out there."

"Excellent, Sergeant! Excellent!"

Ben Cat

"Laureen," Mai Nin pointed down the path, "no candy tonight. Instead, Dui brings a large Cambodian."

"Cambodian, hah! That is a black American. A very large, black American," said Tranh.

"A black American? He is different than the picture books. He smiles. His face is round, his hair short."

"Grandmother! Will Thompson's friend enjoy our hospitality, or is he to be subjected to our scrutiny?"

"Tranh Nhu Lam, the neighbors! Most certainly they will be interested to meet such a specimen. And in honor of this visitor, you must take Ching Phor the black scarf." Mai Nin passed Tranh the scarf.

"Grandmother, is this necessary? Tonight, just tonight, could we not enjoy each other's company? Thompson has told me of this friend. He is very shy. Should we not make him comfortable before we expose him to the whims of our neighbors?"

"Shy? An American? Are the black ones shy? If so, this opportunity may not come again." Mai Nin directed Tranh. "Go to Ching Phor. We will be brief, then you children may have your fun."

Tranh tied the scarf around his neck and ran down the hill nodding to Dui and Mac as he passed.

"*Chao emmoi*," Hodges smiled at Laureen. "This is my very good friend, Donald A. MacKerry. Mac is an honorable man. Unlike me he has no enemies."

"That can't be me he's talkin about," grinned Mac.

"Mac, this," Hodges took Laureen's hand, "is my teacher and special friend, Laureen, Laureen Nhu Lam. And this, this is her inquisitive grandmother, Mai Nin." Hodges extended an open palm toward the grandmother.

"Howdy, Laureen, Mammasan," Mac bowed.

Laureen faced her grandmother. "Mai Nin, Thompson introduces you to his friend, Mac, a man without enemies."

"Has he been to Cambodia? He has the color of a Cambodian."

Laureen bowed to Mac. "You are welcome, please be comfortable." The Americans sat on the steps. "Mac, Thompson says this is the most beautiful view he has ever seen. Do you agree?"

As Mac scanned the valley, Laureen addressed Mai Nin. "He is not from Cambodia. The Americans are sensitive about their color differences. This is not polite conversation. Besides, Thompson may understand more of this conversation than you realize."

"Sensitive about their color? How peculiar. Was it not the way they were born?"

"This is not our affair. They handle this in their own manner. May we be gracious and go beyond this?"

"Is the black American of the soil?"

"Mai Nin! His name is Mac!" Laureen's sharp reply startled the Americans.

"Is this a bad time?" asked Hodges.

"No, Thompson, no. This is a good time. Grandmother's days with the oxen are long. Sometimes she forgets how to converse," Laureen laughed. "Mac, Mai Nin asks what work your family does?"

"Laureen, Dui's right, you sure can speak. I don't have a father. My family works on a horse farm, in Kentucky, that's a state, ya know?"

"You have no father?"

Mac looked away. "No father. My mother, two sisters, and me, that's the MacKerrys... of Hartford, Ken-tuck."

"The MacKerrys of Hart-ford, Ken-tuck," Laureen repeated with amusement. She faced Mai Nin. "Mac has no father. His mother and two sisters raise horses, much as you do your oxen. This was his work before Vietnam."

"Horses, eh? He has the teeth of a horse. Do you see how large they are? Are you certain he is not Cambodian? A Cambodian with crooked and missing teeth?"

"Mai Nin! If you insist on this rudeness, we shall walk to the village!"

"He has the shoulders of an ox."

"Aye, and the width of his shoulders exceeds your hospitality." Laureen turned to the men. "So, Thompson, your friend Mac gains approval from Mai Nin. This is not easily done. It reflects well on you."

"Really? She doesn't seem too pleased. Maybe we should come back another time?"

"Thompson, you must understand the Vietnamese. Please, Mac, do not be offended by Grandmother's..." she scanned her dictionary, "de-mean-or. She teases everyone, even her oldest friends. It is a convenience of old age that one can say foolish things and be forgiven."

"I dunno, Laureen." Mac smiled. "Maybe she's callin em the way she sees em, ya know?"

"Calling them the way she sees them? That saying is unfamiliar to me."

****

Tranh caught Ching Phor on the way to her communion with Buddha. "Again the American! Tonight he brings another. A black one. A large black monkey!" He handed the scarf to her. "She sends you her greeting."

"Ah, and does Mai Nin welcome them?"

"Aye, she does."

"This is good," Ching Phor smiled to Tranh. "Guyan gives thanks this evening. Will you join us?"

They entered the temple filled with worshippers.

"The incense is heavy this evening," noted Tranh.

"Strong incense fends off evil spirits," Ching Phor whispered.

"Then we need more at home."

They chuckled, then bowed until Guyan appeared beside them.

"Good evening, Ching Phor, Little Ox. How are Mai Nin and Laureen this night?"

"They have two guests this evening," Ching Phor laughed. "Little Ox is uncomfortable."

"Understandably so," Guyan sympathized. "But the Little Ox must make a greater effort. After all, the guests can improve your kicking."

"Aye, like all little oxen, you must learn manners. We Vietnamese are very polite. You are the grandson of Mai Nin. You reside in a fine house. You must support her in everything she does. This role is your privilege," affirmed Ching Phor.

Tranh swallowed. "This may be easy for you, Ching Phor, but not for your Little Ox."

"Tonight we have many oxen. The Little Ox should rest and enjoy the peacefulness of Ben Cat," Guyan insisted.

"You dismiss me? To my Americanized house?"

"Not dismissed, brother. Reminded. Reminded of the importance of mathematics. In your situation these things are best learned at home," said Guyan.

"And Tranh, when you return, thank Mai Nin for the scarf." She showed it to Guyan. "It will be returned tomorrow. Now, Little Ox, my time with Buddha grows short." Ching Phor bowed to the floor.

****

The sun began to melt away the mist. Ben Cat finally returned to view. "Guyan, we run late," said Ching Phor.

"Aye. We were further away than usual. We will be near the paddies soon."

"Are we to infiltrate the work force?"

"Aye. Our brothers in the paddies will shield us."

The empty baskets must still be deposited before the carriers dispersed to the paddies. Guarded by eight Viet Cong, the tardy, hungry column slowly forged toward home.

"My Little Ox is missed tonight. My front man tires. He has fallen twice. Why not switch him and Phong? We must move faster before the mist disappears completely."

Guyan waved Phong to the basket. "We fall behind. Soon there will be no cover. Relieve the front carrier of his basket. We must quicken the pace. We have a day's work ahead."

Phong replaced the elderly villager at the front of the yoke. They rushed to close the gap.

Snap! A branch snapped. The enemy!

"Fire!"

Violence exploded into the column.

The ground churned. Weapons opened fire.

Ching Phor dove away from the basket.

"Phong, stay down! Come here! Crawl to me!"

"We must run!"

"Boy! Do not run! Crawl here!"

A grenade exploded thirty feet away. Shrapnel zinged above them.

Phong crawled to her side. "We must run!" The boy's face contorted with fear and the desire to escape.

"No! Stay on the ground!" She reached for him. "Steady yourself! Absorb the turmoil!"

"We must run!"

Bullets tore into their basket. A grenade arched toward them. They hugged the ground.

"Retreat now!"

"No!" barked Ching Phor. "Wait for the artillery! They will cover themselves. By then we must be behind that tree," she pointed. "When they cease firing, we will escape to the sky." She stripped away her outer layer of clothing. "Discard anything heavy. We crawl, then we climb."

Ahead more mines detonated. A woman stood. Her flaming torso shrieked in horror.

Ching Phor crawled to the tree. Bullets spat into the ground.

A panicked carrier got up to run. Shots rang out. His chest flew through the back of his shirt. He stood, momentarily suspended in death.

Phong froze. Ching Phor yanked his hair.

Another grenade landed nearby. They buried their heads. The grenade launcher had bearings!

Ching Phor inched behind the tree. Another mine severed the front of the column. Fear screamed out.

Ching Phor and Phong lay still.

"Now Ching Phor? Now? Up the tree?"

"Wait!"

She listened. He wondered. She listened.

More grenades. More bullets.

"Hold your fire! Hold your fire!"

The barrage stopped.

"Incoming!"

"Now! Phong, now!" She seized on a swinging vine on the far side of the tree. They climbed above the enemy, above their comrades.

Artillery whistled in. Fires ignited in the ravine.

With each explosion, they clutched tighter.

****

LZ - Ben Cat

"Major, I don't understand. We should've been there."

"Nothing personal, Hodges, nothing personal."

"Yes, sir, but..."

"But? But nothing. My call, you understand."

"Yes, sir. It's just that... these are our guys, our team, our job. We should've been there."

"Hodges, you're pushing. That's enough. Dudley thought he was getting rusty. That's it." The major drew a deep breath. "You and MacKerry take these ARVNs, report to Dudley. Find your friend."

White, Hodges, and MacKerry stood at the Ben Cat landing zone awaiting the Lai Khe choppers that would carry them to the ambush site. Thirty ARVNs sat off to the side.

"That won't be easy." Mac shook his head. "The Ghost, he finds us. We never know where he's at."

"That may be, MacKerry, but now Scott needs you. He's Missing In Action." White pointed to the approaching helicopters. "You get on those choppers, find him. We, uh, we're running out of time on this. The rest of your team is out there, they been working all night. They're tired. They want to come home. You got four hours, four hours, that's it. There's no time to worry about your personal agendas. Got it?"

"Yes, sir."

Hodges and MacKerry boarded the first chopper, joined by one of the three ARVN squads. Twenty minutes later the platoon jumped to the ground, moving to rendezvous with the ambush patrol.

"Jesus!" Hodges stood at the crest of the ravine. The smell was as devastating as the images. Hodges covered his face with a yellow bandana and surveyed the wreckage. Splintered Viet Cong baskets marked the path below them.

"Artillery." MacKerry pointed across the ravine. Smoke still rose from the craters.

Several ARVNs piled VC bodies up along the trail. Other soldiers dragged remnants of the baskets toward a raging bonfire.

"A signal to Ben Cat." Hodges motioned to the heavy smoke billowing above the jungle.

"Yeah," agreed Mac. "Think they'll get the message?"

"They got it hours ago," nodded Hodges, "with the breakfast no-shows."

"Uh huh."

Down the ridge Ringhyter leaned against a rock, cleaning his M-60. Weaver sat holding his grenade launcher across his lap. A pile of unspent claymores lay next to a reclining Hosmach.

Dudley came from the north. "Hodges, MacKerry, we got work to do." He pointed across the ravine. "I want you to follow that ridge south. Keep your eyes open. You never know who might be hanging around. Be back in three hours... with Scott."

"Jesus, Sergeant. What happened?"

"Clockwork. 0600, they came up the ditch. Walked into us. Neva had a chance. The claymores froze them. Ducks on the pond."

"Where was Scott?" Hodges asked.

"We had an exit lane up here behind us. Last I knew he cleared the lane, then headed south." Dudley waited. "We had artillery," he pointed, "across the way and south. I'm hoping he was out of the way."

"Okay we go, Sergeant?"

"Good hunting, gentlemen. You got three hours." Dudley shook his head. "Then we got to go."

Hodges and MacKerry crossed to the top of the west bank before turning south along the ridge.

"He ain't over here," said Mac.

"What d'ya mean?"

"I just know. He ain't over here."

"What d'ya think?"

"He knew they were comin."

"Yeah?"

"I think he went south."

"Why?"

"Intuition," Mac looked down the ravine. "Man, no chance. They never had a chance."

"I guess that's the point. Wanna be an Airborne Ranger, Mac? Wanna live through hell and danger, Mac?"

"Uh huh."

The search began. After two kilometers the jungle regained its composure. Each limb had its own personality. Every form shaped their disappointment. With each step their stomachs tensed with discouragement.

The Ghost was gone.

"Mac, we're too far."

"Too far?"

"We gotta get back. He wouldn't be this far."

MacKerry dropped his head. "We got to find him. We shoulda been here."

"Yeah," Hodges winced. "We shoulda been here. Shit!"

"Yeah."

"Mac, we gotta go back. We're too far."

"Let's take the trail. Maybe if we were lookin up the ravine, we could spot him?"

They returned along the enemy's path. Hodges looked east. Mac searched west until they approached two ARVNs struggling with the last basket.

"Here, I'll help," Mac volunteered grabbing the rear of the yoke. Hodges took one more look behind.

Ghost? Into the night... The way I know... shit!

Hodges wiped his hand across his eyes, then turned to follow the basket.

As Mac pushed ahead, his foot grazed a clump of bushes.

Mai Nin's black scarf fluttered to the ground.

Hodges knelt and slid it into his shirt.

What the fuck!

227 days

Ben Cat

The market was unusually quiet.

"Mammasan," Hodges waved. *"Hai bas-mui-bas?"*

"Aye, Dui."

Hodges and Mac set their M-16s against the wall before slumping into their customary chairs.

"Tired?" Mac asked.

"Just another shift."

"You need a shave. How long's it been?"

"Four days."

"Seems like longer."

"It all seems longer."

"We gotta get past it," suggested Mac.

"Past it? That won't be easy. I don't like the ARVN pointman. Our front's suspect."

"Suspect?"

"Maybe worse."

"What are you saying?" Mac leaned back.

"Every night we go out, it feels worse, a sick feeling. Empty."

"Uh huh. I know what ya mean." Mac lifted his bottle. "One more shift, one less day. We're getting there."

"Most of us, yeah."

Mac stared into the marketplace. "Ben Cat's changin."

"Everything's changing."

"C'mon, Dui, you're just missin Laureen. This night shift's got you outta kilter. Let's go on up there and say good mornin. She's probably wonderin what's up."

"Maybe she is. So am I."

"What d'ya mean?"

"I'm not sure. Not too sure about much right now. Could be the wrong time, the wrong place again." Hodges sipped his beer. "You know, Mac, I never thought the enemy was here, in the village, but they are. They're everywhere."

"Yup, they are. Like Dudley said, they been here a long time."

"We're not making any progress with this conversion thing. We give em food, we give em doctors, we keep the bad guys out. What the hell! They spend their nights sneaking around in the fricking jungle. LaVelle, Ghost. Who's next? Shit, maybe we ought to waste the whole village."

"Hey, man, you're tired. You're not thinking right. We better hit the sack. We're on the pad at 1800."

Hodges set his beer down and lifted his rifle. Placing his elbows on the table, he lay the stock into his right shoulder sighting the weapon into the marketplace. "Now let's see, how do you do this?"

"Hey man, that's enough," Mac placed his hand over the barrel.

"Pow! Pow!" Curious shoppers turned to stare.

"That's enough, man. Let's get outta here."

"Why? Where we gonna go?"

"Well, we aren't in the mood to see Laureen, that's for sure."

"No, we're not."

****

"Is everyone accounted for?"

"Captain, almost everyone," offered Guyan.

"Almost everyone? Was everyone notified?"

"All seventeen families," answered Guyan.

"Good. And how many have arrived?"

"Twelve widows, four widowers, and the children are ready for relocation."

The captain walked around the table, seating himself across from the entrance to the cell off the tunnel. He motioned for Guyan to sit. "You have done well, but who does not respond?"

"Ban Dong. She has no family. Now that her husband is dead, she sees no reason to leave."

The captain raised his eyes. "This is not a matter of choice. This is a matter of security. Theirs and ours. This was made clear, was it not?"

"Aye, Captain. Your message was delivered. We have sixteen families in the tunnel ready to go. Thirty-two children, eighteen boys, fourteen girls. They carry their lives in their baskets." Guyan shook his head. "They are shaken by their losses and by their relocation. Ben Cat is all they know."

"Perhaps they will return one day. To a better Ben Cat."

"Captain, they feel betrayed."

"Betrayed? A strange choice of words. Certainly not by us. We struggle to protect them, to return them their heritage." The captain became stern. "War does not select victims or survivors. The dead were lost for the cause. They sought their independence. There is a price."

"The Americans!" hissed Guyan. "They were waiting. We were too slow. Now Ben Cat has thirteen fatherless families, four without mothers. The responsibility is mine. The failure is mine."

"How many dead?"

"Thirty. Five soldiers, twenty-five carriers. Seventeen from Ben Cat, eight from Ben Suc. There was no time to react. Fear overcame us all."

"Guyan, you must take hold of yourself. You must! This is war! Did you expect less? These intruders do not come out of friendship. Losses are inevitable."

"The American pigs!"

"Not only the Americans. Yes, the American pawns are repugnant and they have no souls, but the dogs from Saigon are just as bad. In time they will both be dealt with."

"In time? When? When do we avenge our brothers? When can we look these families in the eye? When will the fatherless children, the husbandless women, not resent me! It was my ignorance that betrayed them. My ignorance and the Americans! We must retaliate."

"There will be no retaliation."

"Why?"

"Because this is not the time. In war we take losses as do they. Your mission is to prepare. Ben Cat still serves its purpose."

"What purpose? To relocate our families? To tolerate their arrogance? To leave our dead unburied so that the snakes slither through their bodies? Will the children forget their fathers? It is unacceptable! We must avenge our losses. These were humble men."

"They were soldiers," said the captain.

"Defenseless soldiers with baskets. Under my care! The children in this tunnel will never forgive me. First the deaths, now relocation. It is unforgivable!" Guyan slouched forward.

The captain stood. Walking behind him, he placed his hands on Guyan's shoulders. "In time we shall avenge the loss. But for now we must preserve Ben Cat."

"Captain, we are surrounded by the enemy. What type of sanctuary can this be?"

"We have sympathizers. You must believe. These families," the captain pointed to the tunnel, "understand loss. Even the children know loss. Our supporters are prepared to cope with loss. The enemy is not. You are a leader in this village. You have respect. Do not betray yourself. Your mission is to lead. When the time is right, you shall have your revenge. This is no time for self-doubt or self-pity. You are not alone in dealing with loss." The captain moved away. "Ban Dong must go."

"Ban Dong? She is harmless. She will not move. She chooses to remain."

"This is not her decision."

"She will not leave with the others. She is adamant. She was born in Ben Cat."

"Guyan, do you know Ching Phor?" asked the captain.

"Of course. One of our bravest. She survived the attack."

"Aye," confirmed the captain. "Did you know she once lived elsewhere?"

"Ching Phor? Lived elsewhere? Are you certain?"

"Her husband was killed by the French. She relocated here to Ben Cat, as these survivors will do in another village. Ching Phor understands loss, understands security. Soon the MPs will identify Ban Dong. You are to explain this. Tonight we will take these families. In two days we shall return for Ban Dong. She must be ready."

"In her grief she pays me no mind," said Guyan. "Could you speak with her?"

"Guyan, you must assert yourself. The woman has no choice. She must come."

"And if not, what do we do? Kidnap her?"

"No! If she will not leave, you will deliver a message that will not be misunderstood."

Guyan stood and stumbled into the tunnel. Everything was sliding toward him. To stabilize himself, he leaned against the wall gasping for space and time.

Ben Cat – Command Compound

"Eyes front!"

White stood beside an easel, holding his curious brass-headed cane. The squad occupied eleven of the twelve chairs facing him.

"Gentlemen, opportunity is now before us." The major smiled. "And we have our friend Scott to thank for it."

Dudley opened the door of the tent. The Ghost strode forward.

"Holy shit!" Hodges yelled. "Ghost!"

"Where you been?" asked MacKerry.

"In the bush," Ghost laughed. "Just a strollin in the bush." He took the seat next to Hodges.

"For five days?" asked Balman.

"Not exactly."

"Gentlemen," White began, "Ghost followed two escapees from the ambush, then somehow found his way to Lai Khe. Sergeant Scott," White paused to let the promotion sink in, "we are glad to see you."

"Way to go... Sarge," congratulated Hodges.

"Gentlemen, unfortunately we do not have time to celebrate Sergeant Scott's return. He has furnished us with information, classified information. Eyes front, pay attention." White lifted the cover sheet on the easel, revealing a map.

"This spot," he placed the tip of the cane on the map, "we will call the kitchen. The kitchen is filled with little chefs and busboys, all wearing black."

The tip of his pointer bored into the spot.

"The kitchen cupboards are filled with goodies. And where there are goodies, there is Charley. Two companies minimum. Is that right, Sergeant?"

"Yes, sir," answered Ghost.

"And Charley lives underground in the kitchen?"

"Yes, sir."

White lowered the cane. "There will be no easy way in, no easy way out. North Vietnamese Regulars are a definite probability." He hesitated. "We are going in. Operation Manhattan commences now! Sergeant Dudley has the details."

The major walked over to Scott. "Scott, good job. You have done well. Welcome home." The major shook Ghost's hand.

"Home?"

"Back with us."

"Yes, sir."

The major checked the squad, turned, and exited.

Dudley stood before them.

"Were you listening? Did you hear the man? This is the reason you are here."

Dudley stood taller.

"We are going to hit the fucker where it hurts. In his lifeline." He paced in front of them. "This is not a patrol. This is search, seal, destroy... in a free-fire zone, in a hot, free-fire zone."

Dudley lowered his voice. "This is my third tour. Not once before have we stung the bastards. We are going to sting him today!"

"Today?" squeaked Balman.

"Today. Now get your heads togetha. Get focused. He's out there in the bush. Waiting, waiting in the bush. We are going to him in broad daylight. We are going to him. We will. Kick ass."

Dudley unsheathed his bayonet and marked the kitchen again. "In three hours the Air Force will commence aggressive action in and around the kitchen." He pointed the bayonet at Hodges. "At 1400 hours we rendezvous with Black Horse Bravo and Delta Companies, 2nd - 28th, at this LZ," he jabbed the bayonet, "which we call the pantry."

"The pantry is a valley surrounded by these hills," the pointer encircled the pantry. "It is the only place open enough, flat enough to land." He surveyed the men, then continued. "From the pantry we head east along this line," the bayonet moved across the map, "up the foothills, into the kitchen. This is jungle. This is uphill. Hot and heavy." He flicked the point. "Over here, on the other side of the kitchen, Black Horse Alpha and Echo Companies will touch down," he marked the spot. "At the back door. Charley's in the kitchen, between the pantry and the back door." Dudley silently contemplated the map.

"He's dug in. We expect resistance, heavy resistance. He don't give up easy." The chin raised. "The strong. Will survive."

Dudley issued a hard look. "In five hours we are on the ground heading up the hill. If you are ready, if you follow your training," he hesitated, "we got a good chance."

"Think about it. First, there is daylight. Second, we know where they are. Third, we," his hand raised over his head, "will have big birds overhead. Ain't they beau-ti-ful?"

Dudley bore down. "This mission is for your ears only! Not one word leaves this tent. 1200 hours on the pad." The chin relaxed. "This just don't happen. Maybe once in a lifetime. Make the most of it. Dismissed."

Hodges stood first.

"Where you going?" asked Mac.

"To the crapper."

"Uh huh. Right behind you."

****

"Write your mother," Hodges instructed Mac.

"Uh huh. You write yours."

"I don't think so, she wouldn't want to know, but I might write Laureen."

"Laureen?" Mac asked. "Our ears only, ya know?"

"Not about this."

"Oh! A love letter?"

"Not quite," Hodges hesitated. "A package."

****

At 1215 hours the squad's helicopters linked up with the Black Horses.

At 1245 they touched down in the pantry.

Artillery shattered the hillside.

Dudley and Ghost flanked Captain Chelius of Bravo Company.

Ghost pointed up the hill. "Into the night, Dui, into the night."

Mac and Hodges fisted each other. "Watch my ass."

"Yeah, Mac, you too. Keep it down."

The jungle danced around them. Jungle eyes! Images darted left, right, up, down.

Jesus! Settle down!

The silence roared.

They moved ahead.

The jungle thickened. The air surrendered. The jungle eyes closed. A high-pitched symphony of insects began.

At 1425, the artillery ceased. Two jets spun out of the sun to make a final deposit.

"Let's go home," mumbled Hodges.

The column turned abruptly east.

At 1600, they halted.

The kitchen door!

A platoon of Black Horses edged parallel to the squad along the crest of the hill. Another platoon covered their north flank.

Shit! Here we go! I can do this! I can do this!

Hodges cradled his weapon.

Be lucky! His fingers checked his clips, his grenades. He straightened his helmet.

He stared down between his legs, into the ground. A deep breath. He inspected his boots, scraped away the buildup.

Three deep breaths. He crouched lower. This is it!

Dudley peered through his binoculars. Weaver slithered over to him. They raised their heads above the crest.

The muzzle of Weaver's M-79 pointed up.

The column hoisted their weapons.

Hodges peered forward at the smoldering potholes and severed trees.

Weaver pulled back, squeezing the trigger. A grenade thudded away, initiating a string of explosions from the Black Horse grenadiers.

The riflemen waited.

One grenade struck an ammunition cache, setting off a series of detonations.

Balman's M-60 blasted away. Small trees fell. Balman fired on.

Ringhyter's M-60 joined in.

Ghost crawled thirty meters forward. The squad bellied ahead.

Ghost fisted them to halt.

He leaned on his left side, looked up, arched a grenade. He raised himself to one knee, fired a five-bullet burst, then ran forward, diving from view.

Dudley sprinted fifteen meters, sprawling behind an ant hill.

Ringhi dove beside him.

Dudley pointed to a camouflaged shelter.

Ringhi laced the site.

Two choppers buzzed overhead.

Yes!

Hollowed bunkers sprung at them. Unoccupied! Trapped? Resistance?

Behind! Behind!

Nothing!

Everything moved. Except the enemy. Where are they?

"Watch your fucking step!"

Booby traps!

Hodges pulled the pin of a grenade, rose to one knee and threw it into a bunker. He discharged a burst.

Two quick breaths. He charged.

Mac jumped to his feet. Three short bursts left. He rushed toward Hodges, who emptied his clip into the bunker, then ducked back, staring blankly at the onrushing MacKerry.

Mac dove next to Hodges. "Where are they?"

"Nobody home! Nobody home!"

"The artillery?"

Hodges locked in a fresh clip. "Look in there! They're fucked."

"How many?"

"Who knows! Cover me!"

Hodges fired at the next bunker. "Fuck! Fuck! Fuck!" Hodges pivoted away from Mac sprinting deeper into the kitchen.

****

At 2030 hours, the Black Horse sentries secured the perimeter. Where were the enemy?

Dudley addressed his squad. "In the morning Alpha and Echo Companies will return to the pantry. They will escort engineers, tunnel rats, and the dogs back here." He smiled. "Charley hates those dogs."

"This place gives me the creeps," said Mac.

"They're dead!" Balman reminded.

"Yeah, they're dead," mumbled Mac. "If that's what you call it."

"Jesus Christ, MacKerry! This is the safest place we could be."

"Yeah, well, where are the rest? They ain't all dead. Where are the ones from the tunnels?"

"Not here, MacKerry, not here," Dudley answered. "But they left beaucoup in the tunnels. You can bank on that. We got what we came for, we did the job."

****

Escorted by gunships, Alpha and Echo Companies departed for the pantry at 0700. Bravo and Delta Companies remained behind to guard the encampment.

Dudley approached Captain Chelius.

"Sir?"

"Sergeant?"

"Sir, request permission to run the flank."

"Run the flank?"

"Yes sir." Dudley opened his map. He pointed to a line across the map. "Below this crest there is a ridge where the pantry is visible. My squad could observe and cover the flank."

"I see, Sergeant. Sounds solid. I like it. I'll notify Major Hughes. You are Matchmaker, right?"

"Yes sir, Matchmaka."

"Hughes is Cornhusker. Major Greagan is with Alpha and Echo Companies. Greagan is Buckeye."

"Cornhusker in the kitchen, Buckeye to the pantry."

"Right."

Dudley approached the squad. "Gentlemen, we are moving out."

"Moving out?" Balman reacted.

"To the flank."

"But Sergeant," Ringhyter began, "they got choppers."

"Gentle-men! This is not a request. Saddle up!"

At 0800 Ghost led them over the crest, down the hillside.

"Hodges!"

"Yes Sergeant."

"Get up here with Parker."

Dudley spread his map across Greenfeld's back. "Here we are. Here is the pantry, here is the kitchen." He traced the line from the kitchen to the pantry. "And here is Buckeye. At 1045 Buckeye secures the pantry. The engineers arrive around 1130. At 1230 they'll head back to the kitchen. Keep your eyes open. Buckeye's got hueys overhead. Mark em. Scott and I are going to have a look around."

From the observation post south of the heavy jungle, Hodges viewed the pantry. Across the valley, high peaks descended into a series of foothills. The remains of an old farmhouse lay at the base of the valley. A forgotten dirt path wound its way up the slope, then vanished.

Once, someone had lived here.

Heavy clouds hung over the hills to the west. Hodges trained his binoculars on a gunship patrolling above Buckeye.

He scanned the pantry until the radio came alive.

"Cornhusker, this is Buckeye, over."

"Buckeye, this is Cornhusker. What's the score?"

"Cornhusker, we are in the pantry. Area will be secure in three-zero."

"Buckeye, we have a watchman in the tower, south of the border. Matchmaker, do you read?"

"Cornhusker, this is Matchmaker, over," Hodges responded.

"Matchmaker, any score?"

"Negative, Cornhusker. All clear from here."

"Roger that."

Hodges watched a squad of Black Horses fan out along the north treeline.

"Bulldog Six, this is Buckeye, over."

No response.

"Bulldog Six, this is Buckeye, over."

Static blipped in. "Buckeye, this is Bulldog Six, over."

"Bulldog Six, we are looking good down here. Let's get em in and get you out."

"Uh, Bulldog Six, here. Roger that. ETA zero-five, over."

"Come on down!"

A row of choppers drifted from behind the west foothills.

Yes!

"All clear?" Dudley asked.

"All clear, Sergeant. The perimeter's secure. Choppers touching down."

"Very good," Dudley raised his binoculars.

Two squads emerged from the trees running towards the Bulldogs.

The Black Horses escorted sixty members of Alpha Company back to the jungle. Four teams from the canine corps jumped from the last chopper and followed the engineers.

The Bulldogs lifted off.

The pantry looked empty.

Hodges lowered his glasses. Dudley maintained his vigil.

"Looks good, Sarge. They'll be moving soon. We gonna meet them half way?"

"We watch, we listen, Hodges."

The 200 American troops completed their meal at 1230 hours.

"Cornhusker, this is Buckeye, over."

"Cornhusker here, go."

"Cornhusker, we are departing pantry. ETA 1600 hours. Do you copy?"

"Copy that. How's the weather?"

"All clear. Thunder overhead. Taking the easy way home."

"Buckeye, this is Cornhusker, copy that. We're holding dinner. Hurry on home now, you hear?"

"Roger, out."

"Son of a bitch!" barked Dudley grabbing the transmitter. "Buckeye, Matchmaka here, ova."

"Come ahead, Matchmaker."

"No can do easy way home, ova."

"Matchmaker, can do, easy way home. My men are tired. Tired of climbing up and down this frigging hill. Got it?"

"You know the rule."

"There are no rules. We're coming up. Out."

Dudley threw the transmitter to Parker. "Dumb fucker! Neva take the same trail. Hodges! Stay on the peepers!" The sergeant looked west. "Scott! Round em up. We're moving out."

"Again?" Balman asked.

"Three times! This asshole used that fucking trail. Three times. West Point, my ass!" Dudley fumed. "Cornhusker, this is Matchmaka, ova."

"Go, Matchmaker."

"Moving out."

"Moving out?"

"Down the hill. Ova."

"Uh, why?"

"Unfriendlies were here yesterday... sir! Ova."

"Roger that... Sergeant. Stay in touch."

"Hodges, anything happening?"

"Nada. Gunships moving up the hill. Buckeye's near the first ridge."

Dudley studied the map. "At the second ridge they'll turn south, toward us. Then they'll move here to start the heavy climb."

He looked at Ghost. "Scott, take us here," he pointed at the map. "Straight down. We'll run interference on the flank."

"Will do, sergeant."

"Gentlemen, we're out of here."

Hodges tucked away his binoculars and followed Parker downward.

At 1400 they settled on the third ridge.

Hodges raised the binoculars. Gunships buzzed perpendicular to their tier. Buckeye would now be turning south along the second ridge.

Hueys scanned the tier. Hodges followed them.

Suddenly, one shuddered.

Smoke belched from the rotor.

The bird fell from the sky.

"Holy shit!"

Rockets! Automatic weapons! A barrage of weapon-fire.

"Sarge! Sarge! They're hit! One chopper's down!"

The radio kicked in. "Bulldog Two! This is Buckeye! We're in a cross-fire! Need firepower now! Right on us!"

Crack! Buckeye's panic ended.

"Buckeye, this is Bulldog Two. Cover up. We're coming in!"

A gunship dove into the fray discharging two rockets. The chopper swerved away.

A second huey charged the ambush. Two more rockets. Doorgunners vibrated violently.

The chopper's tail exploded. The Bulldog fell from view.

"Jesus!" Hodges called out. "Another one's down!"

The ground fire intensified.

"Saddle up!" barked Dudley. "We're shooting the rapids! They're gonna run. We're gonna seal this flank. Now!"

The squad hustled to the ridge below.

"Buckeye, this is Matchmaka. Ova."

No response.

Dudley tapped the transmitter. "Buckeye, this is Matchmaka, do you read?"

Desperate sounds sputtered back. Small arms fire!

"Matchmaker, this is Lieutenant Young. Greagan is down."

"Lieutenant, how many and where?"

"Heavy losses. They're on the bank... east and south! Must be a regiment! Regular Army! We're falling back!"

"Lieutenant, this is Matchmaka, hold your ground! Dig in! You move, you're done! Hang in there!" Dudley turned to his squad. "They're gonna come. Dig in across this ridge."

The radio started again. "Buckeye, Bulldog Four. Heavy air on the way? ETA two-fiver minutes."

"Lieutenant, this is Matchmaka. Do you copy? Two-fiva minutes. Hold on!"

"Bulldog Four! This is Young. Dump on two-four Foxtrot, three-seven Papa, fiver-two Hotel, three-six Zebra, four-eight Zebra, fiver-six Whiskey, fiver-fiver Juilette, two-three Lima. Fast!"

"Buckeye, Bulldog Four. Copy that. ETA zero one-fiver."

"Buckeye, this is Blue Moon. Closing fast on you. Dig in!"

"Blue Moon, this is Buckeye. Will do!"

"Bulldog Four, this is Matchmaka, ova."

"Go, Matchmaker."

"We are on tier two, south of Victor Charley. We have the wing. We stack em up, you be ready, ova!"

"Your location, Matchmaker?"

"One-fiva India, three-four Osca, ova."

"Roger that. You hold em, we finish."

The squad lined the ridge.

MacKerry, Hodges, and Ringhyter occupied a small trench. Mac spread the bandoleers to the left of Ringhi's M-60. Ringhi checked the sight.

"I'm takin the claymores!" Hodges darted ahead with six claymores. Hastily he made the connections and ran the lines back to the trench.

They waited.

"You ready?" Dudley stood above them.

"Ready!"

"MacKerry, you feed those belts. We stack em for Bulldog. Pin the fuckers fifteen minutes, we'll kick some ass."

"Bring em on!" Ringhyter's face flushed.

Dudley moved to the next station.

A massive force rocked the earth.

Blue Moon!

Dudley swung back. "One more load! Be ready. Anything happens, go up the hill, not down. Up the hill, you got that?"

The ground quaked four more times.

"Jesus Christ!"

Cortes, Weaver, and Jones were tucked in to the left.

Velasquez, Greenfeld, and Balman had the M-60 to the right.

Dudley, Ghost, Parker, and Hoss were further right.

The woods shimmered.

Balman's machine gun blasted out. Ringhyter opened fire.

Green-clad soldiers materialized before them! Real soldiers!

Hodges squeezed three claymores. Weaver's grenades looped through the air. Bodies fell.

The green wave dove to the ground.

Ringhyter swiveled destruction across them.

Movement left! Hodges spat a burst.

Right! Another form, another burst.

Bullets spit into the dirt in front of them.

Mac fired a burst, ducked back.

Hodges squeezed two claymores.

Screams!

Ringhi strung a rope across their front.

Two Bulldogs charged from behind.

Yes!

Two rockets struck the enemy.

Yes! Yes!

A doorgunner ripped a stream.

Screaming! Yelling!

An NVR rocket slashed over their trench.

They weren't done! They have nowhere to go!

A grenade landed short.

They were gathering.

"More ammo!" Ringhyter yelled. Mac strung a fresh bandoleer into the weapon. Ringhi snapped the cover over the belt.

"Duck!"

An enemy poised to deliver a grenade.

The three cowered.

The grenadier rippled back.

Hodges looked left. Cortes raised his right thumb.

Nice fucking shot!

Ringhyter strung another rope. Mac fed ammo.

Hodges heaved three grenades.

Bulldogs crossed in front. The doorgunners shook.

"Get em! Get em!" Hodges triggered his last mine.

Mac emptied a clip and ducked down to reload.

Ringhyter snapped back, hurtling to the rear of the trench.

"No!" Mac screamed. Hodges swiveled around.

Blood spewed from Ringhi's faceless form.

"Jesus!"

Mac and Hodges lunged to the front of the trench.

MacKerry grabbed the M-60.

"Ammo! Keep the ammo comin!"

Mac squeezed a line.

Hodges looked back. Ringhi's blood sprayed skyward. Hodges vomited.

Mac's rounds spit low, into the ground.

"Higher! Mac!"

A Bulldog tore in from the right.

Another from the left.

Four rockets blasted the enemy position.

The enemy stopped.

Mac fired on.

The Bulldogs returned, firing away.

Dudley appeared behind them. "Shit!" He jumped into the trench. Blood splashed onto Hodges.

MacKerry blasted on. "More Ammo! Dui! More ammo!"

Dudley gripped Mac, who leaned his head against the sergeant's chest and started to sob.

The bunkers on either side stared over.

"It's ova. It's ova." Dudley repeated.

Hodges fell forward, his face in the dirt.

Weaver stood above the trench. "Fuck! Ringhi!" He jumped in. Blood splattered up onto his face. "Mother fucker!"

MacKerry leaned into the dirt, his head buried next to Hodges. "Dui, where are we?"

"C'mon GIs, outta the hole." Ghost extended a hand to each of them. They stood up, turning their backs to the trench.

NVR bodies were strewn across the ridge.

Further north, 118 Americans lay dead.

To the east, more NVR dotted the embankment.

Those who fled north escaped.

"Matchmaker, this is Cornhusker."

"Matchmaka."

"Is it over?"

"Ova."

219 days

Ben Cat

My scholars are athletes! Laureen zipped her books into the compartments of her yellow backpack. Undermined by the arrival of Phong and four other older boys, her afternoon reading had been cut short. Laureen sat at the edge of the field watching the makeshift soccer game take shape. Tranh controlled the ball with surprising dexterity. Closing her eyes, Laureen turned her face up to the sun.

It had been a day like this, very much like this. Laureen and her mother had returned to Lai Khe after a week with Mai Nin in Ben Cat. Mother had opened the high wooden gate to the villa. There stood the house but with the doors removed, the glass windows shattered. They had moved across the veranda into the empty house.

"Mother, where is everything? Where is Father?"

"Come upstairs, Laureen. There will be a note."

They climbed the stairs to the huge master bedroom. Mother went directly to the dressing room and removed a loose floorboard. She retrieved a metal box and loosened a key from the gold chain around her neck. Fitting it into the box, she removed a letter and began to read. Crumpling the paper, she sank to the floor staring blankly. Laureen moved to her side.

"Mother, where is Father?"

"Laureen, there is money in the box. Money for us."

"But, Father?"

"The furniture has been moved to Saigon. To your godparents'. The Chocarts have everything, more money, our clothes, your books."

"Saigon? Is that where Father is? We must go."

"Laureen, Father is not there. He... he has had to leave the country. He tried to send for us, but..."

"Father would not leave us!"

"There was no choice. The plantation men, the Frenchmen, have returned to their homeland."

"But godfather Chocart is French."

"He is an ambassador. It is different."

"Mother, there must be more." Laureen reached for the letter. "What else does it say?"

Her mother handed her the wrinkled letter. "That the Chocarts will have money, our furniture, everything. This money is for now. Father says we must be careful. That we should stay with Mai Nin in Ben Cat." Mother trembled. "He will try to return. He says we must believe that he loves you, that he loves me."

"We must catch Father. We must." Laureen began to cry. "Are we alone? Mother, what will we do?"

"We shall do as your father says." Her mother rose to her feet. "We shall return to Ben Cat, to Mai Nin."

"But, Father..."

"You must not blame him, Laureen." She raised her daughter. "There was nothing he could do. You must know this, Laureen. You must."

"But?"

"Now we go back, little flower. Back to Ben Cat, to Mai Nin. Father says we must be Vietnamese in Ben Cat. Vietnamese in Ben Cat, French with the Chocarts in Saigon."

Laureen leaned against her mother. "Father, oh Father. We are alone." Laureen sobbed. "Are we truly alone?"

The woman held the child firmly. "We are not what we are at this moment. We are what we will become. We are... what we will become."

Laureen opened her eyes.

Thompson, where are you? Are you safe? Do you miss me? When will you come back? An unusual tingling arose within her. When will you kiss me? Oh please, kiss me soon. Hold me. Touch me.

"La, throw the ball!" Tranh called out.

Laureen retrieved the ball and tossed it back onto the field. She waved to the children and began the walk home.

Come back to me. We have so much to learn about each other. Her feelings were swimming inside her. Oh Thompson, hurry, please hurry back. She turned, looked around. Did anyone know? Could anyone suspect? Thompson, do you feel the same way?

Arriving home, she was surprised to find Mai Nin and Ching Phor enjoying tea.

"And how did the established citizens of Ben Cat enjoy their last Wednesday before the rains?" Laureen asked.

"Tea, Laureen?" asked Mai Nin.

"Thank you."

"Our last Wednesday before the rains?" Ching Phor smiled. "It was not very different than other days. We followed the oxen out to graze. We brought them back, or they brought us back. A day that ended where it began."

"A circle, like our lives," added Mai Nin.

Laureen unzipped her pack to remove a pen and pad. "A circle, let us see." She drew a circle on the paper. Next to the circle she drew a crisp triangle. "Many western stories seem concerned with triangles."

"Triangles?" Ching Phor stared at the two forms. "The triangle is too rigid. The lines too straight. The edges too abrupt."

"Life is a circle. It begins where it ends. The turns are subtle. The complexities ongoing. We carry them forward to the end," added Mai Nin.

"From where we began," Ching Phor concluded.

"But, La, while the circle is more peaceful, do not be fooled. Even the circle is misleading." Mai Nin traced the circle with her finger. "You see, this circle looks innocent enough, but the beginning and the ending, they are unknown to us. It simply goes round and round. Each circle has its complexities, but it is true, there is a certain security in the circle." She pointed to the triangle. "That triangle, that triangle looks precarious to me. Of course at my age, everything looks precarious. What say you old friend? The triangle or the circle?"

"The circle. Who would want to know the end or even the beginning, or where we are within the circle? The quiet suspense of the circle has a certain allure."

The two friends looked to Laureen.

"Well, you are both circles then," she laughed. "As usual, my youth..."

"Your enthusiasm," interrupted Ching Phor.

"My enthusiasm, then. My enthusiasm and my youth leave me indecisive."

"Indecisive? You, Laureen? You are far from indecisive. Perhaps you are ahead of yourself, ahead of your time. That can be a difficult path to follow. It is often misunderstood." Mai Nin said.

Ching Phor placed her cup on the table. "Ah, but the joys of such a path can be most rewarding. Such independence! There is no substitute for independence."

"Do you feel independent, Laureen? Or are you forgetful? What have you done with your brother on this holiday Wednesday?" asked Mai Nin.

"This Wednesday was filled with surprise," Laureen answered.

"What surprises could there be?"

"Well, your grandson for one. He is fascinated with his soccer. Many boys who do not usually attend organized a game. Today there was no Carp's Tail."

"Soccer? What is this soccer?"

"A game played with Thompson's ball. A game the boys of the village seem to like."

"Aye, this is true," added Ching Phor. "They play near the doctors' tent."

"Tranh? Tranh plays this game near the tent?" questioned Mai Nin.

"Not often," hastened Ching Phor. "It amuses the villagers. Even the doctors have noticed."

"A waste of time," pronounced Mai Nin.

"It is just a game," reminded Laureen. "They will outgrow it. And soon, with the rains, their field will be mud. Tranh seems determined with this game. Have you noticed Ching Phor?"

"My work keeps me busy."

"She has no time for games," said Mai Nin sternly. "Her work is healing. Distractions are dangerous."

"True. But sometimes they are refreshing," Ching Phor turned to Laureen.

"Refreshing? Well, possibly. Perhaps they are briefly refreshing," mused Mai Nin, "but, they have rarely served that purpose for me.

A distraction is a distraction."

"Who could argue that?" laughed Laureen.

"Speaking of distractions," Mai Nin reached to the table behind her. She handed a small package to Laureen. "It comes with a note."

"A note?"

"From Dui. The American's laundress, Xiam Thong, delivered these this morning," Mai Nin explained.

"Will you open them?" asked Ching Phor.

"What a surprise!" Laureen blushed.

"The package is small," noted Ching Phor.

"And lightweight," added Mai Nin.

"Lightweight?" asked Laureen.

"When Xiam Thong handed it to me, it was noticeably light."

"Oh!" laughed Laureen. "Lightweight, then."

"Will you open it?" pressed Ching Phor.

Laureen laughed. "Thompson seems to find a way to entertain us, even in his absence."

"So it seems," remarked Ching Phor. "He is most generous."

Laureen removed the tape from the awkwardly wrapped package. Tearing away the paper, she held up the tattered black scarf. "What? What is this?" Laureen laughed. "How could Thompson collect your scarf?"

The elders sat motionless.

"Is that your scarf?" Ching Phor finally asked Mai Nin.

"How could it be?"

"When did you last see it?"

"When Tranh took it for you," answered Mai Nin.

"Oh that Tranh Nhu Lam!" Ching Phor shook her head. "He must have dropped the scarf. Dui recognized it. Your Dui is observant." Ching Phor looked to Mai Nin. "More observant than anticipated."

"Aye! Dui found it," Mai Nin agreed.

"Well, let us see," Laureen opened the attached envelope. As she translated, they listened intently.

"Dear Laureen,

Xiam Thong has agreed to deliver this note. Hope it gets to you.

Found this scarf. Thought it looked familiar. Thought Mai Nin might miss it.

When I return, we should continue discussing your ideas about Paris!

Hope to see you soon. I miss you already!

Love, Thompson."

"Found the scarf?" Ching Phor repeated.

"Paris?" quizzed Mai Nin.

"Love!" Laureen exclaimed.

The Dark Zone – Lai Khe

They were all there. The ten of them. Greenfeld was not invited. Sam and Phan, the matron, passed the beers. The room fell silent.

Hodges stood. "To our strongest, to our quiet man, the force behind us all. Ringhi, you'll be missed." He raised his bottle.

The squad stood tapping their bottles. They waited, searching.

"Ringhi!"

They drank.

Gradually all but Hodges sat down.

"Into the night... I go," Hodges recited.

"The way... I must show.

Into the night... I go
Hunting for friend or foe.
Into the night... I go
The signs... I know.
Into the night... I see
It's either... you or me..."

"Ringhi, my friend, you showed us a lot. You held us together. You were there, always there." Hodges paused. "Whatever else we have learned, you have taught me... courage." He looked at the others. "Now it is up to us to follow your example. We are alive. We must respect the gift we have. We must have the courage to make the most of the rest of our lives." Hodges looked through the roof. "Ringhi, wherever you are, watch over us. We are your friends. We know who you were. We miss you."

Hodges then lowered himself onto the bench next to Mac.

"What the fuck are we doin here?" Balman asked.

"Ya mean here, right here?" Hosmach asked.

"I mean what the fuck is happening? What's this all about? Our man, our main man, our biggest, our strongest, he's gone. And LaVelle, shit, he's got no hand. What the hell are we doin here?"

"Try this," Weaver began. "We're running the numbers. When they run out, we go home. That's what we're doing. Running the numbers."

"Maybe we expected too much? Maybe they expect too much of us?" MacKerry suggested.

Balman sighed. "Maybe we were bullshitted! Nothin's gone the way we were told. I mean nothin. We were supposed to be recon. Right? Recon! Instead, we're cooped up in some gook village. Bullshit! We're gettin picked apart. Fuckin picked apart."

"At least we know where we are," said Mac.

"Know where we are? Bullshit! We're riskin our necks for a buncha turncoat gooks who'd just as soon shoot us as look at us. They fuckin hate us. Let's get that out in the open." Balman gulped his beer.

"I don't buy that," Hodges said.

"You don't buy it! Christ, look at you. Sometimes you really are blind. You better get your head outta your ass! You think these assholes are your friends? Bullshit. Let me ask you this. Is one of those fuckers ever gonna help you? You're smart enough to know, not one of those fuckers is gonna help you whether you speak gook or not. They ain't gonna be there when we need em. We're the fuckin enemy."

"Yo, Mop! Lighten up. We gotta stick together," said Ghost.

"Like the world's stickin up for us. What d'ya think's goin on back there? They don't give two shits what's happenin here. They don't care about LaVelle, Ringhyter, or us."

"Mop's right," said Cortes. "Let's face it. No one back there gives a shit. The gooks hate our fuckin guts. We're just doin time."

"Counting days," Balman added. "Counting days."

Hodges pulled a drag. "You think Ringhi's parents think that? You think LaVelle thinks that? You think your folks think that? How bout your friends? They think that?"

Balman swallowed his beer. "Ya know what I think. I think outta sight, outta mind. That's what I think."

"Yeah," agreed Hoss. "They're driving their cars. They're partying, making money, doing their thing. And here we are...."

"Taking their hits," Weaver finished.

"And Ringhi's dead," said Mac.

"Ringhi's dead, LaVelle's fucked," Balman repeated.

Ghost exhaled. "What we got to do... is survive. There's no way out. Ya wanna leave, ya take a hit. Ya don't take a hit, ya stay. No way round it. That simple enough?"

"I ain't takin no hit," Balman stated. "I'm goin home just the way I am, just the way I came. Fuck these gooks."

Ghost faced Hodges. "How about the kitchen?"

"Unbelievable!" Hodges shook his head. "Un-fucking-believable!"

"Fifteen tons a rice," said Weaver. "Fifteen tons! Jesus!"

"Over fifty thousand rounds," Jones added.

"Two thousand mortars," Balman continued.

"And three tons! Three motherfucking tons... of weed. Three tons! A gold mine! A frigging gold mine." Ghost raised his bottle. "What's going down in those tunnels?"

"Just what's happening here, my man," shrugged Hodges.

Balman would not be detered. "They brought in ten more body bags today. Stacked em with the others in front of the hospital. Fuckin sick! They ain't gettin me in one of those fuckers, I'll tell you that."

"Take at least two," laughed Ghost.

"Fuck you, Ghost. Fuck you."

214 days

LZ – Ben Cat

The gathering clouds warned of the morning downpour. The squad lounged beside the Ben Cat landing zone.

"Remember the first time?" asked Mac.

"Uh huh," said Hodges.

"Ringhi threw up."

"Yeah, Ringhi threw up."

"Maybe he knew," suggested Mac.

"I don't think so."

Dudley stood before them. "Perry, stand up."

A young black man rose from his seat.

"Gentlemen, this is Specialist Aaron Perry. Specialist Perry is your twelfth man. MacKerry, you will handle our second M-60. Any problems?"

"No, Sergeant. No problem, Sergeant."

"We knew we could count on you, MacKerry." Dudley faced Perry. "Specialist, how long you been in country?"

"Three months, Sergeant."

"With the 2nd - 28th?" asked Dudley.

"Yes, Sergeant."

"Very good. Perry was hand-picked by Major White and myself. Welcome aboard, Specialist."

The chin raised. "Listen up. Operation Manhattan hurt the enemy. We recovered beaucoup weapons, food, and Mary Jane. We claim over 200 North Vietnamese Regulas dead. The big bad guys. After you left, the engineers cleared the tunnels and blew away the kitchen. There is nothing left. They had a hospital in the tunnels. In that hospital, there were thirteen dead. All with slit throats. That, gentlemen, is your enemy. He does not leave his wounded, he eliminates them. Human life does not have the same meaning to Charley."

"I have played it straight with you. I always will. Ho Chi Minh is willing to sacrifice his troops. This asshole means business," Dudley halted. "One hundred nineteen Americans died on that hill. One hundred nineteen Americans in four hours. Ringhyter was one of them. And why?" The sergeant checked each face. "They died because one mother-fucker decided he was tired, or that his men were tired, or that they were hungry. That is why 119 Americans are dead. Why somebody is writing those damned letters. Why I wrote Mr. and Mrs. Ringhyter.

"And I am to blame. I knew better. I let him do it anyways. Ringhyter is dead because I allowed that cocky son of a West Point bitch to break the most basic rule of jungle warfare. Neva... eva... take the same fucking trail twice. Neva... eva... take the same trail... twice. How many times have you heard me say it? Ringhyter is dead. I accept the responsibility. I have told Mrs. Ringhyter that. His death was not your fault. You men performed well. I have to deal with Ringhyter. You have to put it aside. I will not permit similar mistakes. You men are my men. I will get you home."

Dudley moved to parade rest. "Before we go forward. We must look back. Rememba the ambush. Not only was the enemy on that hillside, he was here in the ditch. We eliminated twenty-seven VC. You can bet some were connected to Ben Cat. That means widows. That means homes without fathers and mothers. Homes without children. We are going to search this village. The ARVNs are useless, you know that. Their MPs are useless, you know that. We're going to let the ARVNs run the patrols. We are going to search this village and get to the root of the problem. That means every hut, every wagon, every chimney, everything. We will take this village apart, one piece at a time. We will ask questions. We will get answers. The major has requested two translators. In two days we begin. All suspicious conduct is to be reported. Something just ain't right. Meanwhile, watch your ass. Any questions?"

"Sergeant, how long we gonna be out of the field?" asked Ghost.

Dudley surveyed the group. "On September third, General Nguyen Van Thieu will be elected president of South Vietnam. Nguyen Cao Ky will be elected vice president. Until that time we are to secure the village and allow no disruptions to the elections. Intelligence suggests that all voting districts should expect resistance. We will upgrade our security." He looked up. "Back to the salt mines gentlemen."

"Sergeant," Hodges rose. "I... I don't think it was your fault."

"Hodges, everything is someone's fault. This one's mine. Dismissed!"

211 days

Ben Cat

"La, what does it mean?" Tranh waved the torn poster at her.

"It says that the people of Ben Cat should not support the election."

"We know that," shrugged Mai Nin, "but are the statements true?"

"And what does Saigon say of the candidates?" asked Ching Phor.

Folding her hands on her lap, Laureen braced herself. "All the candidates reside in Saigon. Their platforms are as different as their backgrounds."

"Platforms?" questioned Mai Nin.

"Platforms are the ideas they expect to accomplish if they are elected. All three candidates have different solutions to the problems of Vietnam."

"The problems of Vietnam or the problems of Saigon?" laughed Ching Phor.

"The problems of Vietnam," repeated Laureen.

"It says here," Mai Nin began, "that Nguyen Van Thieu served in the French army. That he was an officer in the French army. That he has profited greatly from his association with the Americans. Is this true?"

"Nguyen Van Thieu married a Catholic. Later he converted to Catholicism. He joined the French army and was promoted. In Saigon General Thieu is known as a wealthy man."

"But the notice says he overthrew Diem. Were they not the same?" asked Ching Phor.

"General Thieu commanded the palace uprising that ended the Diem regime, that is true. He maintains Diem was corrupt, opposed to the best interests of Vietnam," explained Laureen.

Mai Nin tapped Ching Phor on the knee. "This behavior is puzzling. What do you think, old friend?"

"These are not the actions of a man of integrity. Why do the Americans support a man of such inconsistencies? Do they believe him trustworthy?" asked Ching Phor.

"In Saigon it is said that Nguyen Van Thieu can lead Vietnam into international politics where peace can be found or negotiated."

"International politics?" Mai Nin repeated.

"Yes. The Americans listen to him. According to the journals, he has a sound economic plan to modernize Vietnam," Laureen turned to Tranh, "and to educate our young."

"Modernize Vietnam? Has he a plan to grow better rice?" Ching Phor chuckled. "Before the struggle, our rice was plentiful. Perhaps we need less modernization, more stability, and less interference from Saigon."

"Educate the young? Ha!" spat Mai Nin. "Who will teach us? Nguyen Van Thieu? The Americans? The French? The Japanese? Teach us what? Their customs! Because these Saigon people do not visit us, they forget the age-old lessons that are sustained in the straw huts of Ben Cat. Apparently these lessons are long since forgotten in Saigon. Never has an Elder of this village turned on another! No wonder these people do not visit."

Tranh shifted. "What of the conflict? What does Thieu say of the conflict?"

"General Thieu believes the South should be independent and lead Vietnam into the future. He encourages the Americans to support our independence. He speaks of ruling a democratic government opposed to Communism."

"Do we need Saigon to rule ourselves? Or does she need us? Saigon wants our food," Ching Phor pointed to the south paddy. "And our land. Thieu already takes our young men."

"Not all support Saigon," Laureen reminded her.

"Who are these other names? Are they as confusing?" Mai Nin returned to the notice. "Little flower, please educate us."

Laureen laughed. "May we not argue?" She studied the notice. "Ah, this man is known to me. Truong Ding Dzu. A famous Saigon lawyer." The older women raised their brows.

"A Saigon lawyer? Not a soldier?"

"Not a soldier. A wise lawyer. His beliefs are considered liberal, not conforming to those of the current government. Indeed, a rebel."

"A rebel? How can a rebel survive in Saigon?"

"He survives quite well. Although he is unpopular with the Americans."

"A good man, then," mumbled Tranh.

"The journals say he believes the North and South should return to the peace tables in Geneva. The National Liberation Front should participate in the formation of a new government in the South. He advocates an immediate halt to all bombing. In Saigon his support grows."

"Why do the Americans oppose him?" asked Mai Nin. "Do they not want to go home?"

"Many will not come. Many who are here wish to leave. There is, shall we say, unrest about this war in America. But Truong Ding Dzu opposes General Thieu, who opposes Communism, the enemy of America."

"La, if the Americans are so divided, why do they not go home?" asked Tranh.

Laureen hesitated. "Thompson would say that Americans believe in freedom and that the North supports Communism, which subjugates the people. Thompson believes this."

Mai Nin interrupted. "Tranh Nhu Lam, no one ever leaves Vietnam by choice, except possibly your sister."

Ching Phor pointed to the bottom of the poster. "Tell us of this other man. Is he known to your Saigon friends?"

"The Chocarts know all the candidates. They will be delighted with your interest," Laureen laughed.

"The more we hear, the less interested we are. The notice is correct. You should not cast a vote," Tranh concluded.

"Democracy is based on each vote, each election," Laureen explained.

"That is a problem for democracy, not for Ben Cat," Tranh argued.

"Laureen, bear with us. Who is this other name?"

"He is unfamiliar to me. Phan Khac Suu. The journals downplay his ideas. He opposes Communism. He promotes a new government with representatives elected by all the people in the provinces." Laureen looked to her brother. "Perhaps, Tranh, you could represent Ben Cat?"

"Perhaps," Tranh said truculantly. "Perhaps."

****

The rain poured down.

Hodges, MacKerry, and Dudley sat with Major White in the command bunker with their most reliable translator, Chia Luoi.

"Chia Luoi, what does it say?"

"This is propaganda, negative propaganda. It advises the people not to vote."

Major White slid the poster across the table. "Negative propaganda? What exactly does it say?"

"Major," began Chia Luoi, "it says General Thieu was a French officer, that now he has become an American puppet, a wealthy, corrupt, American puppet who cares not for the people of Vietnam. To become a French officer, he forsook his religion, becoming a Catholic. Now he becomes a prostitute for the Americans. Here," he designated several paragraphs, "it says Truong Dinh Dzu will halt the bombing and will re-establish the Geneva Peace Conference where after the people's victory over the French foreigners divided our country in half. And here," he pointed, "let me see, Phan Khac Suu opposes Communism and has a senseless plan to govern the countryside through his pawns. It concludes that to vote for any of these men is to support the Americanization of Vietnam. It says the people of Ben Cat should not vote."

"Does it threaten the villagers?" asked White.

"No sir," said Chia Luoi. "No threats."

Dudley looked at Hodges. "How many of these things were out there?"

"Sergeant, they're everywhere. Mac and I, we tore a hundred down, but there were more."

"Why did you take them down? Could you read it?" asked White.

"No sir. But every time we got near one, the people walked away. Ignored us, you know?"

"Ran's more like it. They'd see us coming, they'd hit the road," Mac added.

The major turned toward Dudley. "What do you think, Sergeant?"

"I do not give a shit what they say. What I want to know is how they got there. Security is a joke. The rains don't help, but we got to get serious about searching this village. We got to talk to these people. With the ARVN security the way it is, these frigging things could have been hanging on our bunker door. Last night somebody hung these all over town. That is more important than what they say."

"Agreed," said White. "Where were the MPs?"

"Sir, they're supposed to patrol the town at night. Course, they ain't worth a shit. Excuse me, sir. They need supervision."

"I am working on that." White turned to Hodges. "What does your girlfriend say?"

"Girlfriend, sir?"

"Yes, Hodges, your girlfriend."

"Beg your pardon, sir. I haven't seen my teacher since we got back."

"Oh, your teacher. You giving up on the language or on the teacher?"

"Just trying to stay alive, sir. When I get home, I can learn the language, right sir?"

"True, Hodges, true. To be honest, I admire the way you were learning. And from what I hear, you probably won't have as pretty a teacher back home."

Hodges laughed. "Maybe not, sir, but I'd like to live long enough to find out."

Dudley reacted. "Hodges, you think this girl's some sort of problem?"

"No, Sergeant."

"No way," added Mac.

"Well, what gives? You got the clap?"

"No, Sergeant! I've been thinking about Ringhi. I don't want to make a mistake. I want to get home."

"Hodges, your time ain't that short. Not short enough to be thinking about going home. Ringhyter is gone. That's the way it is. We got a long way to go."

Hodges looked down.

"You want we should see her?" Mac asked.

"I want you to be smart," said Dudley. "Be smart, be safe. If you are safe, see her. If you are not safe, tell me."

"The girl is straight," Hodges said. "I'll think about it."

"Good," said White. "Dismissed."

Hodges saluted and left the bunker. Away from the bunker, Mac caught up with him, grabbing Hodges' shoulder. "Hey, man. There something I should know?"

Ben Cat

On the floor in the middle of the room twelve white pebbles formed a neat circle. Hodges shook his head. "The fourth one in two days! Look, the same pebble is laid over flat. It's gotta be a sign."

Ghost and Chia Luoi looked down. Mac waited outside.

"This is gettin too weird. What's with the circle?" Ghost asked Chia Luoi.

"Is the home unoccupied?"

"Clean and empty," Hodges answered. "Looks like somebody swept it out."

"They do not leave easily," Chia Luoi began. "Their lives were this home, this village. Most certainly they were compelled to leave."

"Where do they go?"

"Where they are told. These are not decisions of choice." The translator addressed Hodges. "Who lived here?"

Hodges flipped through the registration booklet. "Linh Dung Cam, aged thirty-eight, his wife, Con Soc, thirty-four, two sons, twelve and sixteen, and a daughter, eleven. Somebody must have been caught in the ambush."

Chia Luoi nodded agreement. "They knew we would come. This makes four plus three from the other squads yesterday. We are late."

"Yuh, we're late, but what's the circle?" pressed Ghost.

"A local ritual. I have not seen it elsewhere. They believe in the cycle of life. Most likely this circle has something to do with that. The turned stone represents where they perceive themselves within that cycle. Or possibly it is a warning." He shook his head. "I do not know."

"Warning? Warning who?"

"The other villagers. A reminder that sacrifice is part of the cycle. I am not sure."

"Weird how they leave it so clean!"

"They clean the house out of respect for Ben Cat and their neighbors. They leave it this way so they will be accepted when they return."

"The neighbors know who is missing, don't they?" Hodges asked.

"Most likely, but they will not say. Betrayal is disdained."

"Betrayal?" Ghost began to pace. "I keep forgettin, we're the enemy."

Chia Luoi smiled. "This was their village long before you changed it. We are outsiders. They do not see that we are here for them."

"They just want to be here when it's over, right?" Hodges asked.

"Correct."

"And the VC?" asked Ghost. "Are they the good guys?"

"They did defeat the French."

"Man, what are we doing here?"

"If you were not here, this village would belong to the enemy. You make progress, but you will never convert them all. Change is slow in Ben Cat. They must see the benefit."

"That won't be easy with all the thieving the ARVNs do," suggested Ghost.

"It does not help," Chia Luoi agreed.

"Let's get outta here." They joined Mac outside.

"Dui! You gotta see this! Get over here!" Hosmach called from across the path.

"Fucking suicide!" Balman yelled. "C'mon over here, Dui. See if you can talk to this one."

Chia Luoi lingered at the door as the Americans entered the hut.

An elderly woman, dressed in black, sat upright in a wicker rocker. Her eyes were closed. Her bare feet pointed rigidly upwards. Her hands lay crossed in her lap.

"Damn! She died in her chair!" Mac exclaimed.

"I doubt it," whispered Hodges.

"That's the way we found her," said Balman. "Dead as a doornail."

Hodges pointed at the floor. "The stones, they're all turned over, except one. Chia Luoi," Hodges called. "What's the deal?"

"Who gives a shit!" Balman said impatiently.

"Who is this woman?" Chia Luoi asked.

Hodges checked the roster. "Ban Dong, fifty-eight. Married to Khia Kieng, sixty-two. No children."

"Caught in the ambush. For sure." said Ghost.

"Who gives a shit! She's dead."

"But how did she die? How did they kill her?" Mac studied the scene. "There's no blood."

"Poison. Suicide?" Hodges asked.

"Rare, but not impossible," Chia Luoi nodded to the stones. "She begins a new circle."

"That's her problem. Let's get outta here," insisted Balman.

"Do they really believe that?" continued Hodges.

"They do."

Hodges walked into the back room. A small trunk sat apart from the bed. Across the room a chest rested against the wall. An empty rack for clothing was next to the chest.

"Chia Luoi, what's with the trunk?"

"Everything in its place. She moves on."

"Who gives a shit!" complained Balman. "C'mon, I'm hot, hot and thirsty."

"Should we open it?" asked Mac.

"It's her legacy. What d'ya think?" Hodges looked to the translator.

"She's a VC, for Christ's sake. Who gives a shit?" Balman fumed.

Ghost intervened. "Maybe there's a clue. If we don't check it out, the MPs'll steal everything anyway."

"It should be cremated with her," suggested Chia Luoi.

"Good luck," said Ghost.

Balman ended the debate. "Screw her and the MPs too. Open the fucking thing! We're supposed to search these places, right?"

"This goes beyond that."

"Screw you, Hodges. Cut the gook shit!" Balman unlatched the chest. "There probably isn't shit anyway." He opened the cover. "Look at this, nothing."

A container of rice lay at the top next to a supply of incense. A wood carving of Buddha was neatly placed in the left corner, near two pairs of crude sandals. A small box lay in the right corner. Neatly folded clothes lined the bottom of the trunk.

"Let's see what we have here." Opening the box, he revealed a picture of a stiff young man and woman dressed in elaborate costume.

"Their wedding picture," offered Chia Luoi.

Balman handed the translator an envelope, then held up another picture. "Look at this! Brother Ho Chi Minh himself. Son of a bitch!"

"Their liberator," explained Chia Luoi.

"Our fucking enemy!" exclaimed Balman.

"Her life," realized Hodges. "Chia Luoi, read the letter."

The translator scanned the letter before beginning.

"Neighbors,

"Thank you for years of tranquility. My life has been complete. Khia Kieng nursed me through the years. He was a generous man. He died for your future. We hope Ben Cat will long recall our contributions.

"The village must always be self-sufficient. This preserves our integrity. To compromise is unacceptable.

"As we lived with choice, so have we ended.

"Here, where life began, our wishes are that your offspring continue our experience.

"When it is your time to join us, we will be ready.

"On behalf of my beloved husband, Khia Kieng... Ban Dong."

"Her final testimony," said Hodges.

"Not quite," added Ghost. "Her final testimony was puttin herself in that chair and doin the deed."

"Fuck her," said Balman. "You guys talk like she's a martyr. She's a VC. A gook VC. That's it."

"I doubt she wrote this letter," mused Chia Luoi. "Look at this handwriting. It is a young hand. A steady hand."

"Okay, so she didn't write it," Balman conceded. "So what? Maybe she didn't pack everything. Maybe she didn't commit suicide. Maybe that's the way it's supposed to look. Who gives a shit! One less VC."

Chia Luoi turned away from Balman. "The village will care. If the Viet Cong eliminated her, the neighbors will be angry."

"Or scared," smiled Ghost.

"Aye, or afraid. This is a matter for the MPs."

"That'll do a lot of good," Hodges said.

"We should tell Dudley?" Mac suggested.

"Yuh, we better get Dudley," Hodges agreed. "Mop, you and Hoss stay here with Chia Luoi."

"Sure Hodges, sure. Just what I wanna do. Babysit a stiff."

Hodges, Mac and Ghost headed up the hill toward the market. As they turned toward the compound, Tranh unexpectedly raced to them. "Dui! Dui! *Lai dei, lai dei*!"

"Come quick? Come where, why?"

"MPs! MPs! *Lai dei, lai dei*!" Tranh turned and raced back toward his home. The GIs followed.

"Now what?" yelled Ghost.

An MP stood on Laureen's porch. Seeing the Americans, he spoke through the door, into the house.

Tranh leaped up the stairs, pushing aside the startled MP. Just as the Americans entered the home, an ARVN lieutenant struck Mai Nin across the face, knocking her down. Laureen rushed to her side. The lieutenant raised his hand over Laureen.

"Hold it!" Hodges yelled. What's going on, here?"

The lieutenant glared. "You leave, GI!"

Two other policemen were busy picking through the sitting room shelves.

"Lieutenant, what the hell's going on?" shouted Hodges.

Mai Nin staggered to her feet. Her eye had begun to swell. She shook her fist at the lieutenant, yelling angrily. Unable to follow the exchange, Hodges looked to Laureen.

"Thompson, these policemen enter our house! They take our possessions! That one," she pointed at the lieutenant, "ripped a necklace from my neck. It, it belonged to my mother."

"Is this true?" Hodges demanded of the lieutenant.

MacKerry and Ghost moved toward the other two MPs.

"No problem, GI. You leave. We MPs," the officer barked.

Mai Nin crossed the room and grabbed the hand of one of the looters. He kept his fist closed. She slapped him across the face. The looter raised his fist. Mac grabbed his arm.

The surprised corporal looked to his lieutenant, who stared at Hodges. "Sergeant! These my men. This our sector. This not your problem."

"Wrong! These people are my friends. What have they done?"

"Let's see what you got here!" Mac pried open the fist. Three silver birds fell to the floor. As Mai Nin bent to pick them up, the corporal kicked her in the chest. She sprawled across the room. Tranh rushed the corporal, punching him in the face. Blood spurted from his nose.

The third MP reached for his gun.

Ghost swung the butt of his M-16 across the man's head, toppling him backwards into a table.

Laureen gasped.

Flushed with rage, the lieutenant turned on Hodges. "You make big mistake! What your name?"

"My name is Hodges. Who the hell are you?"

"Lieutenant Giam Duoc. You disobey my order. You cause this."

"You steal from us," Laureen flushed. "Why do you steal? You are to protect us."

"We search. We confiscate things." He jabbed his finger at Hodges. "You no can interfere. You be sorry!"

"You're not searching," said Hodges, disgusted. "You're looting. What else have you taken from these people?"

"We take things VC want. They buy weapons with these!"

"He has my mother's necklace," Laureen repeated.

"Give her back the necklace," Hodges insisted.

"Fuck you, GI! These people no can have gold. I keep."

"The necklace belonged to my mother," Laureen looked to Hodges. "A gift from my father."

"Fuck your father! Fuck your mother, you VC bitch!"

"Return the necklace!" Hodges repeated. "Or we take it from you. You decide."

"You no can hit officer!"

"You are not our officer." Hodges shook with anger.

Ghost brushed against the back of the lieutenant. "We ain't goin nowheres. Give the lady her necklace and take your sorry ass outta here, while you still can."

The lieutenant reached into his pocket and dropped the gold necklace on the floor.

"Now, that didn't hurt too much did it," Ghost mocked. "Now you run along home, and don't hurry back. Got it?"

Mai Nin launched another incomprehensible tirade. The lieutenant glared at her, but directed his words at Laureen.

"What did he say?" demanded Hodges.

"The lieutenant says we have made powerful enemies." Laureen looked ashen. "We should bolt our doors, stay in at night."

"Is that right?" Hodges stepped closer. "Giam Duoc, that is your name?"

"Aye, GI! That my name."

"Good. I am Sergeant Hodges. H-O-D-G-E-S. This is Sergeant Scott. This is Corporal MacKerry. You got that. Hodges, Scott, MacKerry!"

"I no forget!"

"Good, you fucker. Remember them. Remember that if you bother these people again, if any of your fucking stooges bother these people, one of us, or maybe all of us will come looking for you. We will find you. Whatever you do to these people, whatever you take, it won't be worth it. Remember that, Giam Duoc. Remember that." A warm sensation eased through Hodges.

"See," Ghost began, "you bother our friends, you are the one's gonna be sorry. One night I'm gonna slide up beside you and cut you, one piece at a time. Shit! You won't even know I'm there. Just one piece at a time. Think about it! What piece would be first? That's what I'll be thinkin about. The first piece. I will do it. I don't give a shit. If you're smart, you'll be sure these people are real safe, cause every time I see them, I'm gonna ask. You best hope I get the right answer. Now get your sorry ass outta here. I ain't gonna say it again." Ghost shoved the officer. "Move out, fucker!"

Laureen sat on the floor, cradling Mai Nin in her arms. Mai Nin was holding her swollen eye.

The Americans followed the MPs out of the house and watched them descend the hill.

Tranh stepped in front of Mac. Grabbing his hand, he shook it in an exaggerated movement. Next he shook Ghost's hand, then Hodges's.

"Why, Tranh, I didn't know you cared," Hodges laughed.

"Everyone loves a winner," chuckled Ghost.

"We gotta get Dudley," Hodges reminded them. "We have to tell him about Ban Dong. Balman's waiting." Hodges turned to the boy. "Tranh, we have to leave. *Di di mao.*"

Laureen called to him. "Thompson, please wait."

The men turned. Mai Nin was now standing at Laureen's side. "Mai Nin wants you to have this." Laureen moved to Hodges. "It will assure you a safe journey. She says you must wear it until you are home. It is her lucky scarf. The one you found."

Laureen's dark eyes locked on his. She looped the scarf around his neck. Holding the loose ends, she pulled his face down to her, kissing him first on the left cheek, then the right. "Thank you, Thompson. You are our protector. You must never again be away so long."

"What about me?" asked Ghost.

"And me?" said Mac.

She nodded, smiling brilliantly at Hodges.

He had never left her. She would never leave him. Nothing else mattered.

206 days

Ben Cat – Command Compound

"Mac," Hodges buried the shovel in the dirt, "feel like an airborne ranger?"

"Dui, this is better than hell or danger. Shoot, we only got a coupla hundred meters left."

Hodges rested on the shovel and stared at the sky. "Who would believe that sky will turn into hours of rain."

"So we'd better finish the trench," Mac smiled. "It would sure help if you'd start digging and stop daydreaming."

Four figures approached. "Mac, looks like we got some help."

Mac looked up. "Well, I'll be. Laureen and Tranh. Who are the other two?"

"Don't know."

"I think we got three diggers and Laureen. She just don't look dressed to dig."

"Hardly. Laureen's not the digging type."

"That's a fact."

"Good morning, Thompson and Mac-Kerry of Hart-ford, Ken-tuck," Laureen smiled. "Tranh brings you two helpers." Laureen motioned to a shorter boy. "This is his friend, Phong, and Phong's sister, Lin."

Lin bowed. Mac and Hodges returned the greeting. Phong and Tranh shook hands with the GIs.

"Laureen, you are full of surprises," Hodges said.

"Laureen, we got to dig this ditch. Do these kids know that?" Mac asked.

"They do," she smiled. "They are eager to help."

"Now that is amazing," Mac chuckled. "I thought I was gonna be digging alone. Your man here, Dui, he isn't the greatest at manual labor."

"Is that so?" Laureen raised her eyebrows. "Thompson, do you not do your part?"

Hodges grinned. "Seems like I'm distracted." He touched the black scarf. "A man with Mai Nin's lucky scarf shouldn't have to dig, should he?"

"That, Thompson, is a question for Mai Nin."

"Hey, Tranh," Mac handed each of the volunteers a shovel. The threesome stared at Mac awaiting instruction.

"Okay," Mac began, "we start here, near this stake." He pointed to the stake near the command compound. "And we dig," he imitated digging, "all the way to the fence over there," he pointed to the perimeter wire. "We gotta keep the water out. You got it?"

Tranh checked the post then, moving his finger to the perimeter wire, traced the line.

"Yes!" Mac nodded. "Yes, Tranh."

"*Bic*," said Tranh lowering the shovel. Lin and Phong moved down the line and began digging.

"Why Mac," said Hodges. "They really respond to your leadership."

"Uh-huh. I see what's comin," Mac smiled. "You're gonna leave me with the kids, right?"

"Well, Laureen shouldn't walk home alone. You know how it is with a lady in distress. Someone's gotta respond."

"I spose it's a one man job."

"Definitely! Just one more job I have to do by myself," Hodges laughed.

"Yeah, well go ahead. I'll run the kindergarten."

"Thank you, MacKerry of Hart-ford, Ken-tuck," Laureen beamed.

"Any time." Mac waved them away.

"Later!" Hodges and Laureen turned toward her house. "Laureen Nhu Lam, you look especially radiant today."

"As do you, Thompson."

"I'm sorry I stayed away. I just had to work some things out." He raised his head. "I missed you. May I take your hand?"

"Yes! Oh yes! But the eyes of Ben Cat will see."

"Then I suppose putting my arm around you wouldn't be good?"

"That would be better, but worse."

"So you came to frustrate me," Hodges laughed.

"Thompson. You need me."

"Yes, Laureen, I need you. When we are apart, things don't make sense. I'm confused."

"This sounds like *chop yeu*."

"*Chop yeu*?"

"Lightning love. The classic ingredient in all Vietnamese love stories," she laughed.

"It's not funny."

"Yes, it is not funny."

"You know?"

"Yes," she smiled. "The feelings we share would be more easily accepted in Saigon. Here in Ben Cat, they are difficult, very difficult."

"Impossible?"

"Nothing is impossible. Is that not an American belief?"

"Yes, nothing is impossible," he brushed his arm against her side. "Could it pass us by?"

"Only if we let it." She leaned momentarily into him. "*Chop yeu* is very powerful, very dangerous."

"Love cannot be more dangerous than war."

"A friend describes it as a tidal wave. The tidal wave within us all."

"Lightning love? Tidal waves?" Hodges laughed. "I was always taught that love conquers all."

"That saying is familiar to me."

"Really? How?"

"To read is to learn. With learning, the world expands. For many years my books have sheltered me."

"From love?"

"And other things. Until now they have served me well." The house came into view.

"And now?" asked Hodges.

"Now everything fails. Thompson, you could understand only if you shared my turmoil."

"Laureen," he shook his head. "I feel the heat."

"Do you?"

He stopped and turned her to him. "The moment I saw you, when you were so nice to me, it was *chop yeu*. It makes no sense. I did not come here, to Vietnam, to fall in love. Now, how can I leave? Nobody understands. It makes me sad, sad for myself, sad for them. I want to tell someone, but who? Mai Nin, Tranh, Dudley, Mac? They wouldn't get it." He took her arms "I want to hold you, to kiss you, to do the things people in love do."

"In love," she sighed. "It is said. What churns within me is not only my love for you, but your love for me. It overwhelms me so. To hear you say it makes me want to cry and laugh, but do neither. It is too personal, too private. You know there are places this could happen. Are we, as you say, in the wrong place at the wrong time?"

"Not this time, Laureen. As long as you're here, as long as I'm with you, this is the right place, the right time."

"Thompson, *em yeu anh, nhieu qua*." Her eyes filled with tears. "*Nhieu qua*!"

They strained not to touch.

"Laureen. I love you now, I will love you forever."

"Yes, Thompson, you will. You must. You must love me forever. It is my opportunity, my responsibility to be sure that you do."

"I will."

Taking his hand, Laureen led him into the house.

****

"You guys are great!" exclaimed Mac.

Tranh nodded.

"We finished the whole thing. I can't believe it." Mac looked back over the trench. "Dudley's gonna be amazed. Anytime you want to work with me, you got a deal."

Reaching into his pocket, Mac handed each of the workers a piaster. "Thanks, guys and gal." He smiled at Lin.

Lin looked at the currency, then beamed up at him before bowing. The boys put the money in their pockets and shook Mac's hand.

"I just gotta get those shovels," he pointed to the shovels at the compound end of the trench. "Then we can call it a day."

Tranh looked where Mac was pointing. "I go!"

He began his practiced stride.

West of Ben Cat

In shovel... lift... turn right... dump shovel... into basket... turn left... slide shovel... lift... turn right... dump... two more hours... five more meters... sweat, this is good. Phong is ahead. Slide shovel... lift... turn right... dump... into basket."

"Tranh, finish that basket, so we can rest."

"Phong, are you tired?"

"Tired and sweaty. This is not the work of soldiers."

"This cave is bigger than the others. Bigger and further from the perimeter," said Tranh.

"A rocket squad will use it."

"But why do they face the village?"

"Guyan says they protect our village."

"Phong, they will destroy the village."

"Tranh, say no more. We have our orders."

"But we enlist to protect Ben Cat, not to destroy it."

"To save the village, we must drive the outsiders away." Phong filled his basket. "Now, they enter our homes."

"Will it ever stop?" Tranh asked.

"They no longer enter your home, do they Tranh?"

"Not since the Americans chased them away."

"The Americans chased them away?" Guyan arrived behind them.

Phong turned to face him. "Guyan! You surprise us. Have the porters returned?"

"Aye, they are behind me. Are your baskets ready?"

"Mine is complete. Tranh will soon be finished."

"Good. The major will be pleased. This is our best vantage point so far."

"But the village is barely visible," noted Tranh.

"Seven thousand meters is far for us, but ideal for the rockets."

"There," Tranh stood. "Another load for the porters. How far do they carry the baskets?"

"A ways," answered Guyan. "For protection, the porters spread the dirt in the jungle."

Four porters lifted the baskets. The three friends moved to the entrance of the cave. In the distance the lanterns of Ben Cat flickered in the twilight.

Tranh leaned against the bank. "The village looks peaceful."

"More peaceful than it is," said Guyan.

"Will they ever leave?" asked Phong.

"Not willingly. Each day they penetrate further. These searches are another display of their arrogance. Would they accept such intrusions?"

Tranh turned to Guyan. "Is it the Americans or Saigon?"

"They are the same, are they not? The Elders have become their pawns. They do not protest, instead yielding with indifference."

"Are they frightened?"

"They are weak. Frightened or not, nothing will change unless they resist. A statement must be made."

"Can such a will be resisted?" asked Phong.

"That responsibility belongs to the Elders. For many years they have sheltered the village. The outside world ended at our gates. Now the Elders welcome the intruders. Ben Cat is compromised. Why?"

"Grandmother says we should not pay attention. If we remain disinterested, they will leave," said Tranh.

"Mai Nin is wise with experience, but do the fortifications seem temporary? They do not intend to leave. Our leaders know this. The Elders' silence is interpreted as acceptance. The National Liberation Front is infuriated. The time for a response grows near."

"Is this why we dig?" asked Tranh.

"We dig because we are told. We are not strategists, merely footsoldiers. We execute the plans borne of military minds." Guyan paced across the entry. "There will be losses."

"The ambush was bad," sighed Phong.

"Aye, the ambush. There is more. Did you know Ban Dong?"

"The old woman who committed suicide?" asked Phong.

"The old woman whose husband the Americans killed," Guyan answered. "The Americans caused her death. And other families were forced from Ben Cat by the Americans. Not only do they intrude, they evict."

"But the families left of their own choice?"

Guyan shook his head. "You are naive, both of you. Our neighbors sacrifice everything, their homes, their privacy, their dignity. What else is there? Tranh, they entered your home? Is Laureen safe?"

"Now she is. The Americans chased the Saigon soldiers away."

"What do you mean?"

"A Saigon soldier hurt Laureen, tore her necklace away. Two others did the looting. One kicked Mai Nin."

"And the Americans interceded?" asked Guyan.

"Three of them."

"How did they know?"

"Laureen told me to summon them. We were in danger. The MPs

were very angry. Mai Nin knocked a soldier over. One of the Americans struck a Saigon soldier with his weapon. The Americans threatened the soldiers."

Guyan spoke as though to himself. "Now they fight amongst themselves. The mercenaries try to outdo each other."

"They saved us. Mai Nin gave a scarf to one." Tranh lowered his head. "We were grateful."

"Grateful to the Americans? Impossible! You forget that if they were not here, your house would not be threatened."

"Are the Americans mercenaries, or just misguided?" asked Tranh. "Some seem friendly."

"Friendly? They invade us for their own gain."

"Did they choose to come here?" asked Phong.

"Or were they ordered?" pressed Tranh. "Most wish they were home."

Guyan glared at Tranh. "What do you say? They torment our village. They kill your neighbors, reduce our crops. Your family must never forget this. You have seen enough. Do not lose sight of your experiences."

"Or the death of our neighbors," added Phong. "Think of Ban Dong dying, rather than accepting life ruled by the outsiders."

Guyan jumped to his feet. "Tranh, does Laureen accept these mercenaries? And Mai Nin? It is inconceivable!"

"They protected us," Tranh repeated.

"One pursues Laureen, is that it? Does he gain her favor?" Guyan flushed with anger. "She is more naive than either of you. This American places her in danger."

Tranh hesitated. "But Guyan. That day in the tunnel the major said we should observe our enemies. Laureen does not pursue the American. He pursues her. Even you and Ching Phor supported their visits to our home. You know how uncomfortable they made me."

"You must not forget that they are the enemy. You are to study them, not befriend them."

"Shall we return to work?" Phong helped Tranh up.

"Aye, continue the digging."

"Will this cave launch rockets at the village?" Tranh asked.

Guyan studied him. "You ask many questions? Have you had a change of heart?"

"Will the rockets land in the village?"

"Tranh Nhu Lam! These bunkers protect Ben Cat."

"But the rockets are powerful. People will be hurt."

"Our people prefer sacrifice to slavery. Our ancestors knew this. The village can be rebuilt more easily than our integrity. You are not too young to understand this. Do not forget how you despised the Americans. You are Vietnamese. Enough of this conversation. Return to work. We all must overcome our doubts. Follow the example of Ching Phor. You must do her honor."

"Aye," Phong added. "She saved my life at the ambush. She is remarkable."

"Aye, Phong, she saved you, so that you could contribute to our cause. If either of you has doubts, you must look to her example. Allow her dedication and bravery to inspire you."

Tranh rose to his feet. Standing at the entry, he peered out toward the lanterns. His shoulders ached. His blistered hands burned. He envisioned the arc of the projectiles that might someday be directed at the village.

"Is it possible," he wondered, "that we bury Ben Cat?"

Ben Cat

Mai Nin's oxen led the parade toward the paddies. The straw hats of Ben Cat followed. The ARVN MPs braced for the usual resistance to the morning checkout.

Hodges tried to look official. Returning the clipboard to an MP, he checked the oncoming work force.

Laureen walked at her grandmother's side. The only one without a hat, her hair glistened in the morning sun.

"Laureen, will Dui join us in the fields?" asked Mai Nin.

"Thompson," she called. "Mai Nin asks if you are ready to work the rice?"

"Hardly," laughed Hodges. "It's my day off."

"A day free from work? This is unlike Ben Cat."

"Unlike Vietnam," smiled Hodges. "But welcome just the same. I hoped we could spend it together."

Laureen blushed. "My studies will wait."

Hodges touched the scarf knotted around his neck. "Does Mai Nin notice?"

"Aye, Dui," Mai Nin did not await Laureen's translation. "You look very handsome today." She turned to Laureen. "The look of Vietnam becomes him. Perhaps there is hope for this American after all."

Mai Nin faced the MP. "We farmers have no time for small talk. The rains will soon begin. Today there is no restraining my oxen, so, MP, have you counted the oxen, or will they be subjected to one of your body searches?"

Disdainfully, the MP waved her through, beginning his count of the labor force. Laureen and Hodges stepped off to the side.

"She is so proud," said Laureen.

"With good reason, Laureen. I know nothing of rice farming, but her work ethic is admirable."

"This is true of all Ben Cat."

"Most of Ben Cat," Hodges agreed. "Does Tranh Nhu Lam work today?"

"Tranh and Ching Phor work the north paddy. They grow inseparable. The village is tired but invigorated. Do you feel it?"

"It is unmistakable, but with the new arrivals, will the crops feed all the people?"

"Ben Cat always has room for her neighbors. You have created a safe haven. The village expands under your watchful eye."

"Under our watchful eye or under our noses? Sometimes it's hard to tell the difference."

"Thompson, there is fear around us. The small villages tremble under the pressure. Their crops are reduced or confiscated by the enemy. They are driven to escape. Ben Cat is their only alternative."

"Uh huh. And now we are over a thousand," he hesitated. "Do you notice more policemen?"

"Very little escapes the eyes of Ben Cat, but this growth increases the importance of our crop and the farmers."

"And of our supplies." Hodges smiled to Laureen. "Shall I walk you home?"

"You must."

They walked against the flow of the labor force.

As they approached the command compound, Dudley loomed at the gate. Standing erect in freshly pressed fatigues, he observed the movements of the village.

"Morning Hodges."

"Good morning Sergeant."

"Seems like your day's starting well."

"Yes, Sergeant, it is. Thanks."

"Remember where you are, Hodges."

"Yes Sergeant."

Laureen and Hodges moved past him.

"Who is this man who makes you nervous?" asked Laureen.

"My keeper."

"Your keeper?"

"Aye, Laureen. He is my instructor, my mentor. He will take me home."

"Ah, then this is a good man for you and a bad man for me."

"What?"

"He will take you away from me."

"Laureen, we will never be apart. We'll figure something out. There are ways you know."

"Aye, there are ways," she smiled. "He still watches."

"He watches everything."

"A guardian, then?"

"Uh huh, a large guardian," Hodges laughed. "I'll tell him you said so. He'll like that."

"Really? What would your guardian say if we were to hold hands?" she teased.

"He would not approve."

"Then putting your arm around me is impossible?" she laughed.

"Not right now, Laureen. Not right now."

"When?"

"When the time is right, Laureen."

"That is vague, is it not?"

"Vague by necessity, not desire. You have become my obsession, all the time. You are everywhere. Inside me. Around me. Everywhere. This fixation is new, the timing bad but it is... inescapable." He halted. "I am hooked."

She turned him toward her. "Will these feelings grow old? In books, they seem to tire."

"We have this moment, then the next," he smiled. "If we continue the moments, they will take us forward to the end, past Ben Cat."

"Why Thompson! You sound Vietnamese. And if past Ben Cat, where then?"

"Where we will be happy."

"And safe?"

"Very safe, Laureen. Very safe."

They resumed the walk. He brushed her side. She leaned into him. Another moment passed.

Ben Cat

"It just ain't right," Mac declared.

"We got our orders," answered Ghost.

"That don't make it right."

While Ben Cat worked, MacKerry, Ghost, and Hodges reluctantly pried into the villager's innermost sanctuaries. Across the road three ARVNs searched eagerly.

"This one's next," Ghost pointed to a hut.

"You guys go ahead. I'll watch the door," suggested Hodges.

"Yeah, sure, you wait here. Don't wanna piss anybody off, right? We don't like this anymore than you," said Ghost. "C'mon Mac, let the prima donna watch our backsides." The Ghost knocked on the door. "Yo hoo! Anybody home?"

Ghost and Mac entered the hut. Hodges watched the ARVNs, who exited a residence and began a muffled conversation. One smirked at him. They passed by the next hut.

"Anything?" Hodges called inside.

"Nada."

"That figures," Hodges muttered.

Suddenly the skies opened with their usual ferocity. Hodges moved under the roof's overhang. "Here she comes!"

"Nothing in there," said Ghost, joining him. "C'mon Mac, let's get this over with."

"Something's wrong," said Hodges.

"What?"

"The ARVNs skipped the hut across from us."

"That's their problem."

"Uh huh."

"We got four more. Let's get on with it."

Lowering their heads, they sprinted next door.

"I'm stayin out this time," Mac said.

"You friggin guys keep this up, I'll be doin em myself," grumbled Ghost.

"I'll go," offered Hodges.

"Good." Ghost knocked. "Anybody home?"

Ghost and Hodges pushed into the house. As usual, everything was in place. The villagers had come to expect the searches. The starkness still surprised the Americans. Ghost inspected the bamboo walls. Hodges checked the cooking utensils, then raised the lids of innocent baskets. Ghost entered a sleeping area. Clothing hung along the wall. Haphazardly, he felt through the pockets. After searching the bunker under the sleeping shelf, he ran his hand along the wall. Satisfied, he returned the bunk to its position and with his M-16 probed the ceiling.

Hodges scoured the other sleeping area. Opening a drawer under a table, he discovered the cigarettes.

"Ghost, something here you might like."

"The stash?"

"Just the usual."

"Amazing, huh?"

"Pretty amazing," confirmed Hodges closing the drawer.

"What a life. It's too simple."

"They're happy," Hodges concluded.

"With all the weed, no wonder. But if this is happiness, they can have it. I'll take the comforts of home."

"How was it?" asked Mac, as they emerged.

"The usual. Where are the ARVNs?" Hodges asked.

"Finishing the last hut. Looks like they're packing it in."

"Uh huh."

Ghost lowered his head. "Onward." They darted next door.

Completing their side of the road, they contemplated the rain.

"This sucks. I'm soaked."

"Welcome to the Nam."

"Here we go!" Hodges ran up the road, but pulled in under a roof. Ghost and Mac followed.

"Hey man! We already did our searches," yelled Mac.

"Yeah," said Ghost, "but we're gonna do the one the ARVNs skipped, right?"

"Right," said Hodges. "We're here. We should do it."

"Go for it!" Ghost ducked across the street.

"Anybody home?" Ghost and Hodges entered.

"Same old, same old," Ghost murmured. "We're wasting time."

"Bedroom or this one?" Hodges offered.

"I'm a bedroom man myself," Ghost smiled.

"Go for it!"

Hodges finished the last basket, then lifted the lid of an urn. "Jesus! What the hell?"

"What you got?" called Ghost.

"That smelly shit! Raunchier than usual." Hodges closed the lid.

"That's real exciting, Dui. A real find."

Hodges entered the bedroom where Ghost lay on the bunk.

"Sorry, GI!" Ghost rose. "Wondered how this would feel."

"C'mon, let's get outta here."

Ghost jerked up the stubborn bunk. Two pegs sprang from the frame. "Now there's a twist! Why would you nail down the cover to your bunker?" Ghost slid the bunk aside and stared down at a mattress across the base of the pit. "A mattress and thatched walls? A real first class bunker."

"Maybe they sleep there?"

"Under lock and key?" Ghost questioned.

Leaning on the wall, he raised the mattress. "Seems all right?" He shuffled his foot along the ground. After replacing the mattress, he inspected the thatched flanks.

"C'mon, Ghost, let's go home."

"Hold it! Look at this!" Ghost pulled away the thatch. "Now that, my man, is a hole." He looked up. "I don't do holes. No tunnels, no holes."

"Son of a bitch. What d'ya see?"

"A hole. A black hole." Ghost shook his head. "Could be a tunnel."

"Mac," Hodges called. "Better get Dudley. He's gonna love this. Gonna be hell to pay."

"Yeah," Ghost agreed. "Specially considering the ARVNs walked right by this one."

"Uh huh."

****

"Who lives here?" asked Dudley.

Hodges looked up from the registry. "Chan Chieu, his wife, Thuoc Ve Tam, and two boys. Uh, that's not quite right. The boys have relocated."

"Relocated?"

"Yes Sergeant. They moved south, to Saigon. At least, that's what we were told."

"Right."

"Make yourselves comfortable, gentlemen. We're going to wait for Mr. Chan Chieu and his wife."

"Say Sergeant?"

"Yes, Scott?"

"We're not doing the tunnel, are we?"

"No, Scott. We are not doing the tunnel. Parker, give me the hook." Dudley spoke into the transmitter. "Matchmaka One, this is Two, ova."

"Go Two."

"We got something here."

"Right."

"We need the dogs."

"Roger that. Will do. Out."

The rain slowed. Dusk set in. Ben Cat returned from the fields. Soaked villagers trudged home. Passing the Chan Chieu residence, the workers stared straight ahead.

The Americans waited through the night.

Chan Chieu and Thuoc Ve Tam never returned.

****

In the morning Dudley's detail assembled in front of the hut. Curious neighbors lingered nearby before gradually yielding to the necessity of working the paddies.

"Man's best friend," Ghost pointed up the road. Escorted by their masters, two german shepherds marched down the street. Villagers veered out of their path.

"Sergeant Dudley?"

"Good morning, Sergeant Thayer." Dudley extended his hand. "Glad you could make it. We got something interesting here."

"Forty-two days, Sergeant. There's nothing here that interests me," muttered Thayer. "This is my assistant, Corporal Howe. He's, uh, new at this." Thayer shook his head. "My last guy just bit it outside Cu Chi."

"Morning, Howe," Dudley nodded.

"Lassie and Snoopy, right?" Hodges asked.

"These guys," Thayer started, "are gonna do your dirty work. Mine's Batch. Howe's is Sage."

"You got leashes?" asked Ghost.

"Don't need em. You'll see," Thayer chuckled. "If I were you, I wouldn't be pattin me or Howe on the back," he looked at Dudley, "or raisin your voice too sharply. They don't go for that."

"That right?"

"That's right," said Howe.

"You out of Lai Khe?" asked Ghost.

"We get around," said Thayer. "One hundred nineteenth tunnel. Howe's second."

"One hundred nineteen!" marvelled Mac. "What's it like?"

"What's it like?" Thayer scratched his head. "Like pussy. Ya never really know til ya taste it. It all looks good enough, innocent enough, til ya get in there and really taste it. Once ya do, ya know right away, right?"

"If you say so," Mac shrugged.

Thayer turned to Dudley. "Let's see what we got, Sergeant."

"Inside," Dudley moved towards the door.

"Under the bed, right?"

"That's right."

"Great. Howe, you and Sage take a hike."

Howe stepped forward. "Sage!" He pointed to the ground. The dog put his nose down and moved ahead of Howe. Together they circled the hut.

"After you, Sergeant." Thayer spoke to Dudley.

Dudley led Thayer and Batch into the hut directly to the sleeping room.

"Stay!" Batch sat at the edge of the bunker. Thayer lowered himself into the pit, then raised a flashlight in one hand while holding a long handled knife in the other. Delicately he probed the opening. Pushing a ray of light into the hole, he peered in. "Yessir. We got us a tunnel. Shit! I hate these fucking people." Thayer climbed out of the pit.

"Let's take some air, see if Howe has anything." He shook his head. "Fucking gophers! They live underground for Christ's sake. Howe!" Thayer called. "The fucking tunnel goes from the rear left corner to the trees. Check the surface, will ya? Go fifty meters into the bush. Find the other end, please!"

"Will do." Howe and Sage scoured the surface.

"Hope he finds something." Thayer lit a cigarette, then pointed at the perimeter wire. "He's gonna be awhile."

"MacKerry, you and Scott give him a hand," Dudley ordered.

Sage methodically led them to the perimeter. Ghost and Mac lifted the wire as Howe and Sage slid through. Soon the group disappeared into the jungle.

Dudley turned to Thayer. "One hundred nineteen tunnels, that's a lot of tunnels, Sergeant."

"Too many," grinned Thayer. "This'll probably be my last."

Howe returned. "Nada!"

"That figures. Forty-two fucking days. I hate these people."

"I'll do this one," said Howe.

"No way, rookie. I got it covered."

Thayer knelt beside Batch, petting him from the top of his head down along his backbone. The huge dog stared upwards. "This is it, Batch. One more time, big guy. One more time." Thayer stood. "Go!"

Batch entered the hut but stopped at the bunker's edge. Thayer lowered himself into the bunker again and looked up to the dog. "Easy!" Thayer assisted Batch into the entry of the hole. The dog crawled ahead.

"Anything we can do?" Hodges asked.

"Pray." Thayer squirmed up into the hole. "These fucking people."

Howe lowered himself into the pit and shone his light behind Thayer.

"How far?"

"Shut the fuck up!"

"Right."

They listened.

"Easy!"

"Forward!"

"These fucking people!"

"Stop!"

"Go!"

"Stop! Touchdown! We got something! Jesus Christ! These fucking people! Unbelievable!"

"What ya got?" asked Howe.

"We're coming out! These fucking people! The whole shabang."

Thayer edged backwards, to Howe. His boots appeared. Howe helped him down. "C'mon Batch."

The dog whimpered loudly. "Back! Batch! Back!"

Batch sprang out of the hole.

Hodges sighed.

Thayer stood in the bunker. Perspiring profusely, he smiled up at Dudley. "Nice neighborhood, ya got here."

"That so?"

Thayer climbed out of the bunker. Batch leapt to his side. "Okay, we take some air?"

"Your pleasure."

Outside, Thayer lit another cigarette. "I say again. Nice neighborhood. At least two tiers. I seen em before. Could be more. About thirty feet out, goes straight down. Ladders on both sides of the shaft. We'll need some equipment." He smiled at Dudley. "Nice fucking neighborhood."

"Nice ARVNs," added Dudley .

****

At 0430 two flatbeds cleared the south checkpoint and were directed to the top of the street. After the backhoe and bulldozer were unloaded, Dudley positioned the flatbeds to barricade the street. Today the neighborhood would not work the paddies. Instead they would witness the uncovering of the tunnels.

The backhoe and bulldozer rumbled down the street. Weary civilians peered from their homes, watching the unfamiliar vehicles.

ARVN MPs lined the block.

MacKerry, Hodges, and Ghost helped Thayer, Howe, and the dogs check the area again.

The neighborhood watched as Dudley motioned the bulldozer ahead. The diesel engine thundered forward. Chan Chieu's bamboo hut crumpled to the ground. After the debris was pushed away, the dozer began clearing a path along the roof of the tunnel.

Awestruck neighbors witnessed the devastation, wondered at the machinery.

The backhoe moved over the tunnel area. The bucket tore into the ground, scooped a full load, raised it above the surface, then swivelled neatly depositing the fill. Thayer and Dudley directed the excavation. Howe stood off to the side nervously anticipating his mission.

"They never seen nothin like this," Mac nodded at the neighbors.

"Think what they could do with this stuff," laughed Ghost.

"Think what they do without it," Hodges countered.

"That's a fact."

Finishing a strip, the backhoe retreated.

Thayer dispatched Batch to investigate the freshly exposed ridge. The dog worked the length of the ridge then returned to Thayer's side.

The backhoe began the next dig.

"Hold it! Right there!" exclaimed Dudley. "That's it. Look at this."

Thayer peered down the shaft. "Pretty fancy, huh? Maybe more than two levels."

"Pretty fancy," Dudley agreed. "Who goes?"

"This one's mine," Howe volunteered. "The ladder?"

Thayer shook his head. "No way, Jose. We lower you and Sage down in the bucket." Thayer turned to Dudley. "I saw a guy lose his foot on one of those ladders. Stepped on the wrong rung, detonated a grenade. Boom! That was it."

Howe paled.

Thayer continued. "Can't be too careful in the hole. Put Sage down first, stay low in the bucket til he clears it." He shrugged. "You never know."

"Right."

Hodges joined Dudley and Thayer at the edge of the hole.

The backhoe engine revved, then lowered the bucket near the deck of the first tier. Howe lifted Sage to the rim, where the dog momentarily wavered before jumping to the floor. He pawed the walls. Suddenly Sage froze. Pointing east, he barked ferociously. Howe checked his revolver then jumped to the floor.

"Watch your step!" Thayer yelled down.

Howe surveyed the flooring. Holstering his pistol, he drew his bayonet and pried up several floorboards. Yanking one free, he probed the supports with his knife.

Sage bristled.

"Down!" The dog snapped back on his haunches.

Howe moved on to a hole at the south side. Prone on the floor, he lowered his head into the opening and surveyed the underside of the deck. Finally, he raised himself. His audience exhaled.

Howe looked up at them. "Three tiers! The deck's clear! Sage has a storage bin in the east wall. Gonna check it out." He moved to the east wall.

"Go!" The dog lowered his nose and moved out of sight. Howe shone the light into the cavity.

"Easy!"

Howe followed the dog.

"I hate this part!" said Thayer. "Almost rather be down there." He lit another cigarette.

Eventually Howe, then Sage, moved back into view. Howe smiled up. "Grenades, mortars, ammo, and AK-47s. Beaucoup!"

"Good job! Get up here!" called Thayer.

Howe gave the thumbs up and lifted the dog back into the bucket, then jumped in himself.

The bucket lifted them out.

"We got us one severe storage facility. Must be 200 rifles, a thousand grenades, beaucoup mortars, and crates of ammo," he smiled.

Thayer turned to the backhoe operator. "Time for the ball!"

The backhoe swung to the side where MacKerry and Ghost held a heavy chain attached to a wrecking ball. Linking the chain to hooks on the bucket, the arm lifted, swinging back over the hole.

The neighborhood moved back.

A tail whistled through the air.

"Incoming!"

The soldiers dove to the ground.

The mortar struck west of them.

Then another! And another!

"They're walking them in!" yelled Dudley. "Clear the hole!"

The Americans dove for cover.

Mortars closed on the pit.

The street emptied.

The backhoe operator jumped from the machine diving behind a mound of fill.

Three more mortars exploded. Shrapnel ripped through the huts. A fourth mortar miraculously disappeared down the shaft. The earth slid into the hole.

The backhoe teetered before falling forward to be buried by the collapsing earth.

The mortars stopped.

The GIs lay still for ten minutes.

"Matchmaker Two, this is One, over."

"Two here, ova."

"All clear! How we doing?"

"No casualties. One zeroed the hole."

Thayer surveyed the empty street. "Nice neighborhood!"

183 days

September 5, 1967

Near the South Paddy

"Enough! Be still. Soon we slide into the paddy."

"But what is this work we do? We betray our brethren, we betray our village. Is this patriotism?"

Ching Phor and Tranh lay in water on the fringe of the paddy. Tall grass rose around them.

"Tranh Nhu Lam!" Ching Phor inched her head closer. "These are not your concerns. Instead, ask who you are, what you are. When you have considered yourself, you will understand that we, of Ben Cat, are the same. Your brethren understand that suffering precedes success." She ran her hand through Tranh's wet hair. "What are you?"

"Wet."

"Who are you?"

"A duck."

"Ah, no longer the Little Ox, now the duck."

Tranh chuckled. "Is that progress?"

She laid her hand on his back. "Perhaps you change with the seasons."

"Perhaps the seasons change me."

"Ah, to be fourteen!"

He looked over to her. "Would you prefer fourteen to where you are?"

"Compared to this," she swirled the water around them, "fourteen might be better. But my journey has been long. Never once has it seemed better to look behind. Always forward. You are much the same."

"How can you tell?"

"Because you are who you are. You will make decisions. Good decisions, bad decisions, but none that will be dishonorable. People will come to you to hear your decisions, to help them with their own. You, Tranh, have instinct. Sometimes, you will need to temper it, but do not be over-influenced. Your instincts are to be trusted. They are what you are. Your first thoughts, your first reaction, those are what you are. Your instincts are honorable. Trust them." She patted his head. "You already make me proud."

Tranh smiled. "My conscience says our path is right, but my instincts cry danger."

"There is always danger. Each path encompasses danger."

"But my stomach churns."

"When?"

"When the caves we dig face the village."

"Your instincts are good."

"Ching Phor, what will happen."

"Nothing that has not happened before."

"Look, our farmers come."

"Ah, then we go." The two slithered into the paddy.

****

The Command Compound

"The election is over. Now we must get back to work," White stared across the table at Major Thiut.

"The results are good," said Thiut.

"Some election!" Dudley shrugged. "One hundred twenty-two civilian votes from Ben Cat. Must have been the rain."

"In Saigon the voting was heavier."

"That tell you anything?" Dudley asked.

Thiut straightened. "Sergeant, it was our first election."

"I understand, Major, but do you understand how few votes were cast in the neighborhood?"

"Aye," said the major. "Ben Cat is a primitive village."

"It sure is," said Dudley. "And it's gettin worse."

"What is the meaning of this?" Thiut looked to White.

"You are aware," began White, "of the irregularities. Your troops terrorize certain civilians. They selectively close their eyes to certain situations. You are aware of this?"

"We use discretion, discretionary discipline. Major, need I remind you that our purpose is the same."

"Major Thiut, you are a good soldier, a smart man. Smart enough to know what's happening. Your troops are out of control. They are active in the black market. They steal from the peasants. We are not here for gain. We are here to secure this village, not loot it. Your men are widening the gap. You do see this?"

Thiut crossed his hands on the table. "Some of my troops have ties to the area. Perhaps they are not as serious as they should be. What can we do?"

"What we got to do," Dudley interjected, "is kick ass. Either they shape up, or you ship em out." Dudley leaned back in the chair putting his hands behind his head. "My guys think your guys knew about Chan Chieu."

"Ridiculous."

"Three of your guys walked past the house. The only one they missed."

"Who tells you this?"

"Three of my guys," Dudley smiled. "The ones who found the hole. You know the hole with the mortars, the AK 47s, the 4000 rounds, the rice, the pot. Ring a bell? The hole that took us two weeks to dig out."

Major Thiut looked at White. "You hear things, we hear things."

White raised his brow. "Oh?"

"You have a GI. The one with the scarf..."

"Hodges," said Dudley.

"The one with the scarf. He is Viet Cong sympathizer."

"Impossible!"

"Oh?"

****

LZ – Ben Cat

"I can't believe the way she talks."

"My man, she's a fine lookin woman, no doubt about it." Ghost was serious in his admiration.

"But she learned to talk... like us. I mean that's pretty amazin," said Mac.

"She's a fine lookin woman. There's a lot goin on inside her."

"She reads everything."

"Yeah, with that imagination she's gonna be hard to keep happy."

"What d'ya mean?"

"I mean that flower's gonna bloom. And when it does... wooey! Watch out! That woman's gonna realize this life, this little village, this country, just ain't what she's all about. She's bigger than this. She's a limo in four-wheel-drive territory. Dui's got his hands full."

"She's the prettiest thing I ever saw."

"Yeah, Mac. Ya think he's doin her? He notch her up?"

"Don't know, Ghost. What happens, happens."

"I do believe she's the only woman with legs in the whole damn country."

"Some smile," mused Mac.

"She's got teeth. That's different. Lips, cheekbones..."

"Eyes. He likes the eyes."

"And hair! Shit, why can't we find somethin like that. I mean, it coulda been us, ya know. It coulda been us."

"Maybe it is."

"Mac, what d'ya mean?"

"Well, it could be us. She's ours too. We're not gonna forget her, let's face it."

"Well, there's one thing she could do to make sure we don't. You wanna ask her?"

"You don't mean that."

"I don't?" Ghost laughed. "She is mighty fine. She prances around here like, like she's better than everyone. Fact is, she's here. She stays, she's gonna end up like the rest of them."

"She'll never be like them."

"Hey man, she squats to pee. She may do it classier, but underneath it all, she's one of them."

"You're kiddin, right?"

"Shit Mac, she's a goddess to you and Dui. You're just two buddies with a case."

"They're in love."

"Love!"

"Yeah, they're in love."

"Mac, you got a lot to learn. Love no, horny yes. They both wanna get laid, they just don't know how to go about it."

"I know they're in love," Mac smiled. "They deserve each other."

"Well, man, if they're in love, they better do the deed soon. Who knows what might happen. We are countin down."

"Maybe he'll take her home."

"You kiddin? He don't have the clout. Is he tellin you he's gonna take her with him?"

"Maybe. He says this is one thing he's got to finish."

Ghost shook his head. "That about says it all. You both got some wild ideas!"

"I know him. I know her."

"What's that mean?" Ghost chuckled. "You only known him, what, fourteen months? You don't know him. What's his mother look like? What kinda car's she drive? How many TV's they got? Where do they go on Saturday night? Yesterday we were civilians, today we're soldiers, tomorrow and the rest of our lives, civilians again. As soldiers we only know what the next guy wants us to. As civilians we'll never see each other again. Be real."

"Why you always tryin to start somethin? You know Dui, you know me, you know Balman, and you know you can count on me, an Dui, even Balman. Ya even know Dudley."

"Yeah, I know Dudley."

"And I know Laureen. And I know Dui. They're my friends. They're your friends."

"Yeah, they're friends. And when we get home, we'll have a big old reunion, right?"

"When we get home, we'll be friends, specially cause of this."

"Yeah, and let me get this straight, where will she be?"

"With Dui."

"Uh-huh. They'll have kids. We'll visit on Christmas. Maybe sing a carol? She's beginnin to sound like a regular Tinkerbell. I listen to you long enough, we'll be one happy, black-white-gook family spending Christmas Eve in Never-Never Land." Ghost laughed. "Think about it."

"Ghost," Mac smiled, "them bein together's no stranger than us bein here."

"Man, oh, man! You really are something!"

****

Laureen's Home

Mai Nin studied his tired, drawn frame. "Guyan, you seem troubled. What is it?"

Guyan turned away from her. "Change. Such rapid changes. Will she ever be the same?"

"Are those not the same hills your grandparents awoke to each day? Does the sun still rise in the East? Does the rice grow?"

"Ah, you speak of Ben Cat? And in Ben Cat, has anyone changed as much as your granddaughter?"

"My little flower? You think she changes? Interesting. Perhaps you did not know her as well as you thought."

"We have been friends since she was seven."

"At such an age, she was unknown to herself, as were you. Now she awakens." Mai Nin looked skyward. "Laureen is like her mother. We are unable to control her course. She must be herself, as you must, as we all must."

"She forgets her roots."

"Never."

He hesitated. "She appears disloyal."

"Disloyal? Certainly we speak of someone unknown to me."

"Mai Nin! The American. She... "

"Must be herself," interrupted Mai Nin. "Like her parents were. They also saw no limits. It has forever puzzled this old lady." She shook her head.

"And what will she do next?" He looked down. "Will she leave the village?"

"Laureen will do what she must. She will do what is in her heart. Neither you, nor myself, nor anything else will change her course. You may be certain that her heart will lead her. As does yours, my young friend."

"You think my heart leads me?"

"Aye. And a strong heart it is."

"Perhaps." He shrugged. "Perhaps it is not as strong as once thought."

"You worry about Ben Cat?"

"When was the last time the village was attacked?"

"Not that long ago."

"Did it... ?"

"Aye, it did. It always will."

"So, you know my troubles."

"Possibly."

"Is it fear?"

"It is anguish, the unmistakable anguish of those who must enact grave decisions. A noble quality, this anguish."

"Anguish! Many of my decisions, indeed, many of my actions are irreversible. The permanence of these decisions is overwhelming. My education, my training are insufficient."

"Guyan, these decisions do not belong to you. Do not fool yourself. You comply with the decisions of others, do you not?"

"Some should be resisted. They create suffering, or worse. My actions betray those who support me."

"Guyan, you misunderstand the reason they follow you. Like La, you are young."

He smiled. "Then tell me, wise one, why do they follow such an anguished soul?"

"Do you notice that you are unquestioned? Do they voice their hunger or wear their exhaustion? You see the depth of their commitment, do you think it fragile? Will it disappear tomorrow, next month, next year? Do you think this is the first time? The last?"

"They are loyal. My complaints are not with my supporters."

"Nor with your superiors."

"Not their purpose."

Mai Nin put her hand on his shoulder. "You and Tranh, you are kindred spirits. You are tigers. Tigers amidst the paddies."

"Will the paddies survive the tigers?"

"Will the paddies survive without them?"

****

Saigon

Chocart's finger stirred the ice in his glass. Was he more frail? Was she nervous? Sipping her tea, Laureen stalled for time.

"So child how did Ben Cat receive the opportunity to vote?"

Laureen lowered her glass. "Unenthusiastically, as you might suspect."

Monsieur Chocart chuckled. "What percentage?"

"Possibly ten percent, certainly no more. On the whole it was just another day in Ben Cat."

"No celebrations?"

"No celebrations, quite solemn really."

Madame studied her. "Father, would you get the packet from your bureau? Laureen may want to have it."

"Now?" he asked. "May I first finish my cocktail?"

"Why not take it with you?"

"I see." Chocart rose, shaking his head. "The minds of women. Always so secretive. Someday I may understand."

"We hope not," Madame nodded to include Laureen. "Men should never know our innermost secrets, don't you agree?"

"Then we would have no secrets at all," Laureen smiled.

"I see," said Chocart. "And how long should it take me to retrieve the papers."

"Certainly you will want to replenish your beverage before you return."

"I see. We have been together so long that you know my habits and capacities better than myself."

"I would never say that."

"No, Mother, you never would. But I shall find the papers and await my next wish or your next command. After all they are the same."

"How wonderful! Meanwhile, I shall try to think of something original."

"That may be more than these old bones can bear," Chocart muttered, walking away.

"That has never been the case."

"You are wonderful together," Laureen mused.

"Years of practice, dear. Years and years of practice. Every now and then it comes together." Reaching for Laureen's hand, she probed the girl's eyes. "There is a difference, *non?* The closer we are, the more distinct the difference. Does the village go badly? Should you stay here a while?"

Laureen withheld her response.

"I see. Should we talk another time?"

Withdrawing her hand, Laureen lowered her eyes.

"Are you, are you all right, dear?"

"Madame, it is more wonderful than ever imagined." Her eyes filled with tears.

"Oh, my dear."

"It is a song, a song within me."

"Oh, dear. Papa will have to know."

"Will you tell him?"

"We will tell him."

"Everything has changed. Do you understand?"

"I do," Madame hesitated. "He will not."

"It makes me happy that you do." Laureen laughed through her tears.

"Oh?"

"Sometimes it feels so lonely."

"Child, it is the setting."

"Or the unanswered, the unasked questions."

"Yes, the young question the validity of the emotion. I understand."

Laureen raised herself. "Do you? Do you really?"

"I do."

"This makes me happy, for you."

"Thank you, my dear."

****

"Laureen, today you set out a new soldier? His uniform is colorless."

"Yes, Alicia, what do you think?"

"That he is misplaced."

"Why?"

"He does not belong with the other soldiers. Our French uniforms are much more colorful. Is he Vietnamese?"

"No, Alicia, he is not Vietnamese, but perhaps we should relocate him. Where do you suggest?"

"Umm, not guarding the ladies by the pool, not at the laboratory. Hmm, let me see. Who is he? What does he do?" Have you named him?"

"His name is Thompson. He is American."

"Thompson? Is that his first name or his last?"

"That is the only name we need to know. What do you think?"

Alicia studied Laureen with amusement. "I think that tonight you must tell me of this Thompson." Alicia lifted the figure from the Lai Khe plantation. "Come to bed, tell me more."

Ben Cat

"Incoming!"

The first bird spun through the air.

The village agonized over its destination. The mortar headed toward the supply depot in the northeast sector. A second round barely cleared the perimeter, harmlessly discharging between the wire and a row of huts.

Hodges turned to Mac. "You see it?"

"Nothing, man, nothing."

Beneath the west wire, dark figures crept across the clearing and disappeared into the foliage. After two kilometers they paused at the base of a hill.

Phong moved to the rear of the column where he anchored two

American made bouncing betty mines. Further along the trail he set a trip flare, then rushed to report to Guyan.

Responding to the mortar fire, gunships summoned from Lai Khe sprayed the east paddy while Guyan oversaw his column's ascent of the west hillside.

"Ching Phor, the patrols? Where are the patrols?" Tranh asked.

"What difference to you, Little Ox?"

"But?"

"Put your reservations aside. We follow our leader."

At the third plateau, fifty untended baskets waited beneath camouflaged coverings.

"Someone watches?"

"Aye, Little Ox, someone watches. Nothing escapes those who watch."

Suddenly two distant explosions rang through the night. Moments later Phong's flare soared into the night, lighting the hillside below them.

Tranh recoiled. "They follow us!"

"No longer," smiled Ching Phor. "You see, each plan must have options and preparation. We are as productive as the preparation of our pilot. Guyan surpasses apprenticeship, as will you Little Ox." Ching Phor chuckled. "Where do you suppose that will place me?"

"By my side, Ching Phor," said Tranh. "Where we began."

Ben Cat – Command Compound

He wore no hat. He was dressed in a long white shirt, his hands folded over the grey beard that hung below his waist. Laureen stood to his side, two steps behind. Her yellow backpack was slung over her shoulder.

"Looks like a shotgun deal to me," said Balman. The Americans looked up from their breakfast to the compound gate. "Christ, Dui, what you done now?"

"Gentlemen," White began. "That is Thong Thai, the senior Elder of the village. Let's clear the table. Seems like we're in for a session."

"He's not happy," Dudley observed.

"You can tell?" asked Ghost.

White stared across the table. "Hodges, anything we should know?"

"No sir, nothing. This is a surprise to me."

"Gentlemen, the meal is over. Clean it up, and move out."

The squad cleared the table and retreated to their tent.

"This cannot be good," Dudley cautioned.

White nodded. "Hodges, let's not keep the lady waiting."

Hodges moved to the gate where he exchanged bows with Thong Thai.

"Good morning, Laureen. What's up?"

"Good day, Thompson. This morning Thong Thai has asked me to assist him in a meeting with your officers. He is the village Elder, a man of great dignity and wisdom."

"*Chao*, Thong Thai," Hodges extended his hand.

The Elder declined the handshake, instead bowing again. "*Chao*, Dui." Thong Thai spoke briefly to Laureen, who translated to Hodges. "Thompson, Thong Thai admires your scarf. He asks who gave it to you."

"Did you tell him?"

"Perhaps you should answer this question."

Hodges addressed the Elder. "*Ca nai cavat dai vat thang Mai Nin, vi dai me*, Laureen Nhu Lam." He looked to Laureen. "How'd I do?"

The Elder struggled to reconstruct the explanation until he suddenly grasped the meaning. "Aye! Mai Nin!" He directed a burst of speech to Laureen.

"Thong Thai says you are a fortunate young man to carry the scarf of Mai Nin. You must never be far from it," Laureen smiled.

"Never?" Hodges laughed. "If my memory serves me, sometimes you like it off."

"But Thompson," Laureen blushed, "never far away."

"*Su cam, anh*," Hodges thanked the Elder. "The major asks you to join him under the tent."

Laureen spoke to Thong Thai, who nodded approvingly.

Entering the tent, Hodges gestured to the major, "Laureen, this is Major White, and this is... "

"Sergeant Dudley," said Laureen. She bowed first to the major, then to Dudley, before turning to Thong Thai and introducing the soldiers. Thong Thai bowed to each, then addressed Laureen.

"Major White," Laureen bowed. "Thong Thai asks if this is a bad time?"

"No time like the present," said White. "Young lady, your English is very good."

"My speech is as good as my teacher," Laureen smiled at Hodges.

"That so?" asked Dudley.

"Coffee?" asked White.

"Thank you, no," Laureen bowed, then faced Dudley.

"Sergeant Dudley," she smiled, "do you know the name the villagers give to you?"

"No, ma'am. I didn't know I was so well known."

"Indeed, you are a man known to us all. Ngurai Giu Gin. That is your name. It means the guardian."

"How do you say that?"

"Ngurai Giu Gin. Very honorable."

"And what do the villagers call me?" asked White.

"Major, you are Tho Moc."

"Tho Moc?"

"Yes Major," Laureen removed the backpack, quickly scanning her dictionary. "Tho Moc. Carpenter. You are the carpenter. A very important job."

Laureen looked to Hodges. "Thompson, is that correct?"

"Thompson?" Dudley repeated.

Laureen turned back to Dudley. "Aye, Thompson. This is the name of Dui's mother. Did you not know?"

Dudley shook his head. "As a matter of fact, no, no I didn't." The sergeant looked to White. "Seems like there's a whole lot I don't know."

White nodded. "Well, ma'am, how about a seat?" He motioned to two chairs. Thong Thai nodded, but curiously remained standing.

"After us, I guess," said Dudley. Dudley and White assumed adjoining seats. Thong Thai then moved to a chair across the table. He slowly brushed the chair clean, then seated himself before motioning Laureen to stand by his side.

Hodges moved behind Dudley.

"To what do we owe the pleasure?" White began.

Laureen opened her notebook and began to read.

"The village of Ben Cat is very grateful for the generosity of the Americans. Your food sustains us. Your medicine cures us. Your clothing protects us." She looked across the table at Hodges. "Your soldiers work very hard on our behalf. We appreciate their efforts." She hesitated. "But all is not well in Ben Cat. Things have not gone as planned." She halted. "Or as were represented."

"Ma'am," said the Major gravely, "begging your pardon, but please remind Thong Thai that we are at war. Things happen in war, things beyond our control."

Laureen relayed the words to the Elder, who took the notebook and pointed to a passage.

"Thong Thai says that while Vietnam has been at war for very long, Ben Cat has not. Many of our most loyal villagers believe that you... " she paused to confirm her reading, "you have brought the war to Ben Cat."

Dudley flushed. "Is this for real?"

"Sergeant," cautioned White. "We will hear them out." He looked to Laureen. "What else do the Elders say?"

"Thank you, Tho Moc." She checked her notes. "The village grows beyond its capacity. With this growth comes overcrowding and undernourishment."

"Maybe the village should dig up some of its storage bins," suggested Dudley sourly.

"At ease, Sergeant!" White placed his hand on Dudley's forearm. "Continue, please?"

Thong Thai spoke. Laureen faced Dudley. "Thong Thai asks why you anger?"

"We are not angry," White interposed. "We are concerned. Like the Elders."

"This is good," said Laureen, who explained to Thong Thai. He nodded, then waved for her to continue. She referred to her notes.

"It has been a long time since rockets penetrated our village."

"Mortars," interrupted Dudley. He looked at White. "They know those are mortars, not rockets. Christ, we found 300 of them, right here in their precious village."

"Sergeant, at ease. Continue, ma'am."

"The policemen of Saigon loot our homes, terrorize the population. The Elders feel the Saigon soldiers are but a poor imitation at defense. Thong Thai expresses the village's concern that now that you have brought the war to Ben Cat, you will fail to protect our families, our homes, and our fields without which the village will disappear." Laureen raised her eyes. "These words may seem harsh, but the Elders need answers. The town grows restless."

"At least we agree on something," Dudley mumbled.

"Answers?" White deliberated. "Thong Thai wants answers. Tell Thong Thai, he is not alone. We also have questions. Why did only 100 villagers vote? Where are all the young men? How many more tunnels are under Ben Cat? Where are they? Why do so many villagers still resist us? We'd like to know." White hesitated. "Seems like he wants food, is that right? Seems like he wants more housing? Is that right? Clothing? Doctors? The whole nine yards?"

"Nine yards?" Laureen looked to Hodges.

"The works," said Dudley. "He wants more help. Let me ask you, what... what do we get?"

Laureen faced Dudley. "Ngurai Giu Gin, we relay the concerns of the Elders. Ben Cat has little to give. This you know."

Dudley rose from his chair, placing his hands on the table. He stared down at Thong Thai, who did not divert his gaze from White. "Little to give! To whom? There was plenty underground!"

"Are these statements for Thong Thai?" Laureen asked.

"Yes," confirmed White. "We're interested to hear his answer."

Laureen addressed the Elder.

Dudley turned to Hodges. "You believe this shit? Hodges, I hope you didn't know about this."

"No Sergeant. They must have had a meeting last night. I didn't know."

"You will find out, right Hodges?"

"Yes Sergeant."

Laureen faced Major White. "Major, Thong Thai responds that the soldiers of South Vietnam do not perform in the best interests of the village, in the best interests of their country, or, for that matter, in your best interests. We come to you because the Elders feel these soldiers should be replaced. You are correct that Thong Thai asks for more food, more medicine, materials for housing. Our village is more than four times what it was. We need these supplies to sustain ourselves. Regardless, the Elders fear the impact of our own soldiers. They undo your good work. We regret to say these things."

"Finally, we agree," said Dudley. "I knew it."

"Knew what, Sergeant?" asked White sharply.

"The ARVNs, sir. They're a big part of the problem, a big part."

White stood. "Young lady..."

"Laureen... Laureen Nhu Lam."

"Yes, ma'am, Laureen. Tell Thong Thai, we will see what we can do. I think increased rations are a possibility, and, uh, probably other things." White turned to Hodges. "Hodges here will get back to you in a week or so."

"A week or so?"

"About our next meeting."

"Oh, thank you, Major," she laughed. Thong Thai rose, giving Laureen a tired look of annoyance. "Thompson..."

"Yeah, Thompson," interrupted Dudley.

"Thompson will schedule the meeting in one week."

"Approximately."

"Aye, approximately."

She explained to Thong Thai, who bowed to White, then turned to leave.

"Thank you, Tho Moc," Laureen bowed.

"Thank you, Ngurai Giu Gin," she bowed again.

"Thank you, Thompson. Your teaching goes well, you see."

"Not as well as your learning," Hodges bowed.

119 days

Ben Cat – Command Compound

Outside the compound gate, six boys sat in a circle around Lin, who was playing a shrill tune on her bamboo fife.

"What the hell is that?" asked Balman.

"That, my man, is the call of the wild," laughed Ghost.

"Let's see what's up." Mac walked over to the children, where he waited for Lin to finish.

Lowering her instrument, she beamed up at Mac. "Mac, *annoi, chao*."

"Uh, howdy, Lin. What's up?"

Tranh stood. He bounced his ball twice, prompting the other boys to their feet. Tranh kicked the ball to another boy, who neatly footed the ball and spun kicking it ahead to Phong.

"I got it. A game. You wanna play?" Mac simulated a kicking motion.

Tranh smiled and nodded.

"You got it!" yelled Balman. "C'mon Mac, let's get some of the guys. We'll kick their asses."

"I wouldn't bet on it," said Mac.

"The pygmies against the giants," declared Balman.

"Mop, you ever hear of David and Goliath."

"I always liked Goliath."

"Figures."

Mac, Hodges, Ghost, Balman, Cortes, Perry, and Hosmach joined the children outside the compound.

As the warm-up began, Tranh moved to the third post of the compound. He paced off twenty meters toward the tenth post of the checkpoint wire. There he stopped, marking the spot with a sandal.

"Looks like these boys know what they're doin," laughed Hodges. "We're gonna have a real field."

Tranh resumed his measured stride away from the compound. At 100 meters he placed his other sandal.

"Hey man, you got no shoes," Hoss pointed at Tranh's feet.

"Okay, GI, okay." Tranh smiled turning across the field to complete the line. Arriving at the far corner, he marked the spot with a heel mark, then retrieved three sticks. He placed the first one at the corner, then moved to the center of the line and stuck a stick at each side of the goal.

"Okay, we got us a field!" yelled Balman. "Let's kick some ass."

Lin positioned herself in the goal as the boys removed their sandals.

The game was a spirited contest from the start. Each team quickly gained respect for the other. An hour flew by before Ghost declared a break. The sunburned Americans sought water. The children assembled around Lin.

Tranh stood, then limped to the corner post. Once there, he began to pace, stretching his cramped legs.

LZ – Ben Cat

"Sergeant Dudley, you're going to like this," beamed Major White, walking away from the chopper.

"Good news from Lai Khe?"

"Big changes, Sergeant. Big changes are going to happen."

"Sir, you got my ear."

"First, we are getting more MPs. Our own MPs. A company of our own."

"Sir, that is. Good news. A step. In the right direction."

"Arriving a week from today."

"Very good, sir."

"And, Sergeant," White turned to enjoy his reaction, "we're going to replace the ARVNs."

"Replace the ARVNs!" Dudley grinned. "Now you're talking. Begging the Major's pardon, but how the hell did you pull that off?"

"The storage bin under our noses didn't hurt. The increased population, our recommendations for a shift of personnel, who knows? Apparently someone is listening."

"Very good, sir. May I be the first to shake your hand." Dudley smiled broadly. "Who we getting?"

"Ever hear of the Queen's Cobras?"

"Thais?"

"Very good, Sergeant. Exactly. We're getting four companies of Thai marines."

"And rid of the ARVNs?"

"Yes Sergeant, rid of the ARVNs."

"The Thais, they any good?"

"Your guess is as good as mine. They've been operating in the south, with the 9th Infantry. My understanding is they are not completely trained in the delicacies of jungle warfare."

"Not completely trained?"

"But eager. And aggressive on defense, very aggressive inside the perimeter."

"That fills a big hole."

"We'll be responsible beyond the perimeter."

"Uh-huh, I like that. We gonna get some of our own to help?"

"Everything in time, Sergeant. Remember, little steps?"

"Yes, sir. Little steps."

"We keep one company of Major Thiut's finest to help our guys until December 1. Then we get our own."

"December 1. When do the Thais... "

"November 1. The day after Nguyen Van Thieu is inaugurated. Then we send most of the ARVNs packing. Ironic, huh?"

"You could call it that. We're going to have quite a..."

"Smorgasbord? Right here in Ben Cat, a smorgasbord."

"Sir, we still got to batten down the hatches. Fortify the perimeter. Keep checking the locals. They're over 1700 now."

"And that's where it stops. Our orders are to redirect newcomers."

"Redirect or refuse?"

"Discourage. We will have to explain to the Elders... "

"Our good friend, Thong Thai," interrupted Dudley.

"Right, Thong Thai. We will inform our good friend that our supplies are now limited. We have surpassed our food allotment. Our medical staff is reduced to visiting physicians. Wednesdays only."

"Sounds good, sir," Dudley smiled. "You, sir, have done. Real well."

"Thank you, Sergeant. Thank you."

111 days

Ben Cat – Laureen's home

"*Nhieu qua, emmoi... nhieu qua,*" Laureen writhed beneath him.

"Laureen... Laureen... " he pushed further into her. "It must never end."

"*Con cuong! Oh con cuong*!" Her legs wrapped higher on his back.

"Now, now take this! Please! Take this."

"Thompson, it, it is mine. It is mine. Now! Please! Now!"

He released.

Her legs lowered to his sides. Hodges collapsed beside her, kissing her perspiring cheek.

"It's happening. My God, it's happening."

"It has happened. Each time is... "

"Perfect! More perfect than... "

"Imagined. Ever imagined. The remembrances make me... quiver." She smiled up at him. "It embarrasses me when we are apart, and..."

"It happens when we are apart?"

"Thompson, it burns within me. My mind is not cautious enough."

"Our love is... without caution."

"Yes, Thompson."

"You, you're not going to cry?"

"Possibly, very possibly. My senses are beyond my control. They crave, yes, that is the word, they crave each meeting."

"Laureen, will you come with me to America? It could work."

"But, this is unlikely, is it not?"

"Unlikely, yes." He rolled closer to her. "Not impossible."

Her fingers massaged his chest. "This hair. Oh, this hair is so soft. Somehow it makes me feel safe."

He laughed. "Every part of you feels good."

"You, you make me that way. My self is lost in your arms."

"And I am lost in yours. We must never lose each other."

Tears rose in her eyes. "Thompson, how will we survive? Soon, too soon, you will leave."

"Yes, I will leave."

"Would you ever... "

"Ever what?"

"Meet me?"

"Meet you! Where?"

"In Paris."

"Paris!" he laughed. "Where does that come from? Have I missed something? What would I do? How would we live?"

She moved on top of him, her black eyes demanding his attention. "You know my father was French?"

"Yes."

"He left me some money." She hesitated. "Enough money to leave Vietnam. My father was not without friends. Friends in Saigon and in

France. These friends can make it possible for me to leave."

"Leave? Could you really leave? Why haven't you already? Thank God you haven't, but why... "

"Mai Nin, Tranh Nhu Lam, they have refused. Until now they have been my heart."

His hands began to massage her back. "How could we live in Paris? It must be expensive. I haven't finished school."

"Yes, Paris is expensive. For Ben Cat my income is sufficient, but for Paris there would never be enough. My friends think my language skills, and my appearance will provide me opportunity. Indeed, they are surprisingly confident. Certainly more confident than myself."

"Yes, there are many Vietnamese in Paris."

"Aye, many, although none are known to me. My friends are very wealthy and well known. They assure me an opportunity." Her finger traced his smile. "We could be very happy."

"School. I must finish."

"You must, but... "

"My parents have always paid for my education," he laughed. "As wasted as it has been. I don't know if they'd go for Paris."

"You must save your money. We must do this ourselves. We will help each other, as we do now. Thompson, will we grow apart because of money?"

"No, Laureen, no. But, this is quite a switch. I mean, I've been thinking about how to get you to America, not about Paris, and you've heard my French!" he laughed.

"Your French will improve." She smiled. "It is the language of love, is it not?"

"Whatever language we have is the language of love, Laureen."

"French. Now it will be French. Much more practical than Vietnamese." She lowered her breast to his lips. "Thompson, you must think about this. Most people spend their lives seeking what we have found. We are fortunate. We are meant to be."

His hand soothed her. She closed her eyes, feeling him stir beneath her. She straddled him, guiding him inside.

"Never stop, Thompson. You must never stop loving me. Never stop." Her eyes opened wide.

"Laureen, you are my life, but... "

"It must be unqualified."

She moved over him. He raised his hips to her. Her head tilted back, her hair fell behind her.

"Laureen, Tranh will never go. And Mai Nin... "

"We shall see, Thompson. Mai Nin will not resist us. She has seen unlikely things... " she thrust down on him.

"Laureen, don't stop! Oh God! Where did you learn these things?"

"These things?" she moved him to the side, then up, then down. He reached higher for her. She clutched his hand to her breast. "These things are in books, but it never seemed they would happen... for me. *Sung Qua! Sung Qua annoi*!" The moisture erupted from within her. Her warmth flowed over him. He closed his eyes, fixing the moment.

She held him tightly. It could not end here!

North of Ben Cat

"In shovel... out shovel... up shovel..." Tranh dug alone as Ching Phor rested near the basket.

"Little Ox, you do well."

"Now the gravedigger, no longer the little ox!"

"Gravedigger, you are relentless. You grow strong."

"Do gravediggers grow strong? Or do they tire of the graves they dig?"

"You dig safe holes. Holes to protect Ben Cat."

"Aye, many holes. Will the village relocate to my holes?"

"Your holes will set the village free."

"Will it ever be the same?"

"Eventually. Once the smaller villages are safe, our neighbors will depart. Ben Cat will then be herself."

"Until then, we need the American supplies, do we not?"

"Aye, we need their supplies, all of them."

"Do you think they like each other. They are so different."

"You know them better than myself. What say you?"

"They have little in common. Different looks, different interests, some are serious, some are not. They seem ill-matched."

"Ah, then we are not as different as once thought."

"Our interests are more uniform. Our rice, our village. Many of the Americans will never see each other again. Before our war they did not know each other. The one, Mac, he was a farmer. Ghost, he lived in a large city, like Saigon. He is a person of the street. Dui, he studied, played games. The fat one, Mop, he worked with metal in a mill. The one they call Hoss repaired autos. As soldiers, they are misfits."

"But dangerous, just the same. What does the little ox suppose they think of Ben Cat?"

"That we are poor, that we are senseless. That everything we do is... "

"Antiquated?"

"Aye. The work we do, they do with machines."

"One cannot rush the rice."

"They build houses and roads with their machines."

"Perhaps these machines make them lazy? Could it be? Could they rely too heavily on them? Perhaps their equipment weakens them? They manufacture entertainment, do they not?"

"And we are it. Do you see how they stare at us. Were we to subject them to the same scrutiny, they would resist."

"This is true, but we are subtle."

"This makes seven," Tranh finished the basket.

"Loads?"

"Holes."

"Your seventh? A good number. Will we finish it tonight, gravedigger?"

"Not tonight, Ching Phor. My arms are aching."

"The dead are not interested in the tired muscles of the diggers." She rose to assist him with the basket. "If not the gravedigger, then what are you?"

"Tired."

"Who are you?"

"The fate of Ben Cat." Tranh lifted the yoke.

"Ah, then Ben Cat is indeed in very good hands."

Ben Cat – Laureen's home

Laureen placed the teapot and two cups on Mai Nin's tray.

"Ah, Laureen, another day begins. In what direction will your mind wander this day?"

"Far away, Mai Nin. Today, Paris is my destination."

"Paris, again! What about this city consumes you so?"

"To the porch, Grandmother?"

"Aye."

Laureen carried the tray through the front room. As Mai Nin swung open the door, Laureen stepped back abruptly. "Thompson! Mac! So early! Have you not slept?"

MacKerry and Hodges stood below the first step.

"Good morning, Mai Nin, *chao emmoi*," greeted Hodges.

"Morning Mammasan, mornin Laureen," added Mac.

"*Chao annoi, chao* Mac. What a surprise!"

"Laureen, we're here on business."

Laureen translated for Mai Nin.

"Whose business?" asked Grandmother.

"Major White sends a message," answered Hodges.

"Will you have tea?" asked Laureen, placing the tray on the table beside Mai Nin's chair.

Mac looked to Hodges, who shook his head. "Thank you, no."

Mai Nin moved to her chair, pouring a cup for herself, then another for Laureen. "Granddaughter, did you expect guests so early this morning? You know my cattle. They need my care."

"Grandmother, this is unexpected."

"Where's Tranh?" asked Mac.

Hearing her grandson's name, Mai Nin focussed her attention on the man.

"Tranh cares for Ching Phor. Last night she felt poorly, so Grandmother suggested he spend the night with her," answered Laureen.

"Ask the Americans their business," pressed Mai Nin. "The day is already late."

"Mai Nin asks what business brings you so early."

Laureen moved behind Mai Nin's chair, enjoying her first sip of the tea.

"Major White," Hodges began, "asks that you, Laureen, bring Thong Thai for a meeting. He asks if this morning is possible."

"For the meeting he requested?"

"Yes, Laureen."

"Thong Thai has been anxious."

"The major has been in Lai Khe. Maybe now he has answers."

"Thong Thai will be pleased with answers, although he will think their tardiness diminishes their significance."

"Shall we tell the major it's a go?"

"Thong Thai will attend."

"What does Dui say?" Mai Nin asked.

"Thompson schedules a meeting between Thong Thai and Tho Moc."

"Ah, a meeting. Meetings are good. Good for the Americans, good for the Elders. From meetings comes much peace of mind."

"Mai Nin agrees the meeting is a good idea."

"Meetings make the decision-makers comfortable," Mai Nin continued. "For people of the fields, who do not participate, they are of little interest, but it is good that Tho Moc and Thong Thai feel important."

"Mai Nin, meetings like this encourage change. Without these meetings there can be no progress."

"Laureen, you are very learned, but Ben Cat has survived a long time without these meetings."

"Mai Nin thinks the meeting is a good idea," said Laureen, looking up at Mac and Hodges, "but when the day starts late, she is uncomfortable with all around her."

"Nobody likes interruptions," Mac sympathized. "C'mon Dui, we should let her get on."

"Mac, Laureen, I have something more to say," Hodges began.

"Thompson?"

"Laureen," Hodges moved to the top step and faced Mai Nin. "It's a little out of context, not official, but Mai Nin should know." He looked to Laureen. "When I am done, you may translate. I think Mai Nin will understand most of this."

"Thompson, what? What is it?" Laureen laughed.

Hodges knelt before Mai Nin. The old woman's eyes focused on his.

"Mai Nin, your village has changed me. When I came to your country, to Ben Cat, I was unknown, unknown to myself. I feared the future. You, your family, and your village have taught me much. You have showed me where I must go." He looked up to Laureen. "From weakness, you have given me strength, the strength to go forward, to look ahead. Now, I know my course." He smiled at Laureen. "Do you think she understands?"

"She does."

Mai Nin stared icily at him.

Undeterred, Hodges resumed. "I understand your anxiety about me. We are from different worlds. My world is big, yours is smaller. Now I understand that they are equally important. Before I came, your world was a dot on a map. Our worlds are now the same. Laureen's world. You see, I love her. I will always love her." He looked to Laureen. "Translate?"

"Perhaps it is not time?"

"Laureen, it is time."

Laureen blushed as she translated Hodges' declaration.

"So now, now it is said," Hodges continued. "It is said to Laureen, to you, Mai Nin, and to my friend, Mac, the people who mean the most to me. No longer will I be uneasy with my feelings." Hodges smiled to Laureen, "Translate, please?"

Rigidly, Mai Nin listened.

"Laureen, please tell Mai Nin more. Tell her that my love for you goes beyond Ben Cat, beyond Vietnam. Tell her that I welcome Tranh Nhu Lam, and Mai Nin herself as family. I hope they welcome me, but if they cannot see that I am sincere, perhaps time will win them over. I will not stop trying." His eyes lowered to Mai Nin. "Tell Mai Nin that I will join you and welcome her, and Tranh Nhu Lam, wherever it must be, whenever it must be. Tell her that I sense danger, that she and I must do the things we must to protect the ones we love. Tell her, I understand her dilemma, but that Paris is safe. Frightening, yes. Frightening for her, for me, for Tranh, and even, Laureen, for you, but in Paris, there is life, and in Paris we will have each other. From there we can go forward. We can fulfill ourselves. Please Laureen, tell her."

"Thompson, she understands."

"She understands?"

"*Em yeu anh*, Thompson."

Tears spilled down the cheeks of Mai Nin.

****

Laureen stood behind Thong Thai, facing Major White and Sergeant Dudley. White completed a quick review of the notes neatly arranged before him.

"Laureen," the Major looked up, "please tell Thong Thai we appreciate his attendance. We apologize for the delay in our response, but we feel we have made progress."

Laureen reported, then faced White. "Tho Moc, Ngurai Giu Gin, Thong Thai appreciates this meeting. He understands that progress takes time. He hopes you also understand this."

Dudley smiled as White continued. "Indeed we do. We have come to better understand the pace of Ben Cat. Our actions are predicated, uh, designed to expedite, uh, speed up the progress. Do you understand?"

"Aye," Laureen reported to Thong Thai, then replied, "Thong Thai listens."

"First of all, Sergeant Dudley and I understand how change is received by Ben Cat. However, as Thong Thai has suggested, change is required. Understand?"

"Aye," Laureen nodded.

"The MPs. We will reduce the existing Vietnamese force."

"Reduce the MPs?"

"The Vietnamese police," Dudley interjected.

Laureen relayed. "Thong Thai is surprised."

"They will be replaced by our American police." White looked for a reaction but could discern nothing in the old man's expression. "They will have translators, but our people will be the law."

"The law?"

"Enforce compliance," Dudley explained.

"They will be fair. They will not loot. They will provide security," White added.

"*Bic.* Excuse me, understood."

Laureen informed Thong Thai, who had questions.

"When will they arrive? Where will they reside?"

"Our MPs arrive in three days. They will reside in this compound. In tents. Construction begins tomorrow. They will oversee all police action." White checked his notes.

"Like the gates," Dudley began. "They will police the checkpoints. They will search everything. People will have to travel lighter."

"Our police will patrol the village," White added.

Laureen relayed the information. Thong Thai raised another issue.

"Will you continue to enter our homes?"

"Only if someone is home. Only if there is suspicion."

"And who will determine suspicion?"

Dudley intervened. "All is not well. We enter these homes because the enemy still has a presence. That must be eliminated. Thong Thai knows this."

"Thong Thai reports that it is the wish of the people... that these... " she scanned her dictionary, "intrusions... stop."

"His request is noted. However, it is our responsibility to the citizens of Ben Cat and to ourselves that we continue aggressive police action."

"Do you say that the intrusions will become... more intense?"

"Not more intense... " Dudley hesitated. "More meaningful."

"Thong Thai will report your words to the council. He asks that you understand our people have been.... " again, to the dictionary, "belittled... by the inspections. They will further object to... more Americans."

"Our people will be fair. They will not steal," defended White.

"Is there more?"

"Yes, there is," said Dudley with a smile. "We will remove the ARVNs."

"Remove the soldiers of Saigon?" Laureen repeated incredulously. "How so?"

White looked at Thong Thai and also allowed himself to smile. "Because we both agree, they are not to be trusted. You don't trust them, we don't trust them."

Laureen translated. Thong Thai sat erect.

"Who will defend the village?" was his immediate question.

"The Queen's Cobras."

"The Queen's Cobras?" asked Laureen, puzzled. "Are they also Americans?"

"Unfortunately not, ma'am," said Dudley. "They are volunteers."

"Volunteers?"

"From Thailand," said White.

"Tho Moc! The Queen's Cobras are from Thailand?" Laureen tensed.

"Yes. Thai Marines."

"What does Tho Moc say?" asked Thong Thai.

"Is this... definite?"

"Yes, ma'am. It's the best we could do."

Laureen hesitated. "What is it?" pressed Thong Thai.

Laureen looked to White. "Do our soldiers know of this?"

"Only their major," White said.

"Laureen Nhu Lam! Answer me! What does Tho Moc say?"

"Thong Thai, Tho Moc has another change. The meaning is not clear to me. He explains further. Please indulge my, my lack of communication."

Laureen looked to White. "And what does Major Thiut say?"

"Say, ma'am?"

"Tho Moc, what does Major Thiut say of this strategy?"

"He is angry. He is disappointed that his troops have not performed to acceptable standards."

"But does he know he is to be replaced by... Thais?"

"Yes, ma'am. Yes, he does."

"Then perhaps it would be best for Major Thiut to report this himself to Thong Thai?"

"Well... " White was startled by Laureen's reaction. "That's a problem. The major refused to attend the meeting, but he will be staying on for a while. Along with a few, a select few, of his troops."

"Major Thiut stays? Stays with a few soldiers?"

"Yes, ma'am."

"You want me to relay this?"

Dudley looked up. "Is there a problem?"

Laureen put her books on the table. She placed her hands together and bowed to White, then to Dudley.

"Tho Moc. Ngurai Giu Gin," she said. "You are soldiers. We are humble people. It is now clear, more clear than ever before, how confused we have become. Your efforts are military, not political, not social. This is clear to me. The people of Ben Cat will never accept the soldiers of Thailand, regardless of your intentions."

"Ma'am," White began, "these soldiers have volunteered to protect your country. They are here for you."

"They are outsiders. They will be regarded as worse."

"They're Asian," said Dudley. "They're not as foreign as we are."

"Aye, Ngurai Giu Gin, they are Asian, as we are." Again she bowed. "The people of Ben Cat perceive that for you, for America, there is no gain in our village. Ben Cat will... feel threatened... by these volunteers. The village does not easily forget the Japanese, or the Chinese before them."

"Ma'am, these are volunteers. They will not stay. You are an intelligent woman. You must tell Thong Thai that they are here to defend Ben Cat, not occupy it."

"Yet their occupation is our defense?"

"Yes, ma'am, yes it is."

October 25, 1967

"Major Thiut, we are in agreement. You are ready?" White asked.

"A strange choice of words, Major. In agreement, no: resigned to your decision, yes." Thiut rubbed the back of his neck. "The preparations are made. Two platoons of our most experienced men will move into the compound across the way. They will work with you, running the patrols outside the perimeter. The rest of my men leave in two days. Our compound will be ready for the Thais." He looked up. "You have our cooperation."

"You know, Major, we do not feel good about this. Sergeant Dudley, here, and myself, both think you are a fine soldier. Things just haven't gone as planned. We know you're not happy. If the shoe were on the other foot, I would feel the same, but we have our orders and you have yours." White studied Thiut. "This is not a reflection on you."

"Not a reflection on me? If the shoe were on the other foot, as you say, would it be a reflection on you?"

"Orders are orders."

"I see." Thiut half-smiled. "If it makes you feel better, I do not blame you. The responsibility is mine."

"Not yours, Major," said Dudley. "It's your men, their training, their background. They just don't get it."

"Thank you, Sergeant. I only hope that my regiment's performance has not further jeopardized our outpost. I have my concerns about the Thais. They will be resisted, but you are aware of this. Now, tell me, are you pleased with your MPs?"

"Yes Major," Dudley began. "Yes, we are. You notice the change?"

"There is lighter traffic, but also less food, and I see the Wednesday lines at the medical tent. I sense discouragement."

"We see... containment," responded White.

"Your MP jeeps are very visible. And with a tank at each checkpoint, you make your point well."

"We like the jeeps. Each of the six carries three MPs and a mounted M-60." Dudley sought a reaction. "We got mobility. We got security. We like it."

"But do the MPs find anything?"

Dudley shook his head. "No, Major. Not a thing."

"And how do the household inspections proceed?"

"Nothing new." White answered. "Fifteen random selections a day. That's it. Just enough to keep em honest."

"You know, Major," Dudley began.

"Yes, Sergeant?"

"These Thais, they can fight. They're not much in the bush, but they're trained in perimeter defense. They even got some experience. With the 9th Infantry."

"If that is what you want," Thiut acknowledged.

"What we need, Major," White interposed. "Not what we want. And," White continued, "we need you, Major. We need you and your platoons to keep em honest outside the wire."

"If that's what you need," Thiut offered a rare smile, "that is what you will get."

Dudley added, "Our squad will work the southeast sector, toward Lai Khe."

"We will work wherever needed."

"Two patrols a day, four at night. Sound all right?"

"Ambitious, but prudent. With your air reconnaissance, that seems enough." Thiut rose from the chair. "Major White, Sergeant Dudley, we have had our disagreements. I compliment your initiative. I know you do the best you can. My men have failed. We must wipe the slate clean and begin again. We both want to succeed. I understand the significance of Ben Cat to Saigon."

White glanced over at Dudley, then rose from his chair and extended his hand. "Thank you, Major. Thank you very much."

****

"A parade, Laureen!" Ching Phor exclaimed. "Truly a parade?"

"To celebrate the inauguration."

Mai Nin turned to Tranh. "Tranh Nhu Lam, the festivities of Saigon are renowned. You may never again have an opportunity like this." Mai Nin turned to Laureen. "You will be safe?"

"Yes, Grandmother, we will be safe. We wish you would come."

"Impossible, but with help from my friend," she took Ching Phor's hand, "you two may celebrate while we tend the herd."

Ching Phor laughed. "As usual, eh Grandmother? Youth enjoys while we must work."

"Aye, good friend."

"So you have made up my mind?" said Tranh irritably. "You send me to Saigon even though the city has neither appeal nor interest for me. Must you direct me so?"

"But Tranh," encouraged Laureen, "there is more than the parade. There is soccer."

"Soccer?"

"In the stadium there will be a game," Laureen teased. "We hear that this distraction, as Grandmother calls it, appeals to you."

"Are you sure, Laureen? A real game?"

"A distraction," Mai Nin threw in.

"Yes, Tranh, a real game. We shall go together. The stadium will be filled."

"Ah, a stadium filled with people from Saigon. First a foolish parade, then the crowds, and, best of all, we will stay with your Frenchman and his family. A perfect week." Tranh said derisively.

"But soccer," Laureen smiled.

"Grandson, perhaps you should reserve judgment until you have actually seen the city."

"Now you, Grandmother! What causes this?" He threw up his arms. "And what say you, Ching Phor? Do you agree?"

"Oh, Tranh, you are filled with tricks. After sixty years with your grandmother, do you think we would disagree? Besides Mai Nin is," Ching Phor chuckled, "so much older than myself, she must certainly be much wiser."

Tranh studied Ching Phor. "What are you?"

She smiled. "Old."

"Who are you?"

"Your conscience, Tranh Nhu Lam. Your family comes first."

****

The tunnel outside the cell was quiet. The captain sat at the table. Guyan stood facing him.

"Guyan, you have done all that has been asked."

Guyan bowed. "Thank you, Captain."

"As Ben Cat grows, the problems become larger. The solutions are beyond us."

"Beyond us? But we have made progress, have we not?"

"One step forward, one to the side." The captain hesitated. "Time runs short." He looked to the map spread on the table. "The boy did well."

"Tranh?"

"Aye, the boy did well. Quite ingenious. He dug this ditch... "

"With Phong and his sister, Lin," Guyan added.

"Aye, from the post to the perimeter?"

"Aye, 317 paces, Captain."

"Um, quite a ditch."

"And from the post to the 10th post, 390 paces."

"Tranh did well. Did you commend him?"

"Aye, Major."

"And how is his sister?"

"Laureen?" Guyan wondered.

"His sister."

"She is well."

"And the American?"

"The American is still here. Like the others, his time grows short."

"As does ours." The captain returned to the map. "These red marks are the bunkers?"

"Aye, Major, all the ones we have dug."

The officer counted the marks. "Twenty-two. Very good. You have been busy. Why only three on the south side?"

"Not enough cover, too many patrols. We attempted three others, but the risk outweighed the gain."

"Now you measure risk and gain, Guyan. This is good."

Guyan bowed.

"These bunkers must be fortified. This is your next assignment."

"Fortify the bunkers?"

"With supplies, not armaments. Each bunker will need enough to last ten men for four days." The captain pressed on. "You have a week."

"A week?"

"Aye, seven days to supply the bunkers. You must be careful. Access becomes more difficult. Do you notice?"

"With the American MPs, there are more restrictions."

"Guyan, the ARVNs will soon leave."

"The ARVNs leave? Are you certain?"

"A regiment of Thai pigs is on the way."

"Thais! Here!"

"They will arrive in six or seven days."

"Thais! Can they be so arrogant?"

"Aye, Guyan." The captain rose and paced to the rear of the cell. "They are unacceptable."

Guyan slumped. "Thais in Ben Cat."

"An example must be made. We are forced to respond."

"Captain..."

"This is beyond your control. An example must be made. We will have assistance."

"Assistance? Who?"

"Soldiers, Guyan. Loyal, dedicated, trained soldiers."

"But Captain, could we not spare..."

"An example must be made." The captain slid deeper into the darkness. "Your preparations are in place. Ben Cat is ready to be set free."

Guyan's eyes opened wide. "How many villagers will be lost?"

"There will be losses, heavy losses."

Guyan slumped to a crouch. "So now the expectations of my followers will be fulfilled."

"Your followers have done well." The captain emerged from the dark. "We fight for them."

"First Americans," Guyan hissed, "now Thais! What next?"

****

"What are you studying now, Dui?"

"French, Mac."

"Uh huh, a French book, a workbook, and a tape recorder." Mac shook his head. "You're losin it."

"Maybe." Hodges smiled returning to his book.

"Tell me again, how's this gonna work?"

"C'mon Mac, it's not that hard. Laureen applies for her passport, I extend for ninety days..."

"We extend for ninety days."

"No, Mac. Not you. I extend for ninety days so I can get the early out. I can't go back to some base in the States and play soldier. When I'm done, I want out." Hodges looked up. "Besides, it'll take Laureen time, extra time to get out."

"Uh huh. You stay, I stay. That was the deal."

"No, Mac. The deal was we do our year, we go home..."

"Together."

"Yeah, after a year. Now I gotta stay. I'm waiting for Laureen. You got to go. This is my problem, not yours."

"Dui, a deal's a deal. You stay, I stay. Besides, I want to see how the Thais fit in."

"That will be... interesting," Hodges grinned. "Laureen says we haven't seen the stubbornness of Ben Cat until we see how they greet the Thais."

"They're already pretty stubborn."

"Yeah, well, so are the Thais. If Dudley likes em, they gotta be."

"Uh huh. Anyway, I'm sorta lookin forward to it. We've come this far, I guess I'll go all the way."

Hodges grinned. "Mac, I want you to go home."

"When you do, Dui, when you do."

"Mac, I'm going to Paris."

Mac smiled. "Yeah, well I'm puttin you on the plane."

"Sure, Mac, sure. We'll talk about it."

Checkpoint East – Ben Cat

Laureen stood enshrouded in Mai Nin's work clothes. Her hair was tucked under a wide brimmed, straw hat. Her backpack lay at her feet.

"What is that muck on your face?"

"The soil of Ben Cat, Thompson. Is it flattering?"

"Laureen, you are still beautiful, just a little less aristocratic."

"Thompson, there are no aristocrats on the road to Saigon."

"So, Tranh," Hodges turned to the boy, "your first trip. A parade and a soccer game. This will be fun, eh?"

"Aye, Dui, Saigon." Tranh shrugged.

Hodges placed his hand on Tranh's shoulder. "You take good care of your sister, okay?"

"Aye, Dui."

The brother and sister climbed aboard the overloaded bus.

Laureen maneuvered to a seat in the back. Tranh stood in the aisle half-way back.

"*Bon voyage*, Laureen," said Hodges, who had followed Laureen's movements.

"*A bientôt, mon amour.*"

They exchanged smiles.

The bus lurched off, beginning the seventy-kilometer trip to Saigon.

Sporadically helicopters buzzed overhead.

About twenty minutes from Lai Khe three men clad in black uniforms sprang into the road, halting the bus.

"What is this?" demanded the driver.

"We want to talk," said a man wielding an AK-47.

"Talk or loot?"

The man discharged a round into the roof of the bus.

"Talk, donkey, talk. Unless you have heard enough."

"We have no quarrel with you. Do what you must," the driver submitted, carefully placing his hands atop the steering wheel.

Two more men appeared on the other side of the road.

The leader, brandishing a pistol, climbed into the bus. The standing passengers huddled towards the rear.

"Good day, citizens! We mean you no harm," announced the leader.

"And where are you from?" he asked an elderly man seated behind the driver.

"We are from Ben Cat. Why do you stop us?"

"Old man! Do you see this pistol? Do you see whose hand holds the pistol? My questions are to be answered, not challenged." The leader examined the travelers. "You come from Ben Cat?"

"Aye."

"And you," the leader pointed at a lady across the aisle. "Where do you go?"

"To Saigon."

"To see the new president?"

No answer.

He shoved the pistol into the woman's cheek. "Did you hear me?"

No answer.

"To see the new president!" he demanded.

"What are you? Who are you?" thought Tranh frantically.

"To seek housing... and food."

"To see the new president!" repeated the leader. He cocked the pistol. The passengers fell still.

"Food... housing," whispered the woman.

"Sir," begged the man next to her. "This woman is my wife. We go to Saigon for food and housing. Ben Cat is overcrowded. We are simple people. We have no quarrel with you."

"Ben Cat overcrowded?"

"Aye."

"With Americans and Thais! Monkeys and pigs! Is this why you leave?"

"Aye. We escape."

"What are you? Who are you?"

The leader withdrew the pistol. Her head sank to her chest. He moved to the next seat, where he pushed back the hat on the woman to his right. "Are you all from Ben Cat? Are you old? Ah hah! You are not so old, are you?"

"Aye," murmured the woman.

He grabbed her chin in his hand, turning her face upward. "Aye? What does that mean? Does that mean that you are not so old?"

"Thirty-two," cried the woman.

"Thirty-two? Tell me, why do you have mud on your face?"

What are you? Who are you?"

"To... to keep... to be... cooler... in the sun. To be cooler... in the sun."

"Ah, to keep cool in the sun," he released her chin and studied the man and woman next to her. "We shall have to try that! Mud to keep cool." He turned to a woman along the side of the bus. "And you, old woman. Do you also wear mud?"

Remarkably, the woman laughed. "With me no mud is necessary. Many years in the sun have conditioned my skin."

"Good answer, old lady. You are unafraid of us?"

"You are ill-mannered. You delay us further, and soon another helicopter will pass overhead."

"Perhaps! But we still have enough time to rob you, or better yet, to sample the women of Ben Cat!"

"You disgrace the cause," said the woman, turning away. "We say no more."

"Feisty! The women of Ben Cat are feisty today," the leader announced to his men, who now peered in from the sides of the bus.

"So," the leader continued. "You people of Ben Cat should know that we are not here to rob... or rape... as the pigs and monkeys would have you believe." He turned and found himself face to face with Tranh.

"No, we are here for one reason. Just one little twenty-three-year-old reason." He laughed. "Her name is Laureen Nhu Lam!"

"What are you? Who are you?" Tranh's heart was pounding in his chest.

"We think she is on this bus. Our commander needs education. He has heard that Laureen Nhu Lam is a very accomplished teacher. The professor of Ben Cat! Laureen Nhu Lam, come forward!"

"What are you? Who are you? Who are you? Who are you?"

"Why? Why... do.... you want this woman?" Tranh stuttered.

"For an American lesson, child. Which one is she?"

"Laureen Nhu Lam?"

"That's right."

"The woman who teaches our children? The woman who brings gifts to the village? The woman who feeds the village from her own resources? The woman whose grandmother raises the oxen who churn the soil of our paddies? The friend of Guyan Dan Quan? Do you know this man?" Tranh's composure returned as he thought of Guyan.

"No, boy. Enough!" he said turning to face the rest of the passengers. "Shall we take all the women or just Laureen Nhu Lam? Where are you, teacher?"

"You do not want this woman!" Tranh shouted. "She is all of us. All we should be! All we have been, all we will be again! She is not... " Tranh gripped the man's shoulder, forcing him around, "for you!"

The passengers rose to their feet, surging forward down the aisle. The bus driver revved the engine.

"Helicopter!" someone called.

The men in the road disappeared into the brush.

The leader glared at Tranh. "We, boy, will meet again!"

"Perhaps." The grandson of Mai Nin, the brother of Laureen, and son of Ben Cat bowed.

The leader bolted from the bus, vanishing into the undergrowth along the road.

The bus lurched into gear.

Huddled in her seat, Laureen sobbed uncontrollably.

Tranh walked down the aisle to her. She reached for him, and they embraced.

"Tranh Nhu Lam, what have you done? What have you become? We," she shivered, "are no longer the same."

Tranh held her firmly. "We never were, Laureen. We never were."

Ben Cat

Anticipation electrified the tunnel. Colonel Con Chuong nodded to a lieutenant who closed the door of the cell, sealing off the six officers from the three North Vietnamese companies awaiting their final orders. A map was spread across the table. Colonel Chuong called for order.

"The time is now! Our mission is specific. We take Ben Cat... regardless of losses." The colonel checked his attentive audience. "The assault has seven stages. Captain, your men," he looked over at the Viet Cong officer, "will commence the operation. Two squads will immobilize the tanks and eliminate the checkpoints. Your other squads will extinguish the two MP jeeps patrolling the west sector. Are you prepared?"

The captain snapped to attention. "Colonel, my men are assembled in the old church. We are disguised in ARVN uniforms. We await your command."

"Captain, there is no margin for error. Disabling the tanks is essential."

"Aye, Colonel. We understand. We are ready."

The colonel nodded. "After the success of our Viet Cong brothers, we will launch a rocket attack to neutralize both the ARVN and American compounds in the east sector." He designated them on the map. "That, Major," he looked to his aide, "is the signal for your three companies to exit the tunnel. Two companies will occupy the marketplace." He pointed to the center of Ben Cat.

"Aye, Colonel. Two companies will take and fortify the marketplace."

The colonel drew a line across the map. "The third company will assault the Thai compound here," he marked the compound, "in the west sector. We expect the Thais from the compound to respond. Two companies are resting while the others are stationed along the perimeter."

Again the colonel turned to the Viet Cong captain. "You have done well." He looked to the officers. "Previously the Thai compound was the ARVN area. Through the captain's resourcefulness, it can be detonated." He looked back to the captain. "Correct?"

"Aye, Colonel. We have wired the barracks."

"Good. After the explosives are detonated, the third company will storm the compound. It is to be destroyed. No prisoners! By the time the Thais are eliminated, our two companies in the marketplace will have established a defensible line." The colonel again drew the line dividing Ben Cat.

"Our rockets will hold the American and ARVN compounds at bay. We have twelve companies in the jungle, positioned to assault the southwest perimeter." The Colonel looked over at his aide. "Major, when the assault begins, you will dispatch two platoons from the marketplace. They will soften the bunkers from behind. Then we shall see how the pigs fight!"

"Yes, Colonel," barked the major. "My men are eager."

"Once inside the perimeter, we dispose of all resistance." The colonel checked each officer. "Questions?"

The colonel's aide studied the map. "What should we expect from Lai Khe?"

"Lai Khe will respond, but not with the usual force. We have unsuspected assistance." The colonel again surveyed his officers. "Each of our assault forces relies on the others. No error! No retreat!"

He snapped to attention. "To the end!"

****

While the women prepared for bed, Tranh examined Laureen's elaborate model of the Lai Khe rubber plantation. He picked up a toy soldier that was painted to look like a GI. "Dui" he laughed to himself. "Ah, Laureen, how you dream!"

Tranh next examined a French soldier decorated in full dress uniform. "This a soldier? Very colorful, a perfect target. Ha!" Returning the soldiers to the landscape, he picked up a figure in a white lab coat. "So this is your father? Mother's first husband?" He set the figure down. Reaching over a miniature ox, Tranh's arm brushed the scientist, knocking him to the floor, where the figure broke into several pieces.

Tranh gasped, then knelt to collect the pieces. The head had rolled under the model. Tranh lay on the floor and slid underneath. A paper was attached to the underside of the model. Carefully he detached the sheet and pushed himself out from beneath the model. Tranh could see the paper contained a list of numbered entries and a series of coordinates. The language was French, but the numbers spoke for themselves. "A map? A map of Lai Khe!"

Folding the paper, he placed it carefully in his pocket and then began to prepare his explanation for Laureen and Alicia.

****

"Hey, honky," the Ghost materialized.

"Jesus, Ghost! You scared the shit out of me!"

"Uh huh. We got company, my man. For sure."

"For sure?"

"Traffic movin north."

"Shit. How much?"

"Hard to tell. At least a platoon."

"For real? You sure, Ghost?"

"They didn't cover their path, man. Broken branches, worn ground. I'm tellin ya, we got company, and they don't give a shit that we know."

"I gotta transmit." Hodges turned to Parker. "We clear?"

"Should be."

"Ghost, spread the word. Parker, crank it up."

"You sure?" Parker hesitated. "I don't like it."

"Give me the fuckin thing."

Parker handed the transmitter to Hodges, who peered down the hillside to the lanterns of Ben Cat, in the valley below. The black of night was descending around them. "Those bright city lights." He clicked the transmitter. "Matchmaker, this is Long Ball, over."

"Long Ball, this is Matchmaka, ova."

"Matchmaker, we got company, over."

"Company?"

"Moving north."

"Movin north? How many?"

"Estimate platoon."

"Visual?"

"Negative."

"Your location?"

"Pete's Post."

"Roga, Pete's Post. Stay put. The fly boys'll check it out. Ova."

"Roger, out." Hodges turned to Parker. "I guess we done good."

****

"What do you think, Sergeant?" White asked.

"Sir. A no-braina. If they got traffic, we got traffic. We make the call."

"Right, Sergeant." White turned to his radioman, "Carr, get Lai Khe."

Carr cleared the transmitter and handed White the microphone.

"Bulldog Six, this is Matchmaker, over."

"Uh... Matchmaker... this... is... uh.... Bulldog Six, over."

"We got traffic in the east. Moving south to north. Need recon... Foxtrot one six to Juliet fiver-niner. Do you copy?"

"Copy that, Matchmaker. We are on the way, over."

"That okay with you, Major?" White asked Thiut.

"Yes, Major," the Vietnamese replied. "It is probably nothing, but..."

"Sir," Dudley interrupted, "mind if I take a ride? Around the perimeter?"

"Yes, Sergeant." White agreed. "Wake em up."

"Yes, sir." Dudley fastened his pistol, secured his helmet, gathered his M-16, then departed briskly.

"Jared!" White startled the private who was dozing in the corner. "Spread the word, we are yellow alert. I want our boys on their toes."

"Yellow alert. Yes, sir." Jared exited the bunker and headed for the MP tent.

"Major? Should we blow the horn?" Corporal Carr motioned to the siren.

"What do you think, Major?" White asked Thiut.

"The pilots will tell us."

"It's probably nothing," reflected White.

"Precisely," responded Thiut.

****

As the Viet Cong left the old Catholic church, their captain patted each squad member on the shoulder. The first group headed directly toward the east checkpoint, the second toward the southwest sector, the site of nightly MP patrols. The third component moved north, while the final squad took up a position close to the west checkpoint. The captain took a deep breath, closed the door of the church, and slipped into a nearby dwelling where Guyan and Phong awaited him.

****

"Matchmaker, this is Bulldog Four, over."

"Bulldog Four, this is Matchmaker, over."

"Uh... Matchmaker... we got nothing. I say again. We got nothing."

"Copy that. Try some live bursts, over."

"Will do. Where you want it? Over."

"East perimeter. From the checkpoint north."

"Roger that."

Two gunships floated across the east perimeter. Red tracers sank into the paddies and surrounding treeline. For thirty minutes Bulldog probed the terrain, firing hundreds of rounds.

"Matchmaker, this is Bulldog Four, over."

"Go Four."

"Nada... We'll be heading home."

"Roger. Thanks anyway, over."

"No problem, Matchmaker. See you tomorrow. Out."

NVR troops squirmed toward the southwest perimeter.

****

At 2230 hours, a red flare rose above the south paddy.

An ARVN staggered in front of the MP jeep.

"Hey asshole!" yelled the driver, halting the vehicle. "What the fuck!" Four AK-47s rang through the air. The three MPs fell from the jeep. Two of the Viet Cong hoisted the M-60 from the jeep mount and scurried toward the southwest corner of the village.

At the east checkpoint the MP guards tried to pinpoint the origin of the shots. Semi-automatic weapons fired into the bunker. A Viet Cong rocket launcher pierced the tank positioned alongside the bunker.

"The horn!" White barked to Carr, who started for the alarm switch.

"Stop!" Thiut's pistol was squarely aimed at Carr. "Major White. Your ignorance is only surpassed by your arrogance!"

"Major!" White was baffled. "This is not the time..."

"Do you understand a patriot's greatest loss?"

"Major!"

"Defeat? Do you think it defeat?"

"Major!"

"Betrayal? Do you think it betrayal?"

"No, Major... neither, we have to..."

"Do you think it dishonor?"

"Corporal! Blow the horn!" commanded White, exasperated.

Thiut fired into the alarm switch. "Halt! I ask again!" Thiut faced White. "The patriot's greatest loss?"

"Major!" White protested desperately.

Thiut pointed at the radio. "You dishonor my country! You replace me with Thais!" He emptied two chambers into the radio. "You, Major, will bear the defeat! The loss is yours! Take it to your grave!" He fired two rounds into White's chest. White jerked forwards, then toppled back, sinking to the floor.

Carr lunged across the table. Thiut backed away, out of reach.

"Corporal! Stand up! You are a soldier!"

Carr rose.

"Tell your soldiers... they have been betrayed, betrayed by the arrogance of their leaders! Tell them this!"

"Fuck you!"

"Ah ha! The cornered patriot speaks." Thiut pressed the muzzle of his pistol against his temple. He smiled curiously at Carr, then pulled the trigger. His head exploded.

"Jesus fucking Christ!" Carr sank to the floor landing in a pool of White's blood.

"We're fucked!"

****

A rocket streaked into the tank at checkpoint west. Another tore into the bunker. Wielding bayonets, six Viet Cong charged through the entry, bayoneting the three MPs inside.

A patrolling jeep sped toward the marketplace, its M-60 swivelled to the left.

A form darted from between two huts. The M-60 opened fire.

A grenade landed in front of the jeep.

"Go! Go! Go!" yelled the co-pilot. The jeep screeched ahead. The machine gun shredded the grenadier. The co-pilot fired his M-16. A dark form slumped to the ground.

Halfway up the hill a figure stood poised with a rocket launcher. The jeep driver swerved left, crashing into a hut. Four Viet Cong stormed the stunned detail.

****

A second flare went up over the south paddy.

"What the fuck?" cursed Hodges. "What's going on down there?" He looked at Parker. "Is the radio on?"

"Yeah, it's on. Nada."

"Give me the mike. Matchmaker, this is Long Ball... Over."

"What gives?" Ghost slid beside them.

"Who knows? Nobody's answering. It looks bad," said Hodges turning back to the radio. "Matchmaker, this is Long Ball. Do you copy?"

The three stared at the silent receiver.

"Call Lai Khe, call Bulldog," said Ghost.

"Bulldog Six, this is Long Ball, over."

"Long Ball, this is Six, over."

"Trouble in River City. We're at Pete's Post."

"Copy that Long Ball. We were just there. No activity. Over."

"We now have bad guys in the fort. Automatic weapons, rockets. Something's going down."

"You sure, Long Ball? We got nothing from Matchmaker, over."

"Matchmaker's on the hot seat! Send the posse, goddamit! The wire's dead. I say again, the wire's dead."

"Roger that. The posse's on the way. Your call! Hold on to your hats! Out."

"What the fuck!" exclaimed Hodges. "Dudley!" He turned to Ghost. "We gotta go back! Dudley's there!"

"We move, we're done," said Ghost grimly. "We wait."

****

Rockets tore into the east sector, scoring hits within the ARVN and American compounds and pinning down the perimeter. Dudley halted the jeep and dove into a bunker, startling three Thais.

"They're comin!" he shouted, shaking his clenched fist. "Be tough!" The Thais nodded. "Where the hell are the fucking choppers? Where's the artillery? What's the major doing?"

The Thais shrugged.

"I'm goin back."

****

In the Thai compound the Queen's Cobras fumbled for their gear.

Guyan and Phong cautiously stood guard sixty meters away, as the Viet Cong captain took an exaggerated breath and detonated the Thai compound.

Flaming torsos shrieked through the darkness.

A whistle blew, and screaming NVR troops surged through the compound gate. Automatic weapon fire blew apart the blazing human torches.

****

"Bulldog Six, this is Four." Finally Hodges' receiver came alive.

"Six, here. Go."

"We got bad guys inside the west wire! Rockets landing in the east. We're working the northeast paddies. Need big guns on rocket sites, over."

"Bulldog Four, Roger that. Hang in there. Our guys are Priority One."

"Roger, Six. Send help!"

"Long Ball, this is Bulldog Six. Over."

"Long Ball, here," Hodges answered.

"Got anything?"

"Rocket flashes south." Hodges stared at his map. "Alpha three-six, Bravo, fiver-niner, Bravo niner-seven, Bravo fiver-fiver, over."

"Roger, coming at you."

****

Back in his jeep, Dudley accelerated through the wire at the north end of the command compound. A rocket landed near the gate. He jumped to the ground, running toward the MPs.

One of the tents had taken a direct hit.

"To the bunker! To the bunker!" he shouted. Twenty-three men sprinted toward him.

Dudley jumped into the bunker, coming face to face with the corpses of White and Thiut. Carr slammed his fist against the radio.

"What the fuck!" yelled Dudley.

"Thiut!" Carr whispered. "He shot the major! The radio. The horn. He killed himself! We got nothin. We're fucked."

"Not yet, we ain't! Get that thing working."

"Sergeant, I can't. It's wasted!"

"It ain't over! Til it's over. You got that!" Dudley turned to his MP unit. "They're gonna come! We hold! For the choppers."

He traced out a new perimeter. "Spread the claymores! Get your heads outta your asses. They're comin. We hold the line." He summoned an MP. "Corporal! I want six sandbag bunkers. Around this position. Three men. Each bunker. You got it?"

"Got it!" The corporal turned to the men around him. "Let's go! Set it up!"

"You men," Dudley designated a detail, "take the M-60." He pointed to the roof of the bunker. "Set your ropes! Get your bearings. Don't melt the fucker! We hold for the choppers."

****

Lai Khe artillery blasted the rocket sites outside the south perimeter.

"Bulldog Six, this is Four. Over."

"Go!"

"We're in deep weeds! I count two zero our guys bagging the bunker. The Thai compound is fini! Bad guys clustering inside the west wire. Something's happenin in the middle of town. Need help! We're blowing two birds! Over!"

"Hell yes! Take em out!"

"Will do."

Bulldog Four sped toward the marketplace. "One away! Two away!" Two rockets whistled into the town. The first tore into a North

Vietnamese squad. Bodies hurtled upwards. The second buried three huts. Fires burst out in the center of the village.

Bulldog Three crossed from the south, spraying rounds into the marketplace.

The North Vietnamese returned rifle fire. The chopper sped beyond the perimeter, then circled for a return.

"One away!" Bulldog Two leveled an NVR squad as it left the smoldering remains of the Thai compound. Two's gunners fired into another squad trapped along the wire.

****

A third flare rose above the south paddy.

From the north three rockets struck the ARVN compound near the East checkpoint. Three more landed beyond the American compound.

"Six, this is Long Ball," called Hodges urgently. "Mark, Lima three-six, Lima four-six, Lima seven-niner. Pour it on!"

"Roger that!"

Lai Khe artillery blasted the north jungle.

From the southwest mortars rained onto the Thai perimeter.

A whistle catapulted twelve North Vietnamese companies to their feet. Screaming, they charged the Thais in the perimeter bunkers.

The Queen's Cobras opened fire, but the NVR kept coming.

The Thais discharged their claymores, halting the wave.

Bulldog Four rained bullets onto the swirling ground.

"Three, get over here! It's a fucking wave!"

Bulldog Three sped from the east. An NVR rocket slammed into the chopper. Bulldog Three crashed into the paddy.

"Three is down!" called Four.

Hodges clicked in. "Six, Long Ball, here. Southwest perimeter. They're on the wire. Bring it!"

"Bulldogs, this is Six. Clear the zone. Artillery coming at you. Go to our guys! Northeast sector! Move out!"

The four helicopters swooped back toward the northeast sector.

The Thais on the southwest perimeter fired on.

Two platoons of North Vietnamese emerged from the village, lunging into the rear flank of the bunkers. The wave rose again.

Lai Khe artillery exploded in the southwest paddies.

"Six, this is Four. You're on em! Keep it comin!"

Their options eliminated, the North Vietnamese rushed forward, overrunning the Thai bunkers.

"Shit! They're in! Six, this is Four. They're in! Southwest corner!"

The artillery zeroed in on the village.

"Four, this is Six. You cover our guys. Blue Moon's got cluster bombs. Is closing fast! Long Ball! This is your call!"

"My call!" Hodges balked. When would the bombs get here? Dudley! My call!

"Your call, Long Ball! Make the mark!"

Ghost shook Hodges. "The market, man! The market." He pointed at the map. "Do it!"

"But the people!"

"Yeah."

Bulldog Two streaked above the market. Rounds smashed into the NVR.

"Four, this is Six."

"Go!"

"Condition ARVN compound?"

"Dug in. They're dug in! Our guys can't get to em."

"Roger! Our guys are yours."

From beyond the east perimeter, reinforcements Bulldog Seven, Bulldog Eight, and Bulldog Nine charged in. Eight released two rockets.

From the north NVR rockets blitzed the American and ARVN compounds, burying the main ARVN bunker.

The NVR charged the ARVN compound as rockets pulverized the defenders.

A North Vietnamese dove onto the wire, detonating the satchel strapped to his body. The wire collapsed, and the NVR streamed across.

Bulldog Seven rushed to defend. A burst from an AK-47 tore into the rotor blade. Seven crashed inside the compound gate.

The ARVN compound fell.

Two rockets landed inside the command compound. Dudley's force wavered.

The choppers rallied above their remaining compatriots. Bulldog Four concentrated on the main NVR force as it rolled toward its last obstacle. A salvo from Bulldog Eight leveled the first surge. Bulldog Nine cleared the huts west of the Command Compound.

Dudley moved between bunkers.

"Hang tough! Hang tough! They're fightin. For us! When you see the fuckers! When they're in the wire! Blow the mines! Use your grenades! Then. Ya fight! Don't hold nothin back!"

Grenadiers fired into the encampment. A sand bunker took a direct hit.

Four North Vietnamese feverishly cut away at the compound wire. The M-60 opened fire, tearing them to shreds.

Two rockets tore into the compound just as the west wire toppled over.

"Long Ball, this is Blue Moon. Over." The bombs had arrived.

"Go Blue Moon."

"Your call!"

My call! My call? Jesus Christ! The people! Dudley! White! Mai Nin! Ching Phor! "The market, goddamit!" Jesus!

"Coming in."

The ground rocked. Cluster bombs savagely splintered Ben Cat.

Life screamed. Everything changed.

The North Vietnamese troops regrouped, charging over their fallen comrades and through the west wire.

"Blow em! Blow em!" shrieked Dudley. The Americans triggered their claymores. The M-60 shattered the onrushing NVR just before a rocket tore into the compound roof, flinging bodies and gun parts in all directions.

"Fuck em! Fuck em!"

A wave of NVR swelled from north of the market.

Bulldog Six fired two rockets. The wave subsided.

Bulldog Four cleared the gate.

"The gate!" Dudley sprang out of the bunker and charged toward the gate. "Go! Go! Go!" Six MPs followed.

A rocket demolished the bunker.

The wave rose again.

A grenade wiped out two men behind Dudley, who reached the gate and turned to cover the men behind. Four MPs ran past the sergeant toward the checkpoint, the only conceivable escape route.

Dudley fired a burst, then pivoted toward the checkpoint. Two NVR tackled him. A knife cut across his throat.

"Long Ball, this is Blue Moon. Coming back!"

"Our compound! Hit the compound!" Hodges slumped to the ground.

As Blue Moon zeroed in, the North Vietnamese stormed north, seeking escape. Cluster bombs exploded the compound. The eastern sector burst into flames.

The battle ended.

Countless civilians were incinerated.

Eight Viet Cong were killed.

One hundred ninety-four NVR lay dead.

Two hundred Thai marines perished, though a few escaped into the jungle.

The ARVN force was annihilated.

No Americans survived.

****

Fires leveled Ben Cat. The surviving villagers cowered in their underground bunkers.

The Viet Cong captain stood with the remnants of his band under the temple. "We are not finished. We will take our dead, deliver our message."

****

Hodges had made the call. He could not look, could not face it. Death covered the village.

Ghost pressed his fingers into his forehead.

"I wanna be... an Airborne Ranger... I wanna live... through hell and danger..."

Beyond the East Perimeter – Ben Cat

Hodges would have to live with the call.

"Long Ball... Bulldog Six, over."

"This is Long Ball."

"Long Ball. Connect Niner Tank Corp five k south of BC. Rte 13. O700. Do you copy?"

"Roger, out."

Hodges looked at Ghost. "So we're off."

Ghost led them down the hill.

One step at a time. Branch! Duck! Hustle!

What am I?

Dudley! We failed you.

Laureen! What have I done?

We lost. We lost!

Pay attention. I'm losing it!

A man. Am I... a man?

The mist! Can't see shit!

It's over.

Hammered! We got hammered!

What happened!

We should have been there! The past was dismal. The future bleak.

I... failed!

Highway 13

At 0700 hours the squad emerged from the jungle to join the first element of the 9th Tank Corp heading back to Ben Cat.

"Man O War" was emblazoned across the back of the fifth tank. MacKerry, Hodges, and Ghost sat on the rear deck. The rumbling motors made conversation impossible. Each man was trapped in his own reflection.

At 0800, Man O War reached the clearing before the village. The tank turned along the northeast perimeter. Pulling to a halt, the tank's cannon swiveled toward Ben Cat. The other tanks poised for the assault.

Behind them the jungle still smoldered from the early morning napalm attack.

Hodges raised his binoculars. "The bunker... is TKOd. Bodies everywhere."

"Jesus Christ!" Ghost exclaimed, gesturing at the demolished checkpoint. "I'll be damned. It's her! And four cows! She's comin out!"

"She's alive!" gasped Hodges.

Slowly driving four oxen in front of her, Mai Nin walked down the road. GIs rushed at her. She rebuffed them with her walking stick and continued ahead.

"Well," Mac sighed, relieved. "There's survivors."

"But it don't look good," Ghost packed his binoculars away.

Four companies of Black Horses dropped from their helicopters and scrambled behind the tanks lining the perimeter. The engines cranked up and the tanks moved into Ben Cat.

"A graveyard!" Mac declared.

"They're everywhere."

Hodges, Mac, and Ghost headed for the bunker in the command compound.

"No way!" Ghost pulled the dogtags from three American corpses. He stepped back. "No chance."

Hodges pulled up sharply at the edge of the devastated bunker. Mac grabbed his arm, helping him down into the rubble.

Feverishly Hodges cast the debris aside.

"Man, they're not here," Ghost announced.

"They got out," repeated Mac.

"They gotta be here..." Hodges leaned against two fallen support beams.

"At ease, soldier!" barked a Black Horse captain. "Out of the hole!"

"Sir! They gotta be here."

"Sergeant, there's no one home."

"Get him out of there." The captain ordered. "We're clearing this shithole before the tanks do their thing."

"We're... we're gonna level it?" stammered Hodges.

"You bet your sweet ass we're gonna level it. We don't leave it for Charley!"

"But..."

"No buts, Sergeant. Out of the hole! Follow the tanks. There are people, living people, that need help. Get yourself together. Let's go!"

Ghost extended his hand, helping Hodges from the pit. They walked across the compound. "Don't look at em, man. Don't look."

"I don't wanna see no more faces," said Mac.

They walked back behind Man O War, which was positioned in the road leading to the center of town. The hatch was open. The crew were staring down the street.

"Have a look..." the tank driver pointed.

Ghost led them around the tank.

"Jesus Christ!" Hodges buckled against the side of the tank.

"No!" Mac protested.

Six crosses were planted across the road.

White's bloody torso had been staked to the center post. To his right was Dudley. His head had been set in the cavity where his stomach had been. Thiut's faceless, uniformed figure hung beside Dudley. To the other side of White, the naked form of Thong Thai, his eyes scorched in their sockets, confronted them. To the Elder's left were two officers of the Queen's Cobras. Their heads lay at their bootless feet.

Hodges vomited over the treads of the tank. Ghost and Mac squatted on either side of him, staring into the sky.

The Black Horses hurried by them, into the village.

****

By early afternoon the helicopters completed the evacuation of the wounded civilians. The American body bags were stacked up in rows, awaiting shipment back to Lai Khe.

Work details unceremoniously sorted out the remaining dead.

At 1630, 326 civilians were herded into a convoy of transport trucks. Many villagers were still unaccounted for.

Hodges' squad huddled beneath the canvas of a small truck near the end of the line. Mary Jane hung heavy in the air.

Balman sat on the floor, his feet hanging over the tail. His M-60 lay across his lap. He flicked away the stub of his joint.

Hodges sat above him, and Ghost was across from Hodges.

Behind them the 9th Corps methodically set about leveling the village.

Dazed, exhausted civilians witnessed the destruction of their world.

Helicopters patrolled above the convoy.

"Got quite a buzz," Balman announced to Ghost.

"Tell me about it," mumbled Ghost. "Some fucking day."

"Yeah. Ya don't think they'd hit us, do ya?"

"With this air power?" Hosmach answered. "No way."

"Feels tense though, don't it?"

"We're tired, man, that's all," said Mac. "We're beat."

"Yeah," Balman agreed. "Tired and beat. We got our asses kicked."

"Shut up, you asshole! Shut the fuck up!" snapped Hodges

"Fuck you, Hodges!"

The men fell quiet. The truck backfired as it inched ahead.

"Incoming!" Balman lunged from the rear of the truck, diving alongside the road.

"Balman!" Ghost yelled. "That's a backfire!"

Balman lay in the dirt, sighting into the hillside.

"Fuck you! Get outta the truck! That's incoming!"

"Get back in here!" Hodges commanded.

"Why don't ya call Blue Moon, Dui!" Balman hollered.

The driver revved his engine again, causing another backfire.

Balman fired into the hillside. An ox toppled over.

Ghost and Hodges sprang from the truck.

"What the fuck are you doing," screamed Hodges.

"Fuck you!" Balman fired again.

"Enough., you asshole!" Hodges put his foot on Balman's back.

MacKerry and Hosmach jumped from the truck. "C'mon, Mop," Hoss cajoled. "Let's go home."

"Someone shot at us!" declared Balman.

Mai Nin was charging down the hill, angrily waving her walking stick.

Balman opened fire again.

"Mai Nin!" Hodges slammed the butt of his rifle across Balman's head, then sprinted up the hill.

Kneeling alongside the old woman, he cradled her lifeless body.

Saigon

Tranh burst across the patio, kicking his ball onto the broad lawn. Madame Chocart smiled up at Laureen. "The game was a success, dear?"

"A great success, Madame. Thank you." Laureen sat down next to her. "Never has he seemed so excited. It was exhilarating to see." She hesitated. "Tranh still surprises me so."

"It's his age, don't you think? Everything is new. As much as he surprises you, I imagine he surprises himself even more." Madame studied Laureen. "So, do you think he will become a regular guest?"

"Possibly. Undoubtedly new visions dance within him."

"And with each new experience, a new interest?"

"And with each interest, more courage. He was without reservation. His enthusiasm was unmistakable and somewhat... embarrassing," Laureen laughed.

"Embarrassing?"

"He cheered for the opposition. We were sitting with fans rooting for the Saigon team. Tranh, of course, supported Long Anh."

"I see." Madame chuckled. "And who won?"

"Saigon, of course. They seemed more practiced, but the game was good."

"He does not seem disappointed."

"No," agreed Laureen happily. "He was in awe of the game, the skill of the players."

Monsieur Chocart closed the screened door behind them. He walked to Laureen and placed his hands on her shoulders. "Child, I have bad news."

"What is it?" Madame asked.

"There is news from the Highlands. From Ben Cat."

"From the village?" Laureen gasped. "Saigon knows we exist?"

"Ben Cat has been... overrun."

"Mai Nin! Thompson!"

Hearing Laureen's cry, Tranh stopped. "Laureen, what is it?"

"Tranh, the village! The village has been overrun."

Headquarters 3rd Brigade – Lai Khe

"At ease, Sergeant." First Sergeant John Rogers closed the file on his desk and leaned back in his chair. Hodges stood before him. "You get some sleep?"

"A little, Top Sergeant. Thank you."

"Nice bandanna."

"My lucky scarf... from Ben Cat."

"Hodges, there's nothing lucky about Ben Cat, is there?"

"No, First Sergeant." Hodges slouched.

"You know where you are?"

"Lai Khe," answered Hodges.

"That's right, Sergeant. Lai Khe. Headquarters of the 3rd Brigade, First Infantry Division. Here, we, uh, do things different than you're used to. You understand?"

"Top, I understand where we are."

"But do you understand that here, we, uh, do things by the book. Standard Operating Procedure. No freelancing. By the book."

"Yes, Sergeant."

"Now what do you have? Seventy-five days left?"

"A little more," Hodges shrugged.

"How many more?"

"Seventy-eight."

"Seventy-eight days. Not bad. You're almost home." Rogers leaned forward. "This is your... personnel file."

"Yes, Sergeant?"

"I don't know what went on out there, you understand?"

"Yes, Sergeant."

"I mean we know about Ben Cat. We know about White and Dudley, the MPs, and the rest. We can't do anything about them, Hodges. But it, uh, seems like we got a problem, right here, doesn't it?"

"Yes, Sergeant."

"One of your fellow GIs has lodged a complaint."

"That figures," Hodges shrugged again.

"That figures? Uh, let me tell you, Sergeant, we, uh, got enough going on around here without having, uh, morale problems. You understand."

"Yes, Sergeant."

"And we, uh, don't have time for this kind of bullshit."

"Yes, Sergeant."

"Now this thing with you and, uh, Corporal Balman. Near as I can tell, you trained together. You been together, uh, seventeen months?"

"Seventeen months, yes Sergeant."

"And you both want the same thing. To go home."

"Yes."

"So what's the problem?"

"The problem, Sergeant?"

"I don't want a question, Hodges. I want answers. Balman says there's a, uh, problem. In fact, Balman says you're responsible for the, uh, stitches in his head."

"Yes, Sergeant."

"Let me give it to you straight, Hodges. You are to, uh, patch this up. Christ seventy-eight days. Get over it."

Hodges shifted. "First Sergeant, Balman's... an asshole, maybe worse."

"Not interested, Hodges. Fix it."

"I don't think so."

"Don't think so!" Rogers bellowed. "You better think so. Now, you got something to say, say it! And, it better be good. I'm losin patience, here."

"First Sergeant. He... he... killed her."

"For Christ sake, Hodges! This is war. We regard Balman's action as an, uh, act of war."

"An act of war? I see it as something else."

"I do not want to hear this." Rogers flushed. "An act of war, you got it?"

"No, Sergeant. I don't get it."

"Hodges, fix it, or there will be discipline."

"Discipline?"

"That's right."

"Discipline me?"

"You can bet on it, soldier."

"First Sergeant, no disrespect, but that was no act of war. It was... unpardonable."

"Hodges, that's not for you to say. Over here shit happens every day. You know that."

"Unforgivable... Top."

"Hodges! You leave me no choice. I'm pulling the stripe. Consider yourself a corporal. You got that?"

"Yes, First Sergeant."

"You're not pulling rank on that dumb bastard. You and Balman are gonna be together right to the end of your tours. I, uh, do not want to hear about this again, that clear?"

"I understand you do not want to hear about this again. Dismissed?"

"Dismissed! Jesus Christ! Listen Hodges. To me you are just another soldier. Worse yet. A wiseass. Now you get yourself cleaned up. You look like shit. The next time I see you, you better have clean fatigues, polished boots, a haircut. And, you are out of uniform. Lose the scarf!"

Checkpoint South – Lai Khe

"She come?" asked Hodges as he approached MacKerry.

"Not yet," Mac placed a hand on Hodges's shoulder. "She'll be here."

"Yeah, I know."

"How'd you make out?"

"I'm dirty," Hodges smiled. "Out of line... out of order."

"Sounds bad," Mac grinned.

"And," Hodges patted Mac, "we're the same rank." He looked down the road leading out of Lai Khe. "What's the action?"

"Lotsa traffic. All goin south." Mac pointed toward the MPs. "These guys don't mess around. I mean to say, they check everything. That guy, the spit-and-polish guy, his name's Dave Carney. From Dayton, Ohio, and real proud of it. He's in charge and tough, real tough."

Hodges studied the man. "Yeah? What's he do?"

"Screams at em, mostly. Empties everything. They don't understand him. The more they talk, the louder he gets." Mac laughed. "He wears em down. He's only got forty-three days."

"Lucky him. Let's have a talk." Hodges and MacKerry approached the MP.

"Morning, Sergeant. Here's the friend I was tellin you bout," said Mac.

Carney took in Hodges' appearance at a glance. "Morning, Sergeant," he said neutrally.

"Uh, Corporal, really."

"Looks like three stripes to me."

Hodges laughed. "Just lost one this very morning."

"Too bad. You look like shit."

"I'm gonna fix that real soon."

"Good for you." Carney seemed to relax. "You know we got all the comforts of home here in Lai Khe. Spent my whole tour here."

"Pretty good duty, huh?" Mac asked.

"It has its benefits," smiled Carney. "The civilians treat me like a god."

"Sounds good for you," said Hodges.

"Yeah, well, what brings you here?" asked Carney.

"We're looking for someone."

"They all pass through here, my man. Heading south these days. Not much comin our way, except some of the hookers. They sprint down to Saigon, sock away a little do-re-me, buy some clothes, ya know? They all come back." Carney shrugged. "Who ya looking for?"

"A girl from Ben Cat."

"Nobody from Ben Cat the last few days."

"She's coming from Saigon."

"Yeah? What makes this girl so special?"

"She's a friend of mine," Hodges answered.

"How good a friend?" Carney's eyebrows raised.

"A very good friend. She needs help."

"Yeah?"

"Her grandmother was killed at Ben Cat. You know about Ben Cat?"

"We all know about Ben Cat. You guys were there?"

"Nine months."

"Ow! Pretty uncivilized."

"It got that way."

"How'd you get out? I thought there were no..."

"In the bush," Hodges flushed. "We were in the bush."

"What a break!"

"We were lucky," said Mac flatly.

"Well, you wanna wait?"

"If we could."

"When's she coming?"

"Don't know how or when."

"Okay. But while you're here, let me know if you see anything weird. I mean sometimes I miss things. Not too often, but every now and then I feel like they slip something by." Carney smiled. "Forty-three days, ya know?"

"Yea. Congratulations, Sergeant. And thanks. Soon you'll be home watching the Flyers. Isn't that what they are, the Dayton Flyers?"

"The one and only." Carney watched the last family he'd checked as they passed through the gate. "The one and only... the Dayton Flyers!" he bellowed. "Forty-three days!"

****

Ching Phor sat in the shade at the edge of the jungle. Two oxen browsed for whatever grass had not been burned. Guyan and Phong stood behind her.

"What will you do?" Guyan asked.

"The children will come. They will need me." She turned to Guyan. "She rests well?"

"It is a fine... grave. You do her honor."

"And in her favorite place," added Phong. "She sleeps in peace."

Ching Phor sighed. "It will be a shock for them."

"They are not alone," said Guyan. "Will you stay after they have returned?"

"Aye. Ben Cat is my home. Today there are five of us. Next week two more."

"But food?" Guyan persisted.

"We will manage." She smiled. "We are patient, have you forgotten?"

"Patient, aye, but..."

"Guyan, my life is here," she motioned to Mai Nin's grave, "with my friends, my family."

"But Ching Phor, there is no shelter, no food. The earth is destroyed," Phong reasoned. "You should come with us."

"Shelter? My needs are simple. A roof is easily replaced. There are five months until the next rain. My appetite shrinks. Others will come.

When you return, you will be surprised."

"And welcome? Will we... be welcome?" Guyan asked.

"Guyan, you must go beyond this. You must not dishonor the sacrifice of Ben Cat. Only that will be unforgivable."

****

"So Sarge, or Corporal, or whatever the hell you are, aren't you supposed to be somewhere? I mean you been here for what, two days?" Carney asked.

"Am I crowding you, Dayton?" Hodges laughed. "I thought we were getting along pretty well."

"Don't get me wrong, I like new faces, especially round eyes, but everyone's sposed to be somewhere."

"Yeah, well, we got five days off."

"How'd you work that?"

"They don't know what to do with us."

"Five days in Lai Khe, now that's quite a holiday. So what're your buddies doin?"

"Getting to know the locals."

"Oh yeah. I used to be a regular."

"Used to be?" Hodges asked.

"I'm so short, I don't go nowhere. Here, the chow line and the barracks." Carney laughed. "Most of the new guys think I'm a fag. Soon they're gonna be downtown in Lai Khe, and I'm gonna be home, in the world." Carney shook his head. "If I were you, I'd stay close to the barracks. It's just not worth it."

"You've thought this out."

"I've learned from the guys before me. I may not be the smartest guy around, but monkey see, monkey do!"

"Not that simple for me."

"Yeah, yours is more complicated. I mean, I seen a lot of guys fall for some of the hookers."

"Yeah?" Hodges had given up trying to convince Carney that Laureen was not a hooker.

"But they don't take em home, or even think about it. I mean what you're thinking, I gotta say, is a long shot. A real long shot."

"Before I get that far, I got a major hurdle."

"What's that?"

"I gotta tell her we killed her grandmother."

"And how you gonna do that?"

"Don't know." Hodges shrugged. "Any ideas?"

Carney scrutinized Hodges. "Ya know, you're a mess. You ain't shaved in a week. At least you outta put your best foot forward."

Hodges shifted his left foot in front of his right. "Like this?"

"It's a start."

"Yeah, may be as far as I get."

"You love her?"

Hodges looked up, "From the minute I saw her."

"She love you, soldier?"

"She does."

"Well then, maybe you'll figure something out." Carney winked. "You're a good-lookin guy. She good-lookin?"

"When you see her, you tell me."

"If I see her. You ever think she might be standing you up?"

"She's coming, don't worry. She's coming."

Checkpoint South – Lai Khe

Carney stood with the morning detail looking at Hodges' outstretched figure. "That, gentlemen, is how they sleep... in the bush."

Hodges lay on his back, his head resting on a sand bag, his arms crossed over his stomach. His shirt was draped over his face, creating a makeshift mosquito net.

"Sleep? You sure he's alive?" asked a private.

"Well, I wouldn't want to wake him up. Would you?" Carney asked.

"No thanks!"

At 0830, Hodges stirred.

"Four Zero! That is the number. Good morning, Corporal."

"Morning, Dayton. Java?"

"In the bunker. Lai Khe's best. We got lotsa outgoing this morning. Still a little early for your special package."

Hodges returned with coffee. "You guys ever find anything?"

"Anything and everything. Black market stuff, contraband, American currency." Carney smiled. "We especially like to find that."

"Who's got dollars?"

"The hookers, my man. They got everything. Ya see the ones with motorbikes, they're hookers." Carney laughed. "I've had some pretty unbelievable propositions, right here, in broad daylight. Was a time when that interested me. Not any more."

"Chow and the barracks right?"

"Exactly. I don't want to be taking any surprises home, ya know what I mean?"

"Gotcha," laughed Hodges.

"Most of the girls, they know me. They know I'm gonna check em out, top to bottom. They're ready for me. Truth is, it's sorta kinky, ya know?"

"Sure, makes sense to me."

"You don't mean that, but you watch close, you'll see. They warm up to me. Then there's the taxis, those little three wheelers. I gotta do the whole number on them. Til your Ben Cat thing, we had buses. They're a pain in the ass. Every bag, every body, the whole bus." Carney chuckled. "If your friend went through here, chances are I know her better than you."

"Could be, Dayton, could be."

"Then there's the bicyclers. Don't trust them one little bit."

"Yeah, why?"

"They're sneaky. I know they get the better of me. I just can't figure out how."

"What d'ya mean?"

"First of all, who the hell would ride a bike from here to Saigon?"

Hodges laughed.

"Second, if they feel safe enough to ride a bike that far, if they're really going that far in the first place, they must know something we don't. That makes me nervous."

"Okay, I get that."

"And that ain't all. They never take anything and they don't bring much back. Now tell me, why the hell would you ride to Saigon, take nothing, and bring nothin back? Just don't add up." Carney turned to his detail. "We're checking every goddam bicycle today! Every frigging one."

"What's your most unusual find?" asked Hodges idly.

"You won't believe it."

"Try me."

"They're two I'm sorta proud of. One was a hooker. She had, you won't believe this, twenty-six thousand dollars."

"Bullshit!"

"No shit, man. Twenty-six K."

"Man, she musta been real popular."

"And very, very busy." Carney laughed. "At fifteen bucks a pop, I figure she screwed one thousand seven hundred and thirty-three... and a third GIs."

"Now that is special," Hodges agreed.

"And then there was the mammasan from the Dark Side. She had 200 pounds of MJ..."

"Two hundred pounds?"

"Yup, and a generator."

"Bullshit!"

"No bullshit. A fucking generator. Three black guys gave it to her for taking such good care a them."

"Jesus. What did you do to her?"

"Turned her over to the gook MPs. That, my man, is a fate worse than death. We ain't gonna see her again." Carney shuddered. "Those fuckers are bad ass."

"I've seen em in action."

"They do not mess around." After a moment's silence Carney said, "ya know, who knows what's goin on in Saigon. Your friend may not even know about Ben Cat."

"Maybe," Hodges admitted.

"Then again, maybe this is her," Carney pointed down the road at a taxi just coming into view.

"Maybe," Hodges strained to see.

Carney walked to his post. "Okay, guys," he summoned his detail. "We got incoming. Let's move em along."

"Gettin a little anxious for thirty-nine, ain't ya, Sarge?"

"A little."

The taxi stopped at the bunker. A plumpish, drab mammasan jumped from her seat and charged at Hodges.

"Thompson! Thompson!" She threw her arms around Hodges, lifting her feet off the ground.

"Laureen!"

"Thompson!" She kissed him deeply. "We," she sobbed, "we heard all the Americans..."

"We were on the hillside, away from the village."

Carney moved closer.

"*Anh yeu em yeu lam*, forever," Hodges clutched her.

"*Annoi, je t'aime*, forever. You are alive! My faith, my life is restored." She cried softly.

Hodges caressed her cheeks, her lips, her eyes. "Laureen, it is bad. The village... is... destroyed, and," he hesitated, "Mai Nin, Laureen, Mai Nin is... was killed." He pulled her closer. "By one of ours."

Laureen sank into him, burying her head in his chest. "Grandmother... Mai Nin," she sobbed.

"It was horrible. Mai Nin was an accident, so stupid, so unforgivable. I couldn't," Hodges shook, "I couldn't... stop it... prevent it. It was so quick."

"Where?"

"On the hillside. The next day. She had four oxen. Two were killed."

"We hoped for her. We heard... it was devastating. We prayed. We... we could not will it. We failed her. Tranh will never forgive me."

"Dudley, White, Thiut, the Thais, Thong Thai, so many villagers! They are all... dead."

"Thompson," she whispered. "Say no more. Just answer me two things." She looked up at him. "Do you love me?"

"Laureen, you are my life. My future, my self. All that I have. I love you."

"And Thompson," tears ran down her face, "will you take me away?"

"Anywhere! Forever!"

She moved into him. "I... I love you, Thompson."

"I know." He held her tightly to him. "Will you tell Tranh?" he asked.

"Yes. He will want me to go with you."

"Will you tell him about Mai Nin?"

"Yes, Thompson. We must go to her."

"We will."

She walked back to Tranh, who was standing by the taxi.

Carney put a hand on Hodges' shoulder. "You look like shit," he said.

"Uh huh."

"I gotta say, she ain't exactly what I thought."

"Un huh," Hodges marvelled. "She's full of surprises. I love her. God! I love her!"

Headquarters 3rd Brigade – Lai Khe

Rogers looked up from reading the *Stars and Stripes.* "Yes, Corporal Hodges?"

"First Sergeant, do you have a minute?"

"For you, Corporal, exactly one minute."

"First Sergeant, the grandchildren of the woman Balman..."

"Are you crazy? I told you, not one more word!"

"I know, Top. I'm not here to talk about Balman, or what he did. Actually I wanted to talk about the woman's grandchildren." Hodges drew a breath. "They were in Saigon when it happened. They came to the checkpoint yesterday. I told them what happened. The grandchildren, my friends, they want to visit their village. Pay their respects, you know?"

Rogers looked thoughtful. "I've read your file. So what's this girl like?"

"She's hurting, Top."

"I bet she is." Rogers waited. "So you wanna take her back?"

"And the brother, yes, Top."

"You want one of my jeeps?"

"Yes, Top."

"No weapons. No American passengers. You wanna die, you really wanna do this, I guess it's your business. You got two days R & R left, right?"

"Right, Sergeant."

"I cannot authorize a jeep outside the base, you understand?" Rogers leaned back. "But I do need some parts moved from the motor pool sometime in the next twenty-four hours. You would need a jeep for that. Think you could handle it?"

"Yes, Top!"

"Means you'd give up part of your R & R to help little old me."

"Yes, Top." Hodges saluted smartly.

"Bring my jeep back, Hodges."

****

"A jeep! You're full of surprises."

"I'm on a mission, Dayton."

"A mission? With two civilians? Must be special." Carney studied Laureen and Tranh.

"I think you've met Laureen and her brother Tranh. They're a little more rested today."

"This," Carney stared at Laureen, "is the old bag from yesterday? That's quite a transformation!"

"Thank you, Sergeant," Laureen smiled.

"And she understands everything I say, right?"

"Right again," acknowledged Hodges.

"Ma'am, you've lost thirty, maybe forty pounds." Carney scratched his head. "And in all the right places."

"Thank you, Sergeant," Laureen blushed. "This is my brother, Tranh."

"Tranh?"

The boy nodded, "*Chao* MP."

"He doesn't speak much English," said Hodges. "But he's a real good listener."

"Yeah, I bet he is."

"Well, I must say, yesterday I didn't see the attraction, but today..."

Laureen beamed. "We belong."

"Yes, ma'am. I can see that." Carney rested his hand on the hood of the jeep. "Now, what's the mission?"

"I gotta run some parts from headquarters to the 2nd-28th motor pool," Hodges smiled, "by way of Ben Cat."

"By way of Ben Cat? That's sorta round about, isn't it?"

"Sort of. But not as far as Dayton by way of Vietnam, right?"

"You got me there. Now tell me, how exactly did you get these two past the village guards?"

"We are hooch boy," Laureen pointed to Tranh, "and hooch girl."

"Hooch boy and girl? You bet. What's that make me?"

"Our chaperone," said Hodges. "We need a couple favors."

"Thirty-nine, my man. Thirty-nine days," Carney repeated, withdrawing from the jeep.

"I know," said Hodges. "but we were hoping you'd escort us to the north checkpoint and, maybe, pull some strings."

"Shit, man. Thirty-nine. I don't need no problems now."

Hodges pressed on. "And I was hoping you might loan me a coupla those MP armbands, you know?" Hodges pointed to the bands around Carney's arm. "So I could have em in the village."

"There's a bunch a new guys now. I don't know as I have any clout at the north end."

"Will you try, Dayton?" asked Laureen.

Carney flushed. "Well, ma'am, I'll try, but you got to promise me one thing."

"Yes, Sergeant?"

"That you'll root for the Flyers."

"The Flyers?"

"They're a team," Hodges explained. "A basketball team."

"What is basket-ball? Is it like soccer?"

"Not exactly," sighed Carney. "It's a way of life, where I live."

"A way of life for you? And if the Flyers do well, then it is good for you?"

"True happiness."

"Then the Flyers have my best wishes."

"So we're off." Carney climbed in the back of the jeep.

"Thanks, Dayton."

Hodges drove through the base, then parked a short distance from the north checkpoint.

"Let me check this out," said Carney. He walked over to the MP in charge. Twice they looked back. Finally Carney laughed, patted the MP on the back, and returned to the jeep.

"It ain't all bad."

"Yuh?"

"He can't give clearance."

"No?"

"But they're gonna break for lunch. If a jeep went through while they were on break, they sure as hell aren't gonna pursue. They probably wouldn't be able to identify the... uh... vehicle. Ain't it amazing how that can happen?"

"Sure is, Dayton, sure is."

"Course there is one other problem."

"Yeah?"

"How the hell do I get back to my post?"

"Bet you'll find a way."

"Win Flyers," laughed Laureen.

"Thanks, ma'am." He stood away from the jeep.

****

Cresting the last hill, Hodges pulled over to the side of the road. "We were over there." Laureen and Tranh looked where he pointed. "You sure you want to do this?" he asked, handing the binoculars to Laureen.

"We must." Hesitantly, Laureen positioned the glasses.

"Tranh, it is as Thompson has said," she sighed, handing him the binoculars. "The village is gone."

Tranh's face became stern. Then suddenly his voice cracked. "But look there! It is Ching Phor!"

"We must go to her." Laureen turned to Hodges.

They drove down into the ruins of Ben Cat.

"Ching Phor!" Tranh jumped from the jeep and raced to embrace the old woman. "We have returned."

"Little Ox!"

"No longer."

"So what are you?"

"Dreams! Your dreams!"

"Aye, and who then?"

"Ching Phor, do you not recognize your son?"

"Aye, my son," she faced Laureen. "Child?"

Laureen bowed. "We are safe. Suffering, as you, but safe. Thank you, Ching Phor. Thompson has told us of Mai Nin."

"She rests in her favorite place on the hillside. You have passed her by."

"On the hillside?" Laureen and Tranh exchanged remorseful looks. "It is her place."

Ching Phor approached her. "Shall we go?"

"Aye."

"How many others are with you?" asked Laureen as they began to walk.

"So far, just five. But now seven," Ching Phor answered. "Dui, Mai Nin's scarf has served you well."

Laureen translated.

"Please tell Ching Phor that I am honored to return."

They continued climbing to the neatly arranged pile of stones that marked Mai Nin's grave. Three bamboo shafts rose as the headstone. In the middle Ching Phor had tied the tattered green scarf. "She sleeps in peace."

The four stood side by side around the grave. Hodges removed his beret.

Laureen's voice quavered. "Grandmother, you..." she stopped to gather herself. "Even your absence brings us together." She reached for Hodges' hand. "You give us strength to do the things we must. You nurtured us so that we may be who we are." She looked across to Tranh. "Thank you."

"Old friend," Ching Phor began, "once again you have left me to finish the things you started." Tranh trembled, Laureen sobbed. "We will visit you each day. Your oxen will be here. The village will grow again, and undoubtedly," she reached for Tranh's hand, "you will offer advice and criticism with each roof we thatch, with each grain we sow. We understand it is simply your way. And, old friend, when we have finished, you will have company. Please wait for me so that on our next journey we may take each stride together." A tear rolled down her cheek. Laureen clutched her left hand, Tranh squeezed the right.

Tranh stared at the green scarf. "Grandmother, for so long you were a mystery to me. Often your patience frustrated me. Now you lie beneath us. My hope is that the wisdom of your ways will guide us. We go forward separately but with your lessons to show us the way." His eyes shifted to Laureen. "We will remember you, always."

They stood in silence.

Then Hodges released Laureen's hand. "Mai Nin, I thank you for allowing my intrusion." Laureen stared at him. "In my country the departed are measured by their successes. Measured by what they have accomplished, what they have accumulated, what they leave behind." He looked to Laureen. "Your accomplishments, your life would never be understood. I thank you for the opportunity to know your family. The sadness I feel is knowing you will not be present to see the rewards we shall reap from your lessons. Since our first meeting, we have traveled far. I will never understand all that has happened, but I know we have found ourselves. I love your granddaughter. I will honor her."

The mourners turned from the grave and walked down the hill. "Tranh Nhu Lam, where will you go?" asked Ching Phor.

"Home."

"And where is that?"

"With me," Laureen suggested.

Tranh stopped. "No, Laureen, not with you. You, you must go with Dui. My place is here, helping the friends of Mai Nin to rebuild Ben Cat." He resumed walking.

"But Tranh," Laureen protested. "We must see each other."

"Ah sister, you will always know my whereabouts. This time my mission is clear. From nothing we begin again." He placed his arm around Ching Phor. "What say you, housebuilder?"

"Housebuilder, eh?" said Ching Phor, turning to Laureen. "We will be safe. Others will join us. They will call us the housebuilder and the director. Like Mai Nin, Tranh will direct us all."

"And protect you," added Tranh. "Protect what we build. This can never happen again."

Laureen sobbed with resignation.

Hodges tried to console her. "One day we shall return. And you, Tranh, will have to visit us. Can we agree on this?"

Laureen translated.

"We can." Tranh extended his hand.

Laureen pulled Tranh aside. "May we walk home one more time?"

"Aye." Hodges and Ching Phor watched as brother and sister walked to the ruins of their home.

"Brother, you have been patient with me." Laureen hesitated. "My love for this village, for our way of life does not change. Without your love, the love of my brother, my life is pointless. On the bus you saved my life. You are very brave. But we do not agree on the means, do we?"

"No sister, we do not." He held her arm. "But my admiration for you, you must never question. Your happiness means much to me."

"Thank you, Tranh Nhu Lam. And your future means more to me than you realize. Now you must listen. This war will continue."

"Not here, sister," he interrupted. "Not in Ben Cat."

"The war will go on," she insisted. "You know where the Chocarts live. They will always know how to reach me. They will always be willing to help you. They, they were very fond of Mother."

"And of you, Laureen."

"Aye, and of me."

They stood at the crater where their home had been.

Laureen grabbed Tranh's arms, turning him to face her. "Tranh Nhu Lam," she said softly, "you must excavate here. Father left money for me. Some of this money is in a metal box, somewhere here."

"Laureen, you, you had money here?"

"Aye Tranh, enough to make you safe."

"Do you have more?"

"In France, where Father had investments."

"In France?"

"Aye, the Chocarts manage them for me. They will always know how to reach me. They will always help you. Knowing these things, that you have money, that the Chocarts will help you, that you are with Ching Phor, that you are here, these things allow me to leave you. You must tell me that you acknowledge this, and that you will use the money."

"The money is meaningless."

"You must ask Ching Phor. Tell her there are at least eleven thousand piastres."

"Eleven thousand!"

"For you."

"For the village?"

"For you," she softened, "to choose."

"Thank you, sister."

"Tranh Nhu Lam, you must never forget that we are brother and sister."

"Aye! Brother and sister." They embraced.

"Laureen," Hodges said as the two approached, "the time to go has come."

"Yes," Laureen agreed. Reaching into the back of the jeep, she handed her yellow backpack to Ching Phor. "Perhaps the contents will key the minds of your new Ben Cat. Please encourage the children and think of me as they progress," she smiled. "And, good friend, take good care of my brother, your new son. His ideas are ambitious."

"It seems a family trait!" Ching Phor hugged Laureen. "Child, you are as beautiful as your mother. You fulfill her dream. Always think of her." She glanced over at Hodges. "And tell your husband that his true heart was noticed in Ben Cat. We believe him to have once been Vietnamese. Now that he has you, he will always be." She bowed to Hodges, then kissed Laureen on each cheek.

Hodges shook Tranh's hand, then bowed to Ching Phor.

As the jeep pulled away, Laureen placed her hand on Hodges' leg. "Ching Phor called you my husband."

"I thought so. She is very wise."

"You think so, eh Dui?"

"I think I would love to be your husband."

"In the worst of times, when all is lost, you make me happy, you give me hope."

"We have come far, now we must finish. You must be safe."

"With you there is safety. And if not, then we endure danger together. This is acceptable." She pressed his leg again. "Would you mind if we stayed?"

"Stay?"

"The night. Near Mai Nin."

He rolled his eyes. "A week ago, a sergeant, today a corporal, tomorrow a PFC." He squeezed her hand. "But the moment is now, and one thing I've learned, each moment counts." He kissed her. "We stay."

Headquarters 3rd Brigade – Lai Khe

"Corporal Hodges."

"Morning, Top."

"Did you make the delivery?"

"Just finished, First Sergeant."

"Uh huh. Anything else I should know?"

"Nice jeep, First Sergeant."

"I see. Hodges, you and your squad are to meet with Lieutenant Stiles and myself tomorrow morning. I guess we've, uh, found something for you to do for the next 70 days. 0800, standing tall. Got it?"

"Yes, Top. Ah, there is one more thing."

"One more thing?"

"I'd like to extend my tour."

"Extend your tour?"

"You know, Top, for the early out."

Rogers ran his hand through his thinning hair. "I see. The early out. You go home with less than 90 days til your discharge and you're out." He thought for a moment. "Hodges, I'm not the fatherly type, but, uh, you sure you thought this out? You only got 70 days. Why fuck around? Get home, get on with it."

"Appreciate the advice, Top, but no can do."

Rogers walked to the door and closed it. "You know we don't like to lose anybody. We especially don't like to lose em when they're almost home. You probably got good duty left. I mean 70 days, think about it. How many days you need for the early out?"

"Sixty days would put me over the top. I'll be out. That's when it starts for me. I just can't sit around some army base, playing soldier for five more months." He paused. "I can't leave just yet."

"Yes you can, Hodges. That's my point. In seven zero days, you're on the way. I know about Operation Manhattan. I know about the ridge and what you people did there. Go home, son. Put this behind you.

You've, uh, done what was asked. There's people to take your place. Your Miss Sunflower, uh, that's not, uh, a good enough reason to lose it."

"Appreciate the advice. Sixty days First Sergeant? I can make that." Hodges smiled. "Not sixty-one."

"Can she get out?"

"Needs minimum three months, but she can get out. She has friends. She's going to Saigon tomorrow to see about the passport, make some plans, stuff like that. She's pretty organized."

"Hodges, you sure?"

"Top, I'm sure that if I don't do this..."

"I see, Hodges. Sixty more then. You, uh, sure your math is right?"

"Yes, Top."

"Right. Well, I guess you're, uh, now one three zero."

"Thanks, Top."

"And, uh Hodges, we don't like our veterans to be underranked. We'll be giving you that, uh, stripe back. Save your money."

"Thank you, Top. And thanks for the jeep."

"Uh huh, what jeep?"

****

"Bullshit!" Hosmach bolted upright on his bunk.

"You kiddin?" asked Mac, looking to Ghost, who shook his head.

"You really are an asshole," mocked Balman.

"Could be." Hodges moved to his bunk. "But when I leave here, I'm out. A free man."

"Not me, brother," said Ghost. "My number comes, I'm goin. I don't push the numbers."

"Dui, we just came to do the number," said Mac.

"It's more than that now."

"Well, I'll be stayin with you," Mac began. "Like I said before, we came together, we go home together."

"No way!" said Hodges. "This has nothing to do with you. First, Laureen can't get out right away. Second, I want out of the army so we can get together in France. You gotta get home. Your mother's probably going crazy. You and Ghost, you go."

Ghost nodded. "Don't worry, I'm goin. Seven-zero. I am outta here. Nothin's changin that."

"Not me," said Mac. "I'm with you, Dui. I'll tell Rogers tomorrow."

****

"Gentlemen, my name is Lieutenant Stiles. As you were." The squad sat down again. "I'll be brief. You are short. We like short timers here at Headquarters, 3rd Brigade. We respect our short timers. We want you home in one piece. You help us, we help you. You will be attached to our guard detail. Close to Lai Khe at all times. This is secure duty on a secure base. Of course, we count on you and the rest of our guards to keep it that way. As headquarters guards you will have three primary assignments. One is perimeter defense. Two, you secure the officers' quarters, which consist of five homes near this building. And three, you manage the Vietnamese compound gate. The village is off limits. ARVN MPs patrol the compound and resolve civilian-related disturbances. They have their own way of straightening things out. Report to Lieutenant Mangione at 1500 hours today. We require military appearance, clean weapons, the usual." He paused. "Seven zero, gentlemen. No heroes, no mistakes, that's the rule."

Near Ben Suc

"Now you are brothers," the major pronounced.

"We have always been the same," said Guyan.

"Ah, but in our uniforms you now look the same. You must wear these with pride, the pride of the ancestors of the Liberation. You are from Ben Cat?"

"Aye," answered Guyan.

"You served the cause well."

"We think we have," Guyan added, "but what was best for the Liberation destroyed our village."

"Did you expect such a formidable force to leave willingly? Do you realize that each day our brothers from the north endure bombardments on our behalf? Cities, villages, homes are destroyed by American bombers. Men, women, children who will never celebrate our triumph, our freedom, perish for you. Do you not think their families also wonder at the price of liberty? Grief unifies us. You must think of this. Never forget your grief for Ben Cat, your friends, our allies. If you ever have doubts, remember our suffering. You must make it worthwhile. As the bamboo bends in the monsoon, you may bend, but the souls of the departed forbid you to break." The major stepped back. "Guyan, Phong, are you prepared to proceed?"

"We are."

"Good. As your uniforms suggest, you will now become more active in the conflict. We are assigning you to a mortar squad."

"A mortar squad?" Guyan asked. "We have no training."

"Ah ha! Our gunners are trained. What you have is knowledge of the terrain, of movement in the night, of the habits of the enemy. Our gunners need your assistance, your guidance. You are assigned to the squad of Trung Gian."

A small, wiry man stepped from behind the major. An AK-47 was slung over his shoulder. Two bandoleers criss-crossed his chest. He wore American boots. Trung Gian bowed.

The major resumed. "Trung Gian has travelled the Highlands for many years. In Saigon his exploits are legendary. In fact his feats are attributed to many different squads. You are to learn from Trung Gian. You are to follow his example. You will never question his leadership. This man has survived thirty years, three wars, in the Highlands. You will find comfort in his tutelage. Comfort where there appears no comfort, food where there is no food, safety in the unlikeliest of places. Trung Gian is a survivor. He is determined. He is the Liberation!" The major turned to the squad leader. "Do you have any advice for your recruits?"

Trung Gian studied the two young faces. "My squad travels only at night. We carry our rifles and ammunition, no mortars. We carry water, no food. What we need is put in place for us by our supporters, like the villagers of Ben Cat. We do what our supporters expect. We strike, we move. We do not look back. We do not question motive or result. We are soldiers of the Liberation." He stepped back behind the major.

"In the next sixty days," the major said, "you will circle the Highlands. You will visit Lai Khe, Long Binh, Cu Chi, even Ben Suc, then back again. You will make your deliveries, then move on. You are two escorts in a squad of fifteen. Do you understand?"

"We do."

"Should any mishap occur, you will discard your uniforms and take refuge among the nearest locals. You will find us. We are there." The major paused. "Never has a member of Trung Gian's squad been taken hostage. This cannot happen, do you understand?"

"We do."

"Good, then it is settled. Before your first mission you have one assignment. Phong, two of the children you brought, Mot Thu and Lin, your sister, are too young. Your squad will return them to Ben Cat."

"To Ben Cat?"

"Aye," smiled the major. "Already two huts are built. The children will be better off there."

"Two huts in the village?" marvelled Guyan. "This does not seem possible."

"To whom?"

Ben Cat

"Your village grows faster than realized," observed Trung Gian.

The mortar squad had crawled to the edge of the jungle. "Aye," Guyan swelled with pride. "There are some familiar faces."

"Who is the boy builder?"

"Trảnh Nhu Lam. He was helpful."

"Should he be recruited?"

"He is young."

"He is strong."

"We call him Little Ox for his strength and his endurance."

"A good recruit, then. When you take the children in, you must speak to him. He may want to join us."

"Perhaps. Two huts, a third near completion. It is quite remarkable. Only a short time ago there was nothing standing," said Guyan.

"And twenty villagers. How do they feed themselves? Were there supplies left?"

"We will ask."

Phong slid next to them. "The children are excited. They are anxious to return."

"They must wait," said Trung Gian. "We will stay here in the jungle until dark. Then you take them in. We must study the village. How do they proceed so effortlessly? Where do the supplies come from? Perhaps Ben Cat can again be an outpost for the Cause?" Trung Gian tapped Guyan. "You are best suited to determine this."

"Aye."

****

Satisfied that the darkness would shield them, Trung Gian sent Guyan, Phong, and the two children into Ben Cat.

The villagers huddled around three separate fires. As Guyan and Phong moved forward the villagers stopped talking and looked away.

"Mot Thu, Lin!" exclaimed Ching Phor. "We are happy to see you." She walked over to the children. "Welcome, Guyan, welcome, Phong. Do you recognize your home, or do those black uniforms mean that you live elsewhere?"

"We are unchanged, Ching Phor," Guyan stated. "We have watched you working. You do wondrous things."

"Ah Guyan, you recognize the fruits of hard work."

Tranh moved to her side. "*Chao* Guyan, *chao* Phong. You look well. Mot Thu and Lin, welcome home. What say you, Lin, do you still smile?"

"For you, Tranh Nhu Lam," she beamed.

"Are you hungry?" asked Ching Phor.

"Is there enough?" asked Guyan.

"There is always enough for the children of Ben Cat. Please join the meal. Tell us of the world beyond."

They sat around a fire. Four bowls of rice and cups of tea appeared.

"We are not alone," began Guyan.

"Ah," said Ching Phor. "Where are the others? How many are with you?"

"We are fifteen," answered Phong. "We cannot stay long."

"We bring you the children. Are you able to give them sanctuary?" Guyan asked.

"Are they ready to work?" answered Ching Phor.

"Aye," smiled Lin.

"We are." Mot Thu nodded.

"Then stay you must," Ching Phor smiled approvingly. "Ben Cat needs young bodies to relieve the likes of these old bones."

Guyan rubbed his chin. "Ching Phor, how do you proceed?"

"With hope."

"But the supplies, where do they come from?"

Ching Phor looked to Tranh. "From the ground, like all the good things of Ben Cat."

"Aye," answered Phong. "You have dug up several homes," he faced Tranh, "including your own."

"Aye," said Tranh. "It is surprising what is under the ground, is it not?"

"Have you found weapons?"

"For these, we do not look."

"Explosives?"

"We find what we look for. We return the rest. For example, we uncovered these cooking utensils, these bowls, the cups from which you drink."

Guyan studied his wooden cup. "Amazing. What of the building supplies?"

"Most were underground. Remnants of the battle."

"But Tranh, the food. Where does the rice come from?"

"We have uncovered what we need."

"Do the Americans support you?"

Ching Phor cackled. "At first they returned periodically to examine the aftermath. Now they only fly overhead. We have nothing for them, so they merely observe us. As do you."

Tranh sat upright. "We will not accept their assistance."

"Ah, this is good," agreed Guyan.

"Nor do we accept yours."

Guyan set his bowl down. "We do not offer, Tranh. In fact, we ask that when you are healthy, you remember your allegiance."

"We do not forget our allegiance," Ching Phor interceded. "The village accepts these children you return to us. They are our allegiance. We have nothing left for the Front, we have nothing for the Americans. As you can see, we have no fences, no gates. We will try to save a portion of the southeast paddy, but we have no crop. Ben Cat is straw huts and straw hats, nothing more." She waved a finger at Guyan. "And when the conflict is finished, when the last battle is fought, we will have a place for you. That is, if you and Phong have not forgotten how to work. Ben Cat has paid its price. The war is past us."

"Ching Phor, you surprise me. These words seem inconsistent with your past."

"Do they? Perhaps they are merely inconsistent with your thoughts." Her hands included the gathering, "We are all from Ben Cat. Your squad has its own purpose. It has nothing to do with ours, or our survival, or our way of life. We have fought for our village. We have suffered tragedy, lost families, lost friends. Now, young warrior, we choose to begin again. Understand that we do this so that you warriors will have a place you know is home. A reason to fight. We support the struggle, but we fight differently." She looked at the hut behind her. "From the floor up, not from the roof down. If you want to support us, if you believe in us, you will keep your comrades away from our village. Ben Cat will be here when you are finished. You will be welcome. This is what you must know."

Guyan turned to Tranh. "And what of you, Tranh. You are young, you are strong. Will you serve with us?"

"No, Guyan, my place is here with my village."

"You are a soldier."

"Aye, a soldier of Ben Cat. Today the soldier is an architect, tomorrow a farmer."

"No longer the Little Ox?"

"More than ever."

Guyan stood. "Ching Phor, Tranh, you realize that with each hut you build, with each meal you serve, with each villager you reclaim, you are observed. The village will again be recruited by our brothers, patrolled by the Americans, or perhaps even occupied."

Ching Phor shrugged. "Then we must be careful. Each step must be small, each meal measured, each hut fully occupied. You see, Guyan, we now must make choices. Choices that you have already made. These things we have discussed. We have buried our dead. Ben Cat will never again have weapons. This time you carry rifles, but not the next. For anyone bearing arms, the doors of Ben Cat will be closed, our rice bowls empty. We hope that you, Guyan, you, Phong, will respect this. We ask that you deliver this message to your friends in the jungle. Truly we have nothing for them."

"These are bold words, Ching Phor. Are you certain? And Tranh, it seems impossible that you reject us?"

Tranh put his arm around Lin. "My choice is to fight. Do not misunderstand that. But my place is here. My fight is for Ben Cat. Perhaps your effort is more heroic, then again, perhaps not. Mai Nin is dead, Laureen gone, this village becomes my cause. It is my past, my future, my choice."

"Laureen gone?" Guyan colored. "To Saigon?"

Tranh nodded. "And beyond."

"So, like me, you have no family."

"Except Ben Cat, like you. Come, friends," Tranh said, rising, "we shall walk to the jungle."

Before they arrived at the heavy growth Tranh halted them. "Guyan, do you think me cowardly?"

Guyan placed both hands on Tranh's shoulders. "We envy your mission."

"And the people of Ben Cat are sympathetic toward yours." Tranh reached into his pocket. "So that you fully understand, take this chart of the old rubber plantation. You or your commanders may find it useful, although the descriptions seem to be in French."

Guyan held the chart to the moonlight. "It has numbers, coordinates."

"Aye."

"Tranh, where did get this? What is this inscription here in the corner?"

"It is French and the source matters not."

"Well, my friend, one thing is certain, the buildings have not moved, have they?"

"Probably not."

Saigon

"So, child," Chocart rose from his chair, "any progress?"

"Yes, Papa, finally. They accepted the passport application with, shall we say, reservation." Laureen seated herself next to him. "Frankly, my persistence wore them down. In any case my interview is a month from now."

"A month from now," mused Madame. "When would you get approval?"

"At least another month after that. They thought a March departure date would be possible. Perhaps you could arrange the apartment for March 1st. It would be settling to know it was ready."

"Agreed," said Monsieur. "Consider it done. I shall write my brother."

"Thompson will be pleased. You must meet him."

"In Paris?" asked Madame.

"Yes, in Paris! That would be wonderful. You have been so kind."

"La, the apartment is modest. Although for you the location is ideal. The Université is within walking distance. You will be in an alley near Notre Dame. The third floor will not bother two such young lovers, eh?"

"Any floor will be fine."

"Who will cook?" asked Madame. "Your kitchen will have a stove, a refrigerator. There is even a television. Oh my, have you ever watched television?"

"No, Madame, no television, but Thompson knows of these appliances. We will use them together. As we will learn everything."

"It sounds like fun, don't you think, Papa?"

"Might I suggest you take notes, copious notes. If you two can master this, your exploits should be published. The world can learn from your experiences."

"Will your Thompson attend the Université also?"

"Oh yes! But he will not arrive in Paris until April."

"La," Madame began, "the world awaits you."

"Do you really think so, Madame?"

"I do. You must try not to miss Tranh too much."

"At least he is where he wants to be. We both take comfort in that. Madame, Monsieur, it puzzles me, but, for the first time, my direction is in front of me, not behind. My feelings have never been so positive. The excitement keeps me awake at night."

Madame leaned forward. "Laureen, I understand this. You are at peace. Your brother is happy. Mai Nin's death is sad, but beyond your control. Your dreams near fulfillment. Yes, La, I understand your excitement. How many Vietnamese complete such lofty dreams, or dream at all?"

"Not very many Madame. Not many at all. We are a simple people, are we not?"

"For many of your countrymen, that is the case. But certainly not for you, La. Wherever you are, wherever you go, people will see you as somebody special. Once you leave Vietnam, it will not be so painful."

"But here?"

"Here, my child? Look how you must disguise yourself just to travel. In the Highlands there is danger in nobility."

"Yes, Madame. Remember the bus. Tranh saved my life."

"Tranh is brave, and you, my dear, are noble. Soon, you will be free to be yourself."

December 19, 1967

0800 hours – Lai Khe

The squad had completed its night perimeter duty and was going off duty. As they approached the barbed wire of the Vietnamese compound, Ghost stood watch. MacKerry lifted the wire while Hodges slid into the Dark Zone.

"See ya tonight," Mac waved.

"Later," Hodges disappeared between two huts.

The door of her hut was open. Laureen stood in view but back from the entrance. She wore a blue terrycloth bathrobe. Her folded arms secured the robe.

Hodges hastened to her.

"*Emmoi.*"

"*Anh, lai dei,*" she beckoned.

He swung the door closed. "Umm, smells good."

She stayed in his arms, tilting her head back. "*Annoi*, did you miss me?"

"When we're apart, Laureen, nothing's right. You are my greatest distraction and my sole purpose. I cannot live without you."

"And you, Thompson, are my involuntary, voluntary emotion without which life has no meaning." She kissed his cheeks then pressed her lips to his. "Do you like this perfume?"

"A first for Lai Khe."

"But not for Paris," she beamed.

"Ah-hah! You've made progress."

"We have a place to live!" She laughed. "It has a stove." She guided his hand under the robe to her breast. "Madame wants to know who will cook."

He carried her to the bed. "We'll live on love."

"Yes, but..."

His lips caressed her breast. "Can we talk later?"

She pulled his face to hers. "*Annoi*! We can do... anything. We can do everything. We can... we can... we can."

She raised onto her knees. Turning her back to him, she reached between her legs eagerly stroking him. He held her apart. She guided him. His hands moved across her back to her breasts. Her hair flowed everywhere.

She pushed back to him, he thrust forward. Her head lifted then relaxed onto her forearms. She encircled him. He stayed. Every part of him sought her.

"Together! Together..."

Beyond Lai Khe

Soaked in perspiration, his shovel across his lap, Guyan leaned wearily against Phong's back. Trung Gian stood above them.

"So this is what we do?" Guyan asked.

"Aye, at each stop, provisions await us," said Trung. "the newest recruits do the digging."

"This war is about digging," sighed Phong.

"When we have new recruits, your responsibilities will change," offered Trung Gian.

"And when is that?"

"When someone moves on."

"Moves on?"

Trung knelt before them. "We have two hours before we go forward. Use this time wisely. Eat, rest, prepare for the attack."

"Two hours?"

"Aye. Then we move in near the perimeter. We carry the tubes, the others carry the mortars. Suy Ngham has marked the trail."

Phong stretched his tightened muscles. "So we set the tubes, fire the mortars, and withdraw."

Trung sat next to them. "Not exactly. After we reach the site, we hide until tomorrow afternoon."

"Tomorrow afternoon!"

"Through the chill of the night, the heat of the day. We attack when it is to our advantage. We chose the day because at night the flash of the mortars might reveal our position. As we have just ten rounds, we fire when they are congregated. And when the Americans are hungry, they eat. That is our time. Because our coordinates are not precise, we need spotters."

"We have spotters?"

"You of Ben Cat know we have sources."

"So we do not fire on the compound?" Guyan asked.

"No. Good things happen in the compound. The Americans call it the Dark Side. They do not know how dark it is."

"Many of our villagers are located there," explained Guyan, reaching into his pocket. "Perhaps this chart will help. Our friend from Ben Cat gave it to me. It is a map of the old plantation."

Trung studied the chart. "French. When we see the colonel, we shall ask him about this. Perhaps he can identify the buildings and decipher the bearings." He folded the chart into his pocket. "So the boy helps us after all."

"Trung, how do we escape?"

"Follow Suy Ngham. You must pay attention and move quickly. Do not get separated."

"But if we do?"

"Then you are lost. You walk to a village, any village. You will be found. Stay clear of the Americans."

"So we fire our rounds and follow Suy Ngham until he stops."

"Aye, just before daylight."

"This is work," said Phong.

"Aye," Trung stood. "Not a soccer game, not a night carrying baskets through the jungle. This is what we do. There will be helicopters and artillery, much artillery. The Americans will be confused, but they will respond. We strike, we move."

"But how will we know how we did?"

Trung hesitated. "This is not a game. We do not keep score. We fire, we run. Three days from now, we fire, then run again. Someday we will return to Lai Khe. Perhaps with your chart."

Phong fidgeted nervously. "Fourteen hours on their perimeter," he laughed uneasily. "What if we must relieve ourselves?"

"You won't. You will be deep in meditation."

"Meditation?"

"You will see. When you meditate, your senses soften. The heat, the hunger, the insects, the wind, the rain, the night, the day become our allies because they distract the enemy. Your body functions? Your senses will be so keen they will ignore your body's needs. You will see the Americans crawl from their bunkers, stand in the moonlight, and urinate. What have you learned?"

"Their position."

"Aye, and that they are not alert. You will hear their whispers. What have you learned?"

"That they are stupid."

"And afraid. They need to talk. You will see their cigarettes, hear them pop their sodas or their beers. A night near their perimeter is a symphony of carelessness." He pointed to his squad. "And we read every note."

Phong considered. "So?"

"So, Phong, if you meditate and if you are one of us, you will not pee."

****

It was his favorite time. The sun burst from behind the eastern hills. Hodges spread his arms, tilted his head back, and rejoiced in the private beauty of the silent moment. The warmth of the sun signalled the conclusion of another shift, the beginning of another day.

Envisioning the intimacy he would soon share with Laureen, he unbuttoned his shirt exposing his chest to the morning warmth. He spread his legs and closed his eyes.

She danced before him. Her hand caressed his cheek, then trailed lightly down his neck, across the hair on his chest. His groin tightened.

Would she kiss him? Would he be too anxious? He held her breast. She bent down to soothe the top of his penis. Gradually she accepted him deeper. He was powerless. He loved her. She loved him. It would never end.

Each day had become a preface to the next embrace. Each embrace was unique. Each move eagerly craved. He groaned, thrusting his hips into her. She sighed, signalling him to spill into her. He leaned forward, then pulled back to retreat. Her lips held him. It was happening! Every reservation stood before him, then miraculously pinnacled. He released into her. She loved him. He loved her.

They fell forward onto the bed. They laughed. Thank you, Laureen.

He opened his eyes. The day began. Soon he would be in her embrace.

The watch! What was he thinking of!

This is when they would come. They would come with the sun at their backs, in the eyes of the perimeter guards. They would come out of the morning haze. They would sift through the wire. A bayonet would pierce his chest. The coldness of the metal, the warmth of Laureen made him shiver.

Is this how Dudley had felt? Had he known all along? He had!

They would come to kill. He could wait no longer. He must hide. Or fight. He could no longer wait. He must survive. They must endure.

****

Guyan saw him. The bastard! The American bastard. Laureen's lover! He was there! Stretching himself. Guyan slid his weapon forward, then pulled it back into his shoulder. His body pressed down into the dirt.

He should do nothing! He should wait twelve more hours.

What was the bastard doing? Was it a dance? Had he lost his mind? Was it meditation?

Guyan closed his left eye, squinting his right into the sight. The bastard was crazy! He lowered his line to the naked chest.

****

What! Had something moved? What was it? The sun reflected from something low in the dirt. A rifle!

Hodges ducked behind the tower wall. He grabbed the transmitter. "Gallows, this is Long Ball, over!"

"Go, Long Ball."

"Fire for effect. Hotel niner-three. Papa fiver-seven. Say again. For effect!"

"Roger, Long Ball. Coming at you."

Hodges flicked the transmitter switch, connecting him to the bunkers below. "Dirt Devils, this is Long Ball in the tower. Rise and shine. We got houseguests in no man's land. Wake up! Big hitters en route."

He turned toward Mac, asleep on the seat at the rear of the tower. "Mac! Mac!"

"Huh? What?"

"Get down! Get over here! They're out there."

"No shit!" Mac slid next to Hodges. "Where?"

"Outside the wire. Trust me. They're out there."

"Long Ball, this is Dirt Devil Three. What the fuck?"

"Dirt Devils, this is Long Ball in the tower. Wake up, you assholes. We got company."

"Where?" demanded Balman.

Hodges took a breath. "Dirt devils, eyes forward. Beyond the wire about 500 meters."

Shells blasted out from the Gallows.

Hodges raised himself to check the results. The first round landed long. The second buried 300 meters right of his mark. He quickly corrected his calculations.

"Gallows, this is Long Ball. Back it up 200 meters. Give me six across! Go!"

"Roger your call, Long Ball."

Six more shells erupted from the Gallows.

Hodges stood.

Guyan squeezed the trigger as the incoming shells ripped into the mortar squad.

Hodges spun back, falling onto the deck.

Guyan twisted his bloodied torso. Pain! He looked down. His right leg was severed at the knee. He blacked out.

Suy Ngham did not hesitate. He sprinted back into the jungle.

Trung Gian lay dead. Phong stepped over him, following Suy Ngham. He knelt down at Guyan's bloodied body. He bent over, cradling Guyan's head. Life oozed from his comrade. Phong knew. It had to be done. He slid his bayonet across Guyan's throat. Phong dropped the body and ran.

Helicopters charged from behind the perimeter.

"Dirt Devils, this is your tower." Mac began. "Dui's hit!"

Hodges

He set the book down on the blanket and looked across at the River Seine. Laureen's hair flowed gently across her cheek. He slid his hand under her hair. She looked up from her reading and smiled back to him. A boat approached. The sky turned grey. Suddenly it began to snow. He blinked.

Sergeant Rogers was standing over him. Next to Rogers a doctor was reading something on a clipboard.

"Afternoon, Hodges."

"Uh-huh."

The doctor moved down the side of the bed. "You're a lucky man, Sergeant. A very lucky man."

"Uh-huh."

"You have damage to the deltoid muscles, but the bullet missed the brachial artery and the brachial plexus. No nerve damage, minimal loss of blood."

"Uh-huh."

"You will experience some discomfort, a lack of mobility, but with therapy, you'll be as good as new."

"Therapy?" Hodges said quickly.

"You'll have to rebuild the muscle. Three months, maybe more, maybe less. That depends on you."

"You'll be going home Hodges," Rogers announced. "You're not much good to us now."

"Not yet." Hodges looked away.

"Not right this minute, Hodges, but you're done. It's over."

"Not yet."

"Doctor's orders, son. We don't tempt the hand of fate." The doctor moved away.

"You've done your time, Hodges. There's nothing left for you to do," Rogers added.

"Yes there is, Top. You know that."

"Whatever you, uh, feel you have to do, whatever you planned, can still happen. Maybe not the way you want, but it can still happen. Four or five days from now, you cross the water. That's all she wrote."

"Top, I want to finish."

"That's your personal agenda, Hodges. Personal agendas are dangerous, here. Uncle Sam doesn't play that game. He's just not interested. Your tour is over. One month in the hospital, then you're out, an honest-to-God civilian. Right back where you started. A year older, a lot wiser. It's time to move on."

"But, Top?"

"That's it, Hodges. Lieutenant Stiles has signed the orders. Do you know how lucky you are? There's a lotta guys'd like to change places with you."

"Goddamit, Top! I came, I did what I was told. Just let me finish. I'll be on my feet in two days. There must be something..."

"Nothing more to say, Hodges. That's it." Rogers hesitated. "By the way, you got visitors. You up for it?"

"I can't leave. I promised."

"You wanna see these people? They brought the girl."

"Laureen?"

"You got good friends, Hodges."

"Who told her?"

"Your friends." Rogers waved to the front of the ward.

Hodges shrank back. "I'm not... I don't want..."

"Yes you do, Hodges. Yes you do." Rogers patted Hodges' leg. "See you later." Rogers moved away, passing by MacKerry, Ghost, and Laureen.

Ghost grinned. "Pretty cozy, my man. All the comforts of home."

"You'll be there soon," added Mac.

Laureen bent to kiss his cheek. "*Annoi*, do you rest well?"

"They're... sending me home."

She kissed him again. "*Em yeu anh*. It is good. Now you will leave first. Nothing will change. You will be first to leave, first to Paris. Thompson, it is better this way. You will have everything ready. Do not worry. We have much to be happy for. It is a short time."

He tried to read her thoughts.

"Bad wing, huh?" Mac asked.

"Yeh, bad wing."

"Could be worse, my man." Ghost looked at Laureen. "Some guys have all the luck."

"We have so much to be thankful for." Laureen brushed Hodges's forehead.

"You two are peas in a pod, as Momma would say," Mac smiled.

"Somethin like that," added Ghost. "My man, we'll be right behind ya. Six months from now, we'll have a reunion. The four of us. Think about it."

"In Paris!" stated Laureen. "When we are away from this, it will be our time."

"So, Dui, when's the big day?" Mac asked.

"Soon. Four or five days."

Laureen placed a notebook beside the bed. "All the arrangements are here. Our address, the address of Monsieur Chocart's brother. Everything is here. You must read this. Your sergeant has given me permission to visit each day. Today you rest. Tomorrow we will talk."

"Dui, we're with you," Mac smiled. "Don't be worryin bout Laureen. We'll take good care a her. Soon she'll be on that plane headin your way. Pretty soon you two can teach us... French. Think about that."

"Yeah, Mac."

Ghost winked to Hodges. "Into the night, my man. Into the night."

****

Rogers and Stiles stood contemplating the articles spread out before them on the desk.

"A mortar squad for sure," said Rogers.

"Right under our noses. Why didn't they fire?"

"Somebody, uh, screwed up. Probably the sniper. They say that the, uh, other guy was older. He musta shit when the sniper gave away their position." Rogers rubbed his chin. "That old guy, he's, uh, been around."

"Any sign of the rest of them?"

"Nothing, sir. Disappeared into the jungle."

"Anything on the younger guy?"

"Nada. They, uh, finished him off."

"Cut his jugular. So I heard." Stiles shrugged. "No prisoners right?"

"That's it, sir. No prisoners. His leg was wasted. He wasn't going anywhere. They didn't have time to carry him."

"Amazing the way they do that." Stiles shook his head.

"No rules, Lieutenant, no rules."

Stiles reached for a folded wad of paper. "This is interesting," he said unfolding the map.

"Yes sir, it was, uh, in the old guy's pocket. Recognize anything?"

"No doubt about it." Stiles pointed to a marking. "Here we are, right here. Headquarters Third Brigade." He moved his finger. "Here's the hospital, the officer's quarters, the motor pool, the CO's residence. Jesus, look at this. Every building. Where the hell did they get this thing?"

"This map, uh, looks like it's from a long time ago," Rogers reflected.

"It's French." Stiles read the inscription. "Who the hell is Philippe M. Castine?"

"No clue, sir. We're turning this over to the ARVNs."

"Not our own people?"

"Seems like they feel it's of national interest. Civilian matters are, uh, theirs."

"Yeah." Stiles muttered. "We have a copy?"

"Yes sir. We're sending it to, uh, G-6."

"At least we'll know what's going on. With the ARVNs, shit, we'll never know."

"Agreed, sir. Thank you. We'll, uh, get it over there this afternoon."

"The ARVNs coming by for the original?"

"Some time this morning, sir."

"You'll handle it."

"Yes, sir."

"Hodges's girl. She's something to look at."

"Yes, sir."

"What d'ya think?"

"Who knows? Maybe they'll, uh, pull it off. Most guys go home and try to, uh, forget."

"Right, try to forget."

"I don't see that with these two."

Lai Khe

Hodges and Laureen sat in a corner of the hospital veranda.

"Tomorrow, then?" Laureen asked.

"Tomorrow." He hated it. "Will you come to the plane?"

"You know I will."

"Mac and Ghost said they'd be there."

"Our last time together, for a while." She looked at him mischievously. "Do you remember when we met?"

"How could I forget! Mai Nin despised me. Tranh wanted to fight. And there I stood mesmerized by you, the rose amidst the thorns." Hodges suddenly sat upright in his chair, a thought occuring to him.. "Laureen, a long time ago, your father might have sat right here, with your mother?"

"Perhaps, *annoi*. The plantation has memories for me. I used to think about that life. Life with you sharpens, but somehow distances the memories." She took his hand. "You are better today?"

"I screwed up, didn't I?"

"*Annoi*, you have done no wrong. You are disappointed. I love you for that, but you will be safe. Like the first piece of the puzzle, the rest will follow." She leaned forward. "After you leave, I will go to Saigon and stay with the Chocarts. They will assist me in expediting the paperwork. Now there is no reason to linger. A short time apart, and then, Thompson, we begin. It will be wonderful. So new, so exciting. I cannot restrain myself. My mind spins with happiness. Am I so selfish? It will be the longest and shortest of times."

"I'll be there, Laureen. I promise. This time, there will be no army to hold me back."

Her brow furrowed slightly. "Will you miss me? Will you write? The Chocarts' address is in the notebook."

"Each day, you will be my first thought and my last. And while I sleep, you know what happens." Hodges slid a paper across the table. "This is my parents' address. Write me every day."

"Yes, *annoi*, my letters will come." She stood to kiss him. "If you ever doubt my arrival, close your eyes, remember our intimacy. Then you will know. Our destiny awaits us."

He looked over the railing into the sun. "It seems so wasteful, so ridiculous, doesn't it? The village, the destruction. So unnecessary. Mai Nin, Dudley, White, Ringhyter, the villagers. We have been surrounded by idiocy," Hodges shrugged.

She walked behind him, placing her hands on his cheeks. "From the tragedy, from the loss, our bond grew. We were meant to escape. I have often wondered. Was it curiosity? Was it fate? It matters not. Never would I have awakened were it not for you. What we have found, others fail to find in more likely places. You are right. Few will understand the tragedy. Fewer still will understand us. We will be subjected to skepticism. I do not care. For you I will be ever grateful. Someday we shall return with our children. A son named Tranh?" she smiled.

"Tranh Hodges? Wait'll Mac hears that. We might as well go all the way. How about Tranh MacKerry Hodges?" He clutched her hand.

"Thompson, Ben Cat will be with us always, in everything we do. This I know."

"Yes. When I am across the room, when people stand between us, I will catch your eye. I will smile. You will know. I will know. They will not. When we are old, it will still be there."

"When we are old?" Laureen laughed. "Will you still find me attractive? Will you touch me... the same way?"

"Laureen, you know who you are. You will only become more beautiful. Me, on the other hand, I might change so that you will desire me less. You might tire of me?"

Her hands moved to the black scarf. Playfully, she pulled the ends tighter around his neck. "So, already you plan an escape! You had better realize there is no escaping me. And, as you grow older, I will be lighter afoot than you. Perhaps from your shadow, I will emerge to lead the way."

"Ha! From my shadow? That'll be the day. I am putty in your hands."

"Putty? What is this putty?"

"It's a soft material, like clay, that you can shape and bend into unusual forms."

"I see. We have been in unusual forms. But never have you been putty... in my hands." She loosened the scarf bending to kiss him. "Or do you forget so soon?"

LZ – Lai Khe

His squad was there. But Laureen was not.

The plane was ready.

"What d'ya think?" asked Hodges.

"She probably couldn't get out. It's just after seven, too early for the sentries," suggested Mac.

"It figures," said Hodges.

"You're gonna mail the letters, right, Dui?"

"Right, Hoss. The stateside postmarks are gonna shake some people up."

"That's the point," said Weaver. "We wanna shake em up. We're not that far behind you, except for our man Mac," Weaver laughed. "Course when Balman's parents see the postmark, they'll probably start boarding up the house."

"Fuck you, Weaver."

"Uh huh, well, while you guys are drillin rookies in the states, I'll be sittin home in Hartford, Kentuck," said Mac.

Hodges patted Mac's shoulder. "Don't forget. Come home in one piece." He faced the squad. "That goes for all of you."

"Do as I say, not as I do, right?" teased Ghost.

"You got it."

"They're waving you on, my man."

Mac lifted Hodges's dufflebag and walked toward the plane. The squad gathered around. Raising his hand over his head, Hodges fisted each of them.

Ghost dropped his fist. "You're still a honky."

Hodges smiled. "Okay, I'm a honky. A honky with a home." Hodges handed Ghost an envelope. "My address is already written on it."

"Yo man! There goes the neighborhood! What'll the white, middle class think of a black, burned-out, pot-smoking point man?"

"Come to Albany, before I go to Paris. We'll find out." He shook Ghost's hand.

"Yeah, man, you bet." Ghost smiled. "Later."

"In the world, my man. In the world."

At the loading ramp Hodges stopped and turned to Mac. "Mac, I'm sorry."

"Dui, when I get home, I'll be out. You're not the only one with places to go, people to see, things to do."

"Make it!"

"I will."

"I love her, Mac. Tell her. I'll be there. I miss her. I know she tried. Soon Paris! Tell her. Paris!"

"I will."

Hodges handed him a letter. "Give her this, the first of many. And this," he said, giving Mac a note, "is for you. My address, my phone number. When you're stateside, you call."

"Dui," Mac grinned, "you did it."

"Not yet, Mac. Not til Laureen and you guys get back. You'll be last, so when you get home, that's when it's over. You be sure to call, so I'll know."

"I will."

Hodges clutched his shoulder. "Without you, we never would have happened. You got me this far. You were always there."

"That's me. Old Reliable."

"Into the night, Mac, into the night." Hodges walked up the ramp.

****

"Congratulations, Sergeant. You are on the way," the copilot shouted above the engines.

"Sort of."

"Where were ya?"

"Ben Cat."

"Ouch! Not good, my man, not good."

"Yeah. Not good." Hodges stared ahead.

"You're lucky, Sergeant." The pilot shouted. "You want one more look?"

"Yeah, one more."

Clearing the last hillside, Hodges pointed. "That's where we were when it happened. Right over there."

The pilot looked down. "I remember when it was a real village."

"Me too," mumbled Hodges.

"Look," said the pilot. "Now there's what, four, maybe five huts."

"Five," confirmed Hodges. "A while ago, there were none."

"They just keep comin back, don't they?"

"Yes sir, they do. They surely do." Hodges shook his head. "They just keep coming back. But what did we do? Why, why were we there?"

****

"What d'ya think?" Mac asked Ghost.

"I think he done good. I think we done good."

"No, I mean Laureen. What d'ya think?"

"She shoulda been here. Let's take the jeep, check it out." Ghost climbed into the driver's seat.

Mac and Ghost bullied their way through the compound checkpoint, but the Dark Side was deserted.

"Man," Mac looked around. "It's like a ghost town."

At the end of the road they turned right, but were forced to stop by a huddled crowd of villagers.

"What the hell?" Mac asked.

"MPs!" A boy pointed to Laureen's hut. "Very bad. MPs mad."

"Not these assholes again!" Ghost pulled his weapon from behind the seat.

Mac checked his sidearm. They jumped from the jeep and moved through the crowd.

"Halt GIs!" An ARVN blocked their path. "This off limits for you!"

"We're here to see a friend," Ghost moved closer.

"You have pass?"

"We got this!" Ghost raised his M-16.

"What's goin on here?" demanded Mac.

"Bad girl live here. She traitor."

"Bullshit!" said Ghost. "Who's in charge here? Where's the officer?"

"This girl bad news, GI. Give map VC. You no like VC, right GI?"

"I no like ARVN MP, you get it? I'm going in." Ghost stepped forward.

The ARVN stayed in front of him. "I no think so, GI. You off limits."

Another MP opened the door. A naked man appeared behind him.

MacKerry pushed the ARVN down. "Son of a bitch!"

Ghost charged the house. The butt of his weapon knocked the door guard down. MacKerry slammed into the naked MP.

Two ARVNs held Laureen's stripped, bleeding body pinned to the floor. A soldier knelt between her legs. Her mouth was gagged, her battered face inflamed. Her terror-filled eyes cried out.

Mac fired his sidearm into the ceiling. The kneeling soldier viciously slapped Laureen across the face.

"Hey black GI, you likey?"

Ghost lunged into the back of the kneeling ARVN. His bayonet sank into his chest.

Blood sprayed onto Laureen. The other ARVNs jumped back, reaching for their weapons.

A shot rang from the door. Ghost's chest exploded. He gasped and pitched forward onto Laureen.

Mac pivoted. An ARVN slammed a chair up into his chin. MacKerry crashed to the floor, unconscious.

Mac

A medic roughly tied MacKerry's last stitch. "When the novocaine wears off, you're gonna feel it. You can spend the night if you want. Otherwise, come back tomorrow, we'll check it out."

MacKerry shook his head.

The medic stepped back from the edge of the bunk and turned to Stiles. "Well then, Lieutenant, he's all yours."

"Very well, Specialist. Thanks."

Sergeant Rogers moved in front of MacKerry, who rose to sit on the edge of the bed. "Goddamit MacKerry. Scott is dead."

MacKerry stared ahead.

"And for what?" asked Stiles.

"Laureen? Where's the girl?"

"Who knows?" Rogers answered. "The ARVNs got her. They're taking her south, to one of their detention camps. They're real unhappy with her. Real unhappy with us. Shit! You guys killed one of theirs!"

"Have they left?"

"MacKerry, this is serious shit," Stiles began. "We got some pissed off ARVNs here. If I were you, I'd be more concerned with my own ass. They're making lotsa noise. This is gonna go higher up." He shook his head. "Way over our heads."

Mac gingerly put his feet on the floor.

Rogers gripped MacKerry's arm. "MacKerry, this is out of our control. It's a, uh, civilian matter. Their call. We got no jurisdiction. It's that simple."

"They raped her."

"Yeah, they raped her," Rogers agreed. "She's not the only one."

"She did nothing wrong."

"They say she gave the VC a map," Rogers said. "The Lieutenant and I, we saw the map. It was French. Her father, he was French, right?"

"Don't know about no map." Mac buttoned his shirt. "Laureen... was our friend, not a traitor. They raped her." He slumped back onto the bed. "Dui, Jesus, Dui. He just left!"

Rogers released his grip. "He'll never know."

"I gotta find her."

"No way, MacKerry. No way." Stiles said forcefully. "Because of their conduct, because of Scott, we can probably get you out of this. Let's not push our luck. Let it go."

"Ghost!" Mac stared down. "Everybody's dead. Ringhyter, White, Dudley, now Ghost." He looked up at Rogers. "They're all dead."

"Yes, MacKerry, they're dead."

"They're gonna kill her. You know that?"

"Probably," muttered Rogers. "There's nothing we can do."

"She's one of us." MacKerry started toward the door. "She's Dui's."

"He's gone."

"MacKerry!" Stiles called. "You are confined to quarters. Do not leave the barracks!"

Mac turned around. "Ya know, I'm not as smart as Dui, or Ghost, or Laureen." He hesitated. "But I know right from wrong. Some things I don't understand, but I still know right from wrong. What's happening here, this is wrong. I got to go to her. I done everything you asked. Everything they told us. But this I got to do. Where's my weapon? Where's my knife?"

"Soldier, you are confined to quarters."

"I'm going to the checkpoint. If she's gone, she's gone. If she's not, I have to see her. I got a letter from Dui. Maybe it will give her hope. That... that's what she gave us... hope."

Sergeant Rogers looked to Stiles. The Lieutenant threw up his hands. "Shit! Just to the checkpoint. If she's gone, that's it. We close the book."

"Whose drivin?"

****

At checkpoint south, Stiles stepped from the passenger's seat and approached Carney, the sergeant in charge.

After helping MacKerry from the rear seat, Rogers joined Stiles.

For a moment Mac rested against the hood. He slid his bayonet into his boot, and released the safety on his pistol. Then he arched his shoulders, drew a breath, and approached the checkpoint.

"So they have not cleared?" Stiles repeated.

"No sir," answered Carney. "Not yet."

"We'll wait. When they get here, we'd appreciate it if you make sure we get a look. If the girl's there, we want to talk to her."

"Yes sir. They're a little funny about that. They take this prisoner thing real serious."

"I understand, Sergeant, but you hold em here. You detain em as long as it takes, til our man MacKerry gets to talk with this girl."

"Yes sir, but feel free to jump in at any time, sir."

"Will do, Sergeant, will do. If you gotta pull the book, yank it."

"Yes sir! With pleasure, sir!" Carney saluted.

Early in the afternoon a canvas-covered pickup stopped at the gate. An ARVN captain directed the driver. Two other ARVNs perched on each side of the tailgate.

Carney positioned a corporal in front of the vehicle. With rifles at port arms, other MPs circled the truck.

"Lieutenant Stiles!" called Carney. "This one's for you."

"Lieutenant?" began the ARVN captain. "What is the meaning of this?"

"Sorry to hold you up, sir, but we would like to question one of your prisoners."

"Laureen," added Mac. "Laureen Nhu Lam."

The captain looked squarely at Stiles. "Lieutenant, we have three women, two men aboard. They are in no condition to be interrogated. Besides, these matters are not your concern."

"I understand, Captain. This woman knows something about one of our men. We need to speak with her."

"Perhaps we can get the information?" The captain raised his narrow eyebrows. "We are quite good at it."

Rogers stepped up beside Stiles. Placing his hand on the driver's mirror, he twisted it. "So we've heard. What did you get from this girl?"

The Captain sat back. "From this girl? Nothing. Nothing yet." He looked back to them. "We will though. It's a matter of time." He wiped his face. "We have documents, you know. Documents that belonged to her. They were used against us, against the base. A mortar attack, I believe."

"Yeah," said Rogers. "We found the map. We're the ones sent it over to you."

"What?" MacKerry exclaimed. "We found the map?"

"Yes, MacKerry, we found the map on one of the dead VC. The one from the mortar squad," Rogers addressed the ARVN Captain. "It was pretty old."

"It belonged to her father. He ran the plantation. The girl was the daughter of the Frog and his whore." The captain looked at MacKerry. "He enslaved our people."

"Look, Captain," said Stiles, "her background doesn't matter to us. We need to talk with her about our man. Five minutes."

"I think not, Lieutenant. The prisoners are sick, all of them."

"Captain, I know these civilian matters..."

"Matters of national interest, Lieutenant."

"Yes, Captain, I recognize your authority, but we just want five minutes with the girl." Stiles smiled. "You know, Captain, it is our base. A lot happens. Hardly a day goes by you don't have something going through this checkpoint. Isn't that right, Sergeant Carney?"

"That's right, Sir. From what I seen. Hardly a day goes by."

"Aye, Lieutenant, I see what you mean. We are allies." The captain hesitated. "She's in the back. Five minutes! No longer."

"Thank you, Captain. Appreciate your... cooperation."

The Americans moved behind the truck. The ARVN guards jumped down, pivoting to point their weapons at their prisoners.

MacKerry hitched himself up into the truck and stared into the darkness. Four bodies huddled along the sides. Laureen cowered on the floor. Her legs tucked up under her chin, she seemed lifeless.

Mac picked her up and carried her outside.

Laureen trembled in his embrace.

"Jesus Christ!" said Rogers, reaching out to help MacKerry.

Dried blood lined her leg. Her left eye was completely closed, her jaw broken. Sweat and filth matted her hair.

Unable to straighten, Laureen leaned against Mac.

"Captain! This! This is outrageous!" yelled Stiles.

The captain stepped down from the truck. "Lieutenant, need I remind you, this woman has betrayed the Republic of South Vietnam. Betrayal is unacceptable." He spit at Laureen. "Do not be fooled! She is a VC pig!"

Rogers stepped between MacKerry and the captain. "MacKerry!" he said. "You got five minutes!"

Laureen buried her head in Mac's shirt.

"Laureen," Mac cried.

"It is no one's fault."

"Laureen, don't give up. He loves you. He'll be there."

"Thompson," she sobbed, "he loves me. He loves me."

"I have this letter. He left it for you. He will write."

"You know what they have done. You know how they treat their prisoners."

"Laureen, we'll figure..."

"No, Mac, enough." Painfully she lifted her face. "You must promise me. You must."

"Promise what?"

"That you will never tell Thompson what you have seen. What they have made of me. You must promise."

Mac put his arms around her.

"As his friend, as my friend, do you promise?"

"I do."

"Thank you, MacKerry from... Hartford Kentuck. He knows I love him."

"Yes, he always has."

"Thank you, Mac." Laureen trembled. "Now, good friend, go forward with your life."

Her hands slid down his side. Abruptly, Laureen pushed Mac away. She was pointing his pistol to her heart.

"Take me to Mai Nin. I... I am not my mother!" Laureen pulled the trigger.

Ben Cat

Hosmach drove. Weaver sat beside him. MacKerry leaned his elbow out the passenger window, staring at the passing scenery.

"I really appreciate this," Mac said. "So would Dui."

"Yeah," acknowledged Hoss. "Have you written? That's gonna be a tough one."

"I just want you guys to know we appreciate this."

At the crest of the hill, Hosmach pulled to the side of the road.

"Jesus!" said Weaver, "It's the first time since... "

"God!" exclaimed Hoss.

"Remember when we first came?" Weaver reflected.

"It was green. God, it was green then." Hosmach pulled back onto the road. "Here we go. Down to Ben Cat Two."

As the truck approached the huts, the villagers stopped their work.

MacKerry got out and went over to them. Weaver and Hosmach moved behind the truck. Weaver released the latches, dropping the tailgate. They jumped up onto the platform.

Ching Phor came toward Mac.

"Tranh?" he asked.

"Tranh Nhu Lam?" she queried.

"Aye, mammasan. Is Tranh here?"

She scrutinized him, but offered no response.

Mac's eyes began to fill. "Is he here?"

"*Chao*, Mac," Ching Phor bowed. "Tranh Nhu Lam, *lai dei*!" she called.

The boy appeared from the inside the hut, a hammer in his hand. Dumbfounded, he stood outside the doorway.

"Mac? Hart-ford Ken-tuck," he called. "*Ou est Dui? Ou est Laureen Nhu Lam*?"

"Dui is gone." He faced Ching Phor, opening his palm to the back of the truck. "I... I bring Laureen... home, to Ben Cat... to you."

Ching Phor lowered her head.

Tranh dropped the hammer and ran to the rear of the truck. He looked at Hosmach and Weaver, then stared at the black body bag lying on the floor.

"I am sorry, so sorry," said Mac. "There was nothing I could do."

Weaver and Hosmach lifted the bag, passing it down to Mac and Ching Phor, who carefully placed the body on the ground.

Tranh knelt to touch the bag. His eyes turned up to Mac. "Laureen Nhu Lam?"

"Aye. We're so sorry. There was nothing we could do." MacKerry looked to Weaver and Hosmach for confirmation. "We're all so sorry."

Ching Phor pulled at the collar of Mac's shirt, forcing him to bend toward her. Tears streaked down her cheeks. Placing her hands on his face, her weathered hands held him. Suddenly he began to cry. Ching Phor loosened the green scarf around her neck and silently tied it around his. Completing the knot, she leaned forward and kissed him on each cheek.

"Dui?" she asked.

"No, mammasan, no Dui," Mac clutched his shoulder. "Dui got hurt."

Ching Phor hugged MacKerry.

Tranh ran his hands over the black bag.

Headquarters 3rd Brigade – Lai Khe

"Corporal MacKerry."

"Yes, Top."

"Corporal MacKerry, the hearing is set. February 4th."

"Uh huh. Anything I should know?"

"I don't think this'll go too far. The ARVNs don't seem real anxious to, uh, pursue this. Are you?"

"Pursue it? What does that mean? Will it do any good?"

Rogers hesitated. "You could call for a, uh, formal investigation. Don't know as it would do much good, but I know how strongly you feel. I might be able to arrange a meeting with an adjutant, you know, like a lawyer. You could ask him."

"A lawyer?" MacKerry turned away. "Insanity! What good's a lawyer?"

"Not much. Fact is, it might call attention to the situation. The newspapers love this shit. Might even make the papers in, uh, Albany, New York. I, uh, know you, uh, don't want to hear that, but you asked."

"February 4th?"

"That's right."

"The guys'll be gone."

"Affirmative," Rogers nodded. "You'll be the only one left. You'll have light duty, like now. You know, we got a little holiday in there? The Vietnamese New Year, Tet."

"Lawyers? Newspapers? Holidays? Hearings?" MacKerry shook his head. "We've really come a long way, haven't we Top?"

"Some of you, yeah. You've, uh, come a long way."

****

Their gear stood ready. Jones, Hosmach, Weaver, Cortes, Parker, Velasquez, and Balman faced the plane.

MacKerry was in front of the ramp. At attention, he snapped his right hand in a brisk salute. "Rememba... your last parade!"

They hoisted their duffels.

"You should be comin," Jones said, shaking Mac's hand.

"I'll be okay." Mac nodded. "The pact?"

"The pact." Jones patted Mac's shoulder, then walked up the ramp.

"Hartford Kentuck, my man," Hosmach extended his hand. "There!"

"The pact?"

"The pact." Hosmach patted the shoulder, and followed Jones up the ramp.

Each man wished Mac well, confirmed their agreement, patted his shoulder, then entered the plane. Only Balman remained.

MacKerry grabbed his shoulders. "You made it, Mop."

"Yeah, I made it."

"It's done."

"Roga that. It's ova."

Mac strengthened his grip. "Don't make it worse. Let it go. Let him be. There's no need for him to know the details."

"I know, I know. The pact."

"The pact." MacKerry nodded. Balman climbed aboard.

MacKerry sprinted down the runway to be in position for the lift-off. As the plane picked up speed, he raised his hand over his head, extending his fist.

Weaver pressed the victory sign onto the window.

Mac thrust the fist higher. "Into the night! Into the night!" he yelled.

No one heard. He was alone.

January 27, 1968

Dear Mom,

Everyone is gone.

Things have happened. A few good. A lot bad.

I don't know how to say this, but I need time.

Everything is different. It will never be the same. I hope you will give me time.

I will be okay. I love you. I love the girls. I miss you.

I'm just not ready. Not ready for the world.

When I am, I'll be home.

If anyone comes for me, if anyone calls for me, just tell them it's over.

Love,

Mac

****

January 27, 1968

Dear Dui,

Everyone is gone.

Things have happened. Things that I am sorry about.

This will be hard for you. It's hard for me.

After you left, we were mortared. Heavy casualties.

Laureen and Ghost died.

She is buried in Ben Cat. She loved you.

It has taken me a long time to write. I guess I couldn't face it.

I am sad to tell you these things. Sadder than you realize. I guess I feel responsible.

Dui, there was nothing I could do. Believe me.

I hope you are well. I hope your parents will comfort you.

Do they know? I wondered that.

My time is soon. Until then, what would Ghost say?

"Into the night.

Into the night, I go.

The way. The way, I must show."

Mac

MacKerry sealed the envelopes. As the mail clerk applied the postage, Mac absent-mindedly twisted an end of Ching Phor's scarf. The clerk dropped the letters into the outgoing bag.

He was released.

On January 30, 1968, the United States Army listed Donald A. MacKerry as Missing In Action.

June 25, 1984

Survivors bared their souls here. Yet even at this distance the overpowering wall lacked resolution. Besides, by now a certain peace, his personal truce, had emerged.

The threadbare black scarf was eccentric, but the beret would single him out. The survivors would stare. The story-less wall of names really belonged to them. It had nothing for him.

Into the night...

One step at a time, Hodges moved forward, into the past.

Ringhyter was slumped against the rear of the ditch, his body covered in blood.

Hodges moved to the next panel. His cluster bombs exploded in Ben Cat. The staked images of Dudley and White stared back at him.

Two slabs over, the Ghost extended his thumb. Something was wrong. The dreams would continue.

He closed his eyes. She would always be there, distancing him from his surroundings. Laureen remained his private anguish, the one no one knew about, the only thing no one had ever asked about. Hodges had learned to deal with the names on the wall, but Laureen, oh, Laureen...

He had scrutinized the memorial register three times. MacKerry was not listed.

He opened his eyes. Mac? Hodges swivelled around, startling the survivors. It was his final effort.

Laureen led him away. MacKerry never called.